Templar Stone – The Siege of Jacob's Ford
Templar Blood – The Battle of Hattin
Templar Fury – The Siege of Acre
Templar Glory – The Road to Jerusalem
Templar Legacy – The Search for the Shroud
Templar Loyalty – The Battle of Adrianople

**The Otherworld Series**

The Legacy Protocol
The Seventh God
The Last Citadel
Savage Eden
Vampire

# Templar Loyalty

by

## K. M. Ashman

Book Seven of the Brotherhood Series.

## More books by K M Ashman

**The Exploratores**
Dark Eagle
The Hidden

**The India Summers Mysteries**
The Vestal Conspiracy
The Treasures of Suleiman
The Mummies of the Reich
The Tomb Builders

**The Roman Chronicles**
The Fall of Britannia
The Rise of Caratacus
The Wrath of Boudicca

**The Medieval Sagas**
Blood of the Cross
In Shadows of Kings
Sword of Liberty
Ring of Steel

**The Blood of Kings**
A Land Divided
A Wounded Realm
Rebellion's Forge
Warrior Princess
The Blade Bearer

**The Road to Hastings**
The Challenges of a King
The Promises of a King
The Fate of a King

**The Brotherhood**
Templar Steel   – The Battle of Montgisard

MAP

## The Battle of Adrianople

## (April 14 - 1205)

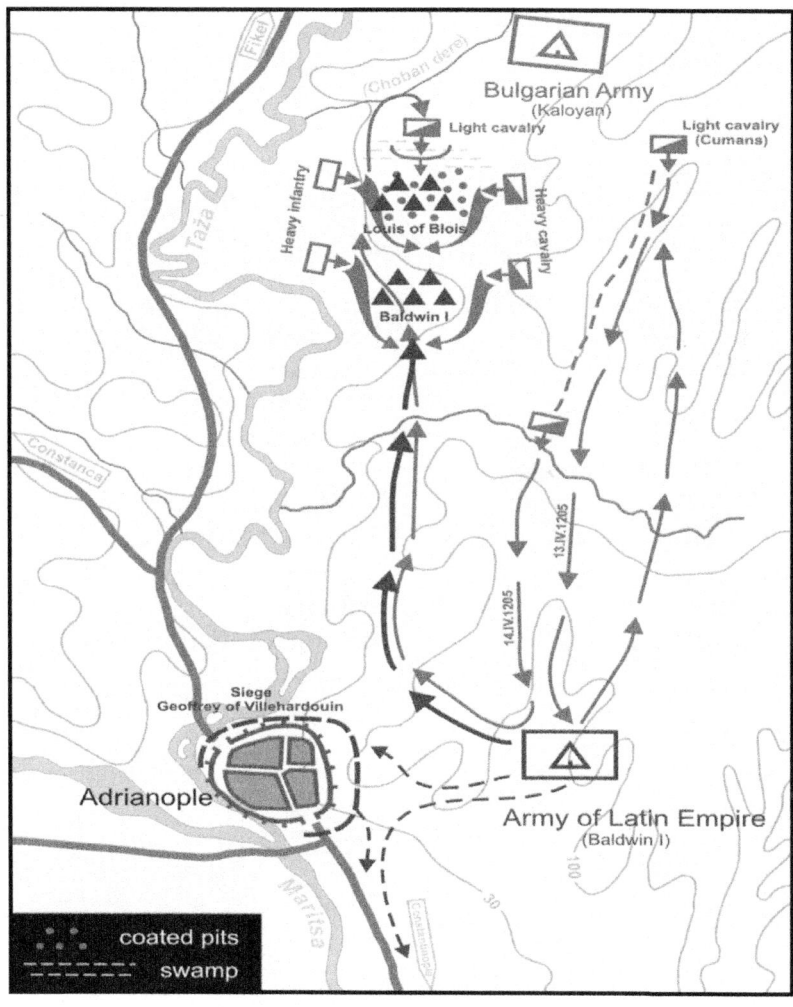

Credit Wikipedia

## CHARACTER LIST

| | |
|---|---|
| Baldwin I | Emperor of Constantinople |
| Boniface I | Marquess of Montferrat |
| Geoffrey of Villehardouin | French Knight |
| Louis of Bloise | Count of Bloise |
| Peter of Bethlehem | Crusading Bishop |
| Doge Dandolo | Leader of Venice |
| Leper Knight | Sir Raymond |
| Thomas Cronin | Templar Knight |
| James Hunter | Scout |
| Sumeira of Greece | Healer |
| Jamal | Sumeira's son |
| Sir Edmund | Ageing Knight |

### The Court of King John

| | |
|---|---|
| John lackland | King of England |
| Hubert Walter | Justiciar |
| Father Edmond | Administrator |

### Bulgarian Forces

| | |
|---|---|
| Tsar Kaloyan | Tsar of Bulgaria |
| Gavril Alexander | Bulgarian Sebastokrator – (The Tsar's second in command) |
| Boris Sigritsa | Bulgarian Boya – (Warlord) |
| Ivan Chelebri | Bulgarian Tarkhan – (General) |

# PROLOGUE

## Bulgaria

### July AD 1014

General Nicephorus Xiphias stood on an outcrop, looking down into the blood-saturated ravine. As far as he could see, the greens, blues, and yellows, so prevalent at this time of year, had been consumed by the never-ending torrent of scarlet poured forth from the tsunami of dead and dying bodies.

It had been almost a full day since the battle, and already the sweet, sickly smell of death was laying claim to the gentle breeze, as if knowing that it would soon own this valley, shared only by the multitude of crows now rallying to the call of the feast.

The battle had been hard-fought and could easily have swung the other way had it not been for the Byzantine commander, Plovdiv Nicephorus, who, faced with a giant, well-defended palisade stretching between the two walls of the ravine, had negotiated a dangerous hidden pass among the hills to lead an army to the rear of the enemy fortifications and fall amongst the Bulgars with overwhelming and deadly force.

The result had been slaughter, and thousands of men now lay dead or dying between the steep valley walls, the latter's cries becoming quieter with each hour that passed.

As he watched, the sound of approaching horses made him and his junior officers spin around, their hands already resting upon the pommels of their swords.

'Stand down, General,' said a familiar voice, 'your work here is done.'

Nicephorus exhaled, realising it was the overall commander himself, the Byzantine Emperor Basil II. Releasing his sword, his hand instead formed a fist, and he struck his chest over his heart.

'Emperor,' he said as the men around him fell to their knees, 'we are truly honoured by your presence, but you should not be here. At least half of the enemy forces are still at large.'

Basil did not answer but dismounted before handing the reins of his horse to one of his accompanying servants. Slowly, he walked over to join the General on the lip of the ravine and stared down at the slaughter below.

'You did well,' he said eventually, turning to face the commander. 'Tell your men that as a reward for their valour, they are welcome to share anything of value they find in the enemy positions.'

'You have my thanks,' said the General, 'but first, we need to pursue what is left of them before they have a chance to reorganise.'

'There is no need to do that,' said Basil. 'They were captured less than three leagues away by General Theopotis. Over fifteen thousand men laid down their arms and surrendered to him without conditions.'

The General's brows raised in surprise. To capture so many men in one battle was almost unheard of, and though it was an extraordinary achievement, it brought risks of its own.

'Fifteen thousand prisoners will take some feeding,' said the General, 'and we will have to take many precautions if we are taking them back to Constantinople.'

'They will not be coming back,' said Basil. 'We will be returning them to Bulgaria as soon as we can.'

'You are letting them go?' gasped the General. 'That is surely a mistake? No matter how heavy the ransom, fifteen thousand begrudged men will surely come back to haunt us.'

'There will be no ransom,' said the Emperor, 'and we will not feed them a single mouthful of bread. Instead, we will release them at dawn tomorrow and let them head home to their cities in the north. Trust me, they will never be back to threaten us again.'

'How can you be so sure?'

'Because,' said Basil, 'we have already separated them into groups of one hundred. Ninety-nine men in each group will be blinded with hot irons, while the last man will lose only one eye so they can find the path north. When the Bulgarians see what we have done to their finest warriors, they will think twice about threatening Constantinople again.'

The General swallowed hard as the response sank in. He was a hard-nosed veteran of many battles and had killed many men in his time and tortured more than his fair share, but always it had been to gain an advantage. To inflict such an overwhelming punishment on so many men whose only crime was to follow the orders of their commanders was abhorrent to him. Despite this, he knew that to voice his distaste was to invite his own punishment despite his recent victory.

'Do you have something to say?' asked Basil, his voice lowering menacingly.

'I do not,' said the General, 'except to say that once more, you display your magnificence across the whole of Thrace. May you live forever.'

Basil nodded and turned away to the rest of his entourage.

'Send messages a hundred leagues in all directions,' he shouted. 'Tell every village and every town that again, the Lion of Constantinople has roared and that anyone, no matter where or whence they come, will feel my wrath. Tell them to come if they will, for I am Basil the Bulgar killer; fear my name now and forever.'

He turned and marched back to his horse before riding away, leaving his General staring after him. For over a year now, the Byzantine Emperor had embraced the nickname given to him by his men and promoted it at every opportunity to instil fear into his ancestral enemies.

It was an apt nickname, for over the decades, he was responsible for the killing of tens of thousands of Bulgarians, but little did he know that less than two hundred years later, his well-earned and brutal nickname would come back to haunt his descendants in a way that not even his warped imagination could ever have anticipated.

----

# CHAPTER ONE

## Constantinople
*One hundred and Ninety Years Later*

Baldwin of Flanders stood at the window of his quarters, gazing out over the darkened city. It had been almost a month since Constantinople had fallen to the Crusaders and their Venetian allies, yet still, wisps of smoke spiralled up into the skies above. The battle to take the city walls had been fierce, with many men losing their lives, but what followed was a hundred times worse.

Just a few weeks earlier, with the Byzantine army having fled overnight, the attackers had formed up to assault the city walls again, as they had done many times, but to their astonishment, they found Constantinople undefended and the city wide open. At first, suspecting a trap, they advanced cautiously, but as they realised the city was indeed unguarded, any restraint and self-discipline fell away. They surged forward into what was once the richest city in Christendom.

Officers and nobles alike tried in vain to rein them in, but to no avail. After years of waiting, months of bloodshed, often hungry and exhausted, the Crusaders unleashed a torrent of violence and destruction on anything and anyone they could find. Churches were ransacked, treasuries, chapels, and prayer houses torn apart, and even tombs were broken open to retrieve any burial goods from long-dead nobles. Buildings across the city were burned to the ground, and many holy places were demolished. Artefacts and relics accumulated over a thousand years disappeared into the pockets and wagons of Christian soldiers and nobles alike, with many hidden away until they could be sent back to the wealthy families and churches in the West.

But worse still was the debauchery. Good Christian men of high morals and strict discipline succumbed to the bloodlust and wickedness surging through their veins. Many women had fled the city, but many more had remained and were now easy prey for the rampaging armies. Darkened alleyways and ruined buildings echoed with the sobs of women suffering the degradation inflicted upon them by lustful men. Some were killed in cold blood, their purpose fulfilled, and though the commanders executed any man found raping a woman, it took several days before order could be restored. By then, Constantinople was a burning shell, a smoke-filled shadow of its former self, filled with fear, pain, and devastation. It had been nothing short of a collapse of Christian civilisation, temporary and localised, but a collapse, nevertheless.

The door opened behind Baldwin, and he turned to see Abbot Martin of Parais enter his room. Martin had been with the crusade since the recruits had started assembling in Venice over three years earlier and was responsible for raising much-needed funds and men before they had set sail for Zara the previous year. Considered a loyal and astute man, he was part of the campaign leadership group that included himself, Marquis Boniface of Montferrat, Count Louis of Blois, and the Venetian Doge, Enrico Dandolo. As well as providing religious guidance, he was also unafraid of wielding a weapon when called for and was particularly skilled with a sword.

'Brother Martin,' said Baldwin, 'you are early.'

'They are ready for you,' said the priest, 'so I see no need to delay.'

'Neither do I,' said Baldwin. 'Let's get this done.'

Both men left the room and walked down the stairs to emerge onto one of the streets. This part of the city was not so damaged as it was mainly constructed of stone, but the signs were still there, with hungry-eyed children, recently orphaned, peering from amongst the remains of any rubble or collapsed buildings.

Abbot Martin and Count Baldwin walked through the streets towards one of the sea walls before arriving at the magnificent façade of the Boukoleon Palace, one of the great royal buildings still untouched in the city. They walked through the gates and past the multitude of crusader tents now erected on what were once the carefully tended lawns and gardens in front of the entrance.

'Ready?' asked Martin, stopping before a closed door in one of the walls.

Baldwin nodded, and the Abbot opened the door to lead the way in. The room was magnificent, with murals adorning every surface, full of colour and movement. Golden candlesticks adorned every surface, and magnificent white marble columns reflected the candlelight, banishing any shadows from the audience chamber.

At the centre, two dozen men sat facing each other at a circle of tables, each silent and lost in their own thoughts as they waited for the meeting to begin. Baldwin recognised most present, having spent years on campaign with them. Some were new to him, mainly the Venetians who had accompanied Doge Dandolo, their very presence at such an important meeting a testament to their significance and authority. He took his seat as the Abbot made his way to the centre of the circle.

'Gentlemen,' he said, 'everyone is now here, so we can proceed. Thank you for attending, for over the next few hours it falls to us to make a decision that will change the world order. Let God be our guide in these matters.' He crossed himself before walking over to take a drink from a crystal glass opposite his empty chair. Once done, he took a deep breath and turned back to face the gathered assembly.

'As you know,' he said, 'the city of Constantinople is leaderless, a giant powerful ship without a rudder. Emperor Alexios has fled to seek safety in a foreign land, from where, I am told, he intends to campaign against us. This is a danger far greater than anything we have seen so far, especially as Constantinople is so vulnerable to others who would wish her ill. Even as we speak, the eastern and northern countries cast covetous eyes this way, and we must move fast to ensure we do not lose what has cost so many lives to gain.' He paused and looked around the room. 'To that end,' he continued, 'we have consulted these past few days to decide who is a suitable candidate to lead this new state, and now, at last, we have three names, each more than capable of uniting us under one banner. Today, it falls to us to choose that leader, so without further ado, I will reveal the names to you.'

He turned to face the elderly Venetian doge.

'The first is Doge Dandolo. It was his vision and treasury that enabled us to get this far. His knowledge and guidance have been and continue to be at the forefront of everything we do, and he has the finances and the support to raise this city from the ashes. He is, without doubt, the preferred option.'

He turned to face a knight sitting on the opposite side of the table.

'The second candidate is Marquis Boniface of Montferrat. His bravery and leadership from the start of the Crusade have been second to none, and he and his men have been the spine upon which this Crusade has been built. When his predecessor, Count Thibaut of Champagne, died at the start of this venture, the whole campaign was at risk of failing before it started, but, answering a call from God, he was the one to step up to ensure it went ahead. He is the preferred choice of the officers and sergeants.'

He turned to face the third man on the list.

'The name of the last candidate was a surprise inclusion,' said the Abbot, 'and was not considered until it was impossible to ignore. That man is Count Baldwin of Flanders. Again, his bravery and pedigree are unchallenged. He was fundamental in negotiating with Venice to form the alliance and has been at the forefront of all engagements. He is by far the preferred choice of the Crusader army. Each man has his own strengths and merits, and all would make excellent leaders. Now it is over to you to make representations on behalf of your preferred choice.' He made his way over to his chair and sat down as the silence was broken by men talking amongst their closest comrades.

After a few moments, one of the Venetian dignitaries got to his feet and waited for the room to fall silent.

'Comrades,' he began, 'this is indeed a monumental decision, and I am sure, with God's guidance, we will make the right one. But first, allow me to lighten the burden upon your shoulders. As you can imagine, this situation has been at the forefront of the Doge's mind for the past few days, and he has come to a decision.' He looked around the room before continuing. 'My master, Doge Enrico Dandolo of Venice, has instructed me to inform you that whilst he is honoured and humbled to be considered for the position, he acknowledges his age would hinder the strong leadership this role will demand. Therefore, you have his eternal gratitude, but he respectfully declines the nomination. Your choices are therefore between Marquis Boniface of Montferrat and Count Baldwin of Flanders, both of whom can count on the Doge's support in equal measure.' He sat down again and waited in silence until, a few moments later, the occupants of the room erupted in shocked conversation.

Martin of Parais allowed them to talk, knowing that in these circumstances, alliances and viewpoints needed to be revised urgently. Eventually, he stood up again and called the room to order and, after summarising recent events, invited comments from around the table. For the next few hours, arguments were made both for and against each man, with the crusading faction favouring their own man, Boniface, and the Venetians leaning towards Baldwin.

The day wore on, with opinions becoming even more entrenched. An outcome seemed unlikely until, at last, the Doge of Venice got to his feet, his sightless eyes pointing towards some unseen distant horizon as the room fell silent. At ninety-six years old, the old man commanded instant respect, and all eyes turned towards him. Despite his age, his voice was strong and carried to all present.

'Fellow Christians,' he said, 'brothers in arms, dear friends. We have come a long way these past few years, and, in a way, it was inevitable that these disputes would eventually present themselves in some form or another. It is natural to argue for what seems the best option for us, but do not forget the many who started out alongside us and have since fallen along the way. They too should have a voice, and it is in their honour that we should avoid this argument growing stronger. Let us end this squabble here and now and march forward in Christ's name, one united army doing God's work. I may have withdrawn from the contest, but that means I now have a vote, and I want to share my thoughts with you.'

All eyes were on the Doge, knowing that his voice carried a lot of influence across all divides.

'Both men are equally qualified to unite us,' continued the Doge, 'with only a blade's thickness between them. However, I feel that one has too strong a link with the former incumbents through marriage. I speak, of course, about my close ally and dear friend, Boniface. As you are aware, his brother, Renier of Montferrat, was married to Maria Comnena of Constantinople before they were both murdered a few years ago, but during that time, the people became very fond of them both and, through no fault of his own, I believe that connection may be a burden upon Boniface, with undue expectations being placed upon his shoulders. Consequently, my vote will go to Baldwin of Flanders, and I urge everyone here to do the same. However, in recognition of the service demonstrated by Boniface, I would also suggest he is suitably compensated by this council. In particular, I am aware that he has often claimed Thessalonica, a city second in size only to the one we stand in, as his by right after being awarded it by his brother's wife, Maria Comnena, before she was killed. My proposal is that this council, using all the powers we possess, support him in his claim, and should he decide to march on Thessalonica, we do so with our combined strength behind him. Upon capturing the city, he should thereafter be declared king of that place from that day onward. That is my recommendation.' He turned around and was led back to his seat by his servant.

Again, there was silence, but eventually, all eyes turned to Boniface for a response. Slowly, he got to his feet and faced the council.

'Comrades,' he started, 'dear friends. I am but a humble servant of God, born by his grace into a family of influence. I have never sought nor expected any sort of elevation above my station, yet here I am, being considered for one of the highest positions in Christendom. I do not doubt that if selected, I would strive every moment of my life to meet and exceed the requirements set upon me. But I have also listened carefully to the arguments made here today by people I look up to.

Now, my path is clear to me, and I have made up my mind.' He turned to face Dandolo. 'Your Grace,' he said, 'you have spoken wisely and clearly, and as usual, your reasoning cuts through the passion of other men's thoughts. I aspire to one day be even half as wise as you, and if God grants me that request, I will die a happy man. Your statement here makes total sense, and whilst it leaves me with a sense of disappointment, I know you are right. We need to move on before the situation is used against us by those who would do us ill. Consequently, I hereby state, in this holy place and in the presence of my peers, that I, Boniface of Montferrat, will be voting for my esteemed comrade, Baldwin of Flanders.'

A gasp rippled around the room as he sat down abruptly. His statement meant there was now only one candidate, and all eyes turned towards Baldwin, who was staring in shock at the man who had just withdrawn. Abbot Martin of Parais stood up and addressed the room.

'We will waste no more time,' he said. 'Is there any man in this room who contests that Count Baldwin of Flanders has won this process in a fair manner before God?'

Nobody spoke, and the priest turned back to face Baldwin.

'Count Baldwin of Flanders,' he said, 'you have been nominated by these men, good and true, as the next leader of Constantinople and its environs. Do you accept the nomination?'

Baldwin got to his feet and looked around the room. Everything was happening so fast, but he knew they had no time to waste. There was so much to do.

'Aye,' he said loudly, 'I do.'

'In that case,' said the Abbot, turning away to face the council, 'I bid all men present to get to their feet and pay homage to Baldwin of Flanders, the next Emperor of Constantinople. May God protect him and guide his hand in whatever trials and tribulations lie before him.'

----

# CHAPTER TWO

## Constantinople

Martin of Parais stood to one side, no longer an instigator of historic change, that role now lay with Bishop Peter of Bethlehem, but as an honoured guest, responsible for getting them this far. He looked up at the breathtaking surroundings of the Hagia Sophia, the most magnificent building in Constantinople. Like the Boukoleon Palace, the cathedral was one of the few buildings untouched by the sacking of the city, and its majesty shone forth like nothing Martin had ever seen. The soaring dome above amplified the sounds of the Catholic Mass below, as if a host of angels approved of the coronation of the first Crusader Emperor of Constantinople, Baldwin of Flanders.

Baldwin had been born into nobility but had spent most of his adult life fighting in various wars, eating and sleeping alongside common soldiers, and his demeanour was humble. Despite this, he was used to authority, but today, as he became one of the most powerful men in Christendom, he realised that this was something beyond most men's imagination.

His attire was like nothing he had ever seen, layer upon layer of long, heavy robes, beautifully decorated in vibrant colours and adorned with gold and precious stones. In one hand, he held the golden orb of his new office, and in the other, the imperial sceptre, signifying his undoubted power. Upon his head, he wore the imperial crown, recently placed by the four bishops in attendance to declare him as the new ruler.

As he watched on, the entire congregation, hundreds strong and each bedecked in their own finery, sang the last hymn of the ceremony, welcoming him to the new life he could never have imagined in even his wildest dreams.

For the moment, he soaked up the ceremony and the adulation, but deep down inside, he knew that before him lay a path of hard work, and if he wanted to have any chance of making Constantinople anything like the city it had once been, he had to start with reconciliation, and that meant winning over the people.

The ceremony came to an end, and the royal party withdrew through a rear door to their private quarters. As the rich and powerful guests made their way from the cathedral to the many feasts and celebrations prepared in their honour, Emperor Baldwin sought a seat in a quiet antechamber, trying to take in all that had happened.

A knock came at the door, but before Baldwin could tell them to go away, Abbot Martin entered and closed the door behind him.

'That was quite something,' said the Abbot eventually.

'It was,' said Baldwin, 'and I'm still not sure how I came to be here.'

'You are here because God wills it,' said Martin.

'But what if it is a mistake, and someone else should be sitting here?'

'God does not make mistakes, as well you know. Just take it one day at a time, and you will grow into your role.'

'But where do I start?'

'For today, just accept the many tributes that come your way with calmness and humility. You will undoubtedly receive riches beyond your imagination, but do not forget, they are for your station, not you as a person.'

'I have never sought riches,' said Baldwin, 'and only ever wanted to serve God. I just hope I can carry the burden that he has placed upon me.'

'You will be fine,' said Martin, 'and you are not alone. You will have many official advisors around you to guide your path, as well as a multitude of others seeking to curry favour. Take what advice you can, be aware of that which comes from deceivers, and then make your own mind up as to which you will implement. There will be a mountain of both, and often, they will be difficult to disentangle from each other, but the more you go on, the easier it will be.'

'I hope so,' said Baldwin, 'for at the moment, I cannot see past tomorrow.'

'Then let me shine a light for you,' said Martin. 'Nobles and the wealthy may have the riches, but in the longer term, never forget that it is the poor who wield the greater power.'

'How so?'

'Because if they are unhappy, it breeds contempt and unrest. Eventually, it will spread like a disease, and then they start looking towards the man at the top, you. Turn the people against you, and your empire will fall, maybe not today, maybe not in your lifetime, but fall it will. Just look around you, for we sit amongst the evidence of such times. But look after the roots, and forests of greatness will soar around your name. Feed the children, the babies, the mothers. Give them homes to grow old in and medicine to ease their pain. Give the men gainful employment and look after those who carry weapons in your name. Reward loyalty at all times.'

'That is a lot to remember,' said Baldwin.

'It is only a scratch upon the surface,' said Martin, 'but it will get you started. But that is for tomorrow. Today, you must meet the nobles and the clerics who have sung praises in your name. Come,' he said, standing up and offering his hand, 'they are waiting.'

Baldwin took a deep sigh and, after replacing the crown upon his head, followed Martin from the room. A few hours ago, he had been a Count of Flanders, but now, much to his own amazement, he was the Emperor of Constantinople.

----

Baldwin woke long before dawn, his mind racing with everything he had experienced over the last few days. His servants had already laid out the attire he was expected to wear during the many audiences scheduled for him, and though they were not of the same magnificence as the robes from the coronation, they were still, by far, the most elegant he had ever seen. What was more, there were another three sets of clothing hanging from ornate hooks embedded into the walls, all as equally beautiful as the first.

'What are they for?' asked Baldwin, nodding towards the magnificent garments.

'They are the changes of clothing you will need throughout the day, my lord,' said a servant.

'I have to change three times?'

'At least.'

'Why?'

'Because it is considered polite, especially when dealing with representatives of foreign countries.'

'And are such people here today?'

'Some,' interjected Abbot Martin, striding into the room, 'for they already had embassies in the city. Others have no doubt sent delegates now the process has been completed and will arrive over the next few weeks.'

'So, which ones are already here?'

'I know that there are ambassadors from Nicaea, Trebizond, and Thessalonica, but there are many more on the way, including Bulgaria.'

'Isn't Thessalonica the place Boniface has cast his eye upon?' asked Baldwin.

Martin turned to the servant.

'Leave us,' he said, and waited until the door closed, leaving them both alone.

'Be careful what you say in front of the servants,' said Martin. 'Remember, they have been here for years, and we know not where their loyalties lie.'

'Understood.'

'To answer your question,' continued Martin, 'yes, Thessalonica is coveted by Boniface, and with little wonder.'

'Why?'

'The city is second only in size to Constantinople, and some say it contains just as many treasures as this city once did. It is a prize worth claiming, and I suspect Boniface will lead his men there just as soon as these celebrations are over.'

'And we will be supporting him?'

'Potentially, yes, but there is another option to consider.'

'And that is?'

'Much of Constantinople's wealth has disappeared, and the treasuries are bare. With Thessalonica so close and an idle army under your command, perhaps it is a conquest you may want to consider yourself.'

'But we promised it to Boniface at the council.'

'Doge Dandolo mentioned the option and the possibility of our support,' said Martin, 'but it was never voted upon. Boniface just assumed it was agreed and withdrew his candidacy without the issue being discussed. If you were to march on the city, the records will show there was no such promise made by those present. Your conscience will be clear.'

'Boniface is an ally,' said Baldwin. 'To do such a thing is tantamount to treachery.'

'You are the emperor now,' said Martin, 'and must do whatever you can to restore this city to its former glory. If that means upsetting a few former comrades, then so be it. Anyway, get dressed, you must break your fast before the first audience.'

Baldwin did as he was told and, once ready, stood before a body-length mirror.

'Now you look like an Emperor,' said Martin.

'I look like a peacock,' said Baldwin, 'and if my wife were here, she would surely die laughing.' He turned to the priest. 'Did you send for her?'

'I did,' said Martin, 'the moment you were crowned. We despatched a ship to Acre to bring her here. With God's will and fair winds, she should be here within a few months.'

'Good,' said Baldwin with a sigh, 'for I think I am going to need her at my side, if only to negotiate all these clothes.'

'Come,' said Martin with a smile, 'we need to get started. It is going to be a long day.'

----

# CHAPTER THREE

## Tarnovo - Bulgaria

Tsar Kaloyan was not an impressive man, at least not physically. His body lacked mass, and his face was dominated by a bent nose. Despite the best efforts of his instructors, his skill at arms could be described as no better than average. However, what he lacked in presence and ability was more than compensated for by guile and cruelty.

Politically astute and hugely ambitious, Kaloyan had been Tsar of Bulgaria for the past seven years, following the murder of his two elder brothers, Theodore and Asen. He was a powerful man with a vast army at his disposal and had cemented his authority by continuing Bulgaria's ongoing fight against the Byzantines, successfully laying siege to the city of Varna.

Varna had been strong and well-defended, surrounded by a moat that protected its walls from any frontal assault. But Kaloyan's army constructed a huge siege engine and, after using it to breach the moat, took the city and captured tens of thousands of prisoners. Being Easter, it was expected that Kaloyan would show some mercy to the defeated garrison, but in an act of revenge for the blinding of 15,000 Bulgars by the Byzantines almost two hundred years earlier, he had every prisoner thrown into the moat and buried alive.

Word of his actions travelled far and wide, and his reputation as a brutal leader of men soared. He continued his campaign of attrition against the Byzantines but was always careful to keep the conflicts close to his own borders, justifying the attacks to foreign ambassadors as acts of defence against raiders from across the mountains.

Today, some of those ambassadors were due to arrive in Tarnovo, having travelled all the way from Rome to discuss his latest request of the Holy Father.

'My lord, they have arrived,' said a voice from behind the Tsar.

Kaloyan took his eyes from the soaring eagle high in the sky above him and turned to see a mounted messenger bearing news from Tarnovo. The royal party had been hunting since dawn with little success, and the Tsar was already growing tired, mainly due to the vast quantities of wine he and his men had drunk throughout the night in anticipation of good news from the Pope's representative. For a moment, he considered calling off the hunt and heading straight back to the city, but he knew it would make him appear weak if he were to react to the needs of others so quickly.

'Make them comfortable,' said Kaloyan, 'and inform them I will receive them as soon as I can.'

'Shall I take them into your palace, my lord?' asked the messenger.

'No. Have the royal tent erected outside the city walls and see to their every need. Smother them with opulence, if necessary, but they are not to set a single foot beyond the gates until I say so. They may be important men in Rome, but they need to understand that in my territories, they are just ambassadors, nothing more, nothing less.'

'As you wish, my lord,' said the messenger, turning his horse away to ride back to Tarnovo.

'Was that wise?' asked Gavril beside him.

Kaloyan turned to the Sebastokrator. Gavril Alexander was one of his most trusted advisors and was allowed the rare privilege of speaking his mind to the Tsar without fear of reprimand.

'Why would it not be?'

'Because whatever you say to these men and however you treat them will be conveyed back to Rome, and you will be judged by those actions alone.'

'They will be treated well,' said Kaloyan, 'but I will bend a knee to no man or organisation who refuses to grant me the recognition I deserve.'

'How long will you make them wait?'

'A few days or so,' said Kaloyan, looking up at the eagle again. 'Come, have the falconers retrieve the birds. We shall try elsewhere.'

----

A week later, Kaloyan sat upon his ornate throne in his palace at the heart of Tarnovo. The usual day's business had been concluded, and at last, the visitors from Rome were being allowed their audience.

The two cardinals approached, robed in their religious finery. Servants provided two silk-covered stools, and after reciting a meandering welcome speech extolling the virtues of the Bulgarian king, Kaloyan's own bishop, Peter Vladislav, invited the visitors to sit.

'Cardinal Brancaleoni,' he said, 'Cardinal Peter, welcome to Tarnovo. I hope the journey was not too taxing and that you have been treated well since your arrival.'

'God looked after us on the road,' said Brancaleoni, 'and your hospitality has not been found wanting. You have our gratitude.'

'It is, and always will be, a pleasure to serve the Holy Father,' said Kaloyan, 'and I hope that today's meeting will cement that relationship in a mutually beneficial manner going forward.'

Brancaleoni glanced at his fellow cardinal nervously, and the Tsar immediately realised that the news they had brought might not be what he had hoped.

'So,' continued Kaloyan, 'let me remind you of the reason you are here. As you are aware, I have been in correspondence with the Holy Father for many months and have sought the recognition of the Church for my unchallengeable claim to the title of Emperor of Bulgaria. This is an administrative recognition only, as I already bear the title of Tsar. However, I realise that for the Church to fully embrace me, and this Empire into its fold, then we need to have full agreement and alignment on titles and jurisdictions. To that end, I formally requested his recognition of my title, and you are now here to administer his reply. Is that how you understand the situation?'

'It is,' said Brancaleoni.

'Then waste no more time, Cardinal, and read out Rome's response.'

The cardinal got to his feet and took a deep breath.

'Your Majesty,' he said, 'before I continue, may I just say that His Holiness, Pope Innocent III, recognises the immense steps you have taken over these past few years to bring your church in line with the Roman Church. He also acknowledges that you have offered him papal primacy over all Bulgarian religious institutions. Both these matters have impressed him immensely, and he sends untold gratitude for your continued efforts.' He took a deep breath and looked around the audience chamber before continuing. 'However, the Holy Father and the Cardinals of Rome feel it falls just short of the commitment needed to be embraced into the fold and have asked me to explain the last steps required so they can grant your request. They are, however, happy to acknowledge your position as King of all Bulgarians and Vlachs and hope that the recognition of your existing titles by the Roman Church will go some way to proving they are listening to your petitions.'

All eyes turned upon the Tsar. He had not moved a muscle, and his face was as if it had been carved from stone.

'Continue,' he said, his voice as cold as ice.

'Your Majesty,' continued Brancaleoni, 'you have made huge steps towards inclusion, of that there is no doubt, but we are aware that your men still attack the villages and towns across the borders to your south. Hardly a week goes by without us receiving requests for aid for those suffering from the attacks, and we are under constant pressure to publicly decry your actions against the Byzantine Empire. This is something we are, of course, reluctant to do, but it is felt that if you could ease the pressures between the two great empires, perhaps with some sort of truce, then papal recognition will be far easier to administer.'

Kaloyan stared at the two cardinals. Inside, he was seething, but externally, he appeared cool and collected.

'So,' he said eventually, 'let me get this right. My forefathers, who were born in Rome and were responsible for bringing many of its holy teachings into Bulgaria, have no influence upon this situation whatsoever. In addition, the fact that we have suffered decades of pain and suffering at the hands of the Byzantines, who have mercilessly slaughtered tens of thousands of our people, is also not a thing to be considered. Instead, you ask us, who at last are able to defend ourselves against their ruthless campaigns, to stand back and sue for peace.'

'It would be the mark of the greater man,' said the cardinal.

'Can I remind you,' said Kaloyan, 'that as far as I am aware, Constantinople is now a shadow of its former self, having recently fallen to Dandolo's illegal Crusade. Its people have been slaughtered, and those treasures not pocketed by the Crusaders are by now well on their way to the idle kings and queens of the West. The much-vaunted Varangian Guard have fled back to their homes in the north, and any strength the city once had has been destroyed under the heel of the western knights. Yet despite all this, you have come here asking us to prostrate ourselves before what is left of their empire and lick their boots, asking if we can be their friends?'

'That is a particularly one-sided view of the matter,' said the cardinal, 'but surely you can see that to continue the conflict will only bring more pain and suffering to even more Christian souls. Now is the time for reconciliation, and if you extend the hand of peace, our faith can sweep all before it as far as the rising sun and beyond.'

'So, he has declined my request,' said Kaloyan simply.

'With regards to recognising you as Emperor, yes,' said Brancaleoni, 'although as I said, the title of King of all Bulgarians and Vlachs has been gladly acknowledged.'

'A title I already have,' said Kaloyan. He took a deep breath and stared at the two cardinals.

His bishop watched him closely, knowing that the Tsar was not above killing anyone who brought him bad news, even cardinals. For an age, there was silence until, at last, the Tsar got to his feet and turned to his advisor.

'Sebastokrator Alexander,' he said, 'arrange an escort for these people to our borders and make sure they are safely on their way. Give them enough food and water to continue their journey in comfort.' He turned back to the ambassadors. 'Gentlemen, this audience is over.' He turned away and started making his way to a rear door.

'Your Majesty,' called the cardinal, shocked at the abrupt dismissal, 'do you not have a message for the Holy Father?'

Kaloyan stopped and, after a moment's thought, turned to stare at the envoys.

'I do,' he said. 'Tell him that it appears that nothing I have said or can say will explain the disappointment of my people, and as he only seems to recognise actions, he will see my full response soon enough. Now, begone while I am still in control of my temper.'

Without another word, he turned away and left the chamber, leaving an astonished audience behind him.

----

A few minutes later, Tsar Kaloyan entered one of his private chambers and, after slamming the door behind him, vented his rage upon the contents of the room. Precious ornaments and jewels flew across the room, and tables overturned, smashing delicate crystal glasses onto the floor. Rare wines seeped into the plush rugs that had travelled so far along the spice trails to reach his palace, and fabulous tapestries were torn from their hangings as his anger showed no signs of abating.

Outside the door, the two ever-present servants looked terrified, not knowing what to do. There were stories that when the Tsar suffered these episodes, the rage often overflowed onto whoever was in range of his fists and boots, so it was with immense relief when Sebastokrator Alexander appeared in the corridor and ordered them to leave immediately.

The two men scuttled away, and Gavril walked up to the door, listening to the carnage that was unfolding inside. Even though he was the Tsar's most trusted man, he knew it was prudent not to intrude when Kaloyan was in this mood. Slowly, he settled into a nearby chair and waited for the Tsar to cool down, fully aware that it could take quite a while.

----

Several hours later, the corridor was silent except for the servants replacing the candles in the many alcoves set into the walls. Gavril looked at the closed door, wondering if it was worth taking the risk. Kaloyan was a small man, but his tempers were legendary, and his victims knew that if they defended themselves in any way, their fate was sealed, and they would end up as food for the hunting dogs. He got to his feet and walked over to the door, placing his ear against one of the ornate panels. Hearing nothing, he tapped lightly, but when there was no response, he gently eased the door open. Expecting to see the Tsar asleep on one of the several opulent couches in the room, he was surprised to see him standing over a table, examining a document.

'Your Majesty,' said Gavril quietly, 'may I come in?'

Kaloyan looked up, a grim smile across his face.

'Of course,' he said. 'Come over here, there is much to discuss.'

The Sebastokrator negotiated the broken furniture and ornaments littering the floor before arriving at the table. Looking down, he could see it was a map of the Balkan Mountains, the natural range of peaks separating Bulgaria and the newly emerging Latin Empire to the south. He saw that Kaloyan had drawn several circles and other symbols on the map, linked with various lines and scribbles in different coloured waxes.

'You have been busy,' said Gavril, struggling to understand the imagery. 'What does it mean?'

'This, my friend, is something you and my generals should have done for me a long time ago.'

'What is it?'

'It's a map of the mountains from here to the Black Sea,' said Kaloyan. 'The circles indicate the location of all the Byzantine villages and towns, and the squares are potential sites for our forces to set up their camps. As far as I can make out, there is a source of water near each one. The red lines indicate the preferred routes, and the blue lines, routes of escape should they be needed.'

'What do you mean by routes of escape?' asked Gavril. 'What do you intend to do?'

'I want raiding parties placed in all these strategic positions throughout the Balkans,' said Kaloyan, 'each protected by palisades and well-supplied for a protracted campaign. From each, we can move quickly, attacking any of the villages in the area before destroying the palisades and returning here with the spoils of war.'

'You are intensifying the war against the Byzantines?'

'I am. Pope Innocent thinks we are the cause of the ongoing conflict between the empires, so let us show him what we are really capable of.'

'I don't think this is a good idea,' said Gavril, staring at the map.

'Why not? Constantinople has no forces left worth mentioning, and not a day passes without some minor official coming to me seeking an alliance against the Crusaders. There is already talk that their new emperor and the Venetian doge have agreed to divide the city amongst themselves and their fellows, and it is only a matter of time before they seek to expand their influence outwards. I know for a fact that they have eyes on both Thessaly and Adrianople, and if we allow that to go unchallenged, then what is to stop them from coming north?'

'But why now? Is this because of the Pope's decision?'

'Partly,' said the Tsar. 'The threat has always been there since the Crusaders first laid siege to Constantinople, but I thought if we could persuade Rome to accept us into their fold, then the Pope would forbid their expansion northward. It is obvious now that this will not happen any time soon, so we must take matters into our own hands to protect our own lands.'

'What do you want me to do?'

'Once the cardinals have crossed our borders,' said Kaloyan, 'summon all our generals and tribal elders. We have been on the receiving end for far too long, and with Constantinople on its knees, there will never be a better time to start fighting back.'

----

# CHAPTER FOUR

## England

Sumeira sat at the water's edge, watching the lazy stream meander slowly past the overhanging willow trees. It had been several months since they had arrived in England from Venice, aided by good weather and favourable winds, and though the place still seemed strange and unnaturally green to her, she was finally settling into her new home.

Behind her, across the carefully tilled fields of corn and barley, their new home stood proudly on the slopes of a gentle hill, its stone walls and heavily thatched roof serving as armour against the cold and wet weather she had been assured would arrive soon enough.

The many discussions that had taken place during the days at sea about what to expect had failed to prepare her for what lay in wait as the soon-to-be wife of a recognised knight of the realm. She had struggled to come to terms with the reality of having so many servants to tend to her every whim. However, within days, the household staff had fallen for her gentle manner completely and had welcomed her as if she were one of their own, especially as she was only too happy to apply her medical skills to anyone who needed attention.

At first, the physicians in the village had seen her as a threat to their livelihood, but as time passed and they saw what she was capable of, they soon embraced her involvement, keen to learn from the woman who had spent most of her life tending the sick and wounded across the Holy Land and beyond.

Today, however, was a quiet day, and all the villagers were either in their church or resting at home on the one day of the week their new master, Cronin of Jerusalem, had granted them to rest.

The journey had been mostly uneventful until they had docked at Hampton, where her son, Jamal, had tripped over some rigging and fallen from the forecastle onto the lower deck, smashing his head on a barrel. For over a week, he failed to regain consciousness, and eventually, when he did recover, his speech was slurred, and he lacked some coordination in one arm. Sumeira was just happy that he had survived, but Jamal was devastated, having set his heart on becoming the best soldier he could and returning to the Holy Land to fight the Saracens. Sumeira knew he would be unlikely ever to achieve a high standard of weapon skills, but Jamal was blinkered in his approach, refusing to believe that he was unlikely to ever travel south again. As soon as he was able, he started training, and although he was helped every day by the huscarls attached to the manor, it was obvious to everyone that he was fighting a lost cause.

Sumeira shook the sad image from her mind. The fields were quiet apart from the songs of the ever-hungry birds waiting for seeds to drop from the crops and the occasional lowing of cattle in the fields. The sun was warm upon her face, and the faint babble of the brook played in the background, a soothing balm of gentle noise that tried valiantly to erase so many memories of pain that a life of hardship and warfare kept just below the surface.

She picked up a pebble at her side and threw it into the water, watching as the ripples set out to seek new shores, a journey somewhat similar to her own over the past few months. She smiled gently. For the first time in as long as she could remember, she was safe, warm, and secure, but despite this, deep inside, there was an uneasy feeling that taunted her in her quietest moments, a doubt that this peace and security she had so desperately sought throughout most of her life could not last. It was an unwelcome feeling, one she discarded almost immediately whenever it raised its ugly head, but no matter how hard she tried, it was always there, lurking in the shadows of her mind like a weeping infected wound.

She picked up another pebble, but her eyes widened in surprise when a larger stone splashed into the river, making her spin around to see who had disturbed her reverie. Leaning against the trunk of one of the willows was the man she had loved for many years, the same one who was soon going to make her his wife.

'Cronin,' she gasped, getting to her feet, 'you are back.' She ran towards him and flung herself into his arms, smothering him with kisses.

'Steady, woman,' laughed Cronin, 'you will have half the village talking about us.'

'To the devil with them,' said Sumeira, pulling herself away to arm's length, 'I was not expecting you for several days yet. How are you back so soon? Did you conclude your business in London?'

'I retrieved the documents from the commandery,' said Cronin. 'Apparently, they had been deposited there over two years ago by King Richard's representative. He was a man of his word.'

'And, are they all in order?'

'It seems so,' said Cronin. 'The deeds show my name as the legal owner, and the document is signed by Richard himself, so I am now the officially recognised Lord Cronin of Fallswater Manor. All I have to do, as a new knight of the realm, is to pledge fealty to King John.'

'When will you do that?'

'I have been told that he will be back in London in ten days and will be accepting similar petitions from other knights. Once done, we can focus on bringing this manor back up to the standards it once held.'

Sumeira hugged him again, relieved that his promised reward from the previous king had been made good.

'Tell me about your journey,' she said, 'for London sounds like a fascinating place.'

'We will talk more over supper,' said Cronin. 'For now, let us just enjoy the sun while it still shines, for, I assure you, its warmth will be gone soon enough.'

The rest of the evening, the two walked alongside the river and through the fields of the manor, sharing ideas and making plans about how they would manage the vast lands, and several villages gifted to Cronin by Richard. By the time they reached the house, the sun was already on its way down to the horizon. As they walked through the courtyard, one of the manor's stable hands approached them.

'My lord,' he said, 'I have checked your horse as requested. There was a stone lodged in one of its hooves, which was the cause of his lameness. A couple of days in the stable, and he should be fine.'

'Thank you, Karl,' said Cronin, looking over to where the rest of the grooms were feeding the horses. 'He has worked hard these past few days.'

'Where is Jamal's horse?' asked Sumeira. 'Is it in the stable?'

'How would I know that?' asked Cronin. 'I haven't seen him yet.'

'Did he not arrive with you?'

Cronin stopped walking and looked at Sumeira.

'I don't know what you are talking about,' he said. 'I haven't seen Jamal since the day I left. Why would he be with me?'

Sumeira's face fell, and she stared at Cronin with concern in her eyes.

'Cronin,' she said, 'remember how you asked him if he wanted to go with you to London?'

'I do, but he said no.'

'I know, but on the day you left, Jamal came to me and said he had changed his mind and wanted to go with you. You couldn't have been gone more than an hour, so I wasn't worried about him catching up with you. Did he not do so?'

'I have not seen him since that day,' said Cronin, 'and we were delayed for a while on the road, so there was no way he could have missed us.'

'Where do you think he went?'

'I don't know,' said Cronin, turning to the stable hand. 'Karl, did Jamal say anything to you when he collected his horse?'

'No, my lord, only that he needed extra fodder for a long journey.'

Cronin looked towards the horses now being fed.

'Where is the destrier?' he asked, seeing that the thoroughbred warhorse was missing. 'Is it in the stable?'

'No, my lord,' said the groom. 'Master Jamal took it with him. He said that you had asked him to take it to you as it may be needed.'

'I said no such thing,' said Cronin, turning back to Sumeira. 'Listen, I think I know where he may have gone but can waste no time here, I have to go after him. Go into the house and check his rooms. See if there is anything missing, especially any of the training weapons we have been using these past few weeks.'

'Why?' asked Sumeira. 'What's going on?'

'I think Jamal may have signed up to King John's army,' said Cronin. 'There are recruitment officers in all the local towns, and he already expressed an interest a few weeks ago.'

'He isn't ready,' gasped Sumeira. 'He'll never be ready.'

'I know,' said Cronin. 'But he can't see what we can see. You check his quarters, and I will ride to the town to see if he is there.'

'What if he has already signed up?'

'If he has, I will find them and buy his release,' said Cronin. 'Now go. I will return as soon as I can.' He turned to the groom. 'Saddle me a horse, quickly.'

'Take the bay, my lord,' said the groom. 'I was just about to ride her out.'

Cronin walked over and mounted the horse before riding it back towards Sumeira.

'I will be back within a few hours,' he said. 'Don't worry, I will find him.' Without another word, he turned the horse and rode out of the gate, heading down the track towards the town a few leagues away.

Sumeira watched him go, her stomach a knot of worry. The familiar feeling of dread returned to the forefront of her mind, and despite her very best efforts, this time it refused to leave. She knew that something was very, very wrong.

----

An hour later, Cronin reined in his horse outside a tavern and handed his horse to one of the many street boys waiting to carry out such duties. He flicked him a coin and walked into the smoke-filled room. Despite the summer heat, there was a fire in the hearth and a pot of potage hanging from an iron above the embers. The voices died away as the occupants realised who had entered, and Cronin looked around, seeking the recruiters who had made the tavern their home for the past few weeks.

'I'm seeking the king's representatives,' he said loudly. 'Those who were signing up men for the army. Are they here?'

The landlord walked over and bowed his head in deference to his master's station.

'My lord,' he said, 'they left a few days ago, along with all those who had signed. Is there anything I can do for you?'

'Was there a young man with them,' asked Cronin. 'A dark-skinned boy by the name of Jamal?'

'Are you talking about the simpleton?' asked a voice in the corner.

Cronin turned to look at the speaker. Ordinarily, he would have reacted to the insult, but this was a serious issue, and he needed to know the truth.

'The boy has suffered a head injury and is slower than most,' he said. 'He is not responsible for his actions. Was he with them?'

'Aye,' said the landlord. 'He was. On the night before they left, he and all the others were in here and they…' he paused and looked around nervously.

'What is it, man?' snapped Cronin. 'Speak up.'

'They took advantage of him,' said the man in the corner, standing up. 'They got him drunk and then engaged him in a game of dice. A decision he soon regretted.'

'What do you mean?'

'He lost everything he had,' said the man. 'Including his two horses. Someone said one of them was a destrier, a magnificent beast, I am told.'

'It was indeed,' said Cronin. 'But what of the boy? Do you know where he is?'

The stranger walked forward until Cronin could see his features in the candlelight. A vivid red scar ran down the side of his face from a long-healed injury. His breath was heavy with ale, and his stare was cold, totally devoid of respect or fear.

'Aye, I know where they went,' said the man. 'But it will cost you a tankard of ale to find out.'

'Rufus,' said the landlord. 'Curb your manner. This is our new lord and master. Show some respect.'

'He could be the king himself,' said Rufus, his stare still locked with Cronin. 'The price is still one tankard of ale.'

Cronin returned the stare, contemplating whether to teach the man a lesson but knowing he had more important things to do.

'Tell me where he is,' he said. 'And I'll pay for as much ale as you can drink.'

'You witnessed this pledge,' shouted Rufus, turning to face the other men in the tavern. 'If he should renege, we will know the man he truly is.'

'I'm waiting,' said Cronin.

The large man leaned forward until Cronin could feel the spittle on his face.

'They took 'em,' said the man, 'every last one of 'em to serve in the king's infantry. As green as grass, mostly boys. Nothing more than human shields, if you ask me.'

'What do you mean?'

'Many took the king's coin,' said the man. 'All those with experience or with rich fathers rode off in the morning, headed for London to join the royal army. But the others, the poor and the stupid, and I count your boy amongst those, were loaded into a cart and sent in the opposite direction.'

'What are you talking about,' asked Cronin. 'Where have they gone?'

'To Bristol,' said the man. 'And one of the three ships that were moored there, waiting for similar cargo.'

'You are making no sense,' said Cronin. 'Why would they do that?'

'I think the man may be as stupid as his son,' laughed Rufus, turning to face the rest of the men in the tavern. 'Perhaps if we engage him in a game of dice like his son, we could also win a horse.' He turned back to find the point of Cronin's blade pressed against his throat.

For a few moments, there was silence, but with a sudden movement, the man grasped Cronin's wrist with his left hand and pressed his own blade against the knight's heart. Both men stared into each other's eyes, knowing it was a stalemate.

'Now why would you do something as stupid as that?' growled Rufus. 'Just as we were getting to know each other?'

'I just need to know where my son is,' said Cronin. 'Now tell me what you know before I slit your throat.'

The occupants of the tavern held their breath as both men refused to cede the advantage until, eventually, Rufus stepped away and lowered his blade. Cronin did the same, and Rufus turned to pick up his tankard.

'The boy does not look like you,' he said, taking a drink. 'He has dark skin.'

'He is not of my blood,' said Cronin. 'But he is my son, nevertheless. If you know where he is, please stop wasting time and tell me what you know.'

'He is in Bristol,' said Rufus, turning back to face Cronin. 'Or at least, he was.'

'What do you mean?'

'As you know, King John is recruiting, and there has been a troop carrier in the harbour at Bristol for the last month waiting for the recruits to arrive. I suspect your son is amongst them.'

Cronin placed his knife back in his belt before turning to the landlord.

'Give this man what I promised, and I will see that you are paid.' He walked towards the doorway before pausing and turning back. 'This ship,' he said, 'has it already sailed?'

'It has,' said Rufus. 'Two days ago.'

'And are there any other ships sailing to France over the next few days?'

'There are, but why would you want to go to France?'

'To find the boy, of course,' replied Cronin. 'Why do you think?'

'I think there has been a misunderstanding,' said Rufus. 'Those men are not destined to fight in the French wars.'

'Then where are they headed?' shouted Cronin. 'In God's name, will someone tell me what is happening?'

'My lord,' interjected the landlord, 'those men are needed to replace those who have died in God's holy Crusade. They are sailing south, my lord, they have been sent to the Holy Land.'

----

Several hours later, Cronin arrived back at the manor house where Sumeira was waiting at the doors.

'Did you find him?' she asked. 'Is he with you?'

'He is not,' said Cronin, dismounting and handing his reins to the groom. 'Come, we will talk inside.'

A few minutes later, after quenching his thirst with a tankard of ale, Cronin and Sumeira sat at a table in the hall.

'What do you mean, gone to the Holy Land?' asked Sumeira. 'Both you and I know that he is not capable of defending himself yet, nor is he likely to be after his head injury.'

'I know,' said Cronin. 'But it seems that he willingly signed up, albeit after being plied with ale by the recruiters.'

'Can they do that?'

'They can, and do,' replied Cronin. 'As long as they have his mark upon a document, then it is legally binding and will be enforced by the crown. How they came about that mark is never questioned.'

'But surely, we can do something about it. He is certainly no knight and can hardly bear a sword properly.'

'The army needs men of all abilities,' said Cronin. 'He could be used as a cook, a wagon master, or even just for manual labour, but it matters not, for if there is a battle to be fought, then all men bear weapons, regardless of ability.'

'What are our options?'

'As a knight of the realm and lord of this manor, I can seek to buy his freedom from the king's service, but that will mean petitioning King John directly, and his decision will be final either way.'

'And if he agrees?'

'Then I will take the signed affirmation to the Holy Land and present it to the local military commander, who will have to honour it, and Jamal will be allowed to return home.'

'What if the King says no?'

'If he says no, then we will have no further recourse, and all we can do is hope he comes home alive when the fighting is done.'

Sumeira sat back in the chair, her worried eyes reflecting the candlelight.

'You have to go and see the King,' she said. 'You have to leave first thing in the morning.'

'I will go as soon as I can,' said Cronin. 'But I want you to be realistic. This sort of thing is far too insignificant for the attention of a king. Petitions such as this are usually dealt with by lesser officials who have no interest in releasing men from military service. King John may never even see the application.'

'But you already have a forthcoming audience,' said Sumeira. 'Can you not raise it with him then?'

'I will try,' said Cronin. 'But it depends on what sort of audience it is. If it is amongst other knights, then it will be impossible to raise. All I can do is promise that I will do my best.'

She reached out her arm and took his hand in hers.

'Just do what you can, Cronin,' she said. 'He is all I have left.'

----

# CHAPTER FIVE

## Bulgaria

Tarkhan Chelebri and Boyar Sigritsa waited alongside their horses in the vast courtyard of the Tsar's palace in Tarnovo. On the far side, the Tsar was deep in conversation with his political advisor, Gavril Alexander, the only man he trusted with his life. Despite their high positions, both Chelebri and Sigritsa had been kept waiting for most of the morning after being summoned for a military meeting. Now, at last, it seemed that something was happening, and as the distant conversation ended, they were summoned into one of the rooms within the outer walls, its air thick with the scent of burning oils and wax candles.

Both had been in the briefing room on several occasions, and even though the decoration was nothing compared to the opulence of the inner chambers, its grandeur still took their breath away. At the centre of the chamber was a large painted table holding a meticulously detailed map of the southern half of Bulgaria, along with the Balkan Mountains and the lands beyond, leading down past Constantinople to the Mediterranean Sea. Both men stared at the map, suitably impressed by the detail. Small carvings made from animal bone, placed in strategic locations across the map, represented the position of forces across the region, both Bulgarian and Latin, including the many crusader groups in and around Constantinople.

Another man, a junior officer in the Bulgarian army, stood silently at the end of the table, his face indifferent to the newcomers, his eyes fixed on the map. As the two commanders waited for the Tsar to arrive, a messenger ran in and whispered something into the officer's ear. A hushed conversation ensued before the officer walked to the opposite side of the table and moved one of the carvings to a different location deeper into the mountains on the map. Once done, he returned to his position guarding the map and resumed his indifferent stance.

A few minutes later, the Tsar entered the room, followed by Alexander. Everyone present bowed deeply as Kaloyan approached the table to lean over the map, his eyes taking in the altered positions since the last time he had attended. For a few moments, he ignored his commanders as the young officer brought him up to date with all the recent movements, information that was constantly updated by messengers from across the region many times throughout the day. Once done, he waved his hand, and the two commanders approached the table, both men fiercely loyal to their Tsar. Kaloyan's voice broke the silence, a low, self-confident rumble dripping with ultimate power.

'Tarkhan Chelebri,' he began, 'Boyar Sigritsa. You are aware of the situation in Constantinople and the threat it brings to our country. We had hoped that the Holy Father in Rome would embrace us into his fold, which would grant us immunity from the ever-reaching tendrils of the Crusaders, but in his arrogance, he has declined our petition, leaving us adrift to fend for ourselves. However, if he thought this would be a weakness, he is sadly mistaken, for we will not sit back while his foul-mouthed and dirty armies spread like a disease over the Balkans. We will take the fight to them, and while we will not encroach on Constantinople itself, we will make life there as hard as possible until they are forced to take notice of how powerful we are.'

He looked across the vast table, his arm sweeping in an arc.

'What you see before you is the most detailed map of the Balkans and beyond that exists. Our many spies, fast riders, and the use of messenger pigeons ensure that the locations of enemies and allies alike are all recorded here.'

'It is truly remarkable,' said Chelebri, his gaze drifting towards the formidable image of Constantinople and the many forces represented in and around the city. 'With this sort of information, a commander can truly plot a campaign in detail with most pitfalls potentially avoided.'

'You will also see,' continued Kaloyan, 'the position of many hidden supply camps amongst the forests and ravines of the mountains, as well as every village or settlement within fifty leagues of Constantinople. These supply posts are being filled as we speak and will be ready within days.' He pointed towards some of the larger roads leading towards the city. 'These are the veins through which the lifeblood of our enemy flows. Chelebri, I want you to take your men and target their supply routes across the region. Capture their wagons and livestock and deliver them to any of our nearby forces. Any guards accompanying the caravan are to be killed, and their bodies disposed of. It is very important that we leave no witnesses or trace of the attacks. I want it to seem as if they have disappeared into thin air.'

'Understood,' said Chelebri.

'Boyar Sigritsa, your men are renowned for their knowledge of these mountains, their ability to move unseen and strike where least expected. Your task is similar but will take place in the southern mountains of the Balkans. You are to visit every village or town on this map and establish their loyalty. If they are supportive of our campaign against the Crusaders, then we will offer them full protection against any enemy patrols. However, in return, we want men, supplies, and more importantly, a constant stream of information about any crusader movement in or around Constantinople. Direct them to send people into the city to watch everything that is going on, the old, the women, the children, I want all eyes reporting back to me in this room.'

'And if the villages do not display this loyalty?' asked Sigritsa.

'Then burn them down,' said Kaloyan. 'Kill everything that breathes and destroy the crops. Take no prisoners or hostages. I want to be able to remove that village from this map.'

'Understood,' said Sigritsa.

'You have three days to make your plans,' said Kaloyan, 'and report them back to me. Once agreed, your own emblems will be placed upon this map, and you will send riders back to me three times every day with any updates, at dawn, at midday, and at dusk. Once they have imparted their information, your men will return to you, with any intelligence deemed relevant to your continuing campaign. Is that understood?'

'Yes, my lord,' said both men.

'Good. Now familiarize yourself with the map and report back when you are ready.'

He turned around, and as everyone in the room bowed, he left to deal with other business, leaving Gavril Alexander behind with the general and the warlord.

'If you have any questions,' he said, 'you will direct them to me. I speak with the Tsar's authority.'

'I only wonder about the possibility of starting a war,' said Chelebri. 'At the moment, the Latins keep their distance, but as soon as we start hitting their supply lines, they will be forced to retaliate.'

'We are already at war with them politically,' said Alexander, 'and our way of life is challenged at every opportunity. The destruction of Constantinople has severely affected their ability to feed themselves, and their hunger is forcing them further afield to find food for their people. There are reports of their patrols ransacking the villages on our side of the border, and that alone is a good enough reason to attack. But now that the Pope has control of Constantinople, there is nothing stopping him from stretching his influence northwards to swallow us up. This is not only a fight for survival but for the assertion of our sovereignty, the protection of our way of life. They seek to subjugate us, impose their beliefs, their rule.' He paused, letting his hand rest heavily on the map. 'This response is our declaration that we will not yield, not to the Crusaders, not to Rome, and not to Constantinople. We fight for our freedom, for our future.'

'And you believe that we are strong enough to face their armies?'

'We will be,' replied Alexander. 'As we speak, our representatives are mobilizing men from across the region, but we are also in talks with our allies, who also see the Crusaders as a threat.'

'Who?' asked Chelebri.

'There are various peoples who have had enough of the Latin expansion, including the Greeks in Thrace, but chief amongst them are the Cumans.'

'The Cumans are mercenaries who come at a great price.'

'They are, but it is a price worth paying. Their skills as cavalry and with bows are unmatched in the known world, and if we can make an agreement, they will make us unbeatable.'

'Will they come under our command?'

'No. Their deployment will be with the Tsar himself and local control managed by me.'

'It is a long time since you picked up a blade in anger,' said Sigritsa.

'Don't let that bother you,' said Alexander. 'You just concern yourself with carrying out your orders. Now, are there any more questions?'

Both men shook their heads.

'Good. You know where I am if you need me,' and with that, he left the room to allow the men to make their plans.

----

# CHAPTER SIX

## England

For the second time in as many weeks, Cronin headed east towards London. The first journey had been without any concerns as he was going to receive his property deeds and the letters patent confirming his recently acquired status as a knight of the realm. All documents had been deposited by King Richard's officials with the Templar depository in Acre and subsequently transferred to the equivalent building in London after the king's death.

This time it was different. His mind was clouded with worry, for although Jamal was not his son, Cronin had grown very close to him and thought of him as his own. Now the young man was in danger, and even though Cronin wanted to go after him as soon as possible, he even knew that the politics of England demanded he first pledge allegiance to the king before he could think of leaving his newly acquired estate under the management of others.

The timing could not have been worse, for if this had happened just a few weeks earlier, then his documentation would still be in the safe hands of the Templars, countersigned by the previous king. But now that they had been transferred, they were no longer protected, and his ownership had to be ratified by the new monarch. This in itself was a worry, for King John, already known for his arrogant reign and lack of piety, had recently lost Normandy, a jewel in the crown of England. He was now rumoured to be contemplating raising taxes yet again to pay for a fresh campaign against France. As a king, John was unloved, brutal, and cunning, and Cronin, unused to the machinations of court life, knew that if he was to achieve the outcome he desired, he would have to tread carefully.

He arrived in London and took up temporary lodgings in a tavern near the king's residence, the imposing tower on the banks of the River Thames that had been built by William the Conqueror over a hundred years earlier. The tower loomed high above all the nearby buildings, its stone façade contrasting against the wooden structures surrounding it. For over a hundred years, it had been the London residence of royalty whenever they came to the city, but of late, it had also become something far more sinister, a place where the enemies of the king were imprisoned and sometimes disappeared in the depths of the night, never to be seen again. Of course, none of these rumours had been proven true, for no evidence existed of such things. And besides, even if there was, no man was in any position to do anything about it; John was far too strong... and merciless.

Cronin stabled his horse and walked into the lodgings. The tavern was a hive of activity, and the interior, dimly lit by flickering candles, cast dancing shadows across the walls and the faces of its patrons.

The scent of roasted meat and freshly baked bread, mingling with the tang of ale and the earthy aroma of wood smoke, filled the air as the conversation and laughter of commoners and merchants competed with the occasional clatter of tankards and the bard's melodic strumming in the corner. The floor was strewn with rushes, absorbing the day's muck brought in by the patrons' boots, and the tavern keeper, a robust man with a ready smile and an apron stained from the day's toil, directed his serving maids as they navigated the crowded space with trays of food and drink.

Choosing a spot near the fire, Cronin settled at a table and called for an ale, feeling an easing of the day's tensions. The tavern was not just a place for lodgings and sustenance but a sanctuary where the worries of the world outside could be drowned out with a cup of ale and the companionship of strangers.

He looked around the room, listening to the conversations. Some were discreet, couched in secrecy and the need for quiet, accompanied by furtive glances from suspicious-looking men with faces hardened by hardship, while others were raucous, delivered by men with rosy cheeks and fat bellies, the merchants and dealers who made their living off the backs of others, often the poorest in society. It was a melting pot of daily life in the city, and one that Cronin was certainly not used to.

Cronin looked up to see an attractive young woman standing next to him, a tray in her arms laden with empty tankards. She nodded to his half-empty drink.

'Another?'

Cronin nodded and lifted his tankard to finish the contents. The day's ride had been hard, and he had a particular thirst about him. A few minutes later, she returned and placed a fresh tankard of frothing beer on the table before him. The woman looked around and, seeing that her services were not required for the next few moments at least, dropped into the chair opposite him.

'I haven't seen you before,' she said. 'You must be new around here.'

'I am,' said Cronin, instantly on his guard. He had nothing to hide, but tavern maids were notorious for their curiosity, and he did not like sharing anything about his personal life, especially with strangers.

'I'm Alice,' she said. 'The landlord's daughter. What's your name?'

'Cronin.'

'Where are you from, Cronin?'

'I've been overseas for many years,' said Cronin, 'but have just returned.'

'You have the look of a soldier about you. Is that what you are?'

Cronin just smiled and took a sip from his ale.

'Ah, a quiet one,' said Alice with a smile. 'Don't worry, I'm not prying into your business. I just thought it would be nice to have a conversation with someone without drunken lust in their eyes. I'll leave you alone.' She got up to leave, but Cronin put out his hand to touch hers.

'I'm sorry,' he said. 'I did not mean to be rude. Please sit, it would indeed be nice to hear a friendly voice.'

She sat back down and leaned forward, putting her elbows on the table and her chin in her hands.

'So,' she said, a sparkle in her eyes, 'what do you want to talk about?'

'I don't know,' laughed Cronin, 'this was your idea.'

'Let's start with you,' she replied. 'Are you married?'

Again, Cronin's reluctance to share private information reared its head, but he realised it was just everyday conversation, and perhaps his years of service in the Holy Land had made him a little overcautious when it came to dealing with ordinary people.

'Not yet, but I will be soon.'

'Ah, so there is hope for me yet,' said the woman with a smile.

Cronin's brow furrowed, and he stared at the woman in shock.

'I jest,' she laughed. 'You should see the look on your face.'

'Sorry,' said Cronin again. 'I have not been in this sort of environment for a long time and think I may have forgotten how to socialise.' He nodded towards a group of agitated men near the door. 'I suspect you may have some trouble before the night is out.'

'They are harmless enough,' said Alice. 'The ale gives them ideas of grandeur that their station and physique can't match. They will all feel rather foolish in the morning.'

'What agitates them so?'

'Oh, the usual. Poverty, lack of opportunity, that sort of thing. But lately, it has been more about the draft.'

'The draft?'

'Haven't you heard? There are rumours that the king will be drafting a new army to try and take back what he lost in France, and men such as those will be amongst the first to go if it goes ahead.'

'If the king wills it, then they are obliged to obey his commands, are they not?'

'Of course, and I'm sure that if it had been Richard, then men would be lining the streets to serve under his banner, but this is John we are talking about, and he does not command such loyalty.'

'Why not?'

'You really haven't been back long, have you?'

'A few months.'

She looked around to check she wasn't overheard.

'Look,' she said, lowering her voice, 'I don't know why you are here or who you are meeting, but the richness of your attire, and the way you guard that satchel at your feet, suggests you are here to meet somebody at a high level. I may be wrong, but if it is with anyone linked to the royal household, just be careful. The Tower is nothing more than a pit of vipers, hand-picked by the king himself.'

'I will bear your words in mind,' said Cronin eventually.

'So, what's her name?' asked Alice.

'Who?'

'You said you were to be married. What's the lucky lady's name?'

'Sumeira. She is a physician.'

'A female physician, you say. There are not many of those around here. She will do well.'

'She's not in London; we have an estate near Bristol.'

'See, I knew you were rich. You may as well have a placard tied around your chest proclaiming the fact.'

Cronin didn't answer, realising that he had already revealed too much, but the woman was very easy to talk to.

'Listen,' she said, seeing his expression change. 'I have seen men such as you many times, and I suspect you are more than able to defend yourself, but this city is dangerous to those who walk its streets without knowing how its heart beats. I suggest that first thing in the morning, you look for better lodgings, as unfortunately, these may not provide you with the safety you require.'

'Thank you,' said Cronin. 'I can assure you that once I have finished my business, I will leave London as soon as I can.'

'You do that,' she said and got to her feet. 'If you need anything, just call out.' She flashed a lovely smile before walking away to continue collecting tankards.

Cronin sat back and cursed his lack of social skills. The woman had seemed very friendly, and it would have been nice to have some company, even for a few minutes, but his built-in sense of self-preservation made him suspect almost everyone he met for the first time. It was an unfortunate trait, but one that had kept him alive for many years.

For the rest of the evening, he sat at the table, eating a simple but wholesome meal of pork stew and vegetables before going to his room, a tiny cellar with a horsehair mattress on a roughly hewn cot. A jug of water sat on a table next to the bed, along with half a wax candle, already lit by one of the staff. The room was very basic, and the walls were damp, but he had actually paid more for the privacy as the only other options were shared rooms with up to six bunks in each. The poor quality was not a problem, for he had slept in far worse over the years, and although he could well afford better accommodation, until he was familiar with the ways of London, he felt more comfortable with what he was used to.

He sat on the side of the bed and opened the satchel he had kept at his side since he had left Fallswater. He lifted out the documents he had retrieved from the Templar depository and read them again by the light of the flickering candle.

When Richard the Lionheart had knighted him in the Holy Land, Cronin had been promised enough lands and income to ensure he had a comfortable life back in England. And while Cronin had received confirmation of his property while he was still in Acre, it was not until he had attended the depository in London a few days earlier that he had found out the depth of Richard's generosity. Not only had he received the deeds to Fallswater, but included amongst the paperwork were the deeds to another estate in the south of England called Cragsmere. It was a much smaller property with only a couple of acres stretching down to the sea, but apparently, it had its own well and had been managed by the local monastery for years.

He read the document again, still not quite able to believe his good fortune. To receive an estate as wonderful as Fallswater was a dream come true, but to receive two was beyond his wildest dreams, and he wasn't quite sure what to do with it.

As tiredness finally caught up with him, he put the paperwork away and laid back on his bunk. His meeting with the king was mid-morning, and he knew he would have to keep his wits about him if he was to get everything he needed.

----

# CHAPTER SEVEN

## The Tower of London

Hubert Walter and one of his administrators waited in the audience chamber for King John to arrive. As justiciar, Walter had direct access to the monarch almost daily, but since the king spent much of his time in one or more of his many palaces and households, it was often difficult to tie him down to make decisions on important matters of state. On such occasions, the designated responsibility for court affairs often fell to nominated officials such as Walter or other high-ranking officers. Today, however, the king, having returned a few days earlier, had ordered that he would personally oversee any requests for an audience deemed important enough for his attention.

The door opened, and as both men jumped to their feet, King John walked in without ceremony. Indeed, he was dressed rather plainly for such a politically visible day, and Walter guessed that the troubled look upon the monarch's face had a lot to do with it. He waited until the king had taken his seat before walking forward.

'Good morning, Your Grace,' he said, bowing his head in deference, 'I hope you slept well.'

'I did not,' said John. 'So let us just get this done as quickly as possible so we can get this day behind us.'

Despite being used to the king's often abrupt manner, Walter was surprised at the dismissive tone so early in the morning, especially as the audience had been arranged by John himself.

'As you wish,' he said and turned to nod at the other official, who promptly walked over and placed a pile of rolled parchments on a nearby table.

'And who are you?' asked the king.

'This is Father Ecgberht from the chancery,' said Walter, 'he has collated the documentation needed for today's perusal, under my guidance, of course.'

'It will take all day to read all those,' said the king, 'I assume you have a summary of each.'

'Indeed, I do, Your Grace, and I have taken the liberty of selecting the most important for your judgement today, specifically matters of law and any issues with alliances or threats to the crown.'

'What about the treasury?' asked the king.

'Most matters are covered, but we do have some outstanding letters patent issued by your late brother that must be addressed.'

The king's eyes rolled in frustration. It had been almost five years since King Richard had died, but his legacy still came back to haunt him on occasion, and it was growing very tedious.

'So be it,' he said, 'let us begin.'

For the next few hours, Walter summarised each matter recorded on the documents, explaining the implications for the king before waiting for the royal judgement. Any advice given or taken, along with final decisions, was carefully recorded by the administrator, ready to be transcribed into the formal records at a later date. Eventually, the king became bored with the whole process and held up his hand.

'Enough,' he said, 'I need to be somewhere else. Deal with the rest on my behalf and let me know the outcome.'

'Of course, Your Grace,' said Walter, 'but if I may, there are three cases that are above my level of authority and all concern the letters patent that I mentioned earlier.'

'Summarise them.'

'As you know, your brother, before he died, awarded several parcels of land to men close to him. Each bequest is not very large, but all have strong earning potential from the peasant farmers. All three men are attending the court today to request ratification of the awards.'

'All denied,' said the king. 'Pay them a nominal fee and confiscate the deeds. Put them in the name of the crown and install somebody we can trust to manage them on our behalf.'

'Of course,' said Walter, setting down two of the scrolls before turning back, still clutching the third. 'Your Grace,' he continued, 'if I may. This applicant is of particular interest, and before we dismiss his claim, I think there is a discussion to be had.'

'Go on.'

The justiciar turned to the cleric.

'We are done here for the day, Father Ecgberht, you may leave.'

The administrator bowed and left the audience chamber, leaving the king and Walter alone.

'Make it quick,' said the king, 'I have a hunger and a thirst about me.'

'Your Grace,' said Walter, holding up the one remaining scroll, 'the man who has presented these particulars was a Templar of great ability and has risen all the way through the ranks from commoner to knight. Indeed, he fought alongside your brother in the Holy Land and was knighted by Richard's own hand.'

'Why is this of interest to me?'

'Because,' said the justiciar, 'if you recall, a few days ago, you mentioned a situation that needed resolution.'

'I did.'

'Well, I believe that this man may be able to help us resolve the problem. He certainly has the ability, and the property he is claiming is small enough to be of no consequence should it be ratified. I think that if we make a deal, the problem we discussed a few days ago could soon be gone forever.'

'I do not make deals,' said the king. 'I issue proclamations.'

'Of course,' said Walter, inwardly cursing his own choice of words, 'but what I meant was that if you offered ratification of his letters patent in return for his services, those specific worries could be made to disappear very quickly.'

'I have my own men capable of resolving this situation,' said the king. 'Why should I trust a stranger?'

'Because,' said Walter, 'I know him. We served alongside each other in the Holy Land. We never actually spent much time together or conversed much, but he was often in attendance at Richard's briefings, especially in the latter days of the campaign. He was well thought of by nobles and commoners alike, for he is not just a formidable fighter, he is also a man of high intellect and loyal to his core. He would be an excellent choice to carry out your wishes.'

'He may well be,' said the king, 'but as I just said, I have my own people whose loyalty and skills at arms have already been well proven. This man, despite your petition, is unknown to me, so I ask again: why should I engage him?'

'Because, Your Grace, unlike so many others proclaiming their loyalty to gain favour on a daily basis, this man is devoid of any expectations of riches or advancement. He has lived his life and desperately wants to settle down with his family. It will cost you nothing more than that already pledged by your predecessor. He has not been tainted by the machinations of England's courtly life, and it could be said that he is innocent of most things political and even ignorant of other events, especially the one that causes you so much stress. If we bring him on board, he could prove a valuable asset in achieving the result you crave whilst remaining ignorant of your true intentions. Despite his innocence, he could be the strong arm that you need to bring this whole sorry mess to an end.'

'I thought you were that man,' said the king.

'Politically, I am, but as far as military matters are concerned, I am under no illusions that my own skills with a sword fall far short of those displayed by this man.'

'Are you asking that he accompany you to Normandy?'

'I am saying that it is a possibility,' said Walter. 'Every other name you have suggested has given me cause for concern, especially when it comes to loyalty or personal ambition.'

John sat back and stared at the justiciar for a few moments.

'If I sanction this proposal,' said the king eventually, 'it will need to be informal without signing any documentation.'

'I can do all that for you,' said Walter, 'and assuming all goes well, when he returns, you can deny all knowledge of any such arrangement and still confiscate his lands if you so wish.'

'It would be better if he did not return at all,' said the king.

'That too can be arranged.'

Again, the king stared at his justiciar, his calculating mind juggling all the possible outcomes. Finally, realising he had little to lose either way, he made his decision and got to his feet.

'Do whatever it takes,' he said, 'but we are running out of time, and if the situation we discussed is as bad as I have been led to believe, it could be the end of me, and by association, you.'

'Leave it to me,' said Walter. 'Do you require my services any further?'

'Not today. In fact, I think it is about time you headed for Normandy, and I expect your next audience with me will be to report the complete elimination of my potential problem.'

'It will, Your Grace,' said the justiciar, and as he bowed, the king left the audience chamber, his stomach already rumbling at the meal he knew awaited him in his quarters.

Once he had gone, Walter walked across to the window and peered out over the courtyard. The king was unlikeable at best, but Walter knew that if he wanted to continue enjoying his privileged life at court, he had to stretch every sinew to meet the king's demands, no matter how distasteful. A few moments later, Father Ecgberht returned to the room.

'Forgive my intrusion,' said the cleric, 'but I need to know what to do with those who still wait.'

'Tell them they are dismissed, but their petitions are being considered by the king. He will be in touch in due course, but the one called Cronin is to remain. There are things we need to discuss.'

'Shall I bring him in here?'

'No,' said Walter eventually, 'take him to my chambers. We need to talk in private.'

----

A few hours later, Cronin sat at a table in an antechamber connected to the justiciar's rooms. Both men had been served warm, watered wine before being left alone by the servants. Cronin stared at the official, unable to fathom quite what was going on.

'Sir Cronin,' said Walter eventually, 'thank you for waiting. It has been a long day, and I promise I won't keep you any longer than I need. You must be very hungry.'

'I am fine,' said Cronin, 'but question why I am here. I thought I was going to speak to the king.'

'Very few people get to speak directly to the king,' said Walter, 'but I have the authority to speak on his behalf.'

'So, has he considered my petition?'

'He has and is happy to countersign your deeds, but there is a condition.'

'And what is that?'

Walter stared at the knight, not sure how much to tell him. The whole truth would sound alarm bells, but he knew that Cronin needed to know as much as possible in order to understand the importance of the mission.

'Sir Cronin,' he said eventually. 'I know you have recently returned from the Holy Land and may not be as aware of the politics surrounding the king or his relationships with those across the channel.'

'I know he has recently lost Normandy,' said Cronin, 'and there is talk of a new campaign to retrieve what he has lost, but that is about it.'

'You are correct,' said Walter, 'but as is usual in such things, the detail is far more important, and you need to understand the background before we can discuss what it is we want of you.'

'Go on.'

'As you may know,' said Walter, 'King Richard had no sons and designated his nephew, Arthur of Brittany, as his heir. When Richard died, King John decried the decision as illegal and assumed the throne himself. As you can imagine, Arthur was incensed and led an uprising against John in France, eventually kidnapping the king's mother and imprisoning her in the castle at Mirebeau.'

'I did not know that,' said Cronin.

'It was a bloody time,' said Walter. 'But anyway, John laid siege to the castle, eventually rescuing Eleanor and capturing Arthur in the process. He is now held as a captive in this very tower, and negotiations are underway for him to renounce his claim to the throne.'

'Is he likely to do that?'

'It's possible. He is being well looked after and has been offered a very handsome package in return for renouncing his claim. However, it turns out that he may have a son in Normandy who is in danger of being harmed by those who would do him ill. Arthur has indicated that if we can retrieve his son, as well as the child's mother, he will gladly step aside and accept the package John has offered.'

'And you want me to find him?'

'Not exactly, for we know exactly where the babe is, but we cannot go riding in there with a troop of men as they would be slaughtered. However, we believe you are perfect to reach them and bring them back here unharmed. You have the skills and honour to reach places that most men cannot, and, as a Templar, your motives would go unchallenged.'

'If I accept and am successful, would not this child also have a claim to the throne?'

'Not if his father steps aside as promised.'

'And if he does not?'

'The ways of kings and princes are not for us to fathom,' said Walter. 'All we can do is carry out what they both want and let whatever happens after that, happen. Our king desires this child found and brought safely to England. And he believes you, Sir Cronin, former Templar and warrior of repute, are uniquely qualified for this mission.'

Cronin's thoughts raced. Normandy was a land fraught with danger, filled with factions loyal to the French and those still clinging to the Plantagenet reign. To enter such a viper's nest was perilous at best.

'And if I refuse?' Cronin asked, though he already knew the answer.

The justiciar's expression darkened.

'To refuse is within your rights, but unwise. The king does not look kindly upon those who thwart his wishes. You may find your position here... less than tenable.'

Cronin's jaw tightened. The threat was clear, as was the opportunity. He needed to set out as soon as possible to find Jamal, but before he could do so, he had to secure the lands given to him by King Richard, and that meant receiving the recognition of King John. It was all one big, political mess, and he knew he was backed into a corner.

'Tell the king I will undertake this mission,' he said at last, 'but I need to leave as soon as I can.'

'The sooner the better as far as we are concerned,' said the justiciar, a trace of a smile tugging at the corners of his mouth. 'I can provide you with all the provisions and documentation you need by tomorrow, as well as a ship to convey you across the sea. How many men will you need?'

'Just one,' said Cronin, 'you.'

The justiciar stared at Cronin in shock. It was the last thing he had expected.

'Why me?' he asked eventually.

'Because I recognise you from Richard's entourage in the Holy Land, and as far as I am concerned, any man trusted by Richard is good enough for me. Besides, I feel that with you at my side, there is less chance of betrayal.'

The justiciar held his tongue, realising that if he responded with the anger he felt at the accusation, he could likely lose the Templar's involvement. He took a deep sigh before nodding his head.

'As you wish,' he said, 'I will accompany you.'

'One more thing,' said Cronin, 'I need a rider to take a message to Bristol. The woman I am to marry awaits me there and will need to know what is happening.'

'Write your note, Sir Cronin, and I will have it delivered within days by the best rider we have in London. Be at the river dock at dawn the day after tomorrow, and we will set out with the tide.'

With a nod, Cronin stood up and offered his hand to the justiciar.

'So be it,' he said and stepped out into the cool night air, the heavy door closing behind him with a resolute thud. It was a distraction that he didn't need, but he had no other option. The mission was set, the stakes were high, and his path was fraught with unknowns. But Cronin was no stranger to jeopardy; it had been his constant companion for much of his life. Now, it beckoned him again, towards Normandy.

----

# CHAPTER EIGHT

## Off the Coast of France

The old ship creaked ominously as it cut through the rough waters off the coast of France, its sails billowing against the backdrop of a cloud-streaked sky. The deck was a flurry of activity, alive with the shouts of men and the slap of ropes against wood as they prepared for the long journey to the Holy Land.

Jamal stood apart from the commotion, his back to the railing, eyes fixed on the horizon where the sea met the sky. His olive skin and dark, curly hair set him apart from the others, as did the white bandage wrapped tightly around his head, a visible mark of his recent misfortune. Despite the constant movement of the ship, his gaze was steady, though inside, his thoughts churned as tumultuously as the ocean.

Piers and Tom, two of his fellow recruits, approached Jamal, their eyes filled with a mix of amusement and contempt as they towered over him.

'Look at him, lost in his own world,' Piers sneered, leaning close enough for Jamal to smell the stale ale on his breath. 'Do you even know where you are, boy?'

Jamal's eyes flickered with confusion and a hint of fear.

'I, I'm here to help... in the Holy Land,' he stammered, his voice barely above a whisper.

'To help or to spy? Can never tell with your kind.'

The young man's face tightened, the muscles in his jaw clenching, but he remained silent, unable to find words that wouldn't provoke them further.

'Let's see if he even knows how to wield a weapon, eh?' Tom suggested, withdrawing a training sword from a rack on the deck and tossing it over to Jamal. The rusting weapon spun through the air before clattering to the deck as Jamal missed the catch.

Laughter erupted from the crew, the sound cruel, cutting deeper than the salt air against his cheeks, but he knew he had to earn his place among these men bound for battle in the Holy Land.

'I'm here to fight in the name of the Lord,' he said, picking up the sword, 'and secure Jerusalem for Christianity.'

'You? Fight? laughed Tom. 'You can't even wield a mop properly. I've seen you swabbing the decks. Stick to that, son, or it's likely you won't last a day.'

'If you doubt my worth so much,' retorted Jamal, standing up, 'why not test it? I challenge you to a duel.'

Instantly, the mood changed. Banter was one thing, even insults, but to challenge another man to a duel, especially one who was so obviously used to warfare, was a completely different matter.

'Jamal,' said a voice, 'back off. They are only jesting with you.'

Jamal turned to see the ship's cook standing at the cauldron where he was preparing the potage for the evening meal. Inside, Jamal was already regretting the outburst, but there was no way he was going to back out now.

'No,' he said. 'He has given me nothing but trouble since the day we boarded. It can't go on like this.'

The crew fell silent, turning to watch the spectacle unfold as Tom, a broad-shouldered brute with a reputation for brawling, looked Jamal over, a smirk spreading across his face.

'You wish to cross swords with me, boy? Very well, let's see what you've got. Give him a good blade.'

Someone handed Jamal a better sword, and the gathered men opened up to give them space.

Jamal swallowed hard and adjusted his grip on the hilt, his stance uncertain as Tom, wielding his own sword with casual ease, advanced, his movements deliberately slow, almost mocking his inferior opponent. Jamal watched carefully, desperately trying to remember the many hours he had spent with Cronin back in England. The moves came back to him, and he lightened his stance, ready to move the instant a blow came his way. His grip reformed around the hilt of the unfamiliar sword, and he stared into his opponent's mocking eyes.

'Come on, son,' said Tom, 'let's get this done.' He lowered his own blade the slightest amount, and Jamal seized the opportunity to lunge forward. His sword arm rained blow after blow onto his adversary. His skill was surprisingly good, but it was quickly evident that they were the moves from a training field, and he lacked the experience of battle.

Tom countered methodically, blocking each blow without too much effort, chuckling under his breath as he waited for his opening.

'Come now, Jamal, you can do better than that,' he said, dodging another clumsy swing.

Jamal's frustration mounted with each miss, his face flushed with exertion and embarrassment. He renewed his attack, his arm aching with the effort, and in a final desperate attempt, lunged forward, overextending himself.

Tom simply stepped aside, letting Jamal's momentum carry him forward to collide with the mast before falling to the floor. Some of the men started laughing, and the pain of embarrassment cut into Jamal like an invisible blade.

Tom lowered his sword, shaking his head.

'Enough of this,' he said scornfully, 'it's clear you're no swordsman. Pick up a mop and stick to swabbing the decks.' He turned away and joined his comrades as they headed towards the cauldron for their daily ration of food.

Most of the watching men turned away, some in pity, as Jamal leaned against the ship's mast, the weight of the sword in his hand now feeling like the weight of his shame. His chest heaved, his dream of proving himself shattered against the hard deck of reality.

Off to one side, the commander of the recruits watched in silence, witnessing the boy's humiliation. Sir Edmund, an older knight, had lost a son in one of the earlier crusades, and when his wife had also died a few months earlier, he had taken the cross to follow his son's route to Jerusalem. He was a seasoned soldier, and age was catching up fast, but his status meant he had been given authority over this latest cohort of foot soldiers to be sent to the Holy Land.

'Hear me,' he shouted across the deck, causing every man to turn around. 'This ship carries the King's men to a sacred duty, not fools for their playground antics. There is a place for every man on this ship, including those less experienced, and we will not turn on each other like hungry dogs. We are bound by a common cause, and from here on in, you will treat each other as brothers, or answer to me. Is that understood?'

'Aye, my lord,' shouted the crew in reply, and as the commotion died away, the knight approached the boy.

'Jamal,' he said softly, 'courage is not only shown through the sword. There are many ways to serve and prove your worth. Let your actions speak for you in other ways, and given time, their words will become dulled.'

'I came to fight,' said Jamal, 'not swab decks.'

'Keeping the deck clean on a ship is one of the most important jobs there is,' said Edmund, 'for if it becomes dirty with slime, men will fall when the seas get rough and be injured. We need every soul fit and ready to fight at the end of this mission, or it will just be a waste of time. There will be time enough for fighting, and I'm sure your day will come, but if you wade in like that, you will fall in the first rush. Carry out the role designated to you while on board, and whenever we have some time, I promise I will help you with your sword skills.'

Jamal looked up at the knight, surprised at the offer.

'You would do that?'

'You have some abilities,' said Sir Edmund, 'and it is evident that you have had some training, but your movement is wooden, like that of a marionette. I cannot promise to make you a great fighter, at least not yet, but I may be able to give you enough skills to stay alive a little bit longer in the East. After that, your fate is in your own hands, and those of God, of course.'

Jamal nodded, not trusting himself to speak, the knight's words a small balm to his wounded pride. As the sky darkened and the crew dispersed, Jamal settled by the railing towards the rear of the deck, gazing out at the endless sea, knowing the journey ahead would be long and fraught with more than just physical battles.

----

Back in Fallswater, in the main hall of the manor, Sumeira paced by the tall, arched windows that overlooked the green fields of Cronin's new estate. Her face was drawn and pale, a stark contrast to the vibrant tapestries that adorned the walls. Her hands trembled slightly as she clutched a crumpled letter. The words on the parchment had blurred before her eyes, but their meaning was seared into her heart.

The door creaked open, and Hunter entered, his face grave, having heard the murmurs of ill news before he had even crossed the threshold. He closed the door behind him, his boots echoing softly on the stone floor.

'Sumeira, I came as soon as I heard,' he said, his voice steady but his concern evident. 'What has happened?'

Sumeira turned to face him, the letter clutched like a lifeline in her hand.

'It's Cronin,' she said, her voice barely a whisper. 'This letter, it says he's dead, killed in a skirmish in London. And not just that, the crown has seized our lands, our home, everything, on the pretence of debts owed to the king.'

Hunter's brow furrowed deeply as he took a step towards her, extending his hand.

'May I?'

She handed him the letter, watching as his eyes quickly scanned the contents. His jaw clenched visibly with each word he read.

'This is not right,' Hunter said firmly, looking up from the letter. 'Cronin was no debtor, and his loyalty to the crown was beyond reproach. This reeks of deception, Sumeira. Someone is playing us for fools.'

'But what can we do, Hunter?' Sumeira asked, despair tingeing her words. 'If Cronin is truly gone, we have no home, no protector.'

'I could go to London and try and find out the truth of the matter?'

'To what end? You are as much a stranger in these lands as I, and there is no way you would ever get anywhere near the truth.'

'How much time have they given you?'

'One week, along with a purse of silver to tide us over for the journey. The messenger suggested that we go back whence we came, to the Holy Land.'

Hunter handed the letter back to her, his eyes hardening with resolve.

'There is merit in his words,' said Hunter. 'We may not be able to do anything about Cronin, but we can honour his memory by finishing what he intended to do. We both know the Holy Land much better than we know England, and besides, that seems to be where Jamal is headed. I knew Cronin better than he knew himself at times and I will not abandon my friend, nor his family. We face this together, Sumeira; we will go back ourselves and we will find Jamal.'

A determined sigh escaped her as she straightened her shoulders.

'Then there is no time to waste. We need to move swiftly.'

'I will make the arrangements,' said Hunter. 'Trust in me, Sumeira. We will see this through together, for Cronin, for you, and for your son.'

----

# CHAPTER NINE

## Constantinople

Emperor Baldwin, resplendent in his chainmail and surcoat emblazoned with the cross, walked through the streets of Constantinople alongside Abbot Martin and their ever-present bodyguards. The crowds heading for the central square parted to let them pass, then followed in the emperor's footsteps, eager to witness whatever was about to unfold. Rumours had spread rapidly through the city that something significant was imminent, and no one wanted to miss it.

Upon arriving at the square, Baldwin and his entourage were guided to a temporary platform raised above the rubble, an unfortunate remnant of the recent terrible battle and raging fires that had beset the city. The nobles and key members of Baldwin's court were already seated on the platform, positioned in lines of ornate chairs behind the emperor's empty throne, each dressed in their finest attire. The image was a commanding one, designed to convey the strength of their new ruling masters. Yet, despite the powerful message, it was an illusion; the men of the council who had voted Baldwin in still had significant influence over how he governed the city and surrounding areas, albeit behind closed doors.

Baldwin was led to his throne and sat facing the gathering and the empty dais erected between them. Dominating the square was the impressive Column of Theodosius, a towering purple monument, twenty rods high, each rod the height of a tall man, celebrating the last emperor to rule both the eastern and western halves of the Roman Empire over seven hundred years earlier. Against the column rested a multi-platformed tower used by masons to access the higher levels when repairing the damage to buildings and monuments.

The crowd settled, and with a nod from the emperor, Abbot Martin unfurled a scroll to address the throng.

'Loyal people of Constantinople,' he began, 'your suffering has been great, and your patience even greater. The peace and prosperity of this new era are just over the horizon, awaiting us like a fresh dawn. But before we can plant the seeds of renewal, we must deal with the rot that caused this once-great city to degenerate into the hell it became.'

Some of the people murmured quietly. Life had always been hard, but at least they had known peace and had seen food on their tables. The killing of so many and the vast destruction within the city had left many with doubts about the promised benefits the Crusaders proclaimed daily.

'To that end,' continued the abbot, 'we have pursued and punished many of those responsible for so many years of pain and suffering, with many already rotting in their graves.' He paused, scanning the crowd to garner the greatest reaction. 'But today,' he said, 'we have brought the worst of them all to face you and your justice. We have captured and present to you, the warmonger, Alexios Doukas Mourtzouphlos, the monster of Constantinople.' He turned to the marshal standing near the edge of the dais, shouting the last command to be heard above the noise of the crowd. 'Bring him to face his accusers.'

Baldwin glanced at the abbot. He knew they had to use every opportunity to win the hearts and minds of the people, but Martin was going overboard with the theatrics, risking undermining the seriousness of the unfolding events. As the noise increased, a squad of armed men dragged a bound prisoner onto the dais before removing his hood to reveal a dishevelled figure. The man's clothes, though dirtied and torn, hinted at nobility, and his demeanour was defiant despite his predicament. As Baldwin stared, the man straightened, his eyes flashing with a mix of anger and arrogance.

'I am Alexios Doukas Mourtzouphlos,' he declared loudly, his voice echoing off the stone buildings around them. 'I am your emperor, rightful ruler of this city. You have no authority over me, and I demand to be granted the respect of my birthright.'

A murmur ran through the crowd. Baldwin looked at the man, studying his proud stance and the disdain in his gaze, the same man whose failures had partially led to the city's fall into Crusader hands. His predecessor had at least made an attempt at peace but had been overthrown and murdered by Alexios, ultimately leading to the battle that had destroyed the city and resulted in the deaths of many of its inhabitants.

'Silence,' Abbot Martin commanded, the authority in his voice quelling the whispers around him. 'You stand before the emperor as a prisoner. Your claims hold no weight here.'

Alexios's lips curled into a sneer, and he turned to face Baldwin a few steps away.

'You think you can control Constantinople, a city of such wealth and power, by mere force? I wielded true power here, respected by those who understood the gravity of my rule. You are but a foreigner sitting on a borrowed throne.'

Baldwin's eyes narrowed. The former emperor was an unlikeable man, and his arrogance needed curbing, a display that would cement Baldwin's position and quell any thoughts of dissent among the populace.

'Alexios Doukas Mourtzouphlos,' Baldwin began slowly, 'your so-called power has destroyed this city, killed thousands of innocent men, women, and children, caused your religious places to be stripped of everything your people held dear to their hearts, and led you here, bound and defeated. How dare you come here and lecture me on who should sit upon this throne? For even if the meanest beggar in this crowd were to be gifted this position today, he would be a greater emperor than you ever were.' Baldwin rose to his feet and walked forward to the edge of the platform. 'Never let it be said that I am anything other than a just man, so if you insist that you were a kind and just ruler, we will let the people decide your fate.' He looked up at the crowd, unable to judge the mood. 'Those who believe this man to be convicted unjustly, speak now, and he will be free to live out his life in exile.'

The crowd responded with a murmur of assent.

'And those who say he is guilty of brutality and of causing this once-great city of light to fall into darkness,' continued Baldwin, 'then let him know now.'

70

This time there was a huge uproar, sealing the prisoner's fate.

'Alexios Doukas Mourtzouphlos,' Baldwin continued, 'the people have spoken, and your fate will be decided by noon tomorrow.' He turned to leave but stopped in his tracks as Alexios called out again.

'This is an abomination, and even more so in the sight of the man this city honours.' He gestured up at the statue dominating the square. 'Kill me if you will, but history will record that you murdered a man even greater than Theodosius. In times to come, when the truth of your unholy conquest reaches the ears of the outside world, it will be my image that will be upon that column as the man who dared face up to your brutality and godlessness.'

Baldwin turned around and looked down at the prisoner before gazing up at the tower. A few moments later, he returned his focus to Alexios.

'You proclaim great self-importance, Alexios,' he said, 'and in honour of your former position and status, I will grant you your greatest desire.'

A ripple of confusion spread through the crowd, and Alexios himself looked bewildered. As the unrest grew, Baldwin again lifted his hand for silence.

'Alexios Doukas Mourtzouphlos,' Baldwin said, 'for your arrogance and failure to protect this city, and for your delusions of grandeur, I sentence you to live out your life to its fullest extent, free to walk in peace in any direction for as far as you may see, uninterrupted on pain of death by any man under this sun.' Alexios grinned, hardly believing his luck, but as the crowd grew angrier, Baldwin again lifted his hand. 'As promised,' he continued, 'I will also grant you your greatest desire, and you will share the gaze of Theodosius as he overlooks this great city as it once more regains its glory.'

All eyes turned to the statue atop the column, unsure of what was happening.

'You are going to create a statue of me?' gasped Alexios, his heart racing with joy.

'We are not,' said Baldwin, 'for you will soon see that view with your own eyes. Alexios Doukas Mourtzouphlos, you are sentenced to see out the rest of your life in freedom, atop the tower and alongside the statue of Theodosius, able to walk unhindered in any direction you wish. You will have a flask of water and a loaf of bread to curb your hunger, but no man will furnish you with more. Guards, take him away.'

Alexios's brow furrowed. The top of the column was only ten paces across in any direction, and the base of the statue took up most of that. He would hardly be able to stand, let alone walk about.

'I don't understand,' he stuttered. 'There is no way I can survive up there, and if I fall...' He left the sentence unfinished, recognising the steel in Baldwin's stare.

The soldiers gripped Alexios firmly, dragging him to the base of the column as he cried out in protest. The crowd parted, a mix of shock and anticipation hanging heavy in the air. The soldiers forced Alexios into the mason's tower, and at sword point, under the watchful eyes of the assembled crowd, a visibly shaken Alexios was made to climb.

As he ascended, his earlier defiance crumbled with each step, his figure diminishing as he reached the top. There, against the skyline of the city he had once ruled, the former emperor stood small and alone, just a few steps away from oblivion, alongside the statue of a true leader of men, contemplating his fate as the soldiers descended and dragged the wooden tower away.

Baldwin watched, his expression unreadable, and as he turned away to return to the palace, the crowd settled down, entranced by the sight of the man who had caused them so much suffering, clinging for his life to the statue high above the city.

The message was clear: Baldwin was not just a conqueror but a ruler whose authority was not to be challenged lightly.

----

A few hours later, in the dimly lit confines of his private study within the sprawling walls of the Crusader palace, the events of the day already pushed to the back of his mind, Baldwin found little solace. The room, filled with maps and scrolls, echoed the chaos that had engulfed the city since its fall. Amid the clutter of his war planning, the emperor sat across from Abbot Martin, his visage drawn with deep lines of worry and fatigue.

The small chamber was barely touched by the day's dying light that struggled through a narrow window, and a single lamp flickered on the heavy oak table between them, casting their shadows against the rough stone walls as they deliberated the fate of the empire.

'Abbot Martin,' Baldwin began, his voice low, as he poured two glasses of watered wine, the burden of leadership etching a worried furrow between his brows. 'The city groans under our rule as much as it did under the yoke of its previous lords. We have not brought the peace we promised.'

Abbot Martin nodded sombrely. His eyes, accustomed to the tranquil scripts of holy books, now frequently poured over the troubled writings of a city on the brink.

'Indeed, my lord,' he replied, 'and beyond the walls, the realm is growing restless. The granaries run dry, the markets are thin, and the people, our people now, grow desperate.'

Baldwin's gaze drifted to the maps spread before him. 'We took this city by storm and promised the people relief from their previous masters. But to date, we have given them nothing but more hunger, more pain, and an unknown future. We need more resources, Martin, something to give us a firmer standing and hope to a starving population. The people look to us for sustenance, not just sovereignty.'

With a heavy sigh, Baldwin walked over to the window, looking out over the vast expanse of the city that stretched beneath the twilight.

'Thessalonica,' he said, almost to himself, the word hanging in the air like a promise.

'Sorry, my lord,' said the abbot, 'I did not catch what you said.'

Baldwin turned and stared at his most trusted advisor.

'Just a few weeks ago, in this very building, you suggested that Thessalonica could be the salve to our financial predicament.'

'I did,' said the abbot, realising where the emperor's train of thought was heading, 'and I stand by that suggestion. It is rich in resources and will help feed the city. Strategically, it is well placed. Its acquisition would solidify our position here and as well as in the hearts of the Greeks. It might sway them to see us as rulers, not just conquerors.'

Baldwin returned to the table, leaning heavily against it.

'It will mean another march, another siege. More blood to water the soils of this land already steeped in centuries of conflict.'

'But action, my lord, often clears the doubt that festers in idleness. The people need a victory as much as they need bread. If you rally them in support of an attack on Thessalonica, they will see you as a true ruler and not just a conqueror.'

The option lay heavy in the air as Baldwin pondered, his fingers drumming a slow, thoughtful rhythm on the ancient wood. Finally, he nodded, the lines of his face set in determination.

'I see no other option,' he said eventually, 'and although the thought of more bloodshed is abhorrent to me, it is becoming more obvious by the day that we have to take drastic action or face a rebellion within the city. Summon the council, Abbot Martin. We need to have them and the people on our side if we are to march on Thessalonica, so let this be the act that turns the tide. We will bring them not just the sword, but also the grain and the promise of the olive branch.'

----

# CHAPTER TEN

## Normandy

The dawn was grey and unforgiving as Sir Cronin and Walter stepped onto the damp soil of Normandy. The estuary churned behind them, eager to reclaim the English knight and the king's justiciar back to its depths. The air was thick with mist, shrouding the sleepy village from prying eyes. Cronin squinted against the chilly wind that swept up from the sea, while Walter scanned their surroundings with an analytical gaze. He was the king's man through and through, every inch of him schooled to decipher friend from foe in the murky depths of political intrigue.

As their boots sank into the wet earth of the riverbank, leaving deep impressions behind, the local villagers eyed them with a mixture of curiosity and suspicion. Normandy was no stranger to visitors, but the arrival of unknown men, with their cloaks billowing and swords at their hips, was enough to stir a wary buzz among the people. Behind Cronin and Walter, another half a dozen knights led their horses down the ramps to join them on the muddy banks of the estuary, an addition that Walter had insisted on before they had left the dock back on the Thames.

'Are you sure this is the place?' Cronin asked, his voice tinged with doubt. 'It is hardly more than a fishing village.'

'That is exactly what it is,' replied Walter, his tone measured. 'Until recently, it was loyal to our king. We will be safe here.'

'There is no such thing as a whole village without spies,' said Cronin. 'I bet there will be messages heading inland before the sun sets.'

'Perhaps so, but by the time any interest is raised, we will be far away, and the ship long gone. Besides, all they know is that a group of men disembarked from a ship and disappeared into the forests. They have no idea who we are, why we are here, or where we are going. We will stay here tonight and leave before dawn tomorrow.'

Cronin's response was a curt nod. He pulled his cloak tighter against the biting wind and gestured towards a modest building with smoke rising from the chimney.

'There, that looks promising.'

Walter nodded and led the way to the inn, a low, timber-framed structure, its walls weathered by the salty winds. As they stepped inside, the warmth from the hearth fought off the cold clinging to their bones. Walter approached the innkeeper, a stout man with a bushy beard, and requested lodgings for all his men, paying with a healthy purse of silver coins.

'If you feed and water us well and keep your mouth shut, there will be a similar purse before we go,' he said in French. 'We also need a place for our horses.'

The purse quickly disappeared into the innkeeper's pocket, and he turned to issue a range of commands to the old woman stirring a pot above the fire. Within a few minutes, platters of raw fish pieces were added to whatever was cooking in the pot, and a younger woman started bringing clay flasks of rich red wine to the trestle tables. Meanwhile, a boy went outside to show the rest of the English party to the stables.

Within the hour, seven of the travellers were seated around a table, eating a fish-laden stew and tearing into mountains of bread teetering in the middle of the table. The eighth man sat at a narrow window alongside the door, keeping watch on the comings and goings outside the inn.

As the night wore on, tensions eased, and although they knew they would have to move before dawn, they were, for the moment, warm, safe, and with full bellies. Some of the men retired to the two rooms the innkeeper had made available, leaving Cronin and Walter alone.

'Did you send that letter?' asked Cronin.

'I did,' said Walter. 'I told her you had been delayed with service to the king, but you would be back within thirty days. I also sent the signed deeds back to her, granting you and your descendants full lordship over the Fallswater estates in perpetuity. I also have in my possession a writ bearing the king's seal, releasing your son from any servitude placed upon him. All you have to do is present it to whoever commands his unit, and they are bound by royal decree to release him into your custody.'

'You have my gratitude,' said Cronin, completely taken in by the justiciar's lies. 'So, you still haven't told me anything about our destination. I would assume that as the potential heir to a kingdom, the child is secreted away in some fortress hidden from prying eyes.'

'He is certainly hidden away,' said Walter, but not where you may think. The mother and child live in a small village just a few leagues from here, in a range of mountains to the east. She was a serving girl at Arthur's court before he fell out with King John. Arthur took a liking to her and, when she fell pregnant, she was whisked away by his courtiers with a purse of silver to keep the baby's existence secret. Now that he does not enjoy the privileges he once did, it seems he has had second thoughts and wishes to be reunited with his son and, of course, the girl.'

'And you know where she is exactly?'

'I do.'

'How?'

'The same way all such secrets are unveiled, greed. One of the courtiers who helped whisk her away realized the knowledge was valuable and sold the information to one of our spies in the area. As you can imagine, he was paid handsomely, with the promise of more if and when we find them. He is meeting us tomorrow in a forest near here and will lead us to the village where we will take them into our custody and return to England seven days from now.'

Satisfied that they had the beginnings of a plan, Cronin finished his drink and headed for his cot, extremely tired after the sea crossing. Walter watched him go and was soon joined by one of the remaining men at one of the other tables, a man named Peter, one of the justiciar's loyal kinsmen.

'Does he know?' asked Peter.

'Not everything,' replied Walter. 'But I have to keep him engaged, at least until we reach the village. Once we have the child... well, you know what to do.'

'I do,' said Peter.

'Do you have the package?'

'Yes.'

'Good. Keep it to yourself until it is needed. To reveal the contents too soon would garner Cronin's mistrust.'

'As you wish,' said Peter. 'You should get some sleep, my lord. I'll make sure someone stays on watch.'

----

Back in England, the heavy scent of salt and tar mingled as Sumeira and Hunter approached the bustling docks at Bristol, their horses sold, and carrying only two bags between them. Ships of all sizes were moored tightly along the wharves, their masts swaying gently like tall reeds by a riverbank. The clamour of sailors and the creaking of timber filled the air as people filled the dock in all directions, some loading ships, others unloading, and some transporting goods to the merchants or hawking their wares to the passing crowd.

Sumeira and Hunter forced their way through the throng. After making countless inquiries, they had at last found out that there was a ship headed to the Holy Land, but it was due to leave within the hour, taking advantage of the tide, and they were desperate to be on board.

They stopped before a sturdy ship, its hull dark and weathered from many voyages, the name *Spiritus Sancti* painted in flaking letters along its side. Men moved briskly across the deck, loading crates that bore the king's seal, weapons destined for the distant shores of Acre.

'There it is,' said Hunter. 'We need to find someone to talk to.' He approached one of the men standing at the end of the gangway as the last of the stores were wheeled up to the ship on handcarts.

'Greetings,' he said, 'I need to speak to the captain. Is he around?'

'Who needs to know?' asked the man, looking past Hunter at Sumeira.

'My name is Hunter, and this...' He paused, realizing that a single woman would immediately become an object of interest to most men. 'This,' he continued, 'is my wife, Sumeira.' He glared at his companion, his widened eyes begging her to go along with the subterfuge.

Sumeira returned a thin-lipped smile, catching on to the necessary lie.

'The captain is busy,' said the sailor, 'tell me what you want, and I will relay it to him when I can.'

'We need to buy passage on this ship,' said Sumeira, walking forward. 'We understand you are headed to Acre.'

'Aye, that we are,' said the man, 'but if you think you can come with us, you can think again. There is no room for a woman on this ship.'

'With respect,' said Sumeira, 'unless you are the captain, I believe that decision is not yours to make.'

The sailor's eyes narrowed, a mixture of thinly veiled lust and scorn for a woman who dared challenge his authority.

'I suggest you turn right around, lady,' he said, his voice lowering dangerously, 'before I say or do something you are not going to like.'

'That is not going to happen,' said Hunter, stepping forward to place himself directly between the sailor and Sumeira.

The look on the sailor's face immediately changed to one of humour, seemingly delighted to be challenged by this stranger. If it came to blows, he had no doubt there could only be one victor.

'I will say this once only,' he said, 'I don't know and don't care who you are, or where you want to go, but I can promise you this, it won't be on this ship. Now be gone before you get hurt.' As he spoke, another three sailors drew near, their hands resting on the leather coshes hanging from their belts.

'Just let me speak to the captain,' pleaded Sumeira again, 'I can pay well and besides, I am a physician. I can work my passage.'

The sailor turned away, ignoring the plea, but a voice called down from above.

'Harvey, let them through.'

All eyes turned up to see a heavily bearded man watching down from the ship's rail. The man exuded authority, and the firmness in his voice commanded respect.

'Let them come up,' he said again. 'I will listen to what they have to say. And get those last carts loaded. We have to sail with this tide, or we will be stuck here for days.'

Harvey stood aside and scowled at Hunter and Sumeira as they made their way up the gangplank. At the top, the captain waited until they stood before him and looked them both up and down.

'My name is Captain Thorne,' he said, his face just inches away from Sumeira's. 'And I am in command of this ship. You say you are a physician. Have you ever treated scurvy?'

'I have and also know how to avoid it.'

'What about broken bones?'

'I have set hundreds, as well as amputated many that were beyond repair.'

'Infections?'

'With the right ingredients, I can ease most, but there is no guaranteed cure. Some men just die from such afflictions, and nothing man or God can do about it.'

'What about you?' asked the captain, turning to Hunter. 'What skills do you have?'

'Not many applicable to a ship,' said Hunter, 'but I can work as hard as any man and can cook better than most.'

Silence fell again as the captain considered his options.

Sumeira stared back. He was a broad-shouldered man with a red beard and a gaze as sharp as a hawk. His face was a moonscape of ravines and pockmarks from a lifetime facing the cruel weather that aged most men who lived their lives at sea.

'Captain Thorne,' she said, growing impatient, 'we seek, no, we need passage to Acre, and this is the only ship available for the next three weeks. Please, I beg you, allow us to join your crew and I promise that we will be no burden. On the contrary, we will do whatever you require of us to pay for our passage. We also have this.' She reached beneath her cloak and produced the bag of silver given to her by the king's messenger a few days earlier.

'There is more than enough here to pay for passage for twice our number. Allow us to sail with you and it is all yours.'

Captain Thorne eyed them both, his look sceptical. He glanced back at his crew, hard men, rough from years at sea, some nursing old wounds that had never properly healed. He knew the voyage could use someone who could stitch a wound or set a bone.

'It's a hard journey, my lady,' he said, 'and you'll not find much comfort among these dogs,' he gestured broadly at his crew, who had paused to watch the exchange.

Sumeira met his gaze firmly, undeterred.

'I have travelled far and seen much hardship, Captain. I do not seek comfort, only passage.'

Captain Thorne grunted, weighing their resolve against the purse of coins. Finally, he nodded curtly.

'Alright. I will take your silver, and you will serve as the ship's medic. We have no cabins, so you will share a corner below decks. Keep yourselves to yourselves and stay away from my men. We keep a tight ship here, and I'll not have any trouble.'

Sumeira breathed a huge sigh of relief and handed over the purse. It had been close, and there was no guarantee that they would even reach the Holy Land, let alone find Jamal, but at least they had made a positive step.

As the last of the stores were loaded and the ship prepared to set sail, Sumeira looked out over the harbour. Her time in England had been but a brief moment, but despite its greenness and the company of the man she had loved for a long time, she realized she was actually happy to be heading back to the Holy Land, a place filled with danger, hardship, and bloodshed, yet also blessed with a beauty all its own, one that was waiting to welcome her home.

----

# CHAPTER ELEVEN

## Constantinople

The early morning at the camp outside Constantinople was bustling with activity, the air filled with the neighing of horses and the sound of men preparing themselves and their equipment for the march westward to Thessalonica. Baldwin, cloaked in a mantle of responsibility as heavy as his chainmail, surveyed the organised chaos with a critical eye. It had not been hard to convince his nobles of the benefits of the attack on their neighbouring city and, once agreed, things had moved swiftly. However, now that the time was here, the reality of the situation began to sink in. There was no doubt that, of the two cities, he possessed the stronger army by far, but it did not mean it would be easy, and many good men would die before the matter was resolved.

As dawn broke over the camp, Baldwin summoned his commanders to his tent for a final briefing. The air inside was thick with the smell of leather and freshly polished metal. Maps of the region were spread out on a large table, weighted down with stones at each corner.

'Gentlemen,' Baldwin began, his voice firm and commanding, 'as you know, Thessalonica is not just a strategic objective. It is a necessity for securing our hold on this empire. Its wealth and position can support our cause and provide a bastion against any who would challenge our rule.' He stepped forward and looked down at the map. 'Our scouts have reported back, and it seems our path may be trickier than we envisaged.' He pointed at a range of hills between their current location and the intended target. 'The rains have been heavy, and these passes will be muddy and difficult. We must keep the men focused and the supply wagons well-guarded. We will keep the heavy cavalry at the rear to aid any wagons that become mired. I trust you to oversee this.'

'What of the local populace, my lord?' asked one of his commanders. 'How likely are they to support our march?'

'There is no way of telling at the moment, but we do know the rulers of Thessalonica are currently dealing with unrest within its walls. With the right approach, the people may yet see us as liberators rather than conquerors.'

The briefing lasted no more than an hour, and once all the final details of the march had been agreed, Baldwin stepped out of his tent to find the camp in its final stages of preparation. Squires scurried about, attending to their knights' needs, while soldiers performed last-minute checks on their equipment.

Approaching his horse, Baldwin was joined by Abbot Martin.

'You were quiet in there,' said Baldwin. 'Are you having second thoughts?'

Martin looked at Baldwin with a grim sincerity.

'Whichever way we look at this, there is always a risk,' replied the abbot. 'It's a bold move and fraught with peril, but it is necessary. I worry, though, that the deeper we entrench ourselves in Greek affairs, the more we might find ourselves entangled in conflicts not our own.'

'It is a fair point,' said Baldwin, 'but there is no alternative that I can see, so the quicker we get this over with, the better.' He mounted his horse and looked out over the ranks of soldiers forming up in neat rows, their banners fluttering in the morning breeze. 'Let's move them out, my friend, we are going to Thessalonica.'

As the army stirred into life, all thoughts turned to the road ahead and the difficulties they would no doubt face before a single blow had been struck. With all minds focused, nobody noticed the two men on horseback atop a nearby hill, watching them leave, and as the army left the outskirts of Constantinople, they turned their horses away and headed back to Bulgaria.

----

The journey westward was arduous and fraught with challenges. The roads, swollen with autumn rains, proved treacherous as Baldwin's army navigated through the muddied and slippery passes. Each day brought its own set of trials, from wagons stuck deep in mud to sudden downpours that chilled to the bone. Yet, under Baldwin's steadfast leadership, the army pressed on, their spirits bolstered by camaraderie and the occasional dry night under the stars.

On the fifth day of the march, as the army made camp near a broad river swollen by recent rains, Baldwin took a moment to walk among his men, stopping to help a group of soldiers repair a broken axle on one of the supply wagons. His hands, though accustomed to the hilt of a sword, worked deftly with the tools.

'Your Majesty,' said one of the soldiers as he handed Baldwin a wooden peg, 'we've heard stories of Thessalonica, of its grand walls and bustling markets. There is talk that it is a rich city and will be well defended.'

Baldwin, securing the peg with a few firm taps, looked up at the young man. 'All cities are well defended,' he said, 'but this is the strongest army in this part of the world. We are strong, experienced, and have God on our side. I believe it may not come to conflict, and the city elders will negotiate, for there is a place for both cities to exist and thrive side by side. But if not, and they resist our advances, then we are more than capable of bringing down the walls. Do not lose any sleep over that.'

'Thank you, my lord,' said the foot soldier, as Baldwin and his entourage continued forward to the head of the column.

As night fell and the march came to a halt, the men gathered around the campfires to cook the one hot meal they looked forward to each day. Despite the weather and trials, morale was good as they had made good time and still had plenty of supplies.

Baldwin and Abbot Martin sat in the emperor's tent, eating their own meal of goat and vegetables, when one of the guards ducked under the flap.

'My lord,' he said, 'one of the scouts has arrived with important information.'

'Send him in,' said Baldwin, getting to his feet and wiping his hands on a piece of linen.

Moments later, a man, filthy from the dust of the road, entered and bowed slightly. He smelled of sweat and horses and was obviously exhausted.

'My lord,' he began, 'it appears that there is a second army advancing towards Thessalonica from the south. They're moving swiftly and could reach the city before us.'

Baldwin's brow furrowed at the news.

'A second army? Do you know what banner they march under?'

'We do,' said the scout, 'it is being led by the Marquess of Montferrat.'

'Boniface,' hissed Martin. 'I knew it.'

'This cannot be a coincidence,' said Baldwin. 'But we kept our plans close to our chests. How did he know?'

'We must have a spy in our midst,' said Martin, 'and he decided to act before we could reach the city ourselves. If he does, any victory will be a lot harder to achieve. His own men match ours in battle readiness, and behind stone walls, they would be difficult to overcome.'

Baldwin moved over to the ever-present map on one of the tables.

'Show me his positions,' he said, and the scout followed him over, staring at the map to orientate himself.

'We are here,' he said eventually, pointing at the map, 'and Boniface is here, three leagues to the south. He has further to travel, but the road is easier. I also have reports that he has the support of several supply ships, but I have not had that confirmed yet.'

Baldwin stared down at the map. 'There is no way we can beat him to Thessalonica,' he said. 'Even if we quicken our pace, I reckon he has two days on us, more than enough time to enter the city and man its walls.'

'My lord,' said the scout, 'if I may.' He pointed to a junction of valleys further west between them and Thessalonica. 'If we press hard and change our route, you could divert to the south here and intercept them near this river. It is out of our way, but the going is easier, and you could stop him before he gets there.'

'There is no way I am going to commit our men to fight a fellow crusader army,' said Baldwin. 'We share the same blood, and men will die needlessly.'

'I agree,' said Martin, 'but Boniface doesn't know that. If we can block his way and face him with a show of force, he may withdraw before a blow is dealt. Alternatively, it may be an opportunity to parley and agree on terms. If both armies appear before the walls of Thessalonica as one, they will throw open the gates in fear.'

Baldwin considered the alternative plan, tapping a finger against the map.

'A parley is preferable. We must try to join forces or, at the very least, get him to turn back.' He turned back to the scout. 'How long until we get to that valley?'

'Two days for us,' said the scout, 'three for them, but we will have to move quickly.'

'So be it,' said Baldwin. 'Summon the commanders for a briefing. Our plans have just changed.'

----

Hundreds of leagues to the north, deep within the shadows of Tarnavo's stone walls, Tsar Kaloyan of Bulgaria convened with his trusted advisor, Gavril Alexander, in the dimly lit map room. The air was thick with the musk of old parchment and burning torches as they considered the latest information delivered by their spies in the crusader camps.

Both men watched in silence as the map master moved indicators across the map to reflect the new positions of the crusader forces, their sharp minds analysing the information and calculating the options.

Kaloyan hovered over the map, his finger tracing the paths that led from Constantinople to Thessalonica. His brow furrowed deeply as he absorbed the gravity of the advancing Christian armies.

'They push hard upon Thessalonica,' he muttered, his voice a low rumble in the quiet of the room. 'If they were to take the city, as seems their intention, then it would create a much larger crusader state, one that we would struggle to deal with both militarily and economically. We have to do something to stop them, but there is no way we could get there in time to stop any assault. We need more time.'

'My lord,' said Alexander, 'direct confrontation may risk too much at this juncture. We might consider alternatives that could sway the balance without open conflict.'

Kaloyan's gaze shifted to meet his advisor's, a flicker of interest lighting his stern features.

'Explain your thoughts, Alexander. What do you propose?'

The advisor leant over the map, his hand pointing to the walled city of Adrianople.

'Here lies a pressure point. Adrianople is occupied by a small force loyal to Baldwin. The people, however, are not happy to be governed by the invaders and would turn on their occupiers given the chance. If we can destabilise the city, it could serve to distract Baldwin's focus, for they could ill afford to ignore unrest in such a key city.'

Intrigued, Kaloyan considered the suggestion, his mind working through the ramifications.

'You suggest we fan the flames of rebellion, yet keep our hands clean of the ashes?'

'Precisely. At least until we have time to grow our forces and consider more direct action. We have contacts within Adrianople, merchants, disgruntled nobles who chafe under the Empire's dominance. Subtly supported, they could ignite dissent that would force Baldwin to divert resources meant for Thessalonica.'

Kaloyan nodded slowly, the strategy aligning well with his own predilections for indirect warfare.

'Ensure our involvement remains shadowed. We cannot afford direct links to these actions. How will you secure our anonymity?'

'I suggest we divert Chelebri to gain access to the city with a small force of men. They will engage with our sympathisers and lead the revolt. None will know the instigation comes from us.'

'Do it,' Kaloyan commanded, a decisive edge to his voice. He turned back to the map, his finger now hovering over Thessalonica. 'And of Thessalonica, keep a watchful eye. We must be ready to exploit any opportunity or weakness that this distraction might reveal.'

Alexander bowed, a subtle movement that conveyed both respect and the weight of responsibility. 'It shall be as you command, Tsar. Patience and precision will guide our steps.'

As Alexander exited, Kaloyan remained alone in the flickering torchlight, his eyes tracing the intricate web of loyalties and treacheries that the map laid bare. Outside, the wind whispered against the high stone walls, a harbinger of the coming storms that their secret machinations would surely bring.

----

# CHAPTER TWELVE

## Normandy

The following day, Cronin and the rest of his comrades were leagues away from the fishing village by the time the sun rose. The path was good and rose steadily towards the distant mountains, easily visible in the crisp morning air.

'There is a vast forest a few days ahead of us,' said Walter. 'I have been there before, but beyond that, the ground is unknown to me. We will be reliant on the trustworthiness of our guide.'

'Is that not a great risk?'

'It is, but we have made arrangements to ensure we are granted safe passage.'

'What arrangements?'

'All will be revealed,' said Walter. 'Just be patient.'

----

For the next two days, they headed eastward, seeing nobody but the occasional farmer or shepherd along the way. Finally, they saw the looming forest filling the horizon and continued to the edge of the treeline before reining in their horses and dismounting to allow them to drink.

'This is the agreed place,' said Walter. 'We will wait here but keep our wits about us. Our man will bring the guide to us soon enough.'

Within the hour, two riders appeared along the outskirts of the forest and made themselves known to the justiciar. Cronin recognised one of the men as one of the soldiers who had sailed with them from London.

'This is Adam of Kent,' said Walter. 'He was sent ahead two days ago to notify this man of our arrival. He was the one who initially sold us the information about Arthur's son. What is your name?' he asked, turning towards the newcomer.

'Jaques de Londres,' came the reply. 'I have been expecting you. Do you have the second half of my payment?'

'We do,' said Walter, 'and you will receive it in full as soon as we have the woman and child in our possession.'

'She is not far away,' said the Frenchman and looked across at Cronin. 'Is this the man who will retrieve her?'

'He is. His name is Cronin.'

'He looks nothing special,' said Jaques. 'I was expecting someone more imposing.'

'You let me worry about that,' said Walter. 'Now, tell me about this woman. What is her name?'

'She is called Annette,' said Jaques, 'and lives two leagues from here in the village of Brejon. She is totally ignorant of your plot to rescue her and the child.'

'What do you mean, rescue?' asked Cronin. 'Is she here against her will?'

'To an extent, yes. This is not her homeland and although she is not kept under lock and key, she is under strict orders not to move far from the shadows of the chateau walls. Her life here is not unpleasant, but she longs to return to her homeland near the Anjou region.'

'What about the lord of the chateau?' asked Cronin. 'Is he aware of the identity of the child's father and the implications that incurs?'

'He is. And should he discover your plan, he will deploy every resource at his disposal to stop you, so you need to be careful.'

'Does the woman sleep outside the chateau walls or inside?'

'Inside, as does the man she lives with. By day, they help till the fields, but the babe is looked after by a nurse while she is away. He is never allowed out, so you will need to think about how to get in there.'

'And that is why you are here,' said Walter, turning to Cronin. 'We want you to gain access, find the child, and bring him out to us so we can flee back to England.'

'And how am I supposed to do that?'

'With the use of this,' said Walter, nodding to Peter, who was standing to one side.

Peter retrieved a bundle from the back of his horse and placed it on a boulder before producing a knife and cutting away the bindings. As he did, the wrap of linen fell away, revealing the contents inside: a dirty white cloak and surcoat emblazoned with a blood-red cross.

Cronin stared in shock as he realised what he was looking at and lifted his gaze to glare at the justiciar.

'What is this?' he asked, his tone low and his eyes narrowed with suppressed anger.

'You know exactly what it is,' said Walter. 'You wore the same garb for many years. Peter also has the rest of the equipment you may need, sword, dagger, that sort of thing. I think you will find we have thought of everything.'

'But I no longer serve as a Templar Knight. I have already told you this.'

'You also said that once a Templar, always a Templar. Is that not so?'

'In my heart, yes, but to ride wearing the cross of Christ goes against our teachings unless you serve a commandery, which I do not.'

'Look,' said Walter, 'I am not asking you to ride into battle beneath the banner of the Templars. All I ask is if we need to access the chateau, you use these garments to gain entry. As a Knight of Christ, you will not be suspected of any subterfuge, and your lack of local language will not be deemed suspicious. Once in, you can find the child and bring him out to us as soon as an opportunity arises. If you time the abduction well, we can be leagues away before the deed is discovered, without a single drop of blood being spilled.'

'So, you are asking me to lie about my station?'

'Not at all. Once a Templar, always a Templar. Remember?'

Cronin fell silent as he realised what the justiciar was asking. Since he had left the Templars, he was not really breaking any oaths, but his conscience ached at the thought of the deception.

'Why did you not explain this in London?'

'I did. I said that your experience as a Templar would help us gain access.'

'You said nothing about adopting the guise of someone who still serves.'

'Would you have come if I had?'

'No.'

'Then there lies your answer.'

'I refuse,' said Cronin suddenly. 'I will not betray the oaths of all those who have worn the mantle by using it for immoral reasons.'

'It genuinely hurts me to say this,' said Walter, 'but I don't think you have any say in the matter.'

'And why is that?'

'Because, if we do not return with the boy within twenty-eight days, then the king has ordered that your family back in Fallswater will be taken to the gallows and hanged as accomplices to a traitor. On top of that, an order will be sent to Acre to have the boy you seek executed immediately. You have no choice, Cronin: do this, or face the full weight of the king's wrath.'

----

Several hours later, Cronin, Walter, Peter, and Jaques stood hidden amongst the trees just off the road leading to an imposing chateau. A river had been diverted to form a huge lake around the towering building before carrying on its way to the sea many leagues to the west.

Between them and the building lay a village, surrounded by a patchwork of fields filled with crops and livestock, tended by the many villagers who relied on the owner of the chateau for their livelihood. The three men knew they could not rely on any of them to give succour should things go wrong.

'Jaques,' said Walter, 'come closer. There is something you need to know.'

The local man's brow knitted in confusion, and he approached nervously.

'You are a married man, are you not?' asked Walter, still staring towards the chateau.

'Perhaps,' replied the Frenchman, 'but why is that relevant?'

'Because I need to establish some ground rules,' said Walter, 'and actually, it does not matter if you reply, as I already know the answers. You are married to a woman called Marie and have two children: a girl called Ellen, who is currently home with her mother, and a son called Pierre... who is not.'

'What do you mean?' asked Jaques. 'How do you all know this? And what do you mean, my boy is not at home?'

'I know,' said Walter, turning to face him, 'because any man who is willing to sell out his countrymen for a purse of gold is also highly likely to betray his new comrades when they attempt to obtain that which they paid for.'

Jaques's eyes narrowed as he realised what direction the conversation was taking.

'If you are implying I have led you into a trap, then you are mistaken,' he said. 'I just want you to get what you came for, pay what you owe me, and get back to England. Once done, I can use that money to take my family away from here to a better life.'

'And all that could well be true,' said Walter. 'But you will understand that we had to take some precautions.'

'What precautions? What have you done?'

'When Adam of Kent came to find you a few days ago, he was not alone. When you both headed back to us, his comrade, who had remained hidden from sight, invited your son to spend a few days with us, an invitation he could not refuse.'

'You have my son?' gasped Jaques.

'He is being well looked after,' replied Walter, 'for now. Of course, that depends on the outcome of this mission, for if it seems we are betrayed at any point, well, I cannot be held responsible for his safety.'

'What sort of people are you?' hissed Jaques. 'It seems that you hold innocents hostage in everything you do.'

'These are trying times,' said Walter, 'and we have to do everything in our power to stay alive. But worry not; the moment we arrive safely back at our ship, your son will be released, and the balance of your payment handed over to you. Is that understood?'

'You will get your prize,' growled Jaques, 'and live to get back to your ship. Just make sure no harm comes to my family.'

'Just do as we agreed,' said Walter, 'and all this will soon be over.' He turned to Cronin. 'It is time,' he said, 'get ready.'

Cronin sighed deeply, unhappy about what he was about to do, but like the Frenchman, Walter had him over a barrel and he could not back out, not if he wanted to see Sumeira again. He walked into the trees, unfastened his cloak, and threw it to the ground before opening the package that had been revealed to him earlier that day. Ten minutes later, he returned, once more resplendent in the garb he had worn with so much pride for so many years, the uniform of a Templar Knight.

----

# CHAPTER THIRTEEN

## Constantinople

The next morning, Baldwin ordered the army to break camp at dawn and march double time towards the pass that the scout had indicated. The days that followed tested the endurance of every man and beast in the army, and Baldwin rode at the front, often dismounting to walk beside his foot soldiers, sharing their hardships and boosting their morale with his presence.

As they neared the pass, scouts returned with reports that Boniface's forces had been spotted making camp just beyond the narrow gorge to the east. They had made it and now lay directly in the path of Boniface's advancing army.

'Set up camp further back at the base of that hill,' said Baldwin to Louis of Blois, one of his main commanders, 'but create a defensive line across the valley directly in front of Boniface's position. It is important he knows that we mean business, and if we have to fight, then so be it.' He turned to Abbot Martin. 'Once we have our men in position, go to Boniface's camp and arrange a meeting. Let's see if negotiation can defeat conflict.'

----

As the sun continued its rise from behind the rugged hills to the east, the clamour of metal and the shouts of men filled the air. Louis of Blois stood on a gentle rise, overseeing the hasty construction of the camp while Geoffrey of Villehardouin, one of the French knights, managed the positioning of the battle lines.

'Barricades here, and here!' he shouted, pointing towards the front where the land narrowed into a natural chokepoint, perfect for slowing an advancing army. His knights hurried to execute his commands, organising teams of soldiers who dragged felled trees and large rocks to form rudimentary but effective barriers.

The camp itself buzzed with activity. Squires and men-at-arms scurried about, unloading supplies from the packhorses, tents, cooking pots, and most crucially, weaponry. Armour clanked as foot soldiers donned their mail hauberks, the interlocking rings glinting in the waning light. Archers carefully inspected their bows, their strings taut, and chainmail-piercing arrows with bodkin points neatly arrayed in leather quivers.

As night fell, torches were lit, casting flickering shadows throughout the camp. Crossbowmen tested their weapons, the steel of their quarrels gleaming ominously, and men-at-arms rubbed whetstones along the edges of their pikes and swords, many silently contemplating the battle they might face the following day.

By the time the moon rose, Baldwin had a rudimentary, yet effective defensive position in place, ready to repel any attack. As the camp settled down, confident that the many sentries deployed eastward would alert them to any potential danger, one of the horse-mounted patrols returned and made their way to the campaign tent.

'My lord,' said one after dismounting and bowing to the emperor, 'the forces of Boniface are encamped less than a day's march from here. If they continue their advance at dawn, they will be here by midday tomorrow.'

'What about his numbers?'

'Somewhat fewer than ours,' said the soldier, 'but they seem well-equipped with a strong cavalry company.'

'Thank you,' said the emperor. 'I think we are as prepared as we can be. You and your men get some food and rest. We will need you out again before dawn.'

'As you wish, my lord,' he replied, then turned to rejoin his men. As the cool night enveloped the camp, Baldwin stepped out of his tent, looking towards the stars that speckled the vast, dark canopy above. Abbot Martin joined him.

'You have done everything you can,' said the abbot, 'and now only God's hand can decide the outcome.'

'Perhaps there is one more thing I can do,' said Baldwin.

'And that is?'

'I will lead the negotiations myself. This is too important to stay in the shadows.'

'Is that wise?'

'Perhaps not, but if crusaders fight crusaders, there will be no victor except our true enemies. Besides, I know Boniface well, and I think it will go a long way to earning his trust if he sees I am willing to put myself in harm's way. Set it up, Abbot Martin, and you and I will see what we can do to avoid brother killing brother.'

----

The following morning, the air was crisp and charged with tension as Baldwin and a small retinue of his most trusted knights made their way to the agreed-upon clearing. The narrow pass, flanked by steep cliffs, served as a natural corridor leading to a field bathed in the soft light of the morning sun. Boniface and his party were already waiting, the Montferrat banners fluttering gently in the morning breeze.

Boniface, a robust figure with a commanding presence, stepped forward to greet Baldwin as he dismounted. His face bore a cautious smile, but his eyes were sharp, assessing.

'Emperor Baldwin,' he said, extending a hand, 'I appreciate your willingness to meet. These are turbulent times, and the wise seek dialogue over conflict.'

Baldwin clasped Boniface's hand firmly.

'Marquis Boniface,' he replied, 'wisdom dictates we use our strength to stabilise and prosper rather than to divide and weaken. I propose we discuss how best to approach Thessalonica, to ensure we both benefit from its undoubted wealth and strategic location.'

The two leaders, followed by their aides, took seats at a makeshift table set under a large olive tree. Maps and documents were laid out, and a flag of truce hung above them, symbolising the sanctity of their negotiations.

'As you know,' began Baldwin, 'the task of ruling Constantinople is a huge one that demands massive resources. Many of the food stores were burned during the assault, and hunger is the bedfellow of everyone within the city. Winter looms and, although we are confident that trade will return in the new year, we need to find alternative sources to feed the populace.'

'It was always going to be the case,' said Boniface. 'Perhaps more thought should have been given to these matters before you attacked the city.'

'You know as well as I,' said Baldwin, 'things happened quickly, and nobody expected the fleeing guards to torch the city.' He stared at the marquis, both men knowing what was on each other's minds. 'Look,' continued Baldwin, breaking the silence, 'I know you are disappointed that the council appointed me as Emperor, but there is no need for any man to spill blood here. We sailed together from Venice, fought alongside each other at the walls of Constantinople, and you eventually gave your blessing to my coronation. Why has it come to this?'

'You know full well why we are here, Baldwin,' said Boniface. 'I stepped aside to allow you a clear path to becoming emperor, purely on the understanding that I would be granted governorship of Thessalonica. That has not been forthcoming, so I will wait no longer and will take what was promised, by force if necessary.'

'That proposal was discussed but not voted upon,' said Baldwin.

Boniface sneered.

'I knew you would use that excuse,' he said, 'and to be frank, it is beneath you. I agree that there was no vote, but you know as well as I that the promise was real and is the only reason you now sit upon the throne. I am happy for you, Baldwin, but make no mistake. I will take what is rightfully mine and if that means fighting you, then so be it.'

Baldwin stared at Boniface, trying to judge if it was a bluff, but the intensity of the argument and the look on the marquis's face left him under no illusion that he meant every word he said.

'If we fight here today,' he said eventually, 'men on both sides will die needlessly at the hands of those they fought alongside and called brother for the last two years. Both sides will be permanently weakened, and the real victors will be those we have spent so much time fighting. We cannot let this happen.'

'Then turn around, Baldwin,' said Boniface, 'and let me take what belongs to me.'

'I cannot,' said Baldwin. 'Constantinople is starving, and we need the resources Thessalonica can offer. To return empty-handed is not an option.'

'Neither is your expectation that I will relinquish my claim,' said Boniface. 'We will fight to the last man if needs be, but make no mistake, it will be my colours flying over that city, or I will die in the attempt.'

'My lords,' interjected Abbot Martin, 'may I speak?'

Both leaders turned and acknowledged the abbot's request.

'Thessalonica is indeed a wealthy prize, and its lands provide a bounty more than capable of feeding both cities, at least until the next harvest. Perhaps there is an agreement to be made where you both can leave this place with what each of you wants without a single blow taking place.'

'Are you suggesting a joint governance of the city?' asked Boniface. 'For that is not on the table. How do we divide authority? Who commands its garrison?'

'What I suggest,' said Abbot Martin, 'is that you publicly pledge your loyalty to Emperor Baldwin as the undisputed ruler of Thessalonica and the surrounding lands, and in return, you are granted the governorship in perpetuity.'

'I see no benefit in this,' said Baldwin. 'Why would I do that?'

'Because, in return, Marquis Boniface will agree to supply Constantinople with all the food and other necessary goods it needs to see it through the winter. In addition, both sides agree to mutually support the other in a permanent alliance where each city swears to aid the other should one come under attack. A mutually beneficial agreement whereby both parties acquire that which they set out to obtain, now and in the future.'

Both men looked at each other, realising that the suggestions had merit. The details would have to be thrashed out, but in essence, the proposal could work. With a pathway agreed, the negotiations continued throughout the day, each point meticulously debated and documented.

That night, Baldwin sat with his commanders, going over the day's discussions.

'We are close to an agreement that could bring us much-needed peace,' he explained. 'But we must remain vigilant. Boniface is as ambitious as he is strategic.'

The following morning, the parties reconvened with renewed vigour. Adjustments were made to the draft, clarifying terms and responsibilities, and by midday, a final document was prepared, bearing the seals of both Baldwin and Boniface. With the accord signed, Baldwin rallied his commanders and relayed the outcome. War against their comrades had been avoided, and they would return to Constantinople without delay. Boniface, in the meantime, would continue to Thessalonica and, once his reign had been established, send the first of many promised caravans of supplies to Constantinople. It had been a fraught negotiation, but at last, it seemed that their combined strengths would ensure there would be no return to the previous regimes. The power of the Latin armies in the region, at last, was now fully assured.

----

# CHAPTER FOURTEEN

## Northern Adriatic Sea

The ship creaked and groaned under the strain of the relentless sea as it docked in the bustling port of Venice. Soldiers and sailors alike lined the deck, eager to stretch their legs on solid ground and resupply for the journey ahead. Among them, Jamal stood silently, his dark eyes scanning the unfamiliar throng of faces and colours that made up the Venetian landscape. His mind was set on Jerusalem, on the sacred city and the promise of redemption it held for a soul marred by misfortune. As the crew disembarked, Sir Edmund motioned for Jamal to follow.

'We'll need provisions and news,' he said, and Jamal nodded, trailing behind the knight as they made their way through the crowded docks. Since the incident on the ship several weeks earlier, the knight had been true to his word and given him intense daily lessons in the art of warfare. At first, the crew had looked on in amusement, but as the days passed and they witnessed Jamal persevering in all weathers, they started to warm to him, gradually offering help in whatever way they could. Some donated spare equipment, while others took the time to give extra instruction where needed. In a surprising turn of events, even the man who had first belittled Jamal just after leaving England took the time to help wherever he could.

Even the ship's cook had taken him under his wing, and it soon became clear that despite the injury to Jamal's head, which had partly affected his coordination and mental function, he had a talent for cooking. The men soon looked forward to the varied stews he helped concoct with the very limited rations available.

'Have you been here before, my lord?' he asked as he hurried through the busy streets, trying hard to keep up with the knight.

'I have,' said Sir Edmund.

'Then perhaps you would know if there is a place where they sell spices,' said Jamal. 'With even the most common, I could make the food so much nicer.'

'I think I know a place,' said the knight without breaking stride. 'If we have enough time, I will take you there.'

Jamal grinned inwardly. His upbringing in the Holy Land meant that he had been exposed to all sorts of cooking methods and traditions, and if he could just get some spices, he knew the men on the ship would be impressed with the flavours he could conjure up.

Venice was alive with activity, merchants shouting over one another to sell their goods, fishermen hauling in their fresh catch, and children darting between the stalls. As they walked, Sir Edmund kept one hand on his purse and the other on his sword, his eyes always watching, always assessing. Jamal, however, could only marvel at the foreign beauty of it all, the exotic smells and sounds so different from the quiet English countryside and the sea-sodden ship he had known for the past few weeks.

Their first stop was at a local tavern where merchants and sailors often exchanged news along with their ale. Sir Edmund, with a few coins and a steady gaze, gleaned what information he could from a talkative trader.

'The route to Jerusalem is fraught with danger, more so now than ever,' the trader warned, wiping ale from his beard. 'And there's talk of a bigger push for reinforcements for Baldwin in Constantinople. They're mustering more forces, redirecting ships from every corner of Christendom.'

'Why?' asked Edmund. 'The city fell many months ago.'

'The walls may have been breached,' said the trader, 'but Baldwin is finding peace harder to win than war. They need food, clothing, livestock, anything really, just to keep the population on side. Who knows what will happen if Kaloyan marches south.'

'What do you mean by that?' asked Edmund.

The trader looked up scornfully.

'Where have you been these past few months?' he sneered. 'It's common knowledge around here.'

'We are en route from England to Acre,' said Edmund, 'so have not been kept up to date with everything that has happened since the city fell.'

'Well,' said the trader, 'it seems Tsar Kaloyan was rebuffed by the Pope and is now raiding towns and villages throughout the mountains north of Constantinople. People fear he may take advantage of Baldwin's predicament and march his vast army southwards to attack Constantinople. If he does that, there's no way the city will survive. It is already in ruins, and the crusading army is exhausted, so they've sent messages throughout Christendom for reinforcements.'

Sir Edmund listened carefully, not just to the trader, but to other men with different perspectives, gleaning whatever information he could from as many sources as possible. Within a few hours, he had as complete a picture of what was happening as he could. Once he was satisfied, he and Jamal left the tavern and headed back towards the ship.

'Jamal,' he said, stopping by the entrance to a side street, 'there are vendors up there that sell the things you seek.' He produced some coins and handed them over. 'Get what you need and head back to the ship. I will see you there later.'

'Where are you going, my lord?' asked Jamal.

'I need to speak to someone,' replied the knight, 'but will be back by nightfall tomorrow. Tell the men that as soon as they have loaded the supplies, be ready to sail at a moment's notice.'

'As you wish, my lord,' said Jamal, and watched as the knight turned away to head back into the city.

----

A few hours later, Sir Edmund sat in an antechamber of the Doge's palace in the heart of the city. The man who had received him had made it clear the Doge wasn't there, but Edmund had insisted that he speak to someone of high rank who could speak on the Doge's behalf. Eventually, a man appeared, clad in the garb of the Pope's office. Edmund got to his feet and waited as the official approached.

'Sir Edmund?' asked the man as he neared. 'My name is Cardinal Fiacci, and I work on behalf of the Doge in his absence. What can I do for you?'

'Your Eminence,' said the knight with a slight bow of the head. 'Thank you for seeing me; I know you must be busy. I have been blessed by God and King John to be given command of a ship headed to the Holy Land to reinforce those who still occupy Acre. On board, I have a good number of men, skilled at arms and ready to fight under the banner of God. I have heard many rumours today of the situation in Constantinople and have decided that if they are true, then perhaps we may be able to help.'

'In what way?' asked the Cardinal.

'Well,' said Sir Edmund, 'I have to stay true to my orders and head for Acre, but I see no reason why we cannot divert to Constantinople first, if only to deliver supplies to the garrison there. Once done, we can head on our way, but at least we may have helped in a small way to alleviate the privations of our fellows.'

'That is a very kind offer,' said the Cardinal, 'and one that we will gladly accept. How much room do you have for extra provisions?'

'Not much, but we can fill every inch of spare space with whatever they may require.'

'Actually,' said the Cardinal, 'I have a greater task for you. Yes, you can load whatever you can onto your ship, but you say you have a fighting force aboard, so why not use them to greater effect?'

'In what manner?'

'We have plenty of supply ships,' said the Cardinal, 'and we have the provisions to load upon them. We even have the crews to man them, but what we don't have are experienced armed men to protect them on their journey. What if I were to ask that you act as an escort to a group of, say, six supply ships, right up to the docks in Constantinople, and once they are seen safely to their moorings, you go on your way to Acre. Is that something you are willing to consider?'

'I think that more than meets my duty before God,' said Sir Edmund, 'and does not deviate from the task issued to me by the officers of King John. Just tell me where and when to meet the convoy, and I will see it done.'

'Thank you, Sir Edmund,' said the Cardinal. 'Keep your ship docked where she is, and my men will seek you out. I expect it will be at least a few days to arrange, but we will be in touch.'

'As you wish, Your Eminence,' said Edmund, and after leaving the palace, he headed back across the city to rejoin his ship.

A few hours later, he gathered the men on board the ship and explained his decision. Although there were a few grumbles of discontent, the majority accepted the decision without question. After all, who were they to question a man of such noble standing?

Once they had dispersed, Jamal approached the knight with concern etched upon his face.

'My lord,' he said, 'will it take long to carry out this task? For my fate is destined to lie in the Holy Land, and I fear that I may be too late.'

Sir Edmund placed a firm hand on Jamal's shoulder.

'I know this isn't the path you hoped for,' he said, his voice low. 'But sometimes, our fates are steered by forces beyond our control. The fate of Jerusalem is not going to be settled any time soon, and I promise you will be in Acre before the year is out.'

'But what if we are drawn into the conflict? Our lives could be at risk.'

'Does that worry you?'

'To lose my life in the service of God would be an honour, but given the choice, I would rather it be in the land once walked by Christ, not in a place where the people never gazed upon his countenance.'

'Christ is Lord of all lands, Jamal,' said Sir Edmund. 'Never forget that. Besides, even if we were to draw swords against those who challenge our fellows, I will do everything in my power to make sure you survive to see the Holy Land.'

'In what way?'

'You'll stay with me,' replied Edmund. 'I'll need a squire, and you need a direction that isn't led by such fear or despair.'

Jamal met the knight's gaze, the weight of his destiny suddenly anchoring him to the ground.

'I will serve you well, Sir Edmund,' he replied, the words carving a new resolve within him. 'And if my fate is to die in your service, then I will do so while defending you and the Cross.'

----

A few days later, the captain confirmed the news to the crew.

'We have had confirmation,' he shouted, 'the supply ships will be here at first light tomorrow, and we will sail with the tide. This will be a journey of succour, but make no mistake, it will be one fraught with peril. Make sure that your equipment is always at hand in case we need to resort to violence.'

That evening, as the ship was being loaded with the final supplies, Sir Edmund continued Jamal's formal training. On the upper deck, against the backdrop of a sinking sun, Jamal learned to hold a heavier sword, shielding himself against a continued rain of blows. The training was far harder than anything he had done previously, and Sir Edmund was a demanding teacher, but despite the pain and exhaustion, Jamal knew that every moment he spent in preparation was potentially an extra moment he would stay alive if it came to a fight.

'You need to be strong, not just in body but in spirit,' Sir Edmund instructed as he parried a clumsy thrust from Jamal. 'The battles ahead will test more than your skill with a sword.'

Jamal, sweat mingling with determination, nodded and adjusted his stance, his earlier despair morphing into focused intent. He was no longer just a passenger on a journey dictated by others; he was a squire, a fighter under the wing of a knight who had shown him kindness in a world that seemed bereft of it.

As night fell and the ship prepared to set sail, Jamal stood at the railing, looking out over the lights of Venice. Constantinople awaited, with all its perils and promises, but with Sir Edmund at his side, he felt a spark of hope, a belief that perhaps, even in the heart of conflict, he could find his place and his purpose.

----

# CHAPTER FIFTEEN

## Normandy

Cronin and the Frenchman led their horses slowly through the village towards the château, each man fully aware of the cover story and the potential consequences should they get it wrong.

'I hope you're happy with your role in this,' said the Frenchman as they approached the gates. 'The treachery oozes out of you like a bad smell.'

'The only treachery here is that which caused this to happen in the first place,' replied Cronin. 'What sort of man sells out his own countrymen for a purse of silver?'

'You do not know my circumstances,' said Jacques, 'or the tragedy which caused the revelation, but at least I don't hold a child at knifepoint to get what I want.'

'That has nothing to do with me,' said Cronin, 'and I also have an axe hanging over the head of my loved ones. But we are allies of circumstance only, not comrades. Let's just get this done and get out of here.' He adjusted the cloak around his shoulders, the fabric itchy and irritating against his skin. The former Templar, hardened by years of battles and subterfuge, had worn the softer garb of a noble for many months and now felt uneasy in the guise of a serving Templar knight.

Jacques was far more comfortable in his role and the environment, having lived in the area for many years. As they approached the towering gates of the fortified château, his manner was one of nonchalance, his rugged features set in a mask of casual curiosity.

'Remember, let me do the talking,' he murmured, his accent thick but his voice steady.

Cronin nodded, scanning the high walls and battlements. Up until now, their main concern had been how to gain entry, but with the towering walls looming above them, he realised the more difficult question could well be how they were going to get out. As they approached, a man emerged from the smaller gate situated in the base of one of the gate towers and walked up to stand before them.

'State your business,' said the guard, looking them both up and down.

'I am Jacques de Londres,' replied the Frenchman. 'I have a farm far to the south but have been here many times.' He turned towards Cronin. 'I came across this man yesterday on the path northward. He says he is on his way to Flanders with important information from the new emperor in Constantinople.'

'And why is that of interest to us?' asked the guard, eyeing the Templar emblem emblazoned upon Cronin's cloak.

'He has been on the road for a long time,' said Jacques, 'and needs to rest for a few days. Bearing in mind his station, I naturally brought him here, as a hay pile is no bed for a knight of the cross.'

'Can he not talk for himself?' asked the guard.

'I can,' said Cronin before Jacques could answer, 'although I find your language difficult.'

Jacques looked up in surprise. He had no idea that the knight could speak French, albeit badly.

'If your master will receive me,' continued Cronin, 'I will be no bother, and I can pay for my board with a promissory note, redeemable at the nearest commandery. If he is otherwise inclined, then I will be on my way.'

'I will see what he has to say,' said the guard. 'Stay there.'

As he disappeared back through the gate, Jacques turned to face Cronin with frustration on his face.

'You never said you could speak our language.'

'You never asked.'

'Do you not think it was relevant?'

'Sometimes it is better to keep your business to yourself. Besides, I barely understand it, let alone speak it.'

'Have you served in Normandy before?'

'I have not, but I once rode alongside a Frenchman called Jakelin de Mailly, and no greater knight ever donned the cloak of a Templar.'

'Where is he now?'

'He died at the Battle of Hattin. They found his body alone, surrounded by hundreds of dead Saracen warriors.'

'He sounds like a great warrior.'

'He was, and a true friend, but perhaps not so great a teacher of languages.'

Both men looked back at the château as the sound of heavy bolts being drawn back heralded the larger gates being opened. The guard emerged and beckoned them in. 'My lord has extended a welcome,' he said, 'and will gladly offer a bed and food for as long as you need it. There will be no cost.'

'Your master is a true gentleman,' replied Cronin and led his horse through the gates. Jacques followed him but was stopped before he reached the entrance. 'There is no reason for you to stay,' said the guard. 'You say you live a few leagues away, so you can use your own bed.'

'He is with me as a guide and as an interpreter,' interjected Cronin. 'If he cannot be allowed the same courtesy, then thank you, but we will be on our way.'

The guard hesitated but eventually nodded, and as both men entered the courtyard, the two heavy gates closed behind them with a bang.

----

Inside, the château was a hive of activity. Servants bustled about, and the air was filled with the scent of roasting meat and fresh bread. Cronin's stomach growled, reminding him that it had been hours since their last meal. A steward approached, eyeing them with curiosity.

'New arrivals?' he asked.

'They are,' said the guard, 'and will be guests of Sir Gerard for a few days. Take them to the stables, and after that, see to it that they get comfortable rooms and a hot meal.'

'Of course,' said the steward and as the soldier returned to his post, led them both to one of the stone outhouses within the small courtyard. Half an hour later, with their horses safely stabled with fresh food and water, the two men were led through the winding corridors of the château.

Cronin's sharp eyes took in every detail, the guards' positions, the layout of the rooms, and any possible escape routes. Their mission was undeniably perilous, and if they were to succeed, he needed to know as much information as he could glean.

The steward led them to a small but comfortable chamber with two beds, and moments later, a maid brought them a platter of hot meat with bread and a jug of warmed wine. The door closed behind her, and they both finally relaxed on their cots, the table between them. Jacques leaned in closer, his voice barely a whisper.

'We need to find out where they're keeping the child. When she comes back for the platters, perhaps we can engage her in conversation and find out more.'

'No,' said Cronin curtly. 'To ask questions when we have been here only a few heartbeats invites suspicion. You told the guard that I am headed to Flanders, and that is the story we will maintain. Once we gain their trust, then opportunities will open up, but until then, we will act the part. Now try to get some rest.'

'Rest? Why?'

'Because if we were truly weary travellers, that is what we would do. I'm sure their master will want to see us soon enough, but until then, we wait.'

Both men finished their food before laying back on their cots, and despite the reluctance of Jacques de Londres, were soon fast asleep.

----

A few hours later, both men left the room and headed back to the stables to check the horses. While there, the steward approached with an invitation.

'Gentlemen,' he said, 'Sir Gerard has invited you to dine with him this evening. If you can be ready at last light, someone will come to collect you.'

'Thank you,' said Cronin, 'we will be ready.' Once the steward had left, he turned to Jacques. 'We need to be patient,' he said, 'but tonight will be a good opportunity to judge the flavour of this man's rule. The softer he is, the easier our task will be. Keep your eyes and ears open and your mouth closed Our pathway will reveal itself soon enough.'

Throughout the rest of the day, the men wandered around the château under the pretext of genuine interest. Some people, attracted by his Templar attire, approached Cronin to ask him questions, and when he revealed his time in the Holy Land, he attracted quite a crowd. For a few hours, he answered whatever questions he could, playing down his part in the troubles but revealing many interesting facts that most men would never know. With Cronin attracting so much attention, Jacques took the opportunity to wander further afield, trying to get a feel for the château.

As the day eased towards sunset, both men reconvened in their room and looked forward to the forthcoming meal with the lord of the château. They each took the opportunity to wash away the dust of the road before re-donning their clothing and waited for someone to arrive to show them the way. Ten minutes later, the steward reappeared at their door.

'Please follow me,' he said, leading the way through the château. Inside the hall, the visitors were immediately struck by the décor, a striking blend of opulence and military strength. Heavy tapestries adorned the walls, depicting scenes of battles long past, while the flickering candlelight cast dancing shadows across the room. At the head of a long, polished oak table sat Sir Gerard, the lord of the château, a man of imposing stature with keen eyes that missed little. Alongside him sat another man, as yet unknown to either visitor. Sir Gerard rose, extending a hand towards two empty seats.

'Welcome, travellers,' he said, 'please, join us.'

Cronin and Jacques sat down, both painfully aware that the second man was staring at them without having said a word.

'This is Sir Bergerac,' continued Gerard, 'and as you can see, he likes to keep his counsel to himself, but I assure you, he has everyone's interests at heart...especially mine.' He gave a thin-lipped smile, the unspoken warning evident to all in the room. Sir Bergerac was Sir Gerard's personal bodyguard.

'I trust you have been well looked after,' continued the knight, taking his own seat, 'I would have greeted you sooner but had business to attend. I'm sure you will understand.'

Cronin inclined his head in acknowledgement.

'We are most grateful, my lord. The hospitality has been second to none, and your generosity is much appreciated.'

'Indeed, my lord,' added Jacques, 'the château is a haven for weary souls like ours.'

As both sides exchanged pleasantries, servants moved with practised efficiency, setting platters of roasted meats, fresh bread, and fine cheeses before them. Goblets of rich red wine were filled and placed within reach, and as they began to dine, the conversation turned to Cronin's Templar service.

'I hear you enthralled my people today with tales of your service with the brotherhood.'

'It was not my intention,' said Cronin, 'but your people were somewhat insistent, and it was difficult to disengage. I did not want to be rude.'

'Their interest does not surprise me in the slightest,' said the knight, 'you will find that the brotherhood is of particular interest around here, especially with me.'

'Is there a reason for that?'

'Indeed, there is. I have contemplated taking the cross myself, and your arrival has presented me with a unique opportunity to hear the truth from one who has served with such distinction. I have also considered the merits of joining the Templars, so I look forward to hearing what it entails.'

Cronin was shocked. The last thing he had expected was to meet a potential recruit to the order. The situation swirled around his mind, trying to calculate if he could use it to his advantage.

'Well,' he said eventually, 'while I am here, I will be only too happy to answer any questions you may have. What do you want to know?'

'Everything,' said Gerard, leaning forward, 'but why do you not start with your own service. Have you served long?'

Cronin met his gaze evenly.

'I have, for many years, but was initially a sergeant. I was knighted by Richard the Lionheart in Acre before he returned home from the Holy Land.'

'You fought alongside the Lionheart?'

'I did.'

'I want to know all about it,' said Gerard, 'but first, tell me about the battles leading up to that, especially those you were involved in.'

'The tales are many, my lord,' said Cronin, 'and fade in the memory, but I will do my best to recall what I can.'

'That's all I can expect,' said the knight and settled back to listen as Cronin recalled the many battles he had witnessed and fought in throughout his time in the Outremer. The night passed quickly, and soon it was evident that the dawn was only a few hours away. Realising the lateness, Sir Gerard finally brought the fascinating discussion to a close. Everyone stood up to leave, with a promise to dine again the following night, but as Cronin turned away, Sir Bergerac spoke for the first time.

'Tell me, Sir Cronin, how does a knight of such esteem find himself wandering the roads of Normandy?'

Cronin chose his words carefully, aware of the underlying suspicion.

'The world has changed, my lord. One of the men I fought alongside has since become the new emperor of Constantinople and asked me to travel back to his homeland to pass on messages to his family with regard to his succession. I am currently upon that road.'

'Surely it would have been better to take a ship?'

'I did, but the crew developed a disease in southern France. There were no other ships due to leave that port for many days, so I decided to continue on horseback, and here I am.'

'So where are these dispatches you talk of?'

'All up here,' said Cronin, tapping his head. 'Some things should not be committed to parchment.'

'And here you are,' said Sir Gerard, cutting the questions short. 'Just a few days away from your destination.'

'We are very grateful for your hospitality,' said Cronin, 'and will be on our way soon enough.'

'There is no rush,' said Sir Gerard, 'you are welcome to stay as long as you wish. Besides, I want to hear more about your time in the Outremer, especially if I am to take the cross. Now, get some sleep, and we will see you again tonight.'

'As you wish, my lord,' said Cronin with a nod of the head, and both he and Jacques left the room, closing the door behind them.

Once they had gone, Sir Gerard broke the silence in the hall.

'Well, what are your thoughts?'

'It's all very convenient,' said Bergerac, 'and he may well be telling the truth, but any Englishman walking the paths of Normandy risks being killed by those not as understanding as you. Even if he tells the truth, he is either very stupid, or very brave. Either way, I think that perhaps his journey should end here.'

'Keep an eye on him,' said Gerard, 'and once he has outlived his usefulness, get rid of him.'

'And his companion?'

'Him too. Who knows what treachery they are cooking up between them. Let's see what he has to say tonight and then make them disappear.'

'As you wish, my lord,' replied Bergerac, and both men left the room to get a few hours' sleep.

----

# CHAPTER SIXTEEN

## Normandy

When Cronin and Jacques reached their quarters, they sat on the beds, discussing what had happened. Both agreed that it had been an interesting night, but neither had gleaned any useful information about the girl and her baby. Despite this, they both felt they had at least made some progress with the lord of the château. Resigned to trying again the following day, Cronin lay down on his cot as Jacques left the room to go to the latrine.

In the courtyard, against the base of one of the outer walls, a concrete trough channelled the guards' urine out through the walls and into the lake outside. Jacques walked over to relieve himself, taking in the coolness and silence of the night. One of the guards approached and grunted a greeting before doing the same a few steps away. A sound echoed across the courtyard, breaking the silence, causing Jacques to turn his head rapidly towards the source.

'What's that?' he asked, already knowing the answer.

'That, my friend,' said the soldier, 'is the sound of a spoiled brat doing his best to wake those who work hard to keep him safe. It's the same every night. They put him down, and then, halfway through the night, he screams at the top of his lungs until his nurse manages to calm him down. If he were mine, I'd knock it out of him, but apparently, he's some sort of noble and is allowed to do whatever he pleases.'

'What's his name?' asked Jacques.

'I know not and care less,' replied the soldier. 'All I want is the occasional full night's sleep, is that too much to ask?'

'Why does he need a nurse?' asked Jacques. 'Where is his mother?'

'The lady Annette is probably bedding one of the knights. She is well known for that.' He adjusted his clothing and turned to head back to the barracks.

Jacques thought furiously. It could be the babe they sought, but there was no way to be sure. He spoke again, just loud enough to be heard by the tired guard.

'I think you judge her too quickly,' he said, 'all babies cry. It could be anyone.'

'Nope,' said the soldier without turning around, 'it's the brat all right. He's the only one in the château.'

Jacques swallowed hard. If there was only one baby in the château, it had to be the one he sought. He stayed a little longer in the courtyard, listening to the crying, calculating where it was coming from, before heading back to his quarters.

Cronin was fast asleep, and although Jacques wanted to wake him with the news, it was nothing that wouldn't wait. With renewed hope, he lay back down on his bed and, despite his expectations, was asleep in minutes.

----

The following morning, Jacques relayed the information to Cronin as they were breaking their fast with warm oats brought by one of the maids.

'Are you sure about this?' asked the knight.

'Certain,' said Jacques. 'It's the only baby in the château, and his mother is called Annette. It is the one we seek; of that I have no doubt.'

'And you know where they sleep?'

'I do.' He looked up at the ceiling with a satisfied smirk. 'It's the room just above ours.'

'This is too easy,' said Cronin. 'There has to be a catch.'

'There is one problem,' said Jacques. 'I walked up the stairway before you awoke. There is certainly a room there, but it is locked.'

'How do you know?'

'Because it is guarded by one of the château guards. He has a key attached to his belt.'

'Did he see you?'

'He did. But I said I was hoping to access the perimeter wall to get some fresh air. He directed me to the other tower and suspected nothing. Besides, it seems he was one of the crowd you regaled with your exploits yesterday and was more interested in finding out if you would sell your knife.'

'My knife?' said Cronin. 'Why?'

'I don't think you realise the notoriety you have garnered,' said Jacques. 'Templars have a revered reputation around here, and many villages have sent men to the Crusades. That knife would be a great acquisition to a man such as he.'

'Do you think he could be bribed?'

Jacques shrugged his shoulders.

'Probably not for a knife,' said Jacques, 'but if you have any gold about you, well, every man has his price.'

'I have no gold,' said Cronin, 'but if what you say is correct, then we have to come up with some way to get into that room, and we have to do it tonight.'

'Why?'

'Because I did not like the way that Sir Bergerac was examining us. He suspects something, and if they have the child guarded, then it is highly likely they know that they have a potential heir to the throne of England in the château. If that is so, then it won't take long for them to suspect we have motives other than rest from the road. I just hope I can keep Sir Gerard engaged enough until we have an opportunity to act.'

Both men finished their food before leaving their quarters and walking out of the château. For the next few hours, they walked around the village and the lake. Once they reached the bridge crossing the stream, both stopped, and Cronin walked down to the water's edge to fill his water bottle.

'You are late,' said a quiet voice from beneath the bridge. 'You said noon.'

Cronin recognised the voice of Walter and responded without looking around.

'We are being watched,' he said, 'and came as soon as we could. We have moments only, so listen carefully. We have found the babe and the mother and will try to get her tonight but will have no time to get to the stables. Make sure you have three spare horses and are as near as you can get to the main gate without being seen. If we are discovered, we will have to ride like the wind to escape our pursuers, and I don't even know if the girl can ride.'

'Don't worry about her,' said Walter. 'Just make sure you get the child.'

Cronin half turned his head in surprise.

'You said that Arthur wanted both his wife and his child.'

'He does, but if it comes to a choice, I'm sure he would prefer to see his son. Do you understand?'

'I do,' said Cronin eventually. 'But I will do everything in my power to get them both.'

'We will not tolerate failure, Cronin, so just make sure you get your priorities right. Remember, the life of your wife relies on it. Now get back up to the road before someone suspects you are here.'

Cronin replaced the stopper on his water gourd and clambered back up to the road alongside the bridge.

'Well?' asked Jacques. 'Was he there?'

'He was, and everything is arranged. All we need to do now is get the girl and her child out of the château, and to be honest, I have no idea how we do that.'

'It will work out,' said Jacques, 'now come, we should be getting back.'

----

Later that night, they once more headed towards the main dining hall and were once again hosted by Sir Gerard and Bergerac.

'Gentlemen,' said Gerard, 'welcome back. Please, be seated.'

Once they were settled, the servants again started bringing the food and drink, and once the table was laden, they were once more left alone.

'I hear you took a walk today,' said Gerard. 'Did you find what you were looking for?'

'We were not looking for anything,' said Cronin, 'but to pass through your lovely region without seeing what the locale has to offer would be criminal. It is a truly beautiful part of Christendom. You are a very lucky man.'

'My ancestors made the luck, with their swords and their blood,' said Gerard, 'and I have them to thank for the luxury you see around you.'

'Them and God's grace, of course,' said Cronin.

'Of course,' said Gerard. 'Now, please eat and drink. You need to rebuild your strength before you continue on your journey.'

Everyone started the meal, filling their bellies with the abundance of meat and vegetables presented in delicately carved bowls.

Cronin reached for another piece of pork but paused as Bergerac spoke up.

'You have a healthy appetite for a Templar,' he said, 'I have met others who were frugal with the food they consumed. I understood it was a required way of life within the Order. Is that no longer the case?'

Cronin cursed inwardly. The observation was correct, but since he had left the Order, he had developed a more robust diet, including meat, a luxury rarely available during his service in the Holy Land.

'When garrisoned, our meals are indeed humble,' he said, thinking quickly, 'but also change depending on circumstance. If strength and health depend on it, we are allowed to eat what we need to keep serving God to the best of our ability, and besides,' he gestured towards the food-laden table, 'what man could resist such a generous gift?'

'Totally understandable,' said Gerard. 'Tell us more about the ways and traditions of your Order.'

'Is there anything in particular you need to know?'

'Many men such as I consider joining,' replied Gerard, 'but understand that to do so, they would have to relinquish all worldly goods. Is that correct?'

'It is,' said Cronin, 'which is why few rich men go through with it. You could, of course, just take the cross and go to Acre to help in the fight against the infidels. That way, you would be doing God's work but would be able to keep all this.' He gestured around the hall.

'Hmmm,' said Gerard, 'interesting. But there is another subject I wish to discuss with you. One that is a bit, shall we say, delicate.'

'Go on.'

Gerard's eyes narrowed slightly, but then he smiled, a gesture that did not quite reach his eyes.

'It is said,' he continued, 'that the Templars possess vast wealth and influence. I must admit, I find the stories intriguing.'

'The tales have substance,' replied Cronin, 'but the true wealth of the Templars lies in their knowledge and faith, not just in gold and silver.'

Gerard chuckled, lifting his goblet.

'Knowledge and faith are indeed priceless, my friend, yet there are times when material wealth is also necessary. Tell me, Master Cronin, have you ever had dealings with the Templar treasury?'

Cronin took a measured sip of wine before answering.

'I have. The Order's resources are vast, and they have been used to aid many in need, including kings and commoners alike.'

'And would the Order consider extending aid to a noble house such as mine? Hypothetically, of course.'

The former Templar's eyes sharpened.

'The Order has always been willing to consider requests for aid, provided the cause is just and the terms are agreed upon. Is there a particular matter you have in mind, my lord?'

Gerard leaned forward, his demeanour shifting from host to negotiator.

'Indeed, there is. But that conversation should be between me and your treasury commanders, is that not the case?'

'Of course,' said Cronin. 'Forgive me, my lord, I did not mean to pry. Such matters would require formal application and discussion with the Order's representatives. However, if you wish, I could provide guidance on how to proceed.'

A genuine smile spread across Gerard's face.

'That would be most appreciated, Master Cronin. To have the counsel of a Templar Knight is an unexpected boon.'

The atmosphere relaxed further as the evening progressed, the initial suspicion giving way to cautious camaraderie. They spoke of lands and battles, of shared experiences and hopes for the future. By the time the last of the wine had been drunk and the candles had burned low, Cronin and Jacques had secured the lord's trust, and Sir Gerard had gained a valuable ally in his quest for support.

120

As they retired for the night, Cronin felt the weight of their mission pressing upon him. The dinner had been a success, but he had a feeling in his gut that Gerard had been toying with him, finding out whatever he could without any intention of following any of it through.

'That went well,' said Jacques as they reached their quarters. 'I think they do not suspect a thing.'

'I have no idea what they think,' said Cronin, 'but I do know it is not favourable.'

'What do you mean?'

'What sort of honourable man talks of joining the Templars, before changing his mind to just taking the cross and then asking about a loan? He is up to something, Jacques, and that is why we have to act now, before it is too late.'

----

Back in the hall, Gerard and Bergerac remained at the table drinking wine. Gerard's mind was spinning, turning over the possibilities that had presented themselves over the meal.

'What are you thinking about, my lord?' asked Bergerac. 'I recognise that look.'

'I am thinking that we could turn this situation into a very profitable one,' said Gerard.

'In what way?'

'If we use his knowledge and guidance to secure a large loan from the Templar treasuries, we could use it to increase our army tenfold. By doing so, we could dominate our region and become the governing family in this part of Normandy.'

'I suspect that the Templars would not fund such a thing, nor perhaps, recognise your status for such a large amount.'

'They would if I told them we have the future king of England under our roof.'

'That is a huge risk, my lord.'

'I know, but King John is widely reviled, and I believe that if the Templar hierarchy saw an opportunity to join the two nations under the banner of Arthur's son, they might see the merit in such an investment. Don't forget, Lionheart fought alongside the Templars and was widely revered by every man who saw him. It was his dying wish that his nephew would assume his throne, and if the Order felt that they could make that situation happen, then perhaps they would be agreeable to such a transaction.'

'And what would be in it for you?'

'As the babe is so small, he would need a protector until he reached his majority. I would make it a condition that I become regent until he is of age.'

'And what about when he does?'

'Accidents happen to young children, do they not? And if that happened, it would make perfect sense for the regent to stay in power, especially if there were no more claimants in the bloodline.' He looked at Bergerac, his eyes hungry for power.

'To fight King John is a huge risk, my lord. You would need an army a hundred times the size you talk of.'

'The army would be to gain power in this region only, a necessary step to gaining recognition of our banners. With regards to King John, I have no intention of fighting him, but he is just one man, and if he fell to an assassin's hand, then we have the one thing that would stop an all-out war. We have the true heir, Bergerac, and that is worth a thousand armies.'

----

# CHAPTER SEVENTEEN

## Normandy

The château lay in a shroud of silence, the stillness of the early hours broken only by the occasional hoot of an owl. Cronin and Jacques sat quietly in their quarters, the room dimly lit by the dying embers of the fire. They exchanged a glance, each recognising the resolve in the other's eyes. The time had come.

Cronin adjusted his cloak, ensuring his movements would be silent. Jacques did the same, his eyes filled with steely determination. They slipped out of their room and into the corridor, their footsteps muffled by the thick stone walls. The way to the upper floor was a labyrinth of shadows and narrow passages, but both men moved with exaggerated caution, desperate not to fail at the first hurdle.

At the base of the stairs, they paused, listening for any signs of life. Satisfied with the silence, they ascended, their senses alert for the guard they knew would be stationed at the door they sought.

As they reached the top, the flicker of a torch fixed into an alcove in the wall revealed the guard, a burly man leaning against the wall, his eyes heavy with the lethargy of a long night. Cronin motioned to Jacques to stay where he was and crept forward, his heart racing with the imminent danger of being discovered.

When he was only a few paces away, the guard looked up, but before he could react, Cronin seized him in a tight grip, one hand clamped over his mouth, the other holding the blade of his knife against the guard's throat. The victim's eyes bulged in surprise, but Cronin's cold, level stare silenced any thoughts of resistance.

'Stay silent, and you'll live to see another day,' Cronin hissed, pressing the cold steel of his dagger harder against the guard's neck. 'The key. Now.'

With trembling hands, the guard produced a key from his belt. Jacques took it from him and inserted the key into the lock, the soft click loud in the stillness. He pushed the door open, and after a final, furtive look around, they slipped inside, closing it quietly behind them.

Cronin forced the guard to the floor and searched him for any hidden weapons before tying his hands behind him and forcing a rag into his mouth. The guard used his feet to push himself back against the wall, his fear evident in his wide eyes but wisely choosing cooperation over resistance.

Cronin stood up and looked around. The room was modest but comfortable, the warm glow of several candles casting soft shadows along the walls. In the corner was the bedspace, surrounded by heavy drapes hanging from the ceiling to the floor, keeping the light of the candles and the oncoming dawn from anyone sleeping within.

As Jacques peered through the narrow crack between the door and frame into the corridor, Cronin walked over to the bed and gently pulled one of the drapes aside. To his huge disappointment, he found not the Lady Annette, but a wet nurse, dozing in a chair beside a small bed containing a sleeping child.

Jacques frowned and quietly lowered the drapes before heading over to kneel beside the tied guard.

'Listen to me,' he said quietly, removing the gag from his captive's mouth. 'I need to know where the child's mother is.'

'I am telling you nothing,' hissed the guard.

Cronin pushed the gag back in before standing up and staring down at the stubborn guard. He knew he had no time to waste, so without warning, he drove his foot down to snap his victim's shin in two.

The muffled screams wafted through the room, and Jacques looked around in concern.

'Keep him quiet,' he hissed, but Cronin was already kneeling down beside the guard, waiting until the man's cries of pain had subsided.

'If you don't talk,' he said, 'the next one will be your knee. Do you understand?'

The man nodded fervently, tears of pain streaming down his face.

Cronin placed the tip of his knife under the guard's chin, a clear threat as to the consequences if he cried out. Slowly he removed the gag and moved his face closer to the sweating guard.

'Now,' he said, 'I'll ask again. Where is the child's mother?'

'Somewhere you will never get to her,' gasped the man.

Cronin pushed his free hand against the man's mouth before placing his knee down onto the broken leg. Again, the man cried out in pain, his cries muffled.

'I asked where she is,' said Cronin. 'I did not request your opinion.'

'She is where she is every night,' gasped the man, 'in the bed of Sir Bergerac on the other side of the château. There are many guards, and you will never get to her. It is the truth, I swear it.'

Cronin grimaced. If the guard was telling the truth, there was no way he could get to the mother.

'When does she come back?'

'Usually just after dawn.'

Cronin glanced over to the window. There were still a few hours of darkness left, and he knew they could not afford to wait. He replaced the gag and walked over to Jacques.

'The child is here,' he whispered, 'but the mother is not. We have to leave without her.'

'Then hurry,' said Jacques. 'I can hear movement deeper in the château. It may be the cooks, but we can't take the risk.'

Cronin walked back to the bed, and after quietly drawing aside one of the drapes, leaned past the sleeping nurse to pick up the baby. Despite his attempts at stealth, the baby stirred, and the nurse opened her eyes. She gasped in fear as she saw the strange man holding the baby, but before she could scream, Cronin pressed a finger to her lips.

'Stay quiet, and no harm will come to you or the boy.'

She stared at the two intruders, fear filling her eyes. The baby started whimpering, and Cronin knew that without the means to tie up the nurse, he had to make a quick decision.

'Listen to me,' he said, his lowered voice conveying a threat of violence. 'We wish no harm to you or the baby, but whatever happens, he is leaving with us.'

'No,' gasped the woman, 'he is too small. Take me instead.'

'I am not interested in you,' said Cronin, 'and it matters not to me if we leave you here with your throat cut. The only thing that stays my hand is the fact that you are innocent in all this. You have ten heartbeats to convince me why I should not cut your throat right now.'

The woman looked over at the injured guard and knew it was no idle threat. When no answer was forthcoming, Cronin glanced at Jacques, unsure what to do. There was no way he could kill the nurse in cold blood, but she did not know that.

'Bring her with us,' said Jacques suddenly.

'What?'

'We have no other option,' said Jacques. 'Let her carry the babe but keep her at the point of a sword.'

'No,' said Cronin, 'she is innocent in all this and needs to stay.'

'He is right,' interjected the woman suddenly, 'you have to take me also. The child will need feeding and is still on breast milk.'

Cronin cursed inwardly, realising it was something they had not considered. The babe was already whimpering, and he knew they had to move quickly.

'What is your name?' he asked, turning back to the nurse.

'Genevieve.'

'You listen to me, Genevieve,' he said, 'and listen closely. We are taking this child to be with his father and mean him no harm But if we meet any trouble, then we are willing to fight, to the death if needs be, and that means this child could be hurt or worse. If you try to raise the alarm in any way or cause trouble, then his life or death will lay upon your conscience. Is that clear?'

'I will be no trouble,' said the nurse. 'Give him to me.'

Cronin handed over the baby, who immediately settled down, comfortable in the familiar embrace and smells of the woman who looked after him. With the matter decided, Cronin joined Jacques at the door, and after checking the corridor was clear, headed out and towards the entrance. The nurse followed, cradling the baby in a warm wrap, and after locking the door behind him, Jacques brought up the rear.

Outside, the night was still dark, but they kept tight to the walls as they made their way around the courtyard towards the entrance. Cronin hoped there would be only one guard at the smaller gate, two at the most, with the others posted atop the château walls looking outwards. After all, the usual threats to such a building would be from outside, not from within.

As they approached, he raised his hand, bringing them to a stop. Leaning against the gate was a single guard, his body language suggesting he was more than ready to fall into his cot and get some well-earned sleep. Cronin looked around, but seeing no other guards, turned to Jacques.

'See if you can distract him,' he said. 'Try to bring him closer so we can overpower him.'

Jacques gave Cronin a derisory look. There was no way they could overpower the guard without making any noise.

'I will deal with it,' he said, and walked out into the open towards the gate. As he approached, the guard heard his footsteps and straightened up quickly, fearing he had been caught dozing by his superior. The ring of light from the burning torch fixed onto the wall soon illuminated Jacques's face, easing the guard's worry.

'Greetings,' said Jacques as he neared the gate. 'It's a surprisingly cold night.'

'It is,' said the guard. 'What brings you out here at such an hour?'

'I was hoping to leave the château for a few hours,' replied Jacques, 'without anyone knowing.'

'Why?' asked the guard, his eyes narrowing in suspicion.

Jacques grimaced and looked around furtively.

'The thing is,' he said, turning back to the guard, 'there is a certain young lady who lives in the village that I have, shall we say, a certain interest in. She agreed yesterday that I could visit her bed when it was dark but needed to be gone before dawn.'

The soldier grinned. In his experience, such things were not unusual, but the hour was late, and the amorous man was not a local.

'If you were promised such delights,' he asked, 'why have you left it so late?'

'Alas, the red wine flowed too easily last night, and I fell asleep. I only just awoke, but I think I still have a few hours. That is more than enough.'

The guard laughed, and the mood eased.

'I know what you are saying,' he said, 'and you have my sympathy, my friend, but alas, nobody leaves the château during the hours of darkness. Your tryst will have to be postponed.'

Jacques feigned disappointment and, sighing deeply, turned away. He had only gone a few paces before stopping and turning back.

'What if I told you her name?' he said. 'She is extremely beautiful and has a healthy appetite for male company, especially at night. As I am leaving in a day or so, she may be willing to let you take my place.'

The young man's eyes widened at the prospect.

'Who is she?' he asked, and Jacques walked back to whisper in the guard's ear.

'Her name is…'

The young man never heard anything else as Jacques thrust his knife up through his abdomen and into his chest, cutting his heart in two.

The guard gasped in pain and shock, trying to cry out, but it was too late, and as he died, Jacques lowered him into the darker shadows against the wall. With the deed done, he fell silent and looked up for a few moments to see if he had been heard, but there was nothing but stillness and, realising the way was now clear, he made his way back to where Cronin and the nurse were hiding.

'It's done,' he said. 'Let's go.'

'What did you do?'

'Don't ask stupid questions,' said Jacques. 'Now follow me.' He turned away and walked to the gate before withdrawing the four heavy bolts as quietly as possible. Once done, he pulled at the gate but was greeted by the deafening sound of unoiled metal hinges. He stopped suddenly, looking around to see if anyone had heard. When it remained silent, he turned to Cronin. 'If I open this gate fully, someone is bound to hear. What do you want to do?'

'We have no other choice,' said Cronin. 'We just have to do it and head as fast as we can to the trees on the far side of the river. Walter will be there with the horses.'

'And if he is not?'

'Then we are done for.' He turned to the woman. 'Give me the child, I will carry him.'

'No,' said the nurse, clutching the baby tighter to her chest. 'I will carry him.'

'I can't risk it,' said Cronin. 'We need to move fast, so you will struggle to keep up. He is safer with me. Once we get to the horses, I will give him back, I swear.'

The woman hesitated but eventually handed over the child.

'Do not let any harm come to him,' she hissed, 'or I will kill you myself.'

Despite the situation, Cronin smiled. There was no doubt that she was serious about the intent, even though the ability may be lacking. He turned back to Jacques.

'Right, let's do it.'

Jacques took a deep breath, and with one sudden jerk, pulled the gate open. The scream of the hinges echoed through the courtyard, but without waiting to see the consequences, all three ran from the château towards the darker shadows of the distant trees.

Behind them, the guards stationed on the perimeter wall of the château looked at each other with concern.

'That was the gate,' said one and walked over to look down into the courtyard. 'Isaac,' he called, 'why have you opened the gate?' He waited for a response but received nothing but silence. 'Isaac,' he shouted again, 'answer me.' After a few seconds, he turned to his comrades. 'I'm going down to see what is happening. You stay here.'

He entered the gate tower and ran down the stairs to the ground floor. Looking around, he saw no sign of the guard until eventually, he found the slumped corpse hidden in the corner. His heart raced, and he looked up in panic. He had no idea what had happened, but knew there was some sort of danger.

'Alarm,' he roared. 'Everyone to arms. We are under attack.'

----

129

Cronin, Jacques, and the nurse hurried through the underbrush, their breaths ragged from the exertion. Behind them, they heard the alarm bell echoing through the château and the sounds of armed men rushing to their stations.

'They must be around here somewhere,' said Jacques, peering into the darkness.

'Keep going,' demanded Cronin. 'The road is somewhere ahead. They might be there.' They doubled their efforts, but it was obvious the woman was struggling.

'Jacques,' said Cronin, 'take the baby.' He handed him over and turned back to the nurse, grabbing her arm. 'Let me help.'

----

Behind them, in the château, the air was one of confusion. Men ran everywhere, looking for the intruders, but it was soon apparent there were none. Bergerac strode across the courtyard to face the man who had raised the alarm.

'Did you actually see anyone come in?' he demanded.

'No, my lord, but when I saw Isaac's dead body, I assumed…'

'You assumed?'

'My lord…,' he started, but before he could continue, a woman's voice screamed from one of the windows above.

'*My baby, it's gone.*'

'The Templar,' hissed Bergerac. 'I knew it.' He turned back to the guard. 'I'll deal with you later. The rest of you, saddle the horses. They can't have gone far.'

The garrison swung into activity, and less than ten minutes later, two dozen men rode out through the giant gates of the château to find the men who had abducted the future king of England.

----

The three fugitives reached the road and paused, looking either way for any sign of the men who should be waiting for them.

'I don't understand,' gasped Cronin, 'they should be here.'

'If anywhere, they will be amongst the trees,' said Jacques. 'Come on, let's keep going.' They crossed into the forest, pushing away the undergrowth as they ran. With their hopes dwindling, they reached a clearing, and the nurse fell to the floor, completely exhausted.

'We'll have to leave her,' said Jacques, but before Cronin could respond, a voice called out from deeper in the trees.

'Over here, hurry.'

Cronin looked up and saw Walter riding out from the trees, followed by several of his men.

'Thank God,' gasped Jacques. 'We had just about given you up.'

'Who's this?' demanded Walter, reigning in his horse.

'It's the child's wet nurse,' said Cronin. 'We brought her along to take care of the child.'

'Where is his mother?'

'We couldn't find her. This is the best we could do.'

'It matters not,' said Walter. 'Lift her up behind me.'

Cronin and Jacques lifted the nurse from the ground and hoisted her up onto his horse.

'And the baby?'

Jacques lifted the child and waited until it was safely nestled beneath the nurse's cloak.

'Where are our horses?' asked Cronin, looking around.

'We could not find any more; we ran out of time.'

'Then who should we ride behind?' asked Jacques, looking at the other horsemen.

'None of them,' said Walter. 'You will have to make your own way back.'

'What,' gasped Cronin, 'you can't just leave us here?'

'I have no other option,' said Walter. 'It is imperative we get this child back to King John, and you will just slow us down.'

'We will die out here,' growled Cronin. 'You know that.'

'We all have to make sacrifices for the crown, Cronin. Consider this yours.'

'You double-crossing snake,' growled Jacques, and reached for his sword, but before he could withdraw it from the scabbard, a crossbow bolt thudded into his chest, sending him backwards to land on the forest floor. Cronin also reached for his sword, but Walter called out, staying his hand.

'Cronin, hold. That man meant nothing to me, but you will suffer the same fate should you draw your weapon, and I don't want to kill you.'

Cronin looked up and saw three of Walter's men aiming crossbows at his heart.

'I don't want to kill you,' said the justiciar again, 'but will do so in a heartbeat unless you back off now.'

'You killed him in cold blood,' said Cronin. 'Why would you spare me?'

'Because we have something in common. Both of us served alongside Lionheart, and in my eyes, that makes us brothers.'

'I am no brother of yours,' snarled Cronin. 'You have the honour of a rat.'

'Think what you like,' said Walter, 'but I have no doubt that if anyone can survive this, you can.'

'You should kill me while you can,' said Cronin. 'For if I get out of this with my life, I swear that I will seek you out and cut your throat.'

'You may well survive,' said Walter. 'You may even find me, but you will not kill me.'

'And what makes you so sure?'

'Because if you do, you will never find out about your wife.'

'Sumeira? What do you mean? What have you done to her?'

'She is alive,' said Walter. 'Though by now, I suspect that she is no longer in England.'

'Where is she?' gasped Cronin. 'Where have you taken her?'

'Somewhere far away,' said Walter, 'and if anything happens to me, you will never know where. It will be interesting to see if you do indeed survive, Cronin, but as I am now the only man who knows where she is, I will sleep soundly knowing my throat will never feel the edge of your blade. Now, I suggest you leave, for I hear horsemen upon the road. Run, Cronin, or die where you stand.'

As Cronin watched, Walter and his men turned away and spurred their horses to head south, leaving him alone in the forests of Normandy, with a dozen heavily armed Frenchmen closing in fast.

----

# CHAPTER EIGHTEEN

## Constantinople

As the sun began its descent behind the Golden Horn, casting a warm glow over the sprawling city, Emperor Baldwin returned to Constantinople, his thoughts heavy with the weight of recent negotiations. The agreement with Boniface had been a necessary compromise, but Baldwin couldn't shake the feeling that he had given away more than just a city. Still, the promise of food and resources was a lifeline for his beleaguered capital, and he needed every single mouthful of grain that Thessalonica could send.

As the majestic walls of Constantinople loomed nearer, Baldwin straightened in his saddle, readying himself for the inevitable barrage of concerns and decisions awaiting him. The city was already a cauldron of simmering unrest, and he had no illusions about the fragility of his rule. His return would need to be marked by swift, decisive action.

The gates swung open, and Baldwin's party was met by a contingent of the men left to defend the city in his absence. With a curt nod, he acknowledged their salute and proceeded through the bustling streets. The people bowed or cheered as the emperor passed, though there was an undercurrent of anxiety in their eyes. The recent hardships had taken their toll.

As Baldwin approached the palace, he was met by Peter of Bethlehem, one of the crusading bishops still in the city.

'Emperor Baldwin,' Peter greeted him, his horse falling into step, 'welcome back. News of your confrontation with Boniface has preceded you.'

'It was more of a negotiation,' said Baldwin, 'not a confrontation.'

'Yet I hear you set up lines blocking his path and would have crossed swords if circumstances demanded it.'

'It did not come to that,' said Baldwin, 'so we will never know.'

'Call it what you will,' said the bishop, 'as long as the outcome was beneficial.'

'It was as good as could be expected. Thessalonica is his, for now. But the supplies he sends will buy us time.'

Peter nodded, understanding the delicate balance they were attempting to maintain.

'What news of the city?' asked Baldwin. 'Is the peace intact?'

'It is, but it is fragile. As I said, the news of your meeting has preceded you, and the people hope there is an end in sight for their suffering.'

'There is,' said Baldwin, 'but it will take time. Is there anything else?'

'There is another matter,' said the bishop. 'Alexios is dead. His body was found at the bottom of the tower a few weeks ago.'

Baldwin glanced across but did not slow his pace. Everyone knew it would happen, but the ex-emperor had lasted far longer than anyone had expected.

'Did anyone see him fall?'

'Apparently, he did not fall,' said the bishop. 'Before the sun set, he stood up, faced the west and outstretched his arms before allowing himself to fall forward. They say it was both graceful and magnificent.'

'Did he say anything before he met his fate?'

'He did,' sighed the bishop.

'And…?'

Peter looked across again, a look of religious fervour in his eyes.

'He shouted, "*Lord forgive me.*"

Baldwin nodded and turned his focus back to negotiating the crowds filling the streets before him. Alexios had deserved his fate, but now he was dead, there was a risk he could become a martyr to those who still thought of him as the true ruler of Constantinople.

'Where is he now?' he asked over his shoulder.

'His body was taken to the palace and buried in the gardens. I assumed you would want it to disappear.'

'A few weeks ago, I would have wished exactly that,' said Baldwin, 'but now I realise we are all pawns in the same game. We need to exhume his body.'

'Why?' asked the bishop. 'What are you saying?'

'I am saying that when we get back, you will arrange a proper burial for him with full ceremonial honours. Despite his failings, he was once an emperor and deserves to rest in peace.'

'But it will provide a focal point for those who still follow his teachings.'

'The ceremony will be public, and we will use it as an opportunity to stitch together the open wounds that still fester across the city, but we will keep his final resting place secret, and the grave will be unmarked. Make the arrangements.'

Bringing the conversation to a close, he spurred his horse to trot through the gates of the palace, reining it in outside the ornate doors. He dismounted, his heavy boots echoing on the stone steps as he made his way into the palace, the weight of leadership pressing heavily upon his shoulders. He had returned to a city fraught with challenges, both seen and unseen, and although the pact with Boniface might bring temporary relief, it was clear that the road ahead would be fraught with peril. The body of Alexios would be laid to rest with honour, but Baldwin's mind was already turning to the many battles yet to be fought.

----

Fifty leagues away, at the confluence of the Maritsa, Tundzha, and Arda rivers, the walled city of Adrianople thrummed with the pulse of daily life. Thick stone walls, built to withstand sieges and assaults, surrounded the city, punctuated by robust towers that loomed like sentinels over the bustling streets below. These walls were more than mere barriers; they were the city's lifeline, the first and last defence against the chaos of the world outside.

Within the city, the cobblestone streets were alive with activity. Merchants hawked their wares, their voices a cacophony of offers and enticements. Blacksmiths hammered out a relentless rhythm, and the chatter of townsfolk negotiating prices filled the air. The scent of freshly baked bread mixed with the earthy aroma of spices, carried on the breeze from the marketplace at the city's heart.

The marketplace itself was a riot of colour and sound. Stalls overflowed with rich fabrics from the East, exotic spices from distant lands, and glittering jewellery that caught the light in a dazzling display. Greek nobles, their robes embroidered with gold and silver, strolled through the market with an air of detached superiority. Latin advisors, distinguishable by their simpler, more practical attire, moved among them, their eyes sharp and wary.

Despite the vibrant life within the walls, an undercurrent of tension was palpable. The recent fall of Constantinople to the Crusaders had cast a long shadow, and the citizens of Adrianople lived with the constant awareness of potential danger. The city's occupants were mainly Greek, but since Constantinople had fallen, an increasing number of crusader nobles had arrived under the guise of special advisors and recently started assuming more and more authority, an imposition that the city elders tolerated in the interests of peace. The last thing they wanted was for Baldwin to attack. But Baldwin was not the only one to send his ambassadors, for despite the newly signed treaty, Boniface was a very astute man and had deployed his own men among the populace, desperate to keep his finger on the pulse of local politics. Adrianople was simply too strategically important to do otherwise.

The defences were formidable. The walls were not only thick but ingeniously designed, with battlements and arrow slits allowing archers to defend the city from a secure position. Moats and ditches further complicated any assault, and within the walls, key fortifications provided additional layers of defence. The citadel, a fortress within the fortress, stood as the ultimate bastion, its high walls and reinforced gates a final refuge for the city's leaders in times of crisis.

As dusk approached, the city began to wind down. Torches were lit, casting a warm glow on the ancient stones, and the gates were secured with heavy iron bars. The guards doubled their vigilance, eyes scanning the horizon for any sign of trouble. In the marketplace, the day's bustle gave way to a quieter, more subdued atmosphere as vendors packed away their goods, and townsfolk hurried home, casting wary glances over their shoulders.

The taverns, however, were just beginning to fill. Inside, the air was thick with the smell of ale and the sound of laughter and conversation. Patrons shared stories of distant lands, the latest political intrigue, and the ever-present threat of attack. The recent upheavals had taught them to be cautious, to live each day with the knowledge that peace was fragile and could shatter at any moment, and it was in this busy, yet inconsequential environment, in a corner away from the bustle of weary traders, that the seeds of war were already being sown.

----

# CHAPTER NINETEEN

## Normandy

Cronin's heart thundered in his chest, blood pounding in his ears as he lay motionless beneath the dense canopy of leaves. The forests of Normandy, normally a sanctuary of tranquillity, had become a labyrinth of treachery and danger. Morning sunlight filtered weakly through the foliage, casting dappled shadows on the forest floor. The clinking of armour and guttural orders of soldiers were faint but unmistakable, carried on the breeze that rustled the branches above.

For the last hour, Cronin had been hiding from the men who had charged from the chateau to pursue the abductors of the baby prince. The horsemen had ridden past his hiding place almost immediately, but just as he thought he was safe, they were followed by foot soldiers who had obviously been ordered to search the woods. It was a game of cat and mouse. Although confident in his own ability to evade them, the sheer number of soldiers meant he had to stay hidden, at least until darkness provided better cover.

He could see the figures moving in the distance, led by the imposing figure of Bergerac. Cronin's breath came shallow and controlled, each inhale a deliberate effort to remain silent. His mind raced, replaying the events that had led to this betrayal. Trust had been a costly mistake.

Minutes felt like hours as the soldiers trampled through the undergrowth, searching. Cronin's training as a Templar had prepared him for many things, but being hunted like a wild animal was a new and bitter reality. He waited, counting the seconds until the noise of the pursuit grew distant.

Slowly, he eased himself from his hiding place, his muscles protesting after the prolonged stillness. His eyes scanned the forest, sharp and wary, before he began his southward trek, every step deliberate, avoiding the brittle twigs that might betray his position. The underbrush parted reluctantly, branches scratching at his face and hands, but Cronin pressed on, driven by a burning need for retribution.

As the hours slipped by, the dense forest began to thin, revealing patches of cultivated land. The sight of a small farmstead brought a grim smile to his lips. A horse would be essential if he was to catch up with the men who had wronged him. Moving with renewed purpose, he approached the farm, keeping to the shadows.

The farm was quiet, the inhabitants likely tending to their daily chores. Cronin's eyes fell upon a sturdy chestnut mare tied to a post in a paddock. He crouched low, moving swiftly and silently across the open ground. With practised ease, he approached the horse, his hand outstretched. The mare whinnied softly, sensing his presence, but Cronin's soothing murmurs calmed her as he loosened the rope.

There was no time for a saddle. He led the mare to the edge of the farmstead, his eyes scanning for any sign of the farmers. With a final glance over his shoulder, he swung himself onto the horse's back and urged her into a gallop.

----

Several leagues southward, Walter and his men reined in their horses. He looked up at the darkening skies and knew they had to stop for the night. Continuing through an unfamiliar forest using unknown paths invited disaster. He slid off his horse and helped the exhausted nurse down to the ground. Immediately, she stumbled over to a nearby tree and sat against the trunk before removing her cloak to feed the baby. Walter turned to his men.

'We will camp here,' he said, 'and move out again at dawn.'

'Are you sure, my lord?' asked Peter. 'We could cover another league before dark.'

'No, there is water here,' said Walter, 'and we can deploy while it is still light. Get the horses out of sight and post guards in pairs all around the camp. Each man is tasked with keeping the other awake. If even a mouse moves in the undergrowth, I want to know about it, understood?'

'They are already very tired, my lord. Why can we not deploy half and then relieve them when the others are rested?'

'We can't risk it,' said Walter. 'One more night is all I ask. After that, they can sleep for a week if they want. And make sure they are fed and ready to ride at first light. It is a straight gallop from here to the ship. There will be no stopping, understood?'

'Yes, my lord.'

'Good. If you need me, I will be guarding the child.'

'As you wish, my lord,' said Peter, and he turned away to set up the position. It was going to be a long night.

----

The landscape blurred as Cronin pushed the horse to its limits. The path was wide, and the ground was easily covered, but he knew that between him and his quarry was an armed force of at least twelve men. Somehow, he had to avoid them, get past, and reach the ship before Walter. They already had a few hours' start, but he knew he could close the distance by riding through the night. It was a dangerous ploy, but he had no other choice. The life of Sumeira could depend on it.

----

Cronin reined in the mare as the darkness deepened, the forest now a shadowy maze beneath a moonless sky. He was hungry, thirsty, and every bone in his body ached from the relentless ride. The urgency of his mission gnawed at him, yet he knew that haste in the black of night could be his undoing. Besides, the horse was also struggling, but he needed to continue. The path was barely visible, and each step forward was a delicate balance between speed and silence. Cronin leaned low over the mare's neck, his eyes straining to catch any hint of movement, ears pricked for the faintest sound that might betray an ambush. The night's stillness was punctuated by the occasional hoot of an owl or the rustle of small creatures in the underbrush.

The trees thinned gradually, revealing a dim glow in the distance, firelight, unmistakably from an enemy camp. His heart quickened, and he reined the mare to a halt, dismounting before leading her into the cover of the trees. From this distance, he could make out the rough outlines of tents and the flickering shadows of men around a central fire.

Cronin's mind raced. The main path was too close to the enemy, and passing by unnoticed was impossible. He needed another route. His eyes scanned the surroundings and saw the land dip into a marshy expanse to the left. It was waterlogged, treacherous terrain, but it offered the cover he needed.

With resigned determination, he turned the mare toward the marsh. The ground quickly grew soft beneath their feet, each step a struggle as the mud sucked at their boots and hooves. Progress was slow and exhausting, the mare's breath laboured, and Cronin whispered words of encouragement, patting her neck to reassure her. Every now and then, the cold water seeped into his boots, numbing his feet, but Cronin pushed on, the faint murmur of voices from the camp still audible in the distance. He stayed low, eyes fixed on the campfires flickering through the trees, ensuring he remained out of sight.

The marsh was a quagmire of tangled reeds and stagnant pools. More than once, Cronin's foot sank deep into the mud, nearly throwing him off balance. His hands were slick with the muck as he clung to the mare's reins, pulling her free whenever she stumbled. The marsh's chill bit into his bones, but the knight's resolve was unyielding. He would not be stopped.

Finally, after what felt like an eternity, the ground began to firm beneath their feet. The treacherous marsh gave way to more solid ground, and Cronin allowed himself a brief moment of relief. He led the mare up a slight rise, pausing at the crest to survey the land behind him. The campfires were distant now, mere pinpricks of light against the dark horizon.

Satisfied that he had evaded detection, he mounted the mare once more. Gently rubbing his hand against her neck in encouragement, he urged her forward.

'Come on, girl,' he whispered, 'we are almost there.'

The path ahead was clearer now, the trees opening up to reveal the undulating terrain of Normandy. The stars overhead provided a faint, silvery illumination, guiding his way.

His thoughts turned to the men who had betrayed him. Their faces flashed before his eyes, fuelling the fire of his resolve. Each rolling league that passed beneath the mare's hooves brought him closer to his goal, and as the first light of dawn began to creep over the horizon, Cronin knew that the chase was far from over.

----

Walter sat against a tree opposite the nurse. For the last hour or so, he had watched as she fed, cleaned, and finally reassured the frightened child until he had fallen into a fitful sleep. Once done, she wrapped him carefully beneath her cloak and leaned back against her own tree, her eyes closed in exhaustion.

Walter got up and walked over before lowering himself to sit opposite her on a rock.

Genevieve opened her eyes and stared, a look of dislike evident in her gaze.

'What do you want?' she said quietly, desperate not to wake the sleeping child.

'Here,' he said, handing over a pouch of dried beef and biscuits. 'It's not much, but it's all we have. Once we are on the ship, I will ensure you have a hot meal.'

The nurse hesitated before reaching out and taking the food. She had to keep her strength up, if only for the sake of the baby. She chewed on the meat slowly, staring at the man who was trying to take them both from the land of their birth.

'Why are you doing this?' she asked eventually. 'We have done nothing to you.'

'It is not personal,' said Walter. 'My king wants the child and its mother, but it seems she was nowhere to be found, so Cronin saw fit to bring you instead. As it happens, it was a wise choice, and I will make sure you are not harmed.'

'Is he the man you killed outside the chateau?'

'No. The man who died was killed because he drew his sword. It was self-defence.'

'He hardly moved,' said Genevieve, 'it was murder.'

Walter shrugged. The woman's opinions were not of his concern.

'Why does your king want this child?' asked the nurse. 'Why is he so important?'

Walter stared back for a moment, wondering why someone who was so close to the child did not know his birthright.

'You do know this child's father, do you not?'

'I do. A womanising noble from Brittany with neither style nor manners. Why?'

'Have you ever met him?'

'No, but I understand he is no more than a child himself, around sixteen years old.'

'Men of sixteen fight and die all around Christendom,' said Walter, 'and father children, as in this case.'

'But I still do not understand why this child,' said Genevieve. 'You have risked a lot to come here and travel so far inland. What is his importance?'

'You have heard of King Richard the Lionheart?'

'I have. He is dead.'

'He is, and before he died, he nominated his nephew, Arthur of Brittany, as his heir and successor. But when Richard's brother, John, found out, he moved quickly to claim the throne for himself and deny Arthur's claim. Blood has been spilt between them and no doubt more will flow before this matter is sorted, but for now, there is calm, especially as Arthur is in the king's custody in London.'

Genevieve realised where the conversation was going and looked down at the baby before looking back at the justiciar.

'And you think this is his child?'

'We do.'

'But if what you say is true, and Arthur has a legitimate claim, this baby...' She left the sentence hanging as the reality sank in.

'Depending on which side of the argument you stand,' said Walter, 'he could be the rightful heir to the throne of England. That is why we have taken him.'

Genevieve's face fell as she realised what he was saying, the reality finally hitting her like a punch to the stomach. She shook her head slowly, fear appearing in her eyes.

'But if that is true,' she said, her voice hardly a whisper, 'then your king cannot allow either of them to live. To do so risks a challenge to his crown.' She stared at the justiciar, the tears already welling in her eyes before looking down at the baby again. 'You are taking him to his death.'

----

Cronin stared down from the top of a hill. Below him, a few leagues away, lay the vast expanse of the sea, and beyond, England where his lands awaited, looked after by the woman he loved. Down below the hill, at the edge of the estuary, was the village they had stayed in when they first arrived, and offshore, the ship that had brought them here. He sighed in relief. The very fact that the ship was still there meant he had got there in time. He dismounted with a grunt of exhaustion and removed the harness from around the beast's neck.

'You have been majestic, my friend,' he said, 'now go find yourself someone to look after you.' He tapped the horse's rump and watched as it walked away before stopping to feed on the succulent green grass. Cronin knew it would only be a matter of time before the animal was found, and he turned back to the matter at hand. God had been on his side so far, but there was no time to waste, and he turned his gaze towards the sleeping village below.

With an audible groan, he forced his already aching body into motion and headed down the hill into the village, his chainmail whispering with each determined step. The village was slowly awakening, the first signs of life stirring behind shuttered windows and creaking wooden doors, but he paid little mind to the stirring world; his eyes were fixed on the distant docks and the ship beyond, its silhouette stark against the lightening sky.

The scent of salt and fish grew stronger, mingling with the earthy aroma of morning dew clinging to the nets and ropes that lined the pathways. The rhythmic creak of boats swaying gently in the harbour reached his ears, and something else, something so welcoming it made his mouth salivate in anticipation, the smell of fresh fish cooking on a griddle.

As Cronin approached the docks, the source of the smell became clear, a group of four men standing around an open fire, waiting as another fried a pile of small fish on a metal griddle. He walked over and all five turned their heads to stare at him. He was a forlorn sight, filthy from the dust of the road and his clothes covered in the dried, stinking mud from the marsh.

The men stared at the newcomer with suspicion. They suspected that he had something to do with the English ship anchored in the harbour, but they were not fighting men and wanted nothing to do with any conflict between the two countries. They were fishermen, and just needed to feed their families.

'Can I share some food?' he asked, his voice dry. He pointed at the griddle over the flames. His speech was difficult to understand, but the request was obvious, and one of the men scraped half a dozen of the small fish onto a platter and handed it over, all the time staring in silence at the dirty newcomer.

Cronin ate as quickly as he could but kept looking around nervously, unsure of the whereabouts of Walter and his men. As soon as he finished eating, he drank his fill from an offered water flask before handing it back and wiping his mouth with the back of his hand.

'Have any other men come through here?' he asked, using his limited French to the best of his ability.

All the men stared, and Cronin realised the dialect was completely different.

'Men like me,' he asked again, pointing at himself, 'twelve men and one baby.' He used his fingers to indicate quantity and mimicked cradling a child.

Again there were blank stares all around, and Cronin knew he was wasting his time. He looked around and, seeing a water trough against a nearby building, expressed his gratitude and headed over to try and clean away as much of the filth as possible. Half an hour later, with his face and hands clean and the worst of the stench washed away, he sank to the ground against the building and leaned back to rest. The familiar ship in the harbour hadn't moved, and it was evident that somehow, despite all the danger and hardship of the past two days, he had managed to get ahead of his quarry. His hand rested on the hilt of the sword cradled in his lap. All he had to do now was wait.

----

# CHAPTER TWENTY

## Adrianople

Chelebri leaned back in his chair, the rough wood creaking under his weight. The dimly lit tavern, thick with the scent of roasted meat and spilled ale, buzzed with the low hum of murmured conversations. It was a typical evening in Adrianople, a city blissfully unaware of the wolves that had slipped through its gates disguised as sheep.

His four trusted men sat around him, each nursing a tankard of ale, their eyes scanning the room with practiced ease. They wore the garb of merchants, their dusty cloaks and tunics a testament to their supposed travels. For the past few days, they had blended seamlessly into the city's bustling life, observing, noting, and now, ready to report their findings.

Chelebri took a long draught of his drink, savouring the bitter taste as he waited for the tavern's noise to swell and drown out their conversation. Finally, he nodded to the man on his left, a wiry fellow named Boril.

'Speak,' he commanded softly.

Boril leaned forward, his voice barely above a whisper.

'The walls are solid, but old. There are sections near the north gate where the stone is crumbling. It wouldn't take much to breach it with the right force.'

Chelebri nodded, his fingers drumming lightly on the table.

'And the guard rotations?'

A hulking man with a scar running down his cheek took over.

'They change every four hours, day and night. Again, the northern gate is the weakest in terms of manpower. Fewer guards, and they seem less alert.'

Chelebri's lips curled into a faint smile.

'Good. What of the garrison?'

Miroslav, the youngest of the group but sharp-eyed and quick, spoke up.

'The garrison is sizable but spread thin. Many of the soldiers are inexperienced. They rely heavily on a small core of veteran fighters. If we can neutralize those, the rest will fall into disarray.'

'And the townsfolk? How are their spirits?'

The final member of their group, an older man named Asparuh, who had a knack for blending into any crowd, answered.

'The people are weary. Taxes are high, and there's a sense of unease. Many whisper of the coming storm but are too afraid to act.'

'Do you think they can be persuaded to rebel?' asked Chelebri.

'I do,' said Asparuh. 'There are many other taverns like this where the talk is of direct action against their overlords. The population is mostly Greek, and they resent the fact that Latins are slowly taking over their lives. The frustration is building up like water behind a dam, and with the right encouragement, I believe we can break that dam and stand back as the deluge washes away our enemies.'

Chelebri leaned back, absorbing the information. He had expected some weaknesses, but the extent of them was promising. Kaloyan would be pleased.

'Good work,' he said, his voice carrying a tone of finality. 'We'll relay this to our Lord Kaloyan tonight and await his final command. Until we hear back, we will maintain this low profile but start sowing the seeds of discontent. Remember, we are still merchants until we leave this city. No unnecessary risks.'

As the night wore on, the tavern's patrons slowly dwindled, leaving the place quieter, the shadows longer. Chelebri and his men finished their drinks and one by one, stepped out into the cool night air.

The streets of Adrianople were mostly empty, the silence broken only by the distant clatter of hooves and the occasional bark of a dog. Chelebri pulled his cloak tighter around him, his eyes scanning the darkened alleys and moonlit rooftops. His instincts were sharp, and he knew better than to let his guard down, even in these final days of their mission.

As he walked back to his rented quarters, a sense of accomplishment settled over him. They had entered the city as shadows, and soon, a new chapter in their conquest of the south would begin. For now, though, he was just another merchant heading home after a long day's work, blending seamlessly into the night.

----

The horizon blushed with the first light of dawn as the convoy of supply ships finally slipped into the harbour of Constantinople. Behind them came the troop ship from England, carrying reinforcements for Acre, along with Jamal and Sir Edmund.

The masts of the many ships already in the harbour stood tall and proud against the backdrop of the ravaged skyline, each adorned with flags from various corners of Christendom. As the ships docked, the harbour came alive with the sound of creaking ropes, shouted orders, and the bustling activity of men eager to unload the much-needed supplies. The sight of crates filled with food, weapons, and medical supplies bringing a measure of hope to the war-weary inhabitants of Constantinople.

Over the next few days, the process of unloading continued, and Sir Edmund tasked his men with helping. Each was given strict instructions to return by dawn on the third day so they could continue their journey to Acre. Any man failing to do so would be named as a deserter and hung by the local authorities if found. Suitably warned, the men from England surged into the city, some seeking women, others ale, and the remainder, a chance to reconnect with God in one of the hundreds of churches scattered across the city.

Sir Edmund and Jamal stood at the rail, watching them go. Jamal was strangely quiet, his eyes seemingly sightless as he stared at the city walls, now shrouded with timber framework as hordes of masons tried to rebuild them to their former glory. Edmund glanced over. They had worked hard on Jamal's training and were at last forming a bond, but the knight knew that his would-be squire would never reach the standard required for battle. Whatever had caused the boy's head injury had left hidden damage; his reactions were just too slow.

'You can join them, you know,' Edmund said, nodding to the last group of men going ashore. 'Go and explore the city; it is a magnificent place, and you may not see it again.'

'I don't need to,' said Jamal quietly. 'I have been here before.'

Edmund's head spun to stare at the boy. 'What do you mean?' he asked. 'That is not possible.'

'My mother is a physician,' said Jamal, 'and she lived here for a long time. I was schooled in the palace and was here when the city fell.'

'What?' gasped Edmund. 'If that is true, why have you not mentioned it before?'

'I had forgotten,' replied Jamal, a look of confusion in his eyes. 'But those walls, the towers, the spires, I recognise them all, and it is all coming back to me.'

'Are you telling the truth?' asked the knight. 'For if you jest with me, I swear I will give you a beating you will never forget.'

'It is true,' said Jamal, still staring at the city. 'I remember it all. The fear, the fighting, the slaughter, all of it. During the battle, my mother was captured by the Turbasel Knights and held captive in the Palace of Blachernae but was rescued by Cronin.' He stopped and turned his head to stare at the knight. 'Cronin is my father, not by blood, but the man who has been there for me and my mother for many years. I left him behind in England.'

'Well, this is all fascinating,' said Edmund, 'but perhaps it is just a vision, a false memory caused by your injury.'

'It is true,' said Jamal, 'all of it, and I can prove it.'

'How?'

'I can take you to all the places we have spoken of. The palaces, the battle sites, the churches. I can even show you the room where the true Shroud of Christ was kept before Cronin saved it from being destroyed by the Turbasel Knights.'

'I have no idea what you are talking about,' said Edmund, 'but I am fascinated by the account. I'm still not sure if I believe you, but we have a few days, so let's see if you are telling the truth. Get your things together, Jamal, and if you speak truly, take me to where the shroud of our Lord was kept.'

----

150

Later that day, with the sun high in the sky, they set out on their exploration. The streets of Constantinople were a sombre mixture of quiet markets and silent ruins. The war had certainly left its mark, with buildings laying in crumbled heaps and much of the once grandiose architecture now mere ghostly remnants of a bygone era.

'It's so…different,' said Jamal as they walked. 'It was so beautiful, but now…' He left the sentence unfinished and turned away into a barren alleyway.

'Where are we going now?' asked the knight.

'To the Blachernae Palace,' said Jamal. 'This is a shortcut.'

'But surely the shroud was kept in the Pharos Chapel of the Boukoleon Palace?'

'It was,' said Jamal, 'but it was moved to Blachernae prior to the siege. It was there that we saw it.'

The knight paused for a moment but, determined to see what the trainee squire was up to, took a deep breath and followed in his footsteps.

As they made their way through the winding streets, the palace eventually came into view, a majestic testament to Byzantine opulence and architectural prowess, albeit now tarnished by the battle's brutal reality. Inside the palace grounds, the splendour of Blachernae was still apparent despite the destruction. The courtyards, which had once been lush gardens filled with exotic flora and flowing fountains, were now overgrown and untamed, with many people living in temporary shelters due to the destruction of their homes in the main city.

The central buildings of the palace, where the emperors once held court, remained imposing, but it was the smaller chapel on the far edge of the complex that Jamal headed to, his mind flooded with re-emerging memories of how close they had come, not only to being killed but, more importantly, to losing the holy shroud forever. He walked in through the damaged doors, feeling none of the awe that he had experienced the last time. All the relics had now gone, some looted by the crusader armies, others secreted away by clergy desperate to save whatever they could during the destruction.

The main hall, with its high vaulted ceilings and massive columns, had an air of faded glory. Sunlight filtered through the remnants of stained-glass windows, casting fragmented rainbows on the cracked marble floors.

Mosaics, once vibrant with the hues of imperial purple and gold, now showed signs of neglect. The images of saints and emperors, angels and battles, were still discernible, but the tesserae had loosened in places, and whole sections had fallen away. Yet, even in their damaged state, the mosaics exuded an aura of magnificence, a reminder of their former grandeur.

'This is the place,' said Jamal quietly. 'It was here that Faulk of Neuilly killed the Turbasel Knight before the shroud could be burnt and then died from his own wounds. I thought that by placing the shroud upon him, God would let him live, but it was too late.'

'Wait,' said Edmund, 'you actually held the shroud?'

'I did, briefly, and swore right then that I would serve God in whatever way I could.'

'Why have you not said any of this before?'

'As I have said, my mind did not recall any of this until recently. I believe that God has hidden my memories from me since I hurt my head to ease my pain, but since we saw the city, I remember it all.'

'Where is the shroud now?'

'Cronin took it to Venice to protect it from the ongoing unrest in the city. There he gave it to a pious noble called Robert de Clari. He swore upon his life that he and his descendants would protect it.'

Sir Edmund's mind was a maelstrom of thoughts. To be in the actual chapel where the shroud had been kept was one thing, but to realise he was in the company of someone who had actually seen and held it was difficult to comprehend

'You are a revelation, Jamal,' he said. 'Despite your tale being hard to take in, I do not believe you to be a liar. I also think that you have far more tales to tell that may not seem important to you, but need to be told and shared, if only to understand the history and ultimate fate of the shroud. Come, let us see more of this place. It is touching my very soul.'

As Sir Edmund and Jamal wandered through the palace, they were continually struck by the enduring beauty of Byzantine art and architecture, still standing resilient against the ravages of war and time. The air was thick with dust and a sombre silence, and Sir Edmund stood in awe, his imagination painting pictures of the chapel's former glory.

'Imagine what it must have been like in its prime,' he whispered. 'A place of reverence and peace, and now, a symbol of resilience.'

They moved deeper into the chapel, their footsteps echoing in the hollow space. Sir Edmund paused before the altar, his hand brushing away the dust to reveal a faint inscription.

'*In nomine Patris, et Filii, et Spiritus Sancti,*' he read aloud, his voice reverberating off the walls.

Outside, the sun had begun its descent, casting long shadows across the city. Sir Edmund and Jamal walked in silence, each lost in their own thoughts. Edmund, in particular, had come into the city out of curiosity, but had found something more profound: an indescribable feeling that he had experienced a spiritual closeness, no matter how fleeting, to Christ's time on earth.

Eventually, they left the palace to head back towards the ship, and Sir Edmund's mind was again full of conflict. As they walked, a disturbing chain of thoughts started to form, and although they went against everything he held dear, he knew that he would never again be the same man. He had huge decisions to make, and they were certainly not going to be easy.

----

The days that followed were filled with both duty and discovery. While the supplies were distributed and the ships prepared for their return journey, Sir Edmund and Jamal continued to explore, uncovering stories etched in stone and whispered by the winds of Constantinople. Jamal shared all the accounts of his time in the city, and the years prior to that in the Holy Land. Sir Edmund was an avid listener, the roles of teacher and student temporarily reversed, and by the time they were ready to sail, his mind was set. His future was about to change dramatically.

----

# CHAPTER TWENTY-ONE

## Normandy

The sun was already halfway to its zenith when Walter and his men finally reached the village. Since leaving the camp at dawn, they had made good time, but knew they could not rest. To his great relief, the ship that had brought them from England was already offshore, waiting for their return.

'Send some men to find food,' Walter said to Peter as he dismounted, 'the tide is still out, so we have a few hours before they can come into the dock. And post guards on the path, those men from the chateau are probably only a few hours behind us. It could be very tight.'

Peter looked out over the mudflats towards the distant ship. 'Could we not walk out and then transfer in rowing boats?'

'These sands are treacherous,' said Walter. 'The waters can rise in minutes, and if we're caught out there, we have no chance. Our only option is to wait until the estuary is deep enough for the ship to dock. Make the arrangements, Peter. Whatever happens, we need to be prepared.'

As his men turned to their new duties, Walter again helped the nurse down from his horse and shepherded her into the tavern they had used on their first night in Normandy. He led her to a seat in the corner and made her sit down.

'Listen,' he said, 'so far, you've been very compliant, and I thank you for that, but I need you to vow you will not cause any trouble in the next few hours.'

'I will not do anything that may cause harm to the child,' said Genevieve.

'Good,' said the justiciar, and he walked over to the landlord. 'Do you have anything worth eating in there?' he asked, nodding towards the pot hanging over the embers of the fire.

'You're in luck,' said the landlord, 'we put a couple of ducks in there just an hour ago.'

'Then bring us a couple of bowls,' said Walter, 'and a flask of warmed ale.'

'Is there another purse to be had?' asked the landlord, referring to the bounty he had earned just a few days earlier.

'Don't push your luck,' said Walter, tossing a silver coin onto the table. 'Just bring us the food, and don't be frugal with the meat.' He walked back over to the nurse and sat down opposite her with his back to the door. 'The baby is quiet,' he said, nodding to the swaddled child. 'Is he sick?'

'He is tired and hungry,' said the woman, 'and besides, even children can pick up on emotions. I suspect he is afraid.'

'Nonsense,' said Walter. 'He's a baby.'

'What is to happen to us?' asked the nurse.

'In a few hours,' replied Walter, 'we'll be away from here and on a ship to England. After that, I will personally make sure you're well looked after, perhaps with a position in the Palace of Westminster.'

'Why do you not just let us go and tell your king that the baby was killed in the confusion?'

'You know I can't do that.'

'Why not?'

'Because one day, he will probably reappear and stake his claim to the throne of England, and if that happens, then I am a dead man.'

'What if I swore before God himself that I would not allow that to happen?'

'And how could you fulfil that vow? You're not his mother.'

'I'm not, but I am more than a mother than she ever was or ever will be. All she's interested in is whose bed she will be visiting each night, and she leaves the welfare of this baby entirely to me. If you allow us to leave, and perhaps furnish me with a purse to get back to my hometown in Lyon, then I will disappear for good and bring up the child as my own. He will never know who his father was.'

'It's an interesting offer,' said Walter, looking down at the baby, 'but alas, one that I cannot risk.'

'But you know as well as I that once we get to England, this child's days are numbered. The only thing that confuses me is why you've allowed him to live so long. I would have thought it would have been easier just to kill him and be done with it.'

'The king wants him alive.'

'Why?'

'So, he has the leverage to make Arthur sign a declaration renouncing his own claim.'

'And after he does?'

'Then the child and his father will be murdered,' said a voice. Walter spun around to see Cronin standing behind him, sword in hand.

'Cronin,' he gasped, standing up, 'how…?'

Cronin lifted his blade and placed it against the justiciar's throat.

'Shut your stinking, double-crossing mouth,' snarled Cronin, forcing Walter back against the wall. 'Now tell me what you meant back there at the chateau. What has happened to Sumeira?'

'I told you, she is safe,' stuttered Walter, pushing his head as far back from the blade as he could.

'Where is she?' asked Cronin again. 'Spit it out, Walter, or I swear you will die right here.'

'If you kill me, you'll never know.'

'I'm willing to take that risk,' said Cronin. 'Are you?' He pushed his blade into the folds of the justiciar's neck, drawing blood.

'She's on a ship,' gasped Walter quickly, 'on her way to the Holy Land.'

'She would never do that,' said Cronin, 'not until I returned.'

'She thinks you're dead,' said Walter. 'That's why she left.'

'How do you know this? You've been here in Normandy all this time.'

Walter hesitated but then spoke again as Cronin's blade drew more blood.

'Because we sent a message,' he gasped, 'but not the one you wrote. She thinks you died in a fight in London.'

Cronin paused as his mind worked furiously.

'What about my lands?'

'Confiscated by the king. You've been accused of treachery and have nothing left. But as far as I know, she is alive, Cronin, I swear it.'

Cronin stared into the man's eyes, trying to judge if he was telling the truth or not. 'Where is she going exactly?'

'I know not, but you are a man with many contacts. I'm sure if you follow, you should be able to find her. Not many ships carry female physicians to the Holy Land.'

Cronin stared at the man again, unsure how to proceed. If he allowed Walter to live, he would raise the alarm the moment he stepped out of the door, but neither could he kill him in cold blood. He glanced over at the nurse with the baby, but the momentary distraction was more than enough for Walter to react. Twisting to one side, he threw the back of his arm to knock Cronin's sword away before hurling himself behind a table.

Cronin responded quickly, but the advantage had been lost and the air reverberated with the justiciar's roar.

'*Alarm, help me!*'

Cronin turned to flee, but the woman also cried out.

'*Please, take us with you. We are not safe here.*'

'I cannot,' shouted Cronin. 'You will slow me down. I cannot protect you.'

'We are already condemned,' screamed the woman. 'At least give us a chance.'

Cronin looked around, seeing the landlord standing against the far wall, his face creased with fear.

'Is there another way out?'

'That way,' said the landlord, indicating a rear door.

Without wasting a breath, Cronin grabbed the woman by the arm, dragging her to the rear of the inn. Moments later, they burst into the open and ran across the courtyard before ducking down behind a wall.

'Listen,' he said, 'I cannot take you, for they will catch me soon enough. You need to hide, and I will try to lure them away. If I succeed, get out of here as fast as you can, understand?'

'Yes,' said the woman, 'but where?'

'In there,' said Cronin, nodding towards the pigsty in the centre of the filth. 'They will not seek you there, at least until they realise you are not with me.'

'But…'

'It is your only chance,' said Cronin, 'and make sure the baby stays silent. Your lives depend on it.'

The nurse nodded and getting to her feet, ran across to the wooden pigsty before kneeling down and crawling through the filth into the dark shadows within. Once she was hidden, Cronin jumped to his feet and sprinted to the far treeline, again seeking the relative safety of the Normandy forests.

----

Ten minutes later, Walter stood firmly in the courtyard, his eyes fixated on the dense line of trees where his men had disappeared, chasing the fleeting shadow of Cronin. The distant shouts and snapping twigs carried back on the wind, a testament to the furious pursuit within the shadowed woods. Behind him, the inn was eerily silent, the usual bustle of activity stilled by the unexpected violence of the chase. Only the soft grunt of the pigs in the adjacent field and the distant calls of his men broke the quiet.

As he turned to leave, his ears caught an out-of-place sound, a faint whimper, delicate and almost swallowed by the surrounding noise. He paused, brow furrowing. The sound came again, unmistakably the cry of a child, muffled and weak. Intrigued and cautious, Walter crossed the courtyard, his steps measured as he approached the dilapidated pigsty. The structure was old, its wood warped and rotten, more a heap of timber than a shelter for animals. He stood beside it, listening intently.

'Did you hear something, my lord?' asked one of the men walking over from the tavern.

'I don't think so,' said Walter. 'They're probably deep in the forest by now, but Peter will find them soon enough. Return to your men and watch the road. We cannot afford to miss this tide and can waste no more time.'

The soldier nodded, casting a curious glance toward the pigsty before turning to carry out the order. As his footsteps faded, Walter stared towards the distant treeline, his voice quiet but just loud enough to be heard should anyone be hiding within the pigsty.

'I am not a bad man,' he said quietly, 'but I am loyal to my king. If I take you with me, you are correct, you will both probably die. So do what you promised, Genevieve. When I leave with my men, take the child and disappear forever. As far as King John is concerned, the babe is dead, killed by my own hand. Do not give him any cause for doubt, or I will be hung, and he will send another party to find you, wherever you are.'

Without waiting for an answer, he turned away and walked back to the tavern. His task here was done.

----

# CHAPTER TWENTY-TWO

## Adrianople

The moon hung low over Adrianople, casting a silver sheen on the ancient stones of the city walls. Tarkhan Chelebri, having finally received the go-ahead from Tsar Kaloyan, moved silently through the narrow alleyways. A dozen of his chosen men, who had infiltrated the city over the preceding months, followed closely behind. Weeks of careful preparation had led to this moment. They had learned the rhythms of the city, the shifts of the guards, the hidden pathways, and, most importantly, the weaknesses in the defences. Now, as their moment of destiny approached, Chelebri headed for their most important discovery: the location of the city's postern gate.

The walls of Adrianople, built to withstand sieges and invaders, towered high and formidable above the city, but even the mightiest fortifications had their secrets, and within these ancient walls lay a concealed passage known only to a select few.

This hidden gate, a small yet crucial aperture, was expertly crafted into the thick stonework, nearly invisible to the untrained eye and only accessible through a narrow, guarded alleyway. Flanked by buildings whose age matched that of the walls themselves, the postern gate was no more than a heavy wooden door, reinforced with iron bands. Its surface was weathered by time, the wood darkened, and the iron rusted in places, yet it remained sturdy and unyielding. Beyond the gate, a winding passage led through the thick base of the wall, emerging discreetly at the base of one of the towers, its location invisible to anyone approaching the city.

Designed to be used in emergencies, such as during a siege, the gate was an essential necessity for defending the city, but at other times, like this, it could also be its Achilles' heel.

The city was still, save for the occasional bark of a dog or the distant murmur of a guard's conversation. When Chelebri and his men finally reached the alley leading to the gate, they melted deeper into the shadows, waiting for their moment to arrive.

----

A few streets away, in a secluded corner, another group of Chelebri's men ignited a controlled fire against a wooden stable, their faces illuminated briefly by the flickering flames. Fire was the most feared disaster in Adrianople, and within moments, shouts rang out in the darkness, the alarm spreading like ripples in a pond. Smoke filled the narrow streets as the flames flickered upward, and people ran from the surrounding houses, knowing that if any fire spread, it could destroy large swathes of the city within hours. With panic and confusion spreading as fast as the fire, Chelebri's men disappeared back into the shadows, ready to move on to the next phase of the plan.

----

Back at the postern gate, the sounds of the panic reached the ears of the men hiding in the shadows, and Chelebri knew it was time to act. He looked around the corner towards the gate, seeing the two men on guard duty looking upwards at the column of flame and smoke reaching into the night sky.

'Move,' he whispered, stepping aside as two of his men crept forward with knives drawn. Blending with the shadows, their steps were silent, and within moments, the two distracted guards lay face down in the alleyway, the blood from their cut throats spreading across the ground, blacker than the darkest night.

Chelebri stepped over the bodies, drew back the heavy bolts of the gate, and headed through the tunnel beneath the wall. On the far end, another door blocked his way. He opened it to peer outside into the darkness. If everything had gone to plan, his men should be hidden somewhere outside among the undergrowth.

For a few moments, there was nothing, but eventually, much to his relief, a crouched shadow approached out of the darkness and as Chelebri stepped to one side, his men slipped through the gate, a silent stream of shadows pouring into the city.

----

For the following two nights, nobody in Adrianople was any the wiser regarding the unwanted visitors, as the men had immediately separated and merged into the population across the vast city. The bodies of the two gate guards had disappeared, and although their absence caused some concern, it had been put down to desertion, an annoying but common problem among the defenders. The fires had been put out, and normality returned to the city quite quickly. Yet, beneath this veneer of tranquillity, a deadly game was afoot. Over a hundred Bulgarian infiltrators had slipped into the city, their mission clear: to sow chaos, eliminate any defenders loyal to Baldwin or Boniface, and bring Adrianople under the banner of Kaloyan.

On the third night, General Chelebri watched from a secluded rooftop, his eyes scanning the cityscape. His men were in position, each group assigned a specific target and as the church bells struck midnight, they put his audacious plan into action.

Like phantoms, the Bulgarian infiltrators moved through the city, striking with precision and silence. Unsuspecting guards stationed at key points fell quietly, their bodies crumpling to the ground before they could raise the alarm.

In the narrow alleyways and dark corners, outside taverns and barracks, and even in their own beds, crusader soldiers died, never seeing their killers. The Bulgarians moved with lethal grace, slipping in and out of the shadows, their movements fluid and deadly. For several hours, the presence of any infiltrators went unnoticed, but it was only a matter of time until the first bodies were found, and someone sounded the alarm.

More bells shattered the silence, and as confused soldiers ran from the yet unaffected barracks, the remaining Bulgarians set the second stage into action. Again, fires were set in strategic positions, though this time, right across the city. As the defenders raced to try and keep things under control, hidden archers fired arrows from the shadows, and men died in their hundreds.

As the night wore on, the violence escalated, adding to the confusion and panic. The Bulgarians used the chaos to their advantage, striking quickly and disappearing into the darkness. The Crusaders, caught off guard and disoriented, struggled to mount a coherent defence and by the time the first light of dawn began to break over the horizon, Adrianople was a city transformed. The fires had died down, leaving smouldering ruins in their wake, and the streets, once bustling with traders and Crusader soldiers, were now eerily quiet.

Many people had died in the night, and dozens of buildings were burnt to the ground, but apart from one dead body, nobody knew who was responsible for the devastation, especially as there was no army visible outside the walls of the city.

Many of the survivors naturally gravitated towards the city center and the buildings that housed the council, calling for the elders to address the population. For several hours, the giant doors remained closed until finally, around noon, two guards pushed the doors open and a dozen elders approached the top of the steps, accompanied by someone who was not known to anyone in the crowd. The leader of the elders, a frail man with a long white beard, spoke with a tremor in his voice.

'My friends,' he started, his voice hardly reaching those towards the rear, 'we have all lived through a night of fear and bloodshed, and you demand answers.' He half-turned to the man on his left. 'This man is General Chelebri, and he will explain to you what has happened.'

Chelebri stepped forward as the elderly man returned to his place among the others. For the past few hours, he and several of his officers had held the council prisoner, explaining in no uncertain terms what was happening and what was expected of them. At first, there had been vocal resistance, but when Chelebri demonstrated the seriousness of the situation by slitting the throat of one of the members, they finally settled down and listened to his ultimatum. Now it was time for the population to hear what was going to happen, and interestingly enough, this time there were no dissenting voices from the council of elders.

'People of Adrianople,' started Chelebri, his voice much stronger, 'first of all, let me say that last night, the city experienced a wave of bloody, yet necessary violence. But I am here to assure you today that it has now come to an end, and you will not be harmed. Last night, my men, at the invitation of many of your elders and with the support of hundreds of your fellow citizens across Adrianople, took action to return this magnificent city to your control. For the past year, my master, Tsar Kaloyan, has watched from afar with growing concern as the forces of Doge Dandolo, Emperor Baldwin, and the pretender, Boniface, started to assume influence over you by planting their officials and soldiers throughout your administrative centres. At first, it was a minor worry, but as more and more of your ambassadors approached my master with their concerns, it became a situation impossible to ignore. The western invaders have already destroyed Zara and Constantinople, and it was only a matter of time until this city also fell, though this time from the inside.'

A murmur of support rippled through the crowd.

'Consequently, over the last two nights,' he continued, 'aided by many of your own citizens, we started the process of purging the city of the westerner's poison. Many have died, some have fled, and there are many still to find, but make no mistake, we will find them, and they will be cast from the city walls.'

This time, the crowd, realizing what was happening, started cheering and shouting their support. Chelebri picked up on the growing fervour and raised his voice, accordingly, feeding on their enthusiasm.

'The city of Adrianople belongs to the people of Adrianople,' he shouted, 'and with this intervention, Tsar Kaloyan vows to protect you and your families from any further interference from the western invaders. From now on, we stand together, and we fall together.'

The crowd roared their approval, and as Chelebri returned to stand alongside the elders, chants of 'Kaloyan, Kaloyan' echoed from the walls. Chelebri half-turned to the old man who had spoken earlier.

'See,' he said, 'I told you they would give their support. Now all you have to do is reinforce my message at every opportunity, and I promise that your family will not be harmed.'

'History will record you as no different from any other usurpers,' said the old man quietly.

'That is not your worry,' said Chelebri. 'Now get back to work and send your messengers across the city extolling the virtues of Kaloyan's rule. I will be watching you closely, my friend, but make no mistake, this city now belongs to us.'

As the sun continued its journey through the skies, casting its golden light over the city spires, the Bulgarian flag was raised alongside the Greek flag over the citadel. The people of Adrianople watched in silence, some with hope, others with trepidation, but most with relief. The night of shadows had passed, but one thing was clear: the city was now firmly under Bulgarian control.

----

# CHAPTER TWENTY-THREE

## Constantinople

In the opulent halls of the Emperor's palace, Baldwin paced restlessly. The intricate mosaics and rich tapestries that adorned the walls, once symbols of the Empire's grandeur, now seemed to close in on him, reflecting his growing anxiety. News had just arrived from Adrianople, and the messenger's words echoed ominously in his mind: the city has fallen to the forces of Kaloyan.

He stopped before a large window, his gaze drifting over the sprawling city of Constantinople. The reflection in the glass revealed a man burdened by the weight of an empire in turmoil. Baldwin had anticipated threats from the outside, but the swiftness and precision of the Bulgarian infiltration had caught him off guard.

He could almost see the shadowy figures of the infiltrators moving through the streets of Adrianople, their daggers flashing in the moonlight, cutting down their victims with lethal efficiency. The thought made his blood run cold. The Bulgarians had not just attacked; they had executed a masterful campaign of subversion and sabotage, turning the city's own defences against it.

Baldwin's mind raced with the implications. The fall of Adrianople was not just the loss of a key stronghold; it was a devastating blow to his authority and the fragile stability of his empire. He imagined the whispering voices of his courtiers, their loyalty wavering, questioning his ability to lead. What was worse, the Greek population, already resentful of Crusader rule, would see this as a sign of weakness and possibly rise in rebellion.

'Kaloyan,' Baldwin whispered, the name tinged with both fear and grudging respect. The Tsar of Bulgaria had proven himself a formidable adversary, a cunning strategist who had turned the Byzantine Empire's own discontent against it. Baldwin knew he could not afford to underestimate him any longer. He turned abruptly to Abbot Martin, who had brought him the news.

'And you are absolutely sure of this?'

'There can be no doubt,' said Martin. 'Not only do we have witness statements from those who managed to escape, but we have also received a communication from the elders of Adrianople declaring their independence from Constantinople and their new allegiance to Kaloyan until such time as a suitably beneficial peace can be arranged between the cities. Do you wish to see it?'

'No,' said Baldwin, waving the offer away. 'What we need to decide is what we are going to do about it. To allow Kaloyan to keep such a strategically crucial city as Adrianople invites further incursions and eventually a full-scale war, yet it is claimed the Bulgarians were aided by the local population. They see Kaloyan as a liberator.'

'The mood has always been one of resentment within the city,' said Martin. 'We should have removed the elders and installed a ruler in your name while we had the chance. Instead, our presence was weak and allowed the dissent to grow. Now the Greeks see Kaloyan as a saviour and guardian, and it will be difficult to prove otherwise.'

'Yet that is what we must do,' Baldwin said, his voice firming. 'Adrianople lies at the confluence of three rivers and controls the approach from the northwest. If we allow Kaloyan to keep control of the city, not only can he choke off any supply routes from that direction, but he can also fortify it into an important outpost of Bulgaria. If it ever comes to war, he will already have a foothold in our territory. We must act swiftly, Brother Martin. Summon the council. We need to reassess our defences and strengthen our alliances. If Kaloyan thinks he can simply walk into our territories and claim them, he is gravely mistaken.'

As the Abbot left to carry out his orders, Baldwin returned to the window, his thoughts turning inward. He saw the faces of his soldiers, weary and battle-worn, and the eyes of his people, filled with hunger and uncertainty. He thought of the city of Adrianople, now under the control of his enemy, its streets stained with the blood of those who had fought and fallen. He also knew there was only one course of action: to retake the city using every resource at his disposal. He turned to the servant standing by the door.

'Summon the scribe,' he commanded. 'We have many letters to write.'

----

As Brother Martin walked quickly across the courtyard to the rooms he used for administration, a guard approached, causing him to pause.

'My lord,' said the guard, 'there is a knight at the gates named Sir Edmund of Bristol. He has newly arrived from England and begs audience.'

'I am busy,' said the Abbot. 'Tell him to request audience through the usual channels, and I will see him in a few days.'

'My lord,' the guard pressed, 'he says he has a force of fighting men at his disposal, and in the circumstances, I thought he could be useful.'

'What circumstances?' asked Martin, abruptly.

'My lord,' stuttered the guard, 'there are rumours raging across the city that Adrianople has fallen to the forces of Tsar Kaloyan and that they may be marching here in the near future. I thought that any extra men would be a more than welcome addition to our defences.'

Martin sighed in frustration but knew such things were normal in times of conflict.

'First of all,' he said, 'tell the rumour makers that there is no way Kaloyan would ever attack Constantinople. Even if he did, and if he were successful, which is highly unlikely, he would have the full force of Christendom fall upon him like an avalanche of bloody steel within months. However, you are correct; any new forces will be welcomed as brothers. Send the knight to my quarters.'

'As you wish, my lord,' said the guard and turned away to return to the gates.

----

Ten minutes later, Sir Edmund entered the Abbot's rooms, still somewhat surprised about the path his destiny was about to take.

'Sir Edmund,' said the Abbot, standing up, 'my name is Abbot Martin, spiritual advisor and confidante to the emperor.'

'Reverend Father Abbot,' said Edmund, bowing slightly, 'thank you for receiving me. I hear there are things afoot, and you must be a busy man.'

'I am, but I have a few minutes to spare. How can I help?'

'My lord, I have recently arrived from England with a ship full of fighting men destined for Acre. On the way, we stopped at Venice for supplies and were asked by the authorities there to escort a fleet of supply ships to Constantinople on our journey to the Holy Land. However, since being here, I have found out that there are more pressing needs that may benefit from the addition of my men, and I would like to offer their services to Emperor Baldwin.'

'That is a very admirable offer,' replied the Abbot, 'and I'm sure one of our officers will take you up on it. I will make the arrangements.'

'My lord,' interrupted the knight, 'I'm afraid it's not as easy as that. First, I have a problem that can only be solved by the intervention of the church.'

'And what is this problem?'

'The men and I took the cross to fight for God in the Holy Land and had the patronage of King John as our sponsor. If we were to divert from that mission to fight here, we would be falling short in our vows to the crown. Unless, of course, we were instructed by a higher power.'

'Ah, I see,' said the Abbot, gesturing for Edmund to sit. 'Let me explain something to you.'

The knight took a seat opposite the Abbot and listened as Martin spoke.

'Sir Edmund,' he began, 'I don't know if you have heard of me, but I was instrumental in putting this crusading army together across the western countries several years ago and have been with it constantly ever since. I fought alongside Dandolo and the bishops at Zara and was among the first to breach the walls of Constantinople along with our new emperor, Baldwin of Flanders. When we first recruited all those who took the cross, our intended destination was always Egypt before marching on Jerusalem. However, God saw fit to change our path to Constantinople, and we have been here ever since. The path of God's service is seldom clear or straightforward. At the time, all I wanted was to worship in the land where Christ himself once walked, but we are all his sheep and must serve where he needs us most.'

'But how do I know where that is?'

'The fact is that Christianity needs us not just to establish Constantinople as a safe and prosperous city, but also to bring stability and peace across the region. Once done, we can again turn our attention to Jerusalem, though this time with a city of strength at our backs that we can use as a base. We have not abandoned our dream of freeing Jerusalem from the infidels, Sir Edmund; this is just a stepping stone. You are still on God's path; this is just a bend in the road.'

The relief on the knight's face was obvious, and he got to his feet.

'Thank you, my lord,' he said, 'but one more thing: could you or one of your priests explain this to my men?'

'Of course,' said the Abbot, standing. 'Assemble them in the church outside the gates on the next Sabbath, and we will ease their minds together and remind them that by serving here, they will still receive absolution for their sins on earth, should they fall.'

'Thank you, Reverend Father,' said Edmund and after kissing the Abbot's ring, turned to leave the building.

Once he had gone, the Abbot sat down again with a sigh. It had been a trifling diversion but with potential conflict looming on the horizon, every sword would count. Outside the palace, Jamal emerged from a side alley and ran over to the knight.

'How did it go,' he asked, 'did you receive permission?'

'I did,' said the knight, striding down the road with a new purpose, 'and on Sunday we will all receive the blessing of the church. Look around you, Jamal. Constantinople is about to once again become your home, but this time, you will be among those defending it in the name of Christianity.'

----

# CHAPTER TWENTY-FOUR

## Normandy

Cronin's breath came in ragged gasps as he staggered through the dense underbrush of the forest. The twilight sky barely pierced the canopy overhead, casting long shadows in the fading light, and his heart pounded in his chest, every beat a reminder of the relentless pursuit behind him. When Walter's men had called off the search after only a few hours, Cronin had thought he was safe. But it soon became clear that the Frenchmen from the chateau had now turned their attention to him, his escape communicated to Sir Bergerac by the tavern owner, only too pleased to be rid of so many armed men.

For days, Cronin had evaded them, moving silently through the woods, surviving on whatever he could forage, exhaustion weighing heavily on his limbs, each step more laboured than the last. His cloak was now torn and muddied, his face smeared with grime and sweat, but still, he pressed on, driven by a desperate will to survive.

The sound of voices and horses pushing through the undergrowth echoed through the trees behind him, growing ever closer. Cronin knew he couldn't outrun them forever. He glanced back, catching a glimpse of the riders through the trees, dark figures with eyes alight with the thrill of the hunt, led by the relentless figure of Sir Bergerac. He renewed his pace as quickly and as quietly as he could but moments later, he realized he could go no further as he burst out of the trees onto the crest of a bare hill, sloping down into a moonlit valley far below. Realising he had no place to go, he dropped to his knees and closed his eyes. His flight was over.

Behind him, a triumphant yell echoed from the forest, and two men rode out onto the hilltop, closing off any routes of escape to either side. Moments later, the rest of the pursuers joined them, dismounting to form a semi-circle around their quarry. Bergerac rode slowly from the trees, and after dismounting, walked through his men's lines to stand a few paces away from Cronin, a satisfied smile on his face as he realised, he had at last found his man.

'Templar,' he said, staring at Cronin's back, 'if that is indeed what you are, why do you not stand and face me?'

Cronin did not answer. Instead, he just stared at the sweeping valley before him and the snakelike river that crept lazily as far as he could see. The swathes of ancient forest and well-manicured farms created order where there should be none, and through his exhaustion and pain, he realised how incredibly beautiful it all was.

'What's the matter with you, Templar?' snapped Bergerac. 'Are you some sort of coward?'

The beauty overwhelmed Cronin, and he realized that if he was to die, no man could wish for a more serene and peaceful execution site. He knew he could never overcome so many men and did not want to fight anymore. But at the back of his mind was the slightest chance that he could one day find Sumeira, and while the slightest spark of hope remained, no matter how faint, he would use every ounce of his strength to find her. Slowly, he got to his feet and turned around to face his pursuers.

'You've led us on quite the chase, Templar,' sneered Bergerac, 'but it ends here.'

'Do what you must, Bergerac,' said Cronin, 'but I have had enough of talking. Let us get this done.'

'It will be my pleasure,' said Bergerac, drawing his sword, 'but let me ask you one last question. Are you truly a Templar Knight, or are you just a fraud that dons their mantle to kidnap women and children to line your own purse?'

'I owe you no explanation, Bergerac,' said Cronin, 'but I will say this. Once a Templar, always a Templar.' He drew his sword slowly and held it loosely at his side. 'As you are about to find out.'

----

Moments later, both swords crashed viciously together, a meeting of deadly steel that would only end when one or both men lay dead above the scene of so much natural beauty. Bergerac was in far better physical shape than Cronin and used his larger stature and superior strength to great effect, advancing slowly, his strikes powerful and relentless.

Cronin fought with a determination born of desperation, each parry and thrust fuelled by a refusal to succumb. He knew he was far weaker than he had ever been and would not last long against such a skilled swordsman. Desperately, he surged forward, seeking to find some sort of advantage, but Bergerac expertly parried everything he had, even laughing at one point at the weakness of the blows from the exhausted Templar.

'Is that all you have?' he sneered as Cronin backed off to catch his breath. 'To be honest, I am hugely disappointed and have fought more skilled squires.' His men laughed at their master's comments and watched on with amusement, waiting to see the inevitable end that was only moments away.

Once again, Bergerac advanced, his blows raining down upon the Templar Knight, an unstoppable storm of bright, death-giving steel. Over and over again, Cronin parried the blows until finally, he was forced down to his knees, the blade of his sword smashed in half by the sheer force of the attack from the Frenchman now looming above him.

Cronin stared up at his adversary and knew there was no way he could win; he was just too exhausted. Every fibre of his being begged for him to stop, to just cast away his blade and accept his fate. The thought of dying was actually very calming, and he turned his head to stare over the valley, wondering if heaven looked as beautiful as the vision before him. But just as he was ready to meet his maker, the image of Sumeira's smiling face floated gently into his mind, reminding him of why he was fighting in the first place.

Bergerac stood above him, catching his breath and relishing the moment. He was undoubtedly the victor and would revel in the stories of how he beat a Templar Knight for many years to come. But he also recognised that his opponent was a fellow knight and deserved a noble death.

'I will make it quick, Templar,' he said, 'and make sure you have an honourable burial. Make your peace with God.'

Cronin lifted himself to one knee and cast away his broken blade before lowering his head as if in prayer. Moments passed, and every man watched in silence, honouring the man's last moments. Finally, Bergerac altered his grip, ready to administer the killing blow.

'Enough,' he said, 'it is time.' He raised his sword above his head and filled his lungs, ready to cleave his victim's head in two. But before he could bring down the blade, Cronin used every last ounce of his strength to drive himself upward into Bergerac's midriff, sending him backwards onto the ground. For a few moments, both men struggled, shrouded in a mist of dust and bloody spray until, slowly, they both lay still.

The world narrowed to the two of them, the noise of the other men fading into the background as they both stared into each other's eyes, close enough to smell each other's breath.

Bergerac's men closed in, unsure of what was happening, and as they neared, Cronin pushed himself away to fall in the dust. The rest of the men stared in disbelief; their eyes focused on one thing: the hilt of the Templar dagger sticking out of Bergerac's chest.

Cronin staggered to his feet and faced the rest of the men. He was spent but determined to meet his fate on his feet.

For several moments, all the men stared at Bergerac's killer until one of them removed the dagger and walked over to face the Templar. Cronin braced himself for the killing blow but was shocked when the Frenchman reversed the knife and offered it to him, hilt first.

'You fought well, Templar,' he said, his voice gruff but respectful. 'We have heard many stories of how men like you protect those who pilgrimage to Jerusalem, and we recognize the red cross you bear. The fight was fair, and you deserve to live.' He pointed towards a village in the distance. 'That place is called Revouii, and if you are truly a Templar, which I believe you are, you will find everything you need there. Now go, we have a body to bury.'

Cronin stared in disbelief as the men who had pursued him for so many days loaded their dead master onto his horse and led it away into the darkness.

He breathed deeply and said a silent prayer. By some miracle of God, he was still alive, and as long as his heart still beat, there was always the slightest chance that he would see Sumeira again. With renewed faith and determination, he turned his aching body away from the scene of the fight and started limping down the slope towards the distant village, limping with the slow, pained determination of one who has journeyed through hell to reach safety.

The Templar cloak given to him just a few days earlier was now a tattered shroud of mud and blood, a testament to the days he had spent fighting the tangled undergrowth of the forests and the French steel of Bergerac. He staggered toward the fortified gate of the town, his face etched with the lines of exhaustion and pain.

Two guards, their hands steady on the hilts of their swords, emerged from the shadows, blocking his path. Their eyes, narrowed with suspicion, scanned the battered figure before them. 'State your business,' the taller one demanded, his voice a mix of caution and command.

Cronin stopped and stared at the two men, not knowing whether they would be friend or foe, but with nowhere else to go, he had little other choice but to throw himself on their mercy.

'I seek sanctuary and aid,' he said, his voice barely audible over the wind that swept around the walls of the town.

'You and a thousand others,' grunted the guard. 'Be gone, stranger, we accept no beggars here.'

'Wait,' said his comrade, and he walked over towards Cronin, stopping just before him and staring down at his filthy cloak. Slowly, his hand raised, and as Cronin waited patiently, he dusted some of the filth from the heavy woollen garment, his eyes widening as the falling dust revealed the blood-red cross. Once done, he looked up and into the exhausted eyes of the Templar, a look of respect and awe etched upon his face.

'Welcome, brother,' he said. But before he could add more, Cronin collapsed into his arms, leaving the pain and exhaustion far behind him.

----

# CHAPTER TWENTY-FIVE

## Constantinople

Baldwin stood in his quarters, staring out over the ancient city. He knew that retaking Adrianople would require more than just the strength of his own army; they were still recovering from the previous campaigns and were already spread too thin. He needed the support of neighbouring powers, especially Venice, whose naval power was crucial for maintaining supply lines. The Doge, seeing the potential benefits of capturing a new city, especially one as rich as Adrianople, pledged a contingent of ships and soldiers to the cause.

While diplomatic efforts were underway, the emperor turned his attention to strengthening his military. The training grounds of Constantinople were filled with the sounds of drilling soldiers and the clash of weapons. Baldwin personally oversaw the training of his knights and infantry, ensuring that they were prepared for the rigors of what could turn out to be a prolonged siege.

Fortifications around Constantinople were reinforced to prevent any surprise attacks from Kaloyan's forces, and engineers worked tirelessly to repair and improve the city's defences, constructing additional towers and reinforcing the walls with extra layers of stone and mortar.

Baldwin also ordered the construction of siege engines, catapults, trebuchets, and battering rams. Master craftsmen from across the region were brought to Constantinople to oversee their construction, ensuring that they were of the highest quality. To ensure the steady flow of supplies, he negotiated with the local Greek population, promising fair treatment and trade incentives in exchange for their cooperation.

----

In the fortified heart of Adrianople, Chelebri stood before a map spread across a grand oak table, the flickering candlelight casting dancing shadows on his hardened features. His advisors gathered around him, their expressions a mix of confidence and anticipation. Chelebri knew that Baldwin would not sit idly by after the fall of Adrianople, so he had to prepare for the inevitable counterattack with a strategy that would not just repel the emperor's forces but cement Bulgarian control over the region.

The first priority was to strengthen Adrianople's defences. He ordered his engineers to reinforce the city walls, repairing any weak points. Towers were equipped with extra archers and ballistae, while the gates were fortified with iron bracings and spikes to deter any battering rams. He knew that a prolonged siege would test the city's resilience, so he ordered the stockpiling of supplies. Granaries were filled with grain, storehouses with dried meats, and wells were secured to ensure a steady supply of fresh water. Artisans worked tirelessly to produce arrows, bolts, and other munitions, aided by the increasingly loyal Greek population. Promises of protection, fair treatment, and shared prosperity under Bulgarian rule were disseminated through trusted community leaders, undermining any potential resistance from within. Chelebri's efforts aimed to ensure that the populace continued to view the Bulgarians as liberators rather than conquerors.

----

In Venice, the ship *Spiritus Sancti* lay at anchor just outside the bustling seaport, waiting for a berth to take on fresh food and water. The journey from England had been disjointed and often fractious as they had battled storms and wild seas, with many nights spent anchored in remote ports or offshore as they waited for the weather to improve. At last, they had entered the Mediterranean, but after so many delays, it had soon become clear that they needed fresh provisions and had headed for the biggest trading port in the region. But now, after waiting for over two days to berth, the crew was growing frustrated.

'What do you think is happening?' asked Sumeira, as the captain walked over to join her at the rail.

'I don't know,' he replied, 'I have been here many times, and this is the busiest I have seen it.'

'Can we not go elsewhere?'

'That's not an option. That last storm smashed some of our water barrels, and we have only a few left.'

Sumeira sighed. She was just as frustrated as everyone else, probably more so, for she knew that the more time that passed before finding Jamal, the colder the trail would become.

'Look,' said Hunter, nodding toward a nearby boat, 'someone is coming.'

'This may be it,' said the captain. 'It's about time.'

Minutes later, several armed men climbed aboard along with a serious-looking official.

'Are you the captain?' he asked, striding over.

'I am.'

'Good. I hereby inform you that I requisition this ship and its contents on behalf of Doge Dandolo. These men will take over with immediate effect.'

'What?' gasped the captain. 'On whose authority?'

'On the authority of the pope himself,' said the official, handing over a scroll.

'What's going on?' asked Sumeira from one side. 'What are they talking about?'

The captain read the scroll slowly, paying particular attention to the detail of the seal at the bottom, before looking over to his gathering men.

'Stand down,' he said, sensing their growing anger. 'The order is legitimate.' He turned back to face the official. 'Tell me exactly what is going on.'

'There is a situation that needs the support of fellow Christian forces,' said the official, taking back the scroll. 'Kaloyan of Bulgaria is on the move, and we need every man we can muster to repel the threat. Any Christian ships headed to the Holy Land are being re-routed to Constantinople to reinforce Emperor Baldwin's army. Once we have succeeded in that effort, your ship will be returned.'

'And in the meantime?'

'You can disembark and wait until your vessel is returned to you, or you can stay on board and see that it reaches Constantinople safely. After that, you can continue on your journey.'

'And my cargo?'

'What is it?'

'Weapons, armour, saddles, tools…'

'It will also be requisitioned.'

'What about those who wait for those supplies in Acre?'

'The pope has decided that this is a more important cause. Until Constantinople has gained stability under Emperor Baldwin, there can be no serious advance on Cairo, or indeed, Jerusalem.'

'And what about King John? When he finds out his ship and cargo has been sent elsewhere, he will not be happy.'

'Once I take your details, his holiness will write a letter to your king explaining the situation. Now, enough talking, what is it going to be?'

The captain looked around the bay, seeing many Venetian warships at anchor, and knew that if he agreed but then double-crossed the official to head for Acre, he would soon be caught and suffer the consequences.

'I don't see how I have any other option,' he replied eventually. 'What do you want of me?'

'We will take an inventory of your cargo,' said the official, 'and in two days, your ship will join many others to head for Constantinople. Once there, your cargo will be unloaded, and any fighting men on board will be recruited into Baldwin's army. After that, you are free to go wherever you wish.'

'So be it,' sighed the captain. As the official walked away to join his men, he turned to find Sumeira and Hunter staring back at him. 'You heard the man,' he said. 'Tomorrow you will disembark.'

'Why?' asked Sumeira.

'Because Constantinople is no place for a woman such as you. It is just too dangerous.'

Sumeira laughed out loud. She had spent most of her life in the Holy Land and had lived the last few years in Constantinople, including during the sacking by the crusaders.

'Captain,' she said, 'there is no way I am leaving this ship. We have paid our way and will stay with it until we reach Acre or leave of our own free will. Besides, if all ships are being diverted, there is a good chance my son is also there. In a strange way, I hope he is, for he knows the city well.'

'As you wish,' said the captain with a shrug, 'but I will not be held responsible for your security.'

'Understood,' said Sumeira and watched as he walked away to brief the crew.

'Are you sure about this?' asked Hunter at her side.

'What other option do we have?' asked Sumeira. 'It's either that or stay here in Venice, and that will serve no purpose at all.'

'So be it,' said Hunter, 'but now we should get some rest. I feel there is yet more to come on this journey, and I just hope God continues to smile upon us.'

----

# CHAPTER TWENTY-SIX

## Normandy

Cronin's eyes opened slowly, heavy and reluctant. The dim light of dawn seeped through the small window of the stone-walled chamber, casting long shadows across the room. He lay on a straw mattress, rough woollen blankets covering his weary body, and the scent of herbs and burning tallow candles filling his nostrils, a stark contrast to the filth he last remembered.

For a moment, disorientation gripped him. The unfamiliar surroundings, the silence after the stress and pain of the past few days, it all felt like a dream. Panic surged within him, and he tried to sit up, but his body protested, every muscle aching, wounds throbbing. He fell back with a groan.

'Easy now, brother,' came a calm voice from the corner of the room. A man in the white mantle of the Templars stepped into view, his face weathered but kind, a comforting presence amidst Cronin's confusion.

'Where... where am I?' Cronin's voice was hoarse, barely above a whisper.

'You're in the commandery of Revouir,' the man replied, gently pressing Cronin back onto the mattress. 'You arrived at our gates several days ago and have been unconscious ever since.'

'Several days?' repeated Cronin. 'How many, exactly?'

'Six,' said the man. 'We've tended to your injuries, but some of your minor wounds were infected, and your body shut down. We thought you wouldn't make it, but God heard our prayers and, in his mercy, granted you another chance to serve him.'

Revouir. The name sparked a flicker of recognition. He was in a Templar commandery, a sanctuary for his brothers-in-arms. Relief washed over him, but it was fleeting. Urgency replaced it.

'I must go to the Holy Land,' Cronin said, trying to rise again, his voice gaining strength from sheer willpower.

The man, Brother Guillaume, shook his head gently. 'You are too weak, Cronin. Your wounds need time to heal. You cannot make such a journey in your condition.'

'How do you know my name?'

'We learned a lot during your illness,' said the man. 'The delirium made you talk through the pain. It seems you seek someone called Sumeira, which, to be frank, raises some questions that the Preceptor is keen to have answered.'

'What sort of questions?'

'Everything will become clear in time,' said Guillaume, 'but for now, just rest and gather your strength.'

'No,' said Cronin, his voice firm. 'You don't understand. I have to leave as soon as I can. There is no time to waste.'

Guillaume sighed, his expression a mix of sympathy and stern resolve.

'Your spirit is commendable, but your body will not follow. You need rest, nourishment, and time. The journey to the Holy Land is long and perilous. To attempt it now would be to court failure and perhaps death.'

Cronin clenched his fists, frustration and helplessness warring within him as a third figure entered the room, an older Templar with a commanding presence.

'Brother Guillaume speaks the truth, Cronin,' he said.

'I am Brother Robert, the commandery marshal. We all share your zeal, but wisdom must temper our actions. You will recover here, and when you are fit, we will ensure you reach the Holy Land. For now, you must trust in God's plan.'

Cronin's head fell back against the pillow, his breath coming in ragged gasps. The fight drained out of him, leaving only the heavy weight of exhaustion.

'Very well,' he muttered, closing his eyes. 'But promise me... promise me you won't delay any longer than necessary.'

Brother Robert placed a reassuring hand on Cronin's shoulder.

'I give you my word, Brother Cronin. Rest now and regain your strength. Your time will come.'

As Cronin succumbed to the pull of sleep, a sense of peace settled over him. He was among his brothers again, safe for now. His journey was not over, merely paused, and with the grace of God, he would leave soon enough. Slowly, against his will, his body once again slipped into darkness, though this time, the strength-giving sleep he so desperately needed after the exertions faced through infection-induced delirium.

----

The next few days passed slowly for Cronin, but he soon realized that the brothers of the commandery were correct: he had overestimated his strength. Slowly and surely, fuelled by rest and regular food, Cronin's strength began to return. He woke more frequently, his mind clearer, his body regaining some semblance of its former vigour.

One morning, as the first rays of sunlight pierced the small window, Cronin opened his eyes feeling stronger than he had in a long time. He knew he could wait no longer. He pushed himself up, the ache in his muscles now a manageable throb rather than an excruciating pain as Brother Guillaume entered, carrying a tray with bread, cheese, and a steaming bowl of broth.

'Good morning, Brother Cronin,' Guillaume greeted him with a smile. 'I see the colour has returned to your cheeks.'

'Thanks to you and our brothers,' replied Cronin, 'but your work is done, and I am ready to leave.'

Guillaume set the tray on the bedside table.

'Take your time. Eat first, regain your strength fully. Once you are done, there is someone who wishes to speak with you.'

Curiosity piqued; Cronin ate with newfound appetite. The simple fare tasted like a feast after so many days of small but strength-giving meals. When he finished, he swung his legs over the side of the bed, testing his strength. He stood, a bit unsteady at first, but determined.

Guillaume observed him with a mix of caution and approval. '

Very well. Follow me.'

Cronin nodded, and together they made their way through the stone corridors of the commandery. The air was cool, the walls adorned with tapestries depicting scenes of Templar valour until eventually, they reached a large wooden door. Guillaume knocked softly and opened it, gesturing for Cronin to enter.

The room beyond was spacious, with a large table at its centre covered in maps and documents. A man stood behind the table, his presence commanding, his gaze sharp and appraising. He was older, with greying hair and a stern countenance softened by wisdom. This was the preceptor of the commandery, Brother Ricardo.

'Brother Cronin,' Ricardo greeted him, his voice deep and authoritative. 'It is good to see you on your feet. Please, have a seat.'

Cronin lowered himself into a chair, grateful for the opportunity to rest. 'Thank you, Brother Ricardo.'

The preceptor nodded. 'You have shown remarkable resilience. Brother Guillaume speaks highly of your determination, and I understand you wish to return to the Holy Land as soon as possible.'

'I do,' said Cronin. 'My family is in trouble, and I need to get to them as soon as possible.'

'Your family?'

'Yes. The woman I am to marry and her son. They are in terrible danger.'

Silence fell in the room as his words sunk in, and all eyes stared in his direction.

Cronin stared back at the preceptor, not sure what was causing the awkward silence.

'Is there a problem?' he asked eventually.

'Brother Cronin,' said the preceptor, 'when you arrived, you were adorned in the garb of our brotherhood, damaged and filthy admittedly, but the robes of a Templar Knight, nonetheless. If you are truly a brother of our order, then you will understand our shock when you talk of a potential marriage while you still serve. Perhaps you can shed some light on this matter.'

Cronin took a deep breath, now realizing exactly what was causing the concern.

'My lord, preceptor,' he replied eventually, 'of course, you are correct, and I was wearing the red cross upon my chest when I arrived. I am indeed a knight of the cross, or at least I was, and have served God and our order for most of my life in the Holy Land, first as a sergeant and then as a knight, an honour placed upon me by the Lionhearted himself. However, it is also true that I have now left the order to retire to England with my newfound family. Alas, that luxury has been denied to me by the duplicity of King John and his officials, and now I am focused only on saving those that I love.'

'So, you admit arriving here under false pretences, wearing the bloody cross?'

'I did, but the garb was forced upon me under protest and upon pain of death for those near to me. I also felt that after a lifetime of service, God would forgive me this one discretion.'

'Do not assume God's indulgence,' snapped the preceptor. 'We serve only and do not seek favour.'

'Of course,' said Cronin. 'Forgive me.'

'Tell me,' continued the preceptor, 'how do I know you are telling the truth and are not some braggart who pretends to be of our order to gain favour or riches?'

'I have no proof except my memories and knowledge of our ceremonies,' said Cronin. 'Other than that, I have nothing but my faith and reliance on your trust.'

'You say you served under the Lionheart?'

'I did.'

'And were you in Acre?'

'I was.'

'I hear his magnanimity was boundless upon the success of his siege, and his mercy a gift before God. You were surely a witness.'

Cronin stared at the preceptor, quite shocked at the statement. Either the templar officer was badly informed or it was a trick question. Either way, Cronin only knew one way to respond, and that was by telling the truth, no matter what the consequences.

'My lord preceptor,' he said eventually, his words calm and assured, 'I did indeed serve under the Lionheart and was knighted by his hand after our failure to retake Jerusalem. I consider him to be the greatest leader I have ever served under and would have followed him into hell itself, but to claim he was merciful in Acre would be an untruth, one that I am not willing to share.'

'And why is that your stance?'

'Because what he did there was beyond evil, and I only hope God forgave him when he died.'

'I am intrigued,' said the preceptor. 'What possible evil could a king do in a time of war that could be so bad?'

'When Acre surrendered, King Richard had all the prisoners, including the women and children, executed to send a signal to Saladin. It was not necessary and beneath him as a truly great monarch. His hands were ever stained with their blood.'

'Yet you still served under him?'

'We were at war, and we are men of service. We may not agree with our lords and masters, but we were there to serve God and Christendom in that order. We did what we had to do.'

The preceptor stared at Cronin for a moment before the serious look upon his face eased, and he gave a slight nod of satisfaction.

'A lesser man may have taken the opportunity to embellish his loyalty,' he said eventually, 'but you speak the truth, not knowing what the consequences may be. For now, I believe you, but there are many more questions I need to ask.'

'With the greatest respect, my lord,' said Cronin, 'my need to get to the Holy Land is of the greatest importance, and I beg permission to leave.'

'One more day will make little difference, and if I am satisfied that you are who you are, and are worthy of our support, there is a way we may be able to help you. Now, tell us everything there is to know from the time you arrived in England to the time we found you at the gates of Revouir.'

For the next few hours, Cronin recounted the events that had led up to his current predicament, and by the time he had finished, the sun was already descending in the west. The day had been long, interspersed with breaks for food and prayer, but eventually, the preceptor was satisfied that Cronin was not just a knight, but a truthful and honourable man. At dusk, Cronin was once again summoned to the preceptor's chamber. Again, Brother Guillaume and Brother Ricardo sat opposite him.

'Brother Cronin,' said the preceptor as he took his seat, 'your story is certainly unique, and whilst we believe it is true, there was always the concern that you adopted the persona of a brother knight, even though you had already left the order. However, in light of your service and in support of a fellow brother of Christ, we hereby offer you our full support in your endeavours. What are your most pressing needs?'

Cronin breathed a sigh of relief and sat back in his chair. He knew that with their boundless monetary strength and network of castles and commanderies across Europe, at least he would now have a chance of getting to his destination.

'My lord,' he said eventually, 'I will need two horses and fresh clothing if that is possible. I will also need a purse to help pay my way, but all these expenses will be repaid by the one estate I still have lodged with the commandery in London. I will sign whatever documents you see fit to arrange the transactions.'

'That will not be necessary,' said the preceptor. 'Your needs will be met by our own treasury. What else?'

'If I could have a letter of introduction in case I need to seek succour from our estates on the journey, that would certainly help.'

'We can do that,' said the preceptor, 'but there is perhaps one more thing we can offer. It is not ideal, but it would more than halve the time needed to get to the Holy Land.'

Cronin looked between the two men. For the first time, his spirits lifted, and he listened intently to the proposal.

'You may not be aware,' continued the preceptor, 'but over this last year we have had a particularly bad outbreak of Christ's disease in this area, and our commandery has been particularly affected. We now have over a dozen men afflicted who lay idle in their cells or spend their days praying for a cure.'

Cronin nodded; his face lined with concern. Leprosy was a particularly debilitating disease, and he knew that the Templars, like all the other orders, had a policy that once a knight had been confirmed as having the disease, he would be made to leave the order immediately to avoid further infections amongst its ranks.

'These men,' continued the preceptor, 'wish to make their final pilgrimage to Jerusalem while they still have the strength, and to that end, we have arranged a galley to take them to Acre. The ship is the fastest we have, and weather permitting, will not be stopping in any port on the way. If it is your desire, you can seek passage aboard that galley.'

'On a plague ship?'

'Yes. The afflicted will keep to themselves, but…'

'I accept,' said Cronin, interrupting the preceptor. 'When does it leave?'

'Two days from now. If you are certain, then Brother Guillaume will see that all your other needs are met, and you will be escorted to the ship prior to its sailing.'

'Thank you, my lord,' said Cronin, standing up. 'I will never forget your kindness in this matter.'

'There is one more thing,' said the preceptor, standing up. 'Come with me.' He walked through to a side chamber, and on the table at the centre of the room, Cronin could see a complete set of clean Templar vestments alongside all the equipment associated with a knight of the order. He walked over and saw on top of the clothing lay a golden ring, the exact replica of the one he had left with Sumeira all those weeks ago. Emblazoned upon it was an image of two men riding a single horse, the emblem of the order.

'As you know,' said the preceptor, 'that ring will open many doors for you.'

'I do not understand,' said Cronin, turning around. 'I have already told you I am no longer in the order.'

'You are now,' said Ricardo. 'Look on your time away from us as a time of reflection. It is a natural path for many, but most come back in the end. And besides, we can only offer our support to fellow members. All this, the ship, and anything else you need is yours. All you need to do is say yes. Take your time, for it is a big decision.'

'There is nothing to consider,' said Cronin almost immediately. 'I accept.'

'In that case,' said the preceptor, stepping forward to grasp Cronin's forearm, 'welcome back to the brotherhood, Brother Cronin. Now, let's get you to the Holy Land.'

----

# CHAPTER TWENTY-SEVEN

## Normandy

The salty wind whipped through Cronin's hair as he stood on the dock in Normandy, staring at the looming silhouette of the Templar ship. The vessel, a sleek and sturdy carrack, rocked gently in the harbour, its white sails emblazoned with the blood-red cross of the Order. It was the very symbol of the crusade that had called men from many lands, yet today it seemed to carry a shadow, a darkness that clung to its hull like a shroud.

Cronin tightened his grip on the leather strap of his pack, his heart pounding with a mixture of anticipation and unease. Any journey to the Holy Land was meant to be a path of glory, a pilgrimage that would see men fulfil vows made to God, king, and country, but as the crew scurried about, preparing the ship for departure, he could not shake the dread gnawing at the edges of his resolve.

He turned to see Brother Guillaume, staring at him from a few paces away.

'Are you sure about this?' asked Guillaume. 'There is another ship due to leave at the end of the month.'

'I do not have the luxury of waiting,' said Cronin, walking over to take the fellow Templar's wrist in gratitude. 'God alone controls my fate, and whether I fall to Christ's disease or not is down to him and him alone.'

'In that case, travel safely, my friend,' said Guillaume. 'I will pray you find those that you seek alive and well.'

Cronin nodded and turned to walk up the wooden plank, his boots thudding heavily against the worn timber beneath his feet. As he stepped onto the deck, he felt a chill that had nothing to do with the crisp autumn air. The usual bustle of a ship preparing to set sail was muted, subdued. Men moved with purpose, but their eyes avoided the bow, where a group of figures huddled together, shrouded in thick, dark cloaks.

Cronin's breath caught in his throat as he saw them. There were about two dozen of them, Templar knights like himself, but marked by fate with a curse that had driven them from the ranks of their brethren. Many of their faces, what little could be seen beneath their hoods, were pale, their skin mottled with the telltale signs of leprosy. The sight of them stirred a deep, instinctual fear within him, a fear of the unknown, of contagion, of the slow, wasting death that these men had been condemned to.

'These are the Lazarus knights,' murmured a voice behind him, and he turned to see another man standing near the rail, also bedecked in the garb of the brotherhood. 'They were once like us, but now… their path lies in Jerusalem, to see out what remains of their lives in the leper quarter.'

Cronin nodded. He had heard of the Lazarus knights, those who had contracted Christ's disease and were forced to leave not just the Templars but all the knightly orders across Christendom. Leprosy was a terrible affliction, incurable and highly contagious, and no order could risk having their ranks decimated by an uncontrollable outbreak, yet none of those who suffered were treated badly and almost all were offered passage to Jerusalem, a final service in the land where Christ once walked. It was a bitter mercy, but one that offered the afflicted a chance to see out their lives in the land of their Lord.

'They keep to themselves,' Geoffrey continued, his voice low. 'They were men like us once, proud and strong warriors, used to living a life of piety and service. It is a sad and terrible way to end their lives.' He walked forward and offered his arm in brotherhood. 'My name is Geoffrey of Sussex, and we will be sharing this voyage. There are several more who will be joining us.'

Cronin stared at the proffered hand; a hesitation noticed by Geoffrey.

'I am clean,' Geoffrey said, 'and like you, share this ship with them out of convenience only.'

Cronin realised his judgment was uncalled for and took his fellow passenger's wrist.

'Come,' said Geoffrey, 'let me show you where we will quarter.'

The two men made their way to the stern, where the rest of the uninfected knights were gathering. As he passed the Lazarus knights, Cronin felt their eyes on him, sad, resigned, yet dignified. These were men who had fought and bled for the same cause, who had once stood as equals. Now, they were exiles in body and spirit, their only comfort the distant hope of dying on sacred soil.

Cronin found a place on a lower deck amongst a dozen other healthy knights. He put away the few items he had brought with him from the commandery before heading back out onto the deck to breathe in the fresh air. The crew finalised the preparations, and a few minutes later, he felt the ship lurch as it began to move, the sails filling with wind. He was on his way at last, and though some of his fellow passengers may not have been the type he would have chosen as shipmates, his mind was focused on one thing only: finding Sumeira.

The harbour of Normandy receded behind them, and he turned to face the bow. The Lazarus knights were still, their heads bowed in prayer, their murmurs lost in the sound of the waves. Cronin's fear did not dissipate, but he felt it tempered by a strange sense of respect. These men were not monsters; they were his brothers, cast aside by the world yet bound by the same vows, the same faith.

As the ship cut through the waters, bound for Jerusalem, Cronin lifted his gaze above the heads of the afflicted, south towards the Holy Land, and somehow, deep inside, he knew this would be his last such journey. Although the thought was at first shocking, it also brought an incredible feeling of peace. One way or the other, these next few months would seal his fate forever.

----

The ship sailed steadily through the rolling waves of the Channel, its wooden hull creaking as it pressed southward along the coast of France. Days passed in a blur of salt spray and prayer as the knights on board settled into the rhythm of the voyage, but the air was thick with an unspoken tension, an invisible barrier that divided the ship's company into two distinct groups: the healthy and the afflicted.

Cronin spent his days at the stern, where the uninfected knights gathered to train, pray, and pass the time. Despite the camaraderie among his brothers, there was an undercurrent of unease. Every glance toward the bow, where the Lazarus knights kept to themselves, was tinged with fear and discomfort. Whispers of the disease, its horrors, and its slow and merciless progression spread among the men like a contagion of their own.

At first, Cronin shared their anxiety. He avoided the bow as much as possible, keeping his distance from the Lazarus knights. The sight of their cloaked figures huddled in isolation filled him with a deep, instinctual dread, but as the days wore on, something in him began to shift. He watched as the afflicted men went about their routines, praying, cleaning their weapons, and tending to one another with a quiet dignity that struck a chord in him. They asked for nothing, expected nothing, and bore their burden with a solemn grace.

One evening, as the sun dipped low on the horizon, Cronin stood at the rail, staring out at the endless sea. The air was cool, and the sky was painted in shades of orange and pink. He felt a presence beside him and turned to see one of the Lazarus knights standing a few paces away. The man's face was mostly hidden by his hood, but Cronin could see the pale, mottled skin of his hands.

For a moment, neither spoke. Then, the knight bowed his head slightly.

'Brother,' he said, his voice raspy but firm.

Cronin hesitated, then nodded in return.

'Brother.'

It was a simple exchange, but it carried a weight that Cronin hadn't expected. He realized, with a pang of guilt, that he had been avoiding these men not out of fear of the disease alone, but because they reminded him of the fragility of the human body, of the thin line that separated the strong from the weak. He had been afraid to face that truth, to acknowledge that the Lazarus knights were no different from him, save for the cruel hand fate had dealt them.

Over the next few days, Cronin found himself observing the Lazarus knights more closely. He noticed the way they cared for one another, offering comfort and support when one of their number faltered. They moved as a unit, bound not just by their affliction but by a brotherhood that was as strong as any he had known. Gradually, his fear gave way to a deep respect for these men who had been cast aside by the world yet remained steadfast in their faith and duty. But it wasn't until a week into the voyage that Cronin's respect would be put to the test.

----

It was a sweltering afternoon as the ship turned into the Mediterranean Sea, the sun beating down mercilessly on the deck. Cronin had been sparring with another knight when he heard a shout as one of the infected men collapsed to the deck. He turned to see a cluster of Lazarus knights gathering around their comrade. One knelt and lifted the head of the semi-conscious man, and as he did, the victim's hood fell away, revealing his severely infected features.

His scab-covered scalp was almost blood-red with infected sores, interspersed with clumps of tangled hair and severely swollen skin, but it was the nose that caused the gasps of disgust from the crew, or rather, the open voids where the nose had once been, now nothing more than frayed cavities of rotting flesh beneath severely sunken eyes contorted with pain and fear.

Open sores and ulcers covered his lower face, and what was left of his yellow teeth were totally exposed by the lack of lips and flesh around his mouth. It was as if a demon from hell had suddenly appeared, and as the crew watched in horror, he turned his head slowly towards them, his mouth struggling to form the words.

'Water,' he gasped, 'water.'

The ship's crew froze in place, their eyes wide with fear as they exchanged nervous glances. No one moved to help.

The man cradling the dying knight's head looked up in despair.

'Please,' he begged, 'someone bring him a cup of water,' but his plea was met with silent stares.

Cronin felt his heart race as he watched the scene unfold. He could see the panic in the crew's eyes, the terror of coming into contact with the disease, but as he looked down at the suffering knight, he felt something else rise within him, a surge of compassion that drowned out his fear. Without thinking, he stepped forward and dropped to his knees.

'First we need to get him out of the sun,' he said, and carefully, he slipped his arms beneath the man's frail body to lift him off the deck. The knight was lighter than he had expected, his bones sharp beneath his thin robes. Cronin carried him to a shaded area where he gently laid him down to sit against a mast. One of the other Lazarus knights handed him a flask of water, and Cronin held it to the sick man's lips, allowing him to drink slowly.

'Thank you,' the knight whispered, eventually, his voice barely audible.

Cronin nodded, his throat tight with emotion. He could feel the eyes of the other knights on him, but he didn't care. At that moment, there was no difference between them, only a shared humanity, a shared faith. He gave him what little medicine they had on the ship, making him as comfortable as possible, and as time passed, the tension seemed to ease. The crew, seeing Cronin's example, began to move about their tasks with less fear, and the Lazarus knights watched him with a newfound respect.

When the afflicted man finally drifted into a restless sleep, Cronin stood and turned to face the others. One of the Lazarus knights, a man with a weathered face and sad eyes, stepped forward. He placed a hand on Cronin's shoulder, a gesture of solidarity, of gratitude.

'You are a true brother,' the knight said softly. 'I am called Raymond, and I was once as strong as you. We all were, even the dying man who you just helped. Please do not forget that.'

'We are all brothers,' replied Cronin. 'I will pray for him.'

He turned away to rejoin his comrades but immediately saw something had changed. As he approached, each took the slightest step away, the risk of infection foremost in their mind. At first, he was shocked, but within moments, he accepted the situation for what it was. Their fears were probably unfounded, but only God himself would decide if he would get the disease.

With a sigh, he shook his head and walked past to go to his cot below deck, resigned to spending the rest of the voyage in isolation. Reaching his bedspace, he sat down and un-stoppered his flask, taking a long drink of the warm water before leaning over to place it on top of his folded cloak at his feet. As he did, a figure appeared before him and leant forward to pull the flask from his hands. Cronin looked up and watched as Geoffrey of Sussex pulled out the stopper with his teeth, and after a moment's silent pause, took his own long draft of the warm water. Once done, he silently re-stoppered the flask and placed it upon the cloak before grasping Cronin's shoulder and turning away to return whence he came. No words had been spoken, but in those few moments, Cronin had once again regained his faith in his fellow warriors. Disease or no disease, their shared vows meant that nothing could divide them, in times of war or times of peace, and after so much time away from the order, Cronin finally accepted he was once more part of the brotherhood.

----

# CHAPTER TWENTY-EIGHT

## Constantinople

Further east, the Spiritus Sancti had already docked in the Golden Horn, and dozens of workers swarmed over and beneath her deck, unloading the precious cargo that would be crucial in the coming advance to Adrianople. Sumeira and Hunter watched as the ship was stripped bare of everything that could be of any possible use. Even the empty water barrels were taken, leaving the captain with just enough to get either to Acre or back to Venice, should he so choose.

Once done, Sumeira and Hunter gathered their things and walked to the gangplank, ready to step once again onto the soil of Constantinople. As they reached the handrail, they paused and looked over at the imposing walls and the magnificent skyline, pierced by the spires and domes of the many places of worship across the city. The last time they had been here, the sky had been filled with smoke and the screams of the dying, but now it seemed to be being reborn as teams of masons and labourers swarmed over the damaged walls, restoring them to their former glory. The work would last years, but already they could see the difference between the old walls and the repaired areas, now built stronger and bigger than ever before. As they were about to disembark, the captain approached, and they paused, seeing he had something on his mind.

'Are you sure about this?' he asked. 'There is war in the air, and it will be no place for a lady.'

'I have walked this path many times, Captain,' said Sumeira, 'and as I said before, I know the city well. I also have many friends I can rely on. Besides, Hunter here will take care of me.'

'If you stay,' said the captain, 'I will see you safely to Acre or Venice, the choice is yours.'

'Thank you, Captain,' she said, 'but my mind is set. This is where we leave you. My son is out there somewhere, and until I find him or his body, I will never rest. Goodbye, my friend, and thank you for the safe passage.' She turned to leave, but the captain reached out and grabbed her arm.

'Wait,' he said as she turned around, 'you will need this.'

He held out his hand, and in it was the purse of silver she had given him that first day in Bristol for their fare.

'I don't understand,' she said, 'that is yours.'

'You have a greater need than I,' said the captain, 'and besides, I am already a rich man. These coins may buy your safety. Take them with my blessing.'

Sumeira looked over at Hunter, receiving a shrug of acceptance in return. She turned back to the captain.

'Thank you,' she said, 'and if we get out of this alive, perhaps our paths will meet again.'

'Just look after yourselves,' said the captain, 'and if you find that boy of yours, keep him somewhere safe, far away from trouble.'

'I will,' said Sumeira, and after giving him a warm smile, she followed Hunter down the plank onto the jetty. They headed toward one of the gates in the wall, but before they entered the city, Sumeira's eyes fell on one of the ramps used by the masons to take their stones to the top of the walls.

'Wait,' she said, 'let us go up there.'

'Why?' asked Hunter.

'Because I want to see her in her majesty,' said Sumeira. 'Once we enter, the walls can close in and become suffocating. Let me remember how it used to look.'

They both walked up the ramp until they reached the top and, after looking out over the many ships now anchored in the Golden Horn, turned their attention inward to the city itself.

Below them, the labyrinthine streets stretched out like the tangled threads of a spider's web. Sumeira pulled her cloak tighter around her shoulders, the familiar scent of salt and spices in the air doing little to calm the worry within her heart. The city that had once been her sanctuary now seemed like a daunting obstacle in her search for Jamal.

Beside her, Hunter scanned the view with a furrowed brow. His hand rested on the hilt of his sword, a silent promise to protect her, though Sumeira knew that no blade could cut through the fog of uncertainty clouding their path.

'They said all the ships unloaded their cargos near the Golden Horn,' Hunter said, his voice low and measured but laced with concern. 'But his would have arrived weeks ago. He could be anywhere by now.'

Sumeira nodded, her mind racing. The city was a mosaic of cultures, languages, and allegiances, Christian and Muslim, Greek and Latin. Finding one boy among the throngs of merchants, pilgrims, and soldiers seemed an impossible task, yet she had no choice but to try.

'We will start at the government buildings,' she replied, determination hardening her voice. 'There must be a record somewhere. Even conscripted men need to be fed and paid, and his name will be on a list. All we need to do is find it.'

Hunter glanced at her, his eyes softening with empathy. 'We'll find him, Sumeira. We will.'

'I have no doubt about it,' said Sumeira, 'but we will get nowhere by standing here. Come, with this purse, at least we will be able to afford decent lodgings.'

Hunter nodded and followed the physician back down the ramp before heading through the gates and into the vast city of Constantinople.

----

The following few days turned into a blur of unanswered questions and dead-end leads, and despite her initial optimism, Sumeira's resolve began to fray. They spoke to fishermen who claimed to have seen nothing, to merchants too busy haggling to notice a solitary boy among so many soldiers. Even the beggars who haunted the streets offered no clues, only empty palms.

Each night, Sumeira returned to their modest quarters in Galata, the weariness in her bones matched only by the ache in her heart. The city she had once navigated with confidence now seemed foreign and hostile, its secrets buried beneath layers of fear, politics, and mistrust. She began to fear that perhaps Jamal was indeed lost to her, swallowed up by the same fate that had claimed so many in these tumultuous times.

Each day she had tried to reach those in power, seeking an audience with anyone who might be able to help, but each time she was just one more face in the crowds of hundreds who sought similar audience, and the sounds of gates slamming in their faces became all too familiar. Her morale flagged until Hunter came up with an audacious plan... to speak directly to the emperor.

'What?' asked Sumeira in disbelief. 'We can't even get past his guards to speak to any of his officers. How on earth do you plan to get to Baldwin himself?'

'Hear me out,' said hunter. 'I am told he is going to address the people tomorrow in the city centre. All we need to do is position ourselves somewhere where he can't fail to see us and deliver a message that he cannot afford to ignore.'

'What sort of message?'

'That, my lady, is down to you. I'll find us a platform, but you are the one who thinks for both of us. You will find the words.'

'That is a stupid plan,' said Sumeira.

'It is the only one we have,' said Hunter. 'We've exhausted every other option, and Baldwin commands the Latin forces here. If anyone knows where Jamal might be, it's him.'

Sumeira hesitated. The Emperor of Constantinople was not a man to be trifled with, and she knew that appealing to him directly was a risk. Baldwin of Flanders was known as a shrewd and calculating ruler, his loyalty to the Crusader cause unwavering.

'I know it's a long shot,' Hunter admitted, seeing her doubt. 'But you have a history here. If you remind him of that... perhaps he'll listen.'

Sumeira's mind flashed back to the years she had spent in the Emperor's household, tending to the sick and injured with a skill that had earned her respect. Yet, that was in the service of the Byzantine Emperor, not Baldwin. She was a physician, not a supplicant, and the thought of pleading for her son's life filled her with dread. But Jamal's face haunted her, his bright eyes, his innocent smile, and she knew she would do anything to bring him back.

'So be it,' she said eventually. 'Let's do it.'

----

The following morning, the streets of Constantinople filled with people gathering to hear the address by the emperor. The threat from Kaloyan and his hordes was a daily conversation, and having survived one devastating attack on the city, the population was keen to hear what their new leader had planned to keep them safe.

At noon, the bells of the city rang out, and as the great bronze gates of the palace creaked open, Emperor Baldwin emerged, flanked by his personal guard. The sun caught the polished surface of their ceremonial armour, turning the street into a river of molten gold. The emperor rode at the head of the procession, his figure imposing atop a snow-white charger, draped in robes of crimson and gold. His crown, studded with jewels, gleamed brightly against the backdrop of the city he had come to rule.

As Baldwin moved through the streets, the populace of Constantinople stirred. Word of his appearance spread like wildfire, drawing the people from their homes and stalls to witness the rare spectacle. They crowded along the thoroughfare, their murmurs a low hum beneath the clatter of hooves and the rhythmic march of the armoured guards. Soldiers lined the path, their spears held aloft, forming a shimmering corridor of steel through which the emperor passed.

The citizens, a mix of Greeks, Latins, and others from every corner of the empire, bowed their heads as Baldwin rode by, their reverence tinged with both awe and fear. Some whispered prayers, while others simply stared, taking in the sight of the man who had claimed their city and their futures. Baldwin's gaze was steady, his expression one of practiced detachment, though his mind churned with the gravity of the message he was about to deliver.

Ahead loomed the Forum of Constantine, where the emperor would address the people. He would speak to them of the threat posed by Kaloyan, the Tsar of the Bulgarians, whose forces encroached ever closer to the city. Baldwin knew that fear was both his ally and his enemy, it could unite his subjects under his banner or drive them into the arms of those who sought to overthrow him.

As they approached the Church of the Theotokos, a massive structure with high domes and intricate mosaics, the procession slowed. The air was thick with incense, and the chants of priests could be heard within, offering prayers for protection and deliverance. Baldwin's eyes remained forward, fixed on the path ahead, until a solitary sound broke through the hushed reverence of the crowd, a solitary handbell, clear, singular, cutting through the murmurs and footsteps like a shard of glass. Baldwin's head snapped upward, his sharp gaze drawn to the source of the sound, and the crowd, sensing his shift in attention, followed his eyes.

High above, on the balcony of the church, stood a lone figure, clad in a dark, flowing cloak. Her hair hung loose about her shoulders, and although Sumeira hated the thought of using her natural beauty and femininity to garner attention, she knew it was just a means to an end.

The bell in her hand fell silent, and for a brief moment, the emperor's regal composure faltered. His eyes locked with Sumeira's, and he could see the determination in her gaze.

'Archers, watch her,' shouted one of the captains of the guard as they continued past the church.

Baldwin's guards shifted uneasily, their hands tightening on the hilts of their swords, but the emperor raised a hand, staying them. There was no threat in Sumeira's stance, only a silent yet haughty presence that threatened to upstage the grand political theatre unfolding below.

The crowd, sensing the tension, remained deathly silent. Baldwin, recovering his composure, offered a slight nod to Sumeira, an acknowledgment of her presence. Then, with a final, lingering glance, he urged his horse forward, the procession resuming its march toward the forum. Baldwin's gaze turned back to the road ahead, but he reined in his horse as a voice filled the air.

'Your Majesty,' called Sumeira, her voice echoing from the spectacular walls around him. 'I am Sumeira of Greece, and I demand audience.'

In the shadows of the room behind her, Hunter winced at her choice of words. Nobody demanded anything of an emperor.

Down below, Emperor Baldwin continued along the road, a small smile playing about his mouth. The audacity of the woman above was amusing, and the unnecessary overreaction of his bodyguards more so.

'Your Majesty,' shouted the woman again as he passed, 'I need to talk to you, but your security is greater than the walls surrounding this city. Grant my petition, and I will reveal to you the fate and location of the true shroud of Christ.'

The crowd gasped in astonishment, and the emperor reined in his horse again, turning his head to stare at the woman above. Her claim to know the location of the missing artifact was not a new one, for many people claimed such knowledge, but this seemed different. The woman looked familiar and was obviously of western descent.

Behind Sumeira, Hunter gasped in astonishment.

'What are you doing?' he asked.

'You said to get his attention,' she replied, 'and that is exactly what I have done.' She stared down, meeting the emperor's gaze. She knew he was judging whether to believe her or have her thrown into a cell as a lunatic. Behind her, she could hear the running steps of a unit of bodyguards running up the stairs, and she knew she had to act fast.

'Your Majesty,' she shouted again, 'I swear I tell the truth before God, for I was there when the shroud was taken. I held it in my own hands and witnessed the killing of the knight who sought to destroy it. Grant me an audience, and I will reveal all to you.'

Behind her, the guards burst into the room, knocking Hunter to the floor. Seconds later, two of the men climbed out onto the balcony, each grabbing an arm and staring down to await further orders.

Down below, the Captain of the Guard turned to Baldwin. 'Majesty, what do you want us to do? Say the word, and my men will hurl her to the streets before you.'

Baldwin stared up at the now-silent woman.

'No,' he said eventually. 'Take her to the palace and place her under guard. I will see what madness besets her when I return.' He turned away, and with a kick of his heels, urged his horse forward. He had a city to address, and the woman could wait.

As they continued down the street, the crowd whispered among themselves, the image of the emperor and the solitary woman etched in their minds. Baldwin's thoughts were heavy with the challenges that lay ahead, Kaloyan's armies, the fragile unity of his empire, and now, the strange but fascinating claim from the unknown woman. Yet as he neared the forum, he straightened in the saddle, pushing these thoughts aside.

When he finally arrived at the forum, the gathered masses erupted in a wave of cheers and chants. The emperor dismounted, ascending the steps to the platform that had been erected for his speech. The echoes of the solitary bell still lingered in his mind, even as he raised his hand to quiet the crowd, preparing to speak words that could determine the fate of his newly claimed empire. His gaze swept across the sea of faces that filled the Forum. The city's great basilicas and ancient columns formed a majestic backdrop, but it was the people, the lifeblood of Constantinople, who held his attention. Their eyes were wide with anticipation, their hearts heavy with the weight of uncertain times, and Baldwin knew this speech would be crucial, not just for his reign, but for the survival of the empire itself.

He raised his hand for silence, and his voice, when it came, was strong and clear, carrying over the heads of the gathered masses like the sound of a trumpet.

'People of Constantinople! Citizens of this great and ancient city! Today, I stand before you not merely as your emperor, but as your protector, your servant, and your fellow Christian. We are all children of this sacred city, heirs to its glory and its trials. And now, a new trial stands before us, a shadow cast by a distant foe, one who seeks to tear down what we are building together.'

Baldwin paused, allowing the gravity of his words to settle over the crowd. He could see the concern in their eyes, the fear that had gripped the city since the news of Kaloyan's advance had spread.

'The Tsar of the Bulgarians, Kaloyan, marches upon us with fury in his heart and destruction in his wake. He has already taken Adrianople, that great jewel of Thrace, and seeks to spread his tyranny to the very gates of our beloved Constantinople. But we shall not allow this.'

The crowd murmured, a mix of anger and unease, and Baldwin knew he had to strike the right balance between acknowledging their fear and kindling their resolve.

'Kaloyan is a man driven by greed and vengeance. He seeks to unravel the peace that now shines upon us like a spring warmth. He wishes to plunge our city into darkness, to extinguish the light of faith, culture, and learning that has made Constantinople the envy of the world. But hear me now, my people, he shall not succeed!'

Baldwin's voice rose with each word, his conviction a palpable force that rippled through the assembly.

'I have seen the strength of Constantinople,' he continued. 'I have seen it in your eyes, in your works, in the unwavering faith that you hold in your hearts. This city has stood for centuries, weathering storms, repelling invaders, and rising from the ashes stronger than before. We are not merely a collection of stones and walls, we are a beacon of Christendom, a testament to the enduring power of faith and unity.'

He gestured toward the Hagia Sophia, its dome glinting in the midday sun. 'This city was built on the foundations of belief, on the courage of those who came before us. And now, it is our turn to defend it, to ensure that Constantinople remains a stronghold against the chaos that seeks to engulf it.'

His eyes narrowed, his tone sharpening as he prepared to deliver the heart of his message.

'Kaloyan believes that we will cower behind our walls, that we will allow him to ravage our lands without consequence. He underestimates us! He underestimates you! We cannot, and we shall not allow Adrianople to become just another outpost of Bulgaria. To do so would be to surrender not only our lands but our very souls. We must meet him with the full force of our might, with the fire of righteousness burning in our hearts!'

The emperor's voice dropped, his words becoming more intimate as he addressed the young men directly.

'To the youth of Constantinople, I speak to you now. Your city, your families, and your future calls upon you. My men will march upon Adrianople, but we cannot do it alone. We need you, your courage, and your loyalty to God to strengthen our lines as we face the enemy. The time has come for you to take up arms, to stand beside your brothers in defence of all that we hold dear. This is your moment to prove your valour, to write your names in the annals of history as the saviours of Constantinople. The enemy may be fierce, but so too are we. Together, we shall drive Kaloyan from Adrianople and reclaim our rightful peace.'

The crowd began to stir, a wave of energy sweeping through it as Baldwin's words took hold.

'Join me!' Baldwin called out, raising his sword high above his head, the sun catching the steel and making it shine like a beacon. 'Join your emperor in this holy cause! Let us march on Adrianople, let us show the world that Constantinople is not a city to be trifled with! For God, for our city, for our people, rise up and fight!'

The crowd erupted into cheers, their voices merging into a powerful roar that echoed off the ancient walls and soared into the heavens. The young men stepped forward, their faces alight with determination and pride, ready to take up the banner of their city and march into battle.

As Baldwin looked out over the surging crowd, he felt a fierce sense of purpose. The path ahead would be perilous, but with the courage of his army, the support of his people, and the grace of God, he knew they could overcome any threat. Kaloyan's time in Adrianople would soon be up, and when it was, he could turn his attention back to Constantinople and his newly found pledge to return the city to greatness.

----

# CHAPTER TWENTY-NINE

## Constantinople

The Boukoleon Palace stood as a testament to Byzantine grandeur, its halls adorned with intricate mosaics and tapestries that whispered tales of glory and power. The side chamber where Sumeira was escorted was no less impressive, though its splendour did little to ease the tension knotted in her stomach. She clutched the folds of her worn robe, trying to steady her breath as she awaited the Emperor's arrival.

It had been two days since she had first made contact in the streets of the city, and although she had been well looked after, she was growing impatient to continue the search for Jamal. However, at last, one of the servants had told her that the emperor had made some time for her, and she had been escorted to an antechamber to wait for him.

Just over an hour later, the heavy wooden doors creaked open, and Emperor Baldwin entered, his presence commanding even in the intimate setting of the chamber. His crimson robes brushed against the marble floor, and his sharp gaze swept across the room before settling on Sumeira. She immediately fell to her knees, her forehead nearly touching the cold stone as she offered her deepest respect.

'Rise,' Baldwin's voice was firm but not unkind.

Sumeira slowly stood, her heart pounding in her chest. She had imagined this moment countless times, but now that it was here, the words seemed to stick in her throat. Baldwin's expression was unreadable, but she knew she had to speak, to make him understand. Before she could say a word, Baldwin held up his hand to stop her from talking.

'I know you,' he said. 'We have met before.'

'We have briefly, Your Majesty,' said Sumeira, 'but I have not had the honour of addressing you directly.'

'When? My memory escapes me.'

'It was after the battle when you first took this great city,' she said. 'My comrades and I were stuck here until a ship became available for passage to Venice. While we waited, I helped in the hospital, and you visited to see your injured men.'

'I remember,' he said, his voice softening slightly. 'You were helping the physician. You seemed very quiet.'

'I was busy. Moments count when trying to save a life.'

'And here you are again,' said Baldwin, his tone more thoughtful. 'Yet the quiet lady who was focused only on helping others just a year ago this time decides to announce her presence to the world by demanding an audience from the heights of a place of worship in front of thousands. Not only this, she claims to know the secret that all pious men crave to know: the location of the Shroud of Christ. You are an intriguing woman, Sumeira of Greece, so tell me what drove you to such an extreme decision.'

'Your Majesty,' she began, her voice trembling slightly, 'I will get straight to the point. I come before you to beg for mercy for my son, Jamal.'

Baldwin's brows knit together slightly, a hint of curiosity in his eyes.

'Tell me of your son, and why you seek my intervention.'

Sumeira swallowed hard, forcing herself to continue.

'Jamal is... he is a good boy, Your Majesty, but he is different. A few months ago, he received a blow to the head, an injury that should have killed him. He survived but has not been the same. He is slower in thought, easily confused, and struggles to keep pace with others. But he is kind, gentle, and loyal. He was tricked, Your Majesty, deceived by men who spoke of honour and glory in the Holy Land. They filled his belly with mead and his head with promises he could not fully understand. Before any of us could intervene, he was taken to a ship bound for war, for a cause he cannot grasp.'

Baldwin's face remained stoic, but Sumeira saw a flicker of something, perhaps sympathy or understanding, in his eyes. She pressed on, her words spilling out in a desperate rush.

'Please, Your Majesty, he does not belong in this Crusade. He cannot fight, cannot survive such hardship. He is not a warrior; he is a child in a man's body. I beg you, show him mercy. Release him from this service before it is too late.'

The chamber fell silent as Sumeira's plea hung in the air. Baldwin looked at her for a long moment, weighing her words. He had seen the toll of war, the broken bodies and shattered minds it left in its wake. He knew that not all who were sent to fight were suited for the horrors they would face.

'Your son,' Baldwin said slowly, 'is he truly incapable of serving in any capacity? Even as a squire or in some support role?'

Sumeira shook her head, tears brimming in her eyes. 'He would try, Your Majesty, but he would fail. And in that failure, he would suffer. I cannot bear the thought of him lost in a foreign land, unable to find his way, or worse, dead and alone. Please, let him come home.'

Baldwin's expression softened slightly, the weight of his own responsibilities pressing heavily upon him. He knew he could not save everyone, could not right every wrong, but this woman's plea touched something within him, something beyond duty, something human.

'And you are sure he is here in Constantinople?'

'As sure as I can be. We were told in Venice that all vessels coming from the west containing men of war had been diverted to serve you in your fight against Kaloyan.'

'This is true,' said Baldwin, 'but so many have arrived, it will be difficult to find him. And even if we do, your son's release is not a simple matter,' he paused before saying the words that made her heart beat with hope. 'But I understand your concern. I will send word to my commanders to see if he can be found. If so, he will be brought back to you, but know this: if he cannot be located, or if he has already been caught up in the turmoil of war, there may be nothing more I can do.'

Sumeira bowed her head, a tear slipping down her cheek.

'Thank you, Your Majesty. I ask for nothing more than your help in finding him.'

Baldwin nodded, signalling to a scribe who had been standing quietly in the corner. 'Have a message sent to my officers. Describe the boy, Jamal, and his condition. Make it clear he is to be returned to Constantinople if found.'

The scribe hurried to fulfil the order and left the room. When he was gone, Baldwin turned his attention back to Sumeira.

'Now, I have done what I can for you, so it is time to deliver your side of the deal. I recall you mentioned the Shroud. Was that true, or was it just a ruse to gain the audience?'

Sumeira breathed deeply before replying. 'It is true, Your Majesty. My son and I got caught up in a plot to destroy the shroud by a group of men called the Turbasel knights. They got very close to carrying out the unholy deed, but a close friend of mine, a Templar knight by the name of Cronin, '

'You know Cronin?'

'Yes, my lord, we were to marry in England, but this situation with my son drove us apart.'

'Is he here with you now?'

'No, my lord. He was killed in London when petitioning the king for Jamal's release. I am all my son has left.'

'I knew Cronin,' said Baldwin, his voice heavy with remembrance. 'He was a great man. If what you say is true, then he is a great loss to all Christendom.' He paused for a few moments before taking a deep breath and casting the memories from his mind. 'Anyway, tell me about the fate of the Shroud, and leave nothing out.'

For the next hour, Sumeira told the emperor how Cronin had foiled the plot by the Knights of Turbasel and how he eventually retrieved the Shroud before dispatching it into the safe hands of Robert De Clari and his family. When she had finished, Baldwin sat back and stared at her, absorbing the information.

'I had hoped you would reveal a hiding place here in the city,' he said eventually, 'but apparently, it is many leagues away, secreted in the vaults of some French noble, probably never to see the light of day again.'

'Robert De Clari is an honourable man, Majesty,' said Sumeira. 'I am sure he will treat the Shroud with the gravitas and reverence it deserves.'

'I hope so,' said Baldwin, 'and perhaps, if we ever achieve a lasting peace in the region, one day I will seek out this man and cast my eyes upon the holy cloth myself. But alas, that day is still a long way off, and we have a city to take. Do you have lodgings?'

'We do,' said Sumeira, 'in the city.'

'You and your man are welcome to stay here,' said Baldwin. 'My servants will find you quarters.'

'That is very kind,' said Sumeira, 'but there is no need.'

'Nonsense,' said Baldwin, 'you will stay here, at least until my men find out about your son. You will also dine with me this evening. I will hear no argument. Go now and wait for word. Pray that your son is found quickly and that he is unharmed.'

As she was led out of the chamber, the weight of uncertainty again pressed down upon her. The Emperor had promised to help, but the fate of her son was still unknown, adrift on the seas of war. All she could do now was wait and pray that Jamal would be found and returned to her, safe from the horrors that had stolen so many others.

----

# CHAPTER THIRTY

## Off the Coast of Cyprus

Cronin stood in the prow of the ship. The weather had calmed, and the salty breeze of the Mediterranean brushed against his weathered face. Despite the heat, he was clad in the chainmail and surcoat of the Knights Templar, in honour of the ceremony that was about to take place. Around him, the air was thick with the stench of rot and despair, a worsening smell that clung to the ship like a curse. The infected knight whom he had helped just a few days earlier had finally succumbed to the illness, and his comrades had gathered to say their final goodbyes.

Cronin watched as the diseased men, their faces and limbs marked by the telltale signs of their affliction, gathered in a sombre circle, surrounding the body of their fallen brother, wrapped hastily in a shroud that could do little to mask the ravages of death. The knights shuffled uneasily, their once-strong voices now hushed and uncertain. These were men who had fought and bled for Christendom, warriors who had faced death on countless battlefields. Yet now, confronted with the death of one of their own in such miserable circumstances, they found themselves at a loss.

The leader of the afflicted knights, Sir Raymond, looked around, his eyes clouded with sorrow as he began to speak.

'He was… a good man,' the knight murmured, his voice wavering. 'A faithful servant of God.' But the words faltered, falling into silence. The others nodded, their expressions pained, but none could find the strength to continue. The wind whispered through the rigging, as if mocking their inadequacy.

Cronin felt a pang of pity in his heart. These men, who had once been revered as the sword arm of Christ, were now reduced to shadows of their former selves, cast out from the world they had sworn to protect. Everyone was desperate to find the right words, but with no priest among them, the words were difficult to find, and an awkward silence fell upon those gathered on the deck. Stepping forward, Cronin made his way between the infected men and looked around, seeing the faintest glimmer of hope in their eyes.

'He was more than that,' he said, his voice firm but gentle. He looked down at the shrouded form before him, and then at the men who stood in mourning. 'He was a brother, a knight of the Temple, and a man of unwavering faith.'

The others listened, their eyes turning to Cronin with a mix of respect and relief. He continued, his words measured and deliberate, as if each one carried the weight of a thousand battles.

'In life, he served God with every breath, every drop of blood. He carried the cross not just in battle, but in his heart, where it burned as a beacon of hope. Even as this disease took hold, he did not waver. He bore his suffering with the same courage that he faced our enemies, knowing that his trials were but a passage to eternal life.'

Cronin paused, letting the weight of his words sink in. The men around him stood still, their gaunt faces softened by the solace his words offered.

'His last hope was to be buried in the Holy Land, but our Lord has decided otherwise, and he is already embraced in his glory. His fight is over, but ours is not. We must remember his example and carry his memory with us as we continue on this path, however dark it may seem.'

The wind stirred again, but this time it seemed gentler, as if the very air had been calmed by Cronin's words. The knights, though still mourning, straightened their shoulders. One by one, they murmured their own prayers, their voices stronger now, carrying their brother's soul toward the heavens.

As the sun dipped lower on the horizon, casting a golden glow over the ship's weathered deck, Cronin remained by the side of the deceased knight. He whispered a final prayer, a plea for mercy for all of them, and then stepped back, allowing the others to say their farewells before they carried the dead man to the side of the ship and committed his remains to the deep.

The remaining knights stood still, their heads bowed as they watched the ripples widen and then disappear into the darkening waters. Cronin felt the solemn weight of the moment, the finality of it pressing on his heart. He crossed himself, whispering a final benediction for the fallen brother.

The wind picked up as the knights slowly dispersed, each man retreating into his own thoughts. Cronin walked away and stood alone at the ship's rear. He gripped the wooden rail, staring out at the horizon where the sun now dipped into the ocean, setting the sky ablaze with hues of orange and crimson. It was a beautiful sight, yet all Cronin could feel was the deep ache of sorrow that had taken root in his chest.

He heard the shuffle of footsteps behind him and turned to see Sir Raymond approaching. The man's face was partially obscured by the hood of his robe, but Cronin could still see the telltale signs of the disease, the discoloured skin and disfigured features. The knight's eyes, however, remained bright, filled with a mixture of determination and gratitude.

'Brother Cronin,' said Raymond, his voice thick with emotion. 'I wanted to thank you... we all do. For what you said back there. For standing by us when so many others have turned away.'

Cronin felt a pang of sympathy as he looked at the man, who, despite his affliction, still bore the dignity of a knight. These men had once been his comrades-in-arms, men of honour who had fought for the same cause. The disease had stolen their strength, their futures, but it could not take away their spirit.

'There's no need to thank me,' Cronin replied softly, shaking his head. 'We are brothers, all of us. No sickness can change that. I only did what any of you would have done for me.'

The knight lowered his gaze, a tear slipping down his scarred cheek.

'It means more than you know, Cronin. To still be seen as a brother... to not be abandoned... it gives us strength, even now.'

Cronin felt the depth of the knight's gratitude and the pain that lay beneath it. These men had been cast aside by the world, feared and shunned because of their disease. To them, the simple act of acknowledgment, of standing by their side, was a gift beyond measure. Cronin's heart once again swelled with an overwhelming sense of comradeship, a bond forged not in battle, but in shared suffering.

Without hesitation, he stepped forward and embraced the knight, pulling him into a firm, brotherly hold. The man stiffened for a moment, surprised by the gesture. Cronin could feel the man's body trembling, not from fear, but from the release of emotions too long held in check. A sob escaped the knight's lips, muffled against Cronin's shoulder.

'We will face this together,' Cronin murmured, his voice steady. 'Whatever happens, you are not alone.'

The knight clung to him for a moment longer before stepping back, wiping at his eyes with the edge of his sleeve.

'Thank you, Cronin,' he whispered, his voice breaking. 'May God bless you for your kindness.'

Cronin nodded, his own eyes stinging with unshed tears. He watched as the knight turned and walked back toward the others, his steps slow but more assured.

Alone again, Cronin turned his gaze back to the sea, the horizon now fading into the twilight. He knew that most of these men would never see Jerusalem, that they would perish before they could set foot on the sacred soil. Their deaths would be slow, painful, robbed of the glory they had once sought.

But in this moment, Cronin found a strange comfort in the knowledge that, at the very least, they would not face it alone. They would go together, as brothers, as they had lived and fought together. Cronin wiped at his eyes, feeling the cool sting of the evening air. He had always believed that a knight's duty was to protect the weak, to serve God with unwavering faith. Now, he realized, that duty extended beyond the battlefield, beyond the reach of swords and shields. It was in these moments, in the quiet acts of compassion, that true courage was found.

The ship continued its journey, cutting through the darkening waves. And on its deck, Cronin stood, a silent sentinel, watching over his brothers as they sailed toward whatever fate awaited them in the Holy Land.

----

Two days later, as dawn broke over the eastern horizon, the island of Cyprus emerged from the mist, a dark silhouette against the pale sky. The ship, weathered and burdened by its grim cargo, drew closer to the coastline, but kept its distance, hovering like a ghostly spectre on the fringes of the port.

Cronin stood at the bow; his gaze fixed on the distant shore. The sea, calm and glassy, reflected the growing light, but even this beauty could not lift the weight that hung over the ship. Behind him, the diseased knights moved slowly across the deck, their eyes too fixed on the land they would never touch. There was a faint murmur of hope in their voices, but it was tempered by the knowledge of their isolation.

The captain approached Cronin, his face etched with concern.

'We'll send a boat to shore for water,' he said, his voice low and rough, 'but we will not dock. As soon as we have enough, we will be on our way.'

Cronin watched as the boat was readied, its wooden sides worn smooth by years of use. A few of the healthiest among the crew, chosen for their lack of contact with the infected knights, climbed down into the vessel, their movements deliberate and cautious. There was no room for error, no room for compassion that might lead to the spread of the disease.

The boat rocked gently as it was lowered into the sea, the oars creaking as the men began to row toward the shore. Cronin could see the tension in their shoulders, the silent prayers on their lips as they navigated the short distance. On the deck, the knights gathered in silence, their eyes following the boat as it drew nearer to the docks.

The port was beginning to stir with the morning's activity. Fishermen prepared their nets, merchants arranged their goods, and children ran through the streets, their laughter carried on the breeze. But as the boat from the plague ship approached, a ripple of unease spread through the town. People paused in their tasks, their eyes narrowing with suspicion and fear.

The boatmen hailed the dockworkers from a safe distance, their voices carrying across the water.

'We come for fresh water, nothing more,' one of them called out. 'We are from a vessel out of Normandy carrying knights bound for Acre and onwards to Jerusalem. We cannot dock for fear of spreading sickness.'

The dockworkers hesitated, exchanging worried glances. They knew well the dangers of leprosy, the suffering it brought, and the fear it incited. But they also knew their duty to provide aid to those in need. After a tense moment, the overseer nodded and shouted back,

'We'll bring water to you. Stay where you are.'

The boat pulled up short of the dock, the oarsmen holding it steady as they waited. On the shore, barrels of fresh water were rolled out, men working quickly to load them onto a small skiff that would ferry the supplies out to the waiting ship. The mood was tense, the air heavy with the unspoken dread of what lay aboard the vessel anchored offshore.

From the deck, Cronin watched the scene unfold, his heart heavy with the knowledge that even this small exchange was tainted by fear. The people of Cyprus, despite their willingness to help, were keenly aware of the invisible boundary that separated them from the ship. It was a boundary defined not by ropes or chains, but by the deadly disease that clung to the knights like a shadow.

As the skiff set out from the dock, loaded with barrels of water and baskets of fresh fruit and vegetables, Cronin turned his gaze back to his fellow knights. They were watching too, their faces a mixture of hope and resignation. The fresh water would sustain them, but it would not change their fate. Their pilgrimage to Jerusalem would continue, but for how long, none of them could say.

The skiff drew alongside the ship, and the supplies were hoisted aboard, their dull thud against the deck echoing through the tense silence. The knights and crew, still wary of the unseen threat of leprosy, handled the cargo with care, moving quickly to store the precious liquid below. The ship's captain exchanged a few terse words with the boatmen before they returned to shore, but Cronin, standing nearby, caught fragments of their conversation. It wasn't just water they brought; there was news too, news that sent a chill through Cronin's veins. The captain's face darkened as he listened, his expression growing more troubled with each passing moment.

'What is it?' Cronin asked, stepping forward as the captain turned away from the departing skiff.

The captain hesitated, then sighed deeply, rubbing a hand over his weathered face. 'There's talk of war, Sir Cronin. Kaloyan of Bulgaria has begun his campaign against the Latins. They say he's already laying waste to Thrace, and the emperor, Baldwin, is calling for every available ship to bolster his forces.'

'Why would that affect us?' asked Cronin. 'There is no way these men can fight, even if Baldwin's campaign was supported by our order, which it is not.'

'It does not affect us,' said the Captain, 'and I am happy to proceed as planned. But you said that the boy you seek was on a warship sent from England to Acre. If that is true, then I suggest that you are heading to the wrong port.'

Cronin stared at the captain as he pieced together the implications.

'Every ship has been redirected?'

'Aye,' the captain confirmed. 'For the past few months, any ship that was carrying arms or men of war was commandeered to support Baldwin. Apparently, Kaloyan has taken the city of Adrianople, and the emperor has assembled a holy army to take it back.'

Cronin's mind raced. He had no way of knowing where Sumeira was, or even if she had arrived safely in the region, but if all warships had been re-directed to Constantinople, it was a safe wager that Jamal's ship would have been amongst them. And if that was the case, then he had no doubt that as soon as Sumeira found out, she would have made a beeline for that city, despite the dangers. His heart raced, and the realization struck him like a hammer blow.

'I need to go to Constantinople,' he said, his voice steady but urgent. 'I must get there before the battle begins.'

The captain frowned, shaking his head.

'It's impossible, Sir Cronin. We've already risked enough just coming here. This ship is bound for Acre, and that's where it'll go. I can't turn it around on a whim.'

'But this isn't just a whim,' Cronin insisted, stepping closer. 'Lives are at stake, people who could be saved if I can get there in time.'

The captain remained unmoved, his gaze hardening. 'And what of the men on this ship? Their lives are no less valuable. They've placed their trust in me to deliver them to the Holy Land, where they can find peace. I can't abandon them now, not for anything.'

Cronin clenched his fists in frustration, knowing the captain was right. The knights aboard the ship were already living on borrowed time, and to divert the ship's course could mean the difference between dying at sea or reaching Jerusalem's sacred soil. But the thought of Sumeira in danger gnawed at him, a constant, unrelenting fear. He was about to plead his case again when a voice interrupted.

'Brother Cronin.'

Cronin turned to see Sir Raymond standing behind him, the man whom he had embraced at the funerary service a few days earlier.

'Brother,' Cronin acknowledged, bowing his head slightly. 'I didn't mean to disturb you.'

'You've disturbed nothing,' replied the knight gently. He glanced at the captain, then back at Cronin. 'I've heard enough to understand your plight. You wish to save someone dear to you.'

Cronin hesitated, then nodded.

'Yes. A woman and a boy I care for deeply. I promised to protect them at all costs and have let them down.'

The old knight nodded and turned to the captain.

'Captain,' he began, his voice slow but firm, 'these men on this ship, my brothers and I… we are not long for this world. Whether we reach Jerusalem a few days sooner or later matters little to us now. But for Sir Cronin, time is of the essence. Perhaps it is God's will that we offer him this chance, even if it means altering our course.'

The captain looked conflicted, torn between his duty to his passengers and the moral weight of the diseased knight's words.

'But the risk…'

'The risk is ours to bear,' interjected the knight, raising a hand. 'If we can give our brother a chance to save Christian lives, then let us do so. The sea will still carry us to Acre when we are done.'

Cronin felt a surge of gratitude and a deep sense of kinship with these men who had nothing left but their faith and each other. He could see the resolve in the knight's face, the determination to do one last act of kindness before the end.

The captain looked between the two men and, after a long silence, finally relented.

'Very well,' he said gruffly. 'We'll make for Constantinople. But we cannot tarry. Once we've delivered Sir Cronin, we sail for Acre without delay.'

Cronin bowed his head deeply, humbled by the sacrifice these men were willing to make for him.

'Thank you,' he said, his voice thick with emotion. 'You have given me a chance I do not deserve, and I will not forget it.'

The knight nodded, a faint smile touching his lips.

'We will go with God, Brother Cronin. May he guide your path as he guides ours.'

With the decision made, the ship's course was altered, its sails adjusted to catch the wind that would take them toward Constantinople. And as the island of Cyprus faded into the distance, Cronin whispered a prayer for all of them, for the leprous knights, many of whom would never see Jerusalem, for Sumeira waiting somewhere in Constantinople, and for himself, as he faced the uncertain path that lay ahead.

# CHAPTER THIRTY-ONE

## Constantinople

The opulent dining hall of the imperial palace in Constantinople was a grand affair, a glittering testament to the wealth and power of the city under its new Latin rulers. The walls, adorned with tapestries depicting the glories of past empires, seemed to watch over the gathering like silent witnesses to history. A long table, laden with gold and silver platters, stretched beneath the high vaulted ceiling, its surface almost groaning under the weight of the lavish feast. The air was thick with the scent of roasted meats, exotic spices, and the heady aroma of wine, mingling with the muted murmurs of conversation and the occasional burst of laughter.

At the head of the table sat Emperor Baldwin I, his presence unmistakable even in the midst of such opulence. His face, though lined with the ongoing burdens of rule, was softened by a genial smile as he engaged his guests. There was a warmth to him that belied the steel beneath, a ruler who knew that charm could be as effective as force in holding an empire together.

Seated to his right was Sumeira, similarly relaxed, yet beneath her composed exterior, there was a tension, a worry that gnawed at her with every passing moment. Her son, Jamal, was never far from her thoughts, and tonight, the unease was almost unbearable.

Beside Sumeira sat Hunter, preferring to observe rather than participate in the conversations swirling around him, his gaze constantly scanning the room, ever alert to potential threats, even in this seemingly secure environment.

The guests at the table were a varied lot, each representing a different facet of the complex world that Constantinople had become under Latin rule. Closest to the emperor were the high-ranking Latin nobles and knights, men who had earned their places through blood and steel. They were warriors, most of them grizzled and battle-hardened, their conversation revolving around strategies and the logistics of war. They spoke of King Kaloyan's advance with a mixture of disdain and respect, knowing that the Bulgarian monarch was not to be underestimated.

Further down the table, Byzantine nobles, the remnants of a once-great empire, sat with an air of cautious dignity. Their positions were precarious, caught between loyalty to their Byzantine heritage and the need to survive under the new Latin rulers. They spoke less, their words measured, their glances toward Baldwin careful, acutely aware that any misstep could cost them dearly in this new order.

Sumeira turned to speak to Hunter and noticed his attention was firmly fixed on something happening at the far end of the hall. She followed his gaze and watched as a cloaked man passed on a message to one of the stewards standing by the door. Moments later, the steward approached the top table and conveyed the message to the emperor. Baldwin listened intently before dismissing the steward and turning to face Sumeira.

'What is it?' she asked nervously, seeing the worry in his face. 'Is it news of Jamal? Is he dead?'

'It is indeed news of your son,' said Baldwin, 'but fret not, he is alive and well.'

The relief that surged through Sumeira's body was overwhelming, and she thought she would pass out.

'Where is he?' she asked eventually. 'Can I go to him?'

'Alas, that is not possible,' said the emperor. 'Since leaving England, he has been appointed as a squire to a man called Edmund of Bristol, an officer who has been deployed with a unit of fellow knights charged with paving the way for our main army. I'm sorry, Sumeira, but it seems your son is already on his way to Adrianople.'

The words hung in the air. Sumeira's face paled, her hands gripping the edge of the table as she processed the information. Jamal, her son, her life, had been sent to the front lines of a war that threatened to engulf them all.

'When?' she asked eventually, her voice a mere croak as she battled to keep hold of her fear.

'Two days ago,' he said. 'They are tasked with establishing a forward camp from where my forces will campaign onward to Adrianople itself in a few days' time.'

Sumeira could barely hear the emperor's words over the roaring in her ears. Two days. Jamal was already on his way to Adrianople, beyond her reach, thrust into the midst of a conflict that could claim his life. The room, once filled with warmth and light, now felt cold and distant, the faces around her blurring into indistinct shapes.

Hunter's hand on her arm brought her back to the present. His grip was firm, grounding her in the reality of the moment, his voice steady, a lifeline in the storm of her emotions.

'Nothing has changed,' he said quietly. 'We'll find Jamal and bring him back.'

Sumeira nodded, her heart heavy but resolute. She met Baldwin's gaze once more, her expression unreadable.

'Thank you, Your Majesty,' she said, her voice betraying nothing of the turmoil within. 'Could I ask, what fate awaits Jamal and his comrades when they reach Adrianople?'

'Everyone's fate is in the hands of God himself,' said Baldwin, 'especially when it comes to battle, but it may not come to that.'

'What do you mean?'

'When we reach the walled city, we will offer terms for their surrender. If they accept, then there will be no need for bloodshed on either side.'

'And if they do not?'

'Then the city will be placed under siege, and we will either starve them out or wait until they are weak before destroying their walls.'

Sumeira swallowed hard. The information was sobering, but at least it meant that she still had some time.

'Thank you, Your Majesty,' she said, 'but if you will forgive me, I respectfully request permission to leave. I fear this news will make me poor company, and I have to decide what it is I need to do next.'

The emperor inclined his head, a gesture of both understanding and dismissal. As Sumeira rose from the table, the other guests watched her with a mixture of curiosity and sympathy, aware that something profound had just transpired but unsure of its full significance.

As she left the hall, Hunter by her side, the conversations slowly resumed, though the light-heartedness of the earlier evening was gone. The feast continued, but the shadow of war hung heavier over the gathering, and the fate of Constantinople, and all those within it, seemed more uncertain than ever.

----

The heavy wooden door to Sumeira's guest chambers closed behind them with a soft thud, shutting out the muted sounds of the palace corridors and the lingering echoes of the feast. The room was dimly lit by a single candle on the table, its flickering flame casting long, wavering shadows across the rich tapestries that lined the walls. The luxurious surroundings were stifling rather than comforting, as if the very opulence of the space was pressing down on them.

Sumeira moved to the window, pushed aside the heavy velvet drapes, letting in the cool night air, and gazed out over the sprawling city of Constantinople.

Hunter remained by the door, his eyes following her every movement. He had seen her withstand countless pressures, face dangers that would have broken others, yet tonight she seemed more fragile, as if the news had struck at the very core of her being. He knew better than to speak immediately, instead giving her the space she needed to gather her thoughts. Finally, Sumeira turned to him, her expression a mixture of determination and deep sorrow.

'Hunter, I cannot let this happen,' she said, her voice trembling slightly. 'Jamal is just a boy, thrust into the middle of a war he does not understand. If we do not reach him before the war begins...'

Her voice trailed off, the words too painful to complete. The thought of losing Jamal, her only son, to the horrors of war was unbearable. She had fought so hard to protect him, to keep him safe, and now, in the span of a few moments, she had found out he had been sent away, beyond her reach, to face dangers that no mother could shield her child from.

Hunter stepped forward, his presence solid and reassuring.

'We will reach him,' he said firmly, his voice leaving no room for doubt. 'We will leave at first light, travel fast, and catch up with the army before they reach Adrianople. The siege has not yet begun.'

'But what if we are too late, Hunter? What if we do not reach him in time?'

Hunter took a step closer, his voice softening but remaining resolute.

'We will not think of failure, Sumeira. Jamal is strong, like his mother. He will hold on until we reach him, and then we will get him out of there.'

Sumeira looked up at Hunter, her tears threatening to spill over, but she held them back, drawing strength from his unwavering confidence.

'I cannot lose him,' she whispered, her voice breaking. 'He is all I have left.'

Hunter's heart ached at her pain, but he knew he had to remain strong for her. He reached out, taking her hands in his, his grip firm but gentle.

'You will not lose him,' he vowed. 'I swear to you, Sumeira, we will bring him back.'

For a moment, they stood in silence, the bond between them unspoken but palpable. Hunter had been by her side through so much, and now, in this darkest hour, he was her anchor, the one constant in a world that seemed to be falling apart.

Sumeira finally nodded, her resolve hardening.

'We leave at first light,' she repeated, her voice stronger now. 'No delays, no distractions. We will find Jamal and bring him home.'

Hunter released her hands, his eyes never leaving hers. 'I will make the preparations,' he said. 'Rest if you can. We'll need our strength for the journey ahead.'

Sumeira watched as he turned to leave, but before he reached the door, she spoke again, her voice soft but filled with gratitude.

'Hunter... thank you. For everything.'

He paused, turning back to her, his expression gentle, suggesting something more than just affection, before suddenly averting his eyes.

'It's what Cronin would have wanted,' he said. 'Now get some sleep.'

With that, he slipped out of the room, leaving Sumeira alone with her thoughts. She turned back to the window, gazing out into the night, her mind racing with plans and prayers. The road ahead would again be fraught with danger, but she could not, would not, fail her son. The thought of Jamal gave her strength, a fierce determination to protect him, no matter the cost.

As the candle flickered and the night deepened, Sumeira prepared herself for the journey to come, her heart heavy but resolute. She would reach Jamal, she told herself over and over, and together they would survive the storm that was fast approaching.

----

# CHAPTER THIRTY-TWO

## Constantinople

The dawn sky over Constantinople was streaked with hues of pale pink and gold, the first light of day casting a warm glow over the city's imposing walls and the glittering waters of the Bosporus. The air was crisp and cool, a fleeting moment of peace before the city stirred to life. But this morning, the usual sounds of traders setting up their stalls and the calls of fishermen heading out to sea were overshadowed by the rhythmic clang of armour, the snorting of warhorses, and the low murmur of thousands of voices, a city preparing for war.

Emperor Baldwin stood atop the great walls of Constantinople, surveying the scene below. The mighty Latin army was assembling in the vast fields outside the city gates, a formidable force of knights, foot soldiers, and siege engines, all arranged with military precision. Banners bearing the emblem of the Latin Empire, golden crosses on fields of red and white, fluttered in the breeze, a sea of colour against the morning sky. The soldiers moved with purpose, their armour gleaming in the early light, their faces set with grim determination.

Baldwin's gaze swept over his troops. This was his army, forged from the remnants of the crusaders who had taken Constantinople and the local forces now loyal to his rule. They had faced many battles together, and now they were being called upon to defend the empire once more. Kaloyan had been a thorn in their side for too long, and his relentless advance had brought the war to the empire's doorstep.

The advance force had already departed days earlier, clearing the way to Adrianople, where the decisive battle would be fought. Baldwin's own son, Philip of Courtenay, led that vanguard, and though Baldwin trusted his son's abilities, he knew the full weight of the campaign now rested on the army he would lead into the field. The time for strategy and diplomacy had passed; now it was time for action.

Behind him, the gates of Constantinople creaked open, and Baldwin turned to see his officers assembling, their faces reflecting the seriousness of the task ahead. Among them were seasoned commanders who had fought beside him during the Fourth Crusade, men who had earned their places through courage and loyalty. They saluted him as he descended from the walls to join them, their eyes searching his for the confidence and strength they needed to carry into battle.

Baldwin mounted his horse, a powerful white stallion draped in a crimson caparison emblazoned with the imperial cross. As he rode toward the front of the army, the soldiers fell silent, all eyes on their emperor. He could feel the weight of their expectations, the unspoken demand for leadership that would see them through the trials ahead.

At the head of the army, he raised his hand, signalling for his men to gather closer. The sound of armour and leather creaking filled the air as the soldiers tightened their ranks, the hush of anticipation spreading through the ranks like a ripple across still water. The emperor looked out over his assembled forces, his heart pounding with the intensity of the moment.

'Men of the Latin Empire,' Baldwin began, his voice carrying across the field with the authority of a man who had led armies to victory before. 'Today, we march not just for glory, but for the survival of our empire. The threat we face is great, but so too is our resolve. Kaloyan and his forces have ravaged our lands, slaughtered our people, and now seek what is rightfully ours. But they will find no easy victory here.'

The soldiers listened intently, their eyes fixed on their leader, their faces a mix of determination and fierce loyalty.

'We go to Adrianople to meet them in battle,' Baldwin continued, his voice rising with passion. 'There, we will show them the strength of our arms and the power of our faith. We fight for our homes, for our families, and for the cross under which we serve. Let none doubt our resolve, for we march to defend not just this city, but all of Christendom. And when we meet Kaloyan on the field, we will drive him back, or we will die trying.'

A cheer rose from the soldiers, a roar of approval and defiance that echoed across the plain. Baldwin felt the surge of energy from his men, their unity, and their readiness for the fight to come. He nodded, satisfaction settling into his chest as he turned his horse toward the road that led out of Constantinople.

The order was given, and with a great clamour, the army began to move. The creaking of wooden wheels, the clatter of hooves on stone, and the rhythmic march of thousands of feet filled the air as the massive host began its journey. The banners of the Latin Empire fluttered in the breeze, leading the way, while the sun climbed higher into the sky, bathing the soldiers in its golden light.

Baldwin rode at the head of the column, his eyes fixed on the road ahead, but his thoughts were with those who had already gone before him. His son, Philip, was out there, somewhere on the road to Adrianople, along with the other knights and soldiers who had been dispatched to secure the route. The emperor prayed silently for their safety, knowing that the coming days would test them all in ways they could scarcely imagine.

As the city's walls receded into the distance, the full magnitude of the task became clear. The road to Adrianople would be long, and the battle waiting at its end would be fierce. But Baldwin felt no fear, only the fire of determination burning in his chest. He was a crusader, an emperor, and he would not be deterred by the likes of Kaloyan.

The army pressed onward, a relentless tide of steel and faith moving inexorably toward its destination. Behind them, Constantinople stood as a symbol of all they fought to protect, its mighty walls a testament to the endurance of their cause. Ahead, the plains stretched out toward Adrianople, where the fate of the empire would soon be decided.

----

That night, in the northeast, the jagged peaks of the Balkan Mountains loomed like sentinels against the darkening sky, their craggy faces etched in shadow as the sun dipped below the horizon. Nestled deep within this forbidding landscape, far from prying eyes, a vast encampment sprawled across the valley floor, the rough and utilitarian tents forming a chaotic labyrinth that stretched as far as the eye could see. Fires dotted the landscape like fallen stars, their orange glow flickering against the encroaching darkness, casting eerie, dancing shadows across the rugged terrain.

Tsar Kaloyan of Bulgaria stood on a rocky outcrop overlooking the camp, clad in a fur-lined cloak that billowed in the wind. His face, weathered by years of war and harsh rule, was a mask of determination, every line etched with the weight of the decisions he had made and the battles he had fought. His gaze, cold and calculating, swept over his army, his horde, spread out across the valley like a sea of steel and sinew.

The Bulgarian army was vast, a formidable force composed of seasoned warriors hardened by years of relentless conflict. They had followed Kaloyan into battle countless times, and now they waited, restless and eager for the bloodshed to come. But it was not just the sheer size of his force that gave Kaloyan confidence. No, it was the reinforcements he awaited, the Cumans, fierce steppe warriors who had pledged their support to his campaign against the Latins.

Kaloyan's thoughts were interrupted by the approach of Boris Sigritsa, the Boyar who had served him loyally for years.

'Your Majesty,' Boris said, his voice gruff but respectful. 'The men are ready. They know what's at stake. They just await your command. Just say the word and we can sweep down upon the Latins while they are yet strung out, their swords unbloodied.'

Kaloyan nodded, his eyes still fixed on the camp below.

'Good. But we will not move yet. Let them march to Adrianople unchallenged, let them expend their strength upon the walls, shedding blood in what will ultimately be a futile endeavour. We will wait and watch until the time is right, and when it is, when they least expect it, we will fall upon them like the worst of storms, led by the fiercest warriors the steppe has to offer.'

Boris grinned, a savage gleam in his eyes.

'The Cumans will arrive soon?'

Kaloyan's lips curled into a cold smile.

'Yes. They come from the north, swift as the wind. When they arrive, we will have the strength to strike not just at Adrianople, but at the heart of Baldwin's forces. The Latins will never see us coming, not until it's too late.'

Boris looked out over the camp, where thousands of Bulgarian soldiers prepared for the coming battle. The sounds of sharpening blades and the low murmur of voices filled the air, a symphony of war in the making.

'The men will fight to the death for you, Tsar Kaloyan. They believe in your cause, in driving these invaders from our lands.'

'As they should,' Kaloyan replied, his voice laced with steel. 'These Latins are interlopers, thieves who would take what is ours. They think they can conquer Bulgaria, that they can impose their rule on us. But they have underestimated our resolve. We will show them the price of their ambition.'

A gust of wind swept through the valley, carrying with it the faint scent of pine and the distant howls of wolves in the forest. Kaloyan breathed in the cold air, feeling the tension in his chest coil tighter with each passing moment. The Cumans were close; he could feel it. Their arrival would be the final piece of the puzzle, the force that would tip the scales in his favour.

'They say the Cumans are savage,' Boris remarked, almost as if testing the air with his words. 'Fierce fighters, but difficult to control.'

Kaloyan's smile widened, his teeth flashing in the dim light.

'Savage, yes. But that is precisely what we need. The Latins are disciplined, but they do not know how to fight against chaos, against the fury of the steppe. When the Cumans strike, it will be as if the very mountains have come alive to swallow them whole. And in that chaos, we will be the blade that cuts their heart out.'

Boris nodded, his own anticipation mirrored in the tension that rippled through the camp. Every soldier knew what was coming, and though fear lurked in the corners of their minds, it was drowned out by the thirst for victory, for vengeance.

'Keep the men at the ready,' said Kaloyan eventually, 'for when the moment arrives, there will be very little time to prepare. They need to be ready to move at a heartbeat's notice.' He turned away from the camp, his eyes narrowing as he stared into the distance, toward the north where the Cumans would soon appear, and as Boris left to carry out his orders, Kaloyan remained on the outcrop, his mind already picturing the coming battle. He could see the Latins, their ranks breaking as the Cumans swept down upon them, their lines crumbling under the relentless assault. And then, in the midst of that chaos, his army would strike, driving them into the ground, into the rivers, into the dark oblivion from which they would never return.

The mountains loomed above him, dark and silent, as if waiting for the bloodshed to begin. And Kaloyan, Tsar of Bulgaria, felt the cold thrill of anticipation ripple through him, as if the very earth beneath his feet was urging him onward to victory.

A wolf howled in the forests again, a haunting echo of the battle cry that would soon resound from the mountains to the plains, and Kaloyan closed his eyes, savouring the moment, knowing that the time for blood and fire was nearly at hand.

----

At the confluence of the three rivers, the streets of Adrianople were a chaotic tangle of movement, a city on the brink of war. The clang of hammers against iron rang out from every corner as blacksmiths worked frantically to forge weapons and repair armour. The smell of sweat and fear hung thick in the air, mingling with the acrid scent of burning wood as fires roared in the forges and ovens. The city, ancient and proud, had become a fortress overnight, its people driven by a mixture of desperation and defiance as they prepared for the onslaught that loomed on the horizon.

In the shadow of the city's towering walls, farmers hurried their livestock through the gates, their faces lined with worry as they cast nervous glances over their shoulders. The last of the stragglers, peasants, merchants, and their families, pushed their way through the throngs, seeking refuge behind the walls that they hoped would protect them from the coming storm. The gates groaned as they were drawn shut, the heavy wood slamming into place with a finality that sent a shiver through the gathered crowd. Outside, the distant hills remained eerily quiet, but everyone knew that the silence would not last.

Within the walls, the mood was one of frenzied activity, but beneath the surface, fear gnawed at the hearts of the people. Whispers of the Latin army's approach spread like wildfire, rumours growing wilder with each retelling. They spoke of Baldwin's might, of his legions of knights clad in shining chainmail, their swords blessed by the Church, cutting through anything that dared stand in their path. But alongside the fear, there was also anger, a deep, burning resentment that smouldered in the hearts of those whose ancestors had made the city their home for countless generations.

Who was Baldwin to assume that they, the people of Adrianople, would simply bow to his will? Who was he to march his army into their lands, expecting loyalty where there was none? The city had always been fiercely independent, its people proud of their heritage and their strength. They had no love for the Latins, no desire to see their banners raised above their walls. And now, as the enemy approached, that pride was turning to fury.

In the heart of the city, the Bulgarians oversaw the preparations. They were not many, far fewer than the massive host that Baldwin commanded, but they were hardened warriors, men who had fought and bled for their land.

Ivan Chelebri stood at the centre of the bustling courtyard, his sharp eyes assessing the preparations with the practised gaze of a veteran. He was a tall man, broad-shouldered and imposing, his face weathered by years of battle.

'Reinforce the eastern wall,' he ordered, his voice calm but carrying the weight of authority. 'If Baldwin is foolish enough to think we will surrender, he'll likely focus his attack there, expecting it to be weakest point.'

The officers nodded, barking orders to the men around them. Soldiers moved with purpose, hauling barrels of oil to the ramparts, where they would be ready to pour down upon the attackers. Archers inspected their bows, their faces grim as they prepared for the inevitable siege. The Bulgarians were few, but their numbers were reinforced by Adrianople's existing army, Greeks who owed their allegiance only to the elders of the city, the men who had ordered them to do what they could to repel Baldwin's oncoming storm. They knew the terrain, knew the city's defences inside and out, and they would use every advantage they had to hold the walls.

As Ivan Chelebri watched his men work, a scout approached, breathless from running. The man's face was pale, sweat streaking his brow, but his voice was steady as he delivered his report.

'The Latin army is near, my lord,' the scout said, his eyes wide with urgency. 'Their advance forces are already within sight of the city. They'll be at the gates by tomorrow.'

Ivan nodded, his expression unreadable. 'How many?'

'Hundreds, my lord,' the scout replied. 'But their numbers are spread out. We've seen no sign of their main force yet, just the vanguard.'

The Tarkhan considered this for a moment, his mind racing through the possibilities. The vanguard would be testing the city's defences, probing for weaknesses before the main army arrived. It was a tactic he knew well, one he had used himself in battles past. But this time, the stakes were higher

'My lord,' said one of his officers, 'this might be an opportunity to strike early, before they have a chance to get organized. We may not cause huge casualties, but a quick strike could dent their confidence and send a message that we are not to be underestimated.'

'Not this time, my friend,' said Chelebri, 'we need every man we can muster to defend the walls. Make sure they are ready.'

The scout saluted and rushed off to carry out the orders, leaving Ivan alone in the courtyard. He could feel the weight of the city's fate pressing down on him, the responsibility heavy on his shoulders. But he was not a man to falter under pressure. He had fought in countless battles, faced down armies larger than his own, and he had survived through cunning, strategy, and sheer force of will. This would be no different.

As the last of the city's inhabitants were ushered through the gates and the great doors were locked with a resounding clang, Ivan Chelebri climbed the stairs to the eastern wall. From his vantage point, he could see the land stretching out before the city, a patchwork of fields and forests, now eerily still in the twilight. In the distance, just at the edge of his vision, he could make out the faint glimmer of movement, Baldwin's vanguard.

The sight of the enemy filled him with a cold resolve. Adrianople would not fall. Not to Baldwin, not to any Latin invader, as long as he was alive. He had sworn as much to Kaloyan and intended to carry out his vow with every last breath in his body. He turned to the soldiers gathered on the walls, their faces etched with the same determination that burned within him.

'Let them come,' he said, his voice carrying across the ramparts. 'They will find nothing but death and ruin here. Adrianople is ours, and we will defend it with our lives.'

A cheer rose from the men, a fierce, defiant cry that echoed through the night. The fires on the walls burned brighter, casting long shadows over the city, and the soldiers tightened their grips on their weapons, ready for the battle that was fast approaching.

As the last light of day faded and the stars began to emerge, Adrianople stood ready, a fortress bristling with anger and pride. The Latins might be many, but they were not invincible. And Ivan Chelebri, Tarkhan to the great Tsar Kaloyan of Bulgaria, would make sure they learned that lesson in blood.

----

Far to the south, amidst the gentle swell of the Aegean Sea, the wind whipped through the rigging of the leper ship, straining the weathered sails as they cut through the choppy waters heading towards Constantinople. The horizon was a bleak, endless stretch of grey, the sky heavy with the promise of a coming storm.

237

Cronin stood on the deck, his eyes scanning the distant waves, his thoughts consumed with the urgency of his mission. Every moment they spent at sea felt like a precious hour slipping through his fingers, each wave that buffeted the ship another obstacle between him and the safety of Sumeira and Jamal.

The crew, hardened by years of service, moved with practised efficiency, their faces set in grim determination. The leper knights, few in number but resolute, kept to themselves, their hollow eyes fixed on the horizon as they prayed silently for a swift and uneventful journey.

Suddenly, a shout rang out from the bow, breaking through the steady rhythm of the ship's progress.

'Sail ahead! Landward.'

All eyes turned towards the horizon, Cronin's heart quickening as he spotted the looming shape of a ship, its sails catching the failing light as it emerged from the sea mist. The vessel was heading westward, its course taking it away from the Byzantine shores and back toward the open sea. As they drew closer, Cronin caught sight of the banner fluttering from the mast, a red cross on a white field. The captain of the leper ship moved to stand beside Cronin, his face etched with curiosity.

'An English ship, and in these waters,' he muttered, squinting against the spray. 'It rides high, so I suspect it has unloaded whatever cargo it once had.'

'It must have been one of the many diverted to Constantinople,' Cronin replied, his voice tense with anticipation. 'And if so, they may know something of Baldwin's march.'

The captain nodded, and with a quick gesture, he ordered the helmsman to bring their ship alongside the English vessel. The two ships slowly closed the distance between them, the waves growing rougher as they drew near. The ship's name, *Spiritus Sancti*, was visible on its side, the letters weathered but legible.

Cronin's heart pounded in his chest as the ships drew nearer, their hulls creaking as they bobbed alongside each other. The captain of the other ship peered down over the rail to Cronin's smaller vessel, his eyes scanning the leper knights with a mixture of curiosity and pity.

'I am the captain of the *Spiritus Sancti*,' the man said, offering a curt nod. 'We've just come from Constantinople, though we tarried only long enough to unload our cargo. We are now headed for Venice to pick up supplies for his campaign. Where are you headed?'

'Constantinople,' said Cronin. 'We hope to get there before Baldwin sets out.'

'Then your journey is a futile one,' said the captain, 'for he has already marched westward, taking every able-bodied man and beast he could muster.'

'To Adrianople?' Cronin asked, his voice tight with urgency.

'Aye,' the captain replied grimly. 'Kaloyan of Bulgaria now controls the city, and Baldwin means to wrest it from his grip. The roads to the west of Constantinople are thick with men, wagons, and supplies. It is a vast host, but they move slowly. Why do you hurry to join them, for it looks like your comrades are in no fit state to fight?'

'I am seeking a woman who sailed from England to find her son,' replied Cronin. 'The chances of finding her are slim, but it is a quest I cannot abandon.'

'Do you talk of Sumeira?' asked the captain.

Cronin gasped and stared at the man in shock.

'You know of her?'

'Aye, she and her man sailed with me from England. She is seeking her son, and we left her in Constantinople.'

Again, Cronin gasped. To actually find someone who had seen Sumeira only a few days ago was truly a miracle from God.

'How is she?' he asked. 'Is she well?'

'She is feisty and determined, and a difficult woman to argue with,' said the captain, 'but apart from that, she is fine.'

'Do you know where she was heading, or if she has found Jamal?'

'The last time I saw her, she was heading into the city with her husband, a man called Hunter.'

Cronin did not correct the captain, realising that they would have assumed the relationship to protect Sumeira.

'How long ago was this?'

'About a week ago.'

'And when did Baldwin lead his army out of Constantinople?'

'Two days ago.'

Cronin's mind raced. If Jamal had headed west with the army, then Sumeira would certainly have followed, perhaps even travelled with the supply train for safety, which meant she was probably no longer in Constantinople.

'What is the closest port to Adrianople?' he asked, an air of urgency in his voice.

'That would be Ainos,' said the captain, nodding toward the northeast. 'From there, it's a hard ride inland, but it's your best chance of catching up with the army before the battle begins.'

'Thank you,' said Cronin, turning to the captain of his own ship. 'Do you know of this place?'

'I can find it on the charts,' came the reply, 'but the journey may be dangerous. It means sailing into Greek waters, and if Adrianople has declared for Kaloyan, we may encounter some of his own ships.'

'It is a risk I am willing to take,' said Cronin.

'It is not just your decision, remember?' said the captain.

'We are happy to go where he wants,' said a voice behind them, and Cronin glanced over to see Raymond standing nearby.

'Are you sure?' asked the captain. 'You could all be killed before we even reach the port.'

'We are already dead men,' said the leper. 'Take us to Ainos.'

'So be it,' said the captain with a sigh, 'but on your own heads be it.'

Once disengaged, the leper ship surged forward, the wind at their back as they sped toward Ainos. Cronin stood at the bow, his eyes fixed on the distant horizon, where the land of Thrace lay somewhere out of sight. Sumeira and Jamal were out there, somewhere on the road to Adrianople, caught in the midst of a conflict that could consume them all. Their lives had never been in so much danger, but at last, after a mixture of faith and good fortune, he was almost within touching distance. All he had to do was make landfall with his life intact, the rest was in the hands of God himself.

----

# CHAPTER THIRTY-THREE

## The Approach to Adrianople

Sir Edmund tightened his grip on the reins, the leather creaking under the pressure of his mailed hands. The wind, cold and unforgiving, swept across the open plain, carrying with it the scent of distant fires and the faint, foreboding whispers of a city on the brink of siege. Adrianople loomed on the horizon, its ancient walls a dark silhouette against the pale morning sky. For a moment, all was silent save for the occasional coughs of the men, the rhythmic clink of chainmail, and the occasional snort from the warhorses.

Beside him, Jamal stared at their eventual destination, his eyes wide with a mixture of awe and fear, his hand resting on the hilt of the sword that still looked too large for his frame. His brow furrowed in concentration as he guided his horse forward.

The walls of Adrianople were formidable, towering above the surrounding landscape, a seemingly unassailable fortress of stone, wood, and iron. Even from this distance, he could see the faint glimmer of soldiers atop the battlements, their own armour reflecting the pale light of dawn.

'It's... larger than I imagined, my lord,' Jamal admitted, his voice tinged with nervousness.

'Aye,' Edmund replied, his gaze never leaving the city. 'And stronger. But do not let its size fool you, lad. Every wall, no matter how tall, has its weakness. And we shall find it.'

As they drew nearer, the vanguard began to slow, the men spreading out across the plain under the watchful eye of Geoffrey of Villehardouin. The Marshal of Champagne, seasoned and battle-hardened, rode at the head of the column, his banner flapping in the wind. He issued commands with a sharp, practiced efficiency, directing the knights and footmen to establish a forward camp.

'Sir Edmund!' Geoffrey called, his voice carrying above the din of the assembling forces. 'Take your men and secure the northern approach. We will go firm here and await Baldwin and the rest of the army.'

Edmund nodded curtly and led his knights to block off any potential re-supply route from that direction. The ground was uneven, strewn with rocks and debris from past conflicts. His eyes scanned the terrain, assessing the best position to create a temporary camp. His instincts, honed through years of warfare, finally guided him to a small rise topped with trees overlooking the city's northern gate.

'We'll set up here,' he decided, dismounting and handing his reins to Jamal. 'Water the horses but keep them close in case we need to ride.'

As his comrades spread out through the treeline to find better vantage points, Edmund stood at the edge of the rise, watching the city below. The sun was higher now, casting long shadows across the plain. Adrianople was quiet, but Edmund knew that within its walls, the defenders were preparing, just as they were.

Jamal returned to his side, his brow damp with sweat and his breathing heavy.

'We have no tents, my lord,' he said. 'Where are we to sleep?'

'There will be little sleep for us, Jamal,' said Edmund, 'at least not yet. Once Baldwin arrives with the main army, he will decide where to set up camp and we will be relieved. Until then, keep your wits about you and watch for any sign of movement on the road in both directions.'

'Yes, my lord,' said Jamal, and he walked over to sit beside a tree overlooking the city. Edmund watched him go with a feeling of pride and a little sadness. The boy was certainly keen and eager to learn, but his idea of battle was a vision of brave men vanquishing an evil army in a one-sided battle in the name of God. Edmund knew that the reality was something far different, more horrifying, and Jamal, despite his determination to fight on the side of Christianity, would soon realise that war was nothing more than an early demonstration of what hell itself would look like. With a sigh, he turned away and headed over to discuss strategy with his fellow knights.

----

Back at the treeline, Jamal sat on the cold earth, his back pressed against the rough bark of a gnarled tree. Below, the city of Adrianople sprawled out like a beast waiting to be tamed, its high walls both a challenge and a threat. He could still see the faint movement of soldiers on the battlements, their figures mere specks in the distance, yet their presence weighed heavily upon him.

His fingers traced the edge of his sword, the metal cool and reassuring beneath his touch. It was a new weapon, given to him by Sir Edmund, and he had spent countless hours practising with it, though the grip still felt awkward in his hand. He glanced at the city again, his heart thudding in his chest, a rhythm of anxiety that refused to settle.

Fear was there, deep and gnawing, no matter how much he tried to push it away. The tales of battle he had heard, the songs of glory sung by his fellow soldiers on the ship, had never captured the true essence of what it meant to be here, on the brink of war. The thought of charging into battle, of facing men who would do anything to protect their home, made his stomach churn. What if he wasn't fast enough? What if his injury held him back? He had seen the way some of the other men looked at him, pity in their eyes, as if they expected him to fail.

But there was more than just fear. There was excitement too, a fire that burned bright within him, fed by dreams of valour and honour. Jamal had yearned for this moment, the chance to prove himself, to show that he was more than the injury that had marked him, more than the boy who had struggled through the training during their voyage from England. The city below was a test, and he was determined to pass it, to earn his place among the knights and warriors he had always admired, and start on the journey to attain greatness in the service of the Lord.

His gaze remained fixed on Adrianople, and he imagined what lay ahead. The clash of steel, the roar of men in the heat of combat, the cries of victory or the silence of defeat. His thoughts raced between the two extremes, fear of what could go wrong and the thrill of what could go right. Yet even in his nervousness, there was clarity, a singular focus that emerged from the chaos in his mind.

He would fight. He would stand with Sir Edmund and the others, and he would not falter. The fear, the nervousness, they were part of him, but so too was the courage that grew stronger with each passing moment. This was what he had trained for, what he had dreamed of, and now that the moment was nearly upon him, he found that he was ready. Or at least, as ready as any man could be when staring down the gates of a city like Adrianople.

With a deep breath, he pushed himself to his feet, the weight of the sword at his side a reminder of the responsibility he carried. The city below was a challenge, but he was determined to meet it head-on, no matter what fears still lingered in the corners of his mind.

'I am ready, my lord,' he whispered into the morning air. 'My life is yours to take or to spare as you see fit. My destiny is in your hands.'

----

For two days, the knights endured a tense, uneasy stillness. The road that wound through the countryside leading to Adrianople was mostly empty, save for the occasional trader, blissfully ignorant of the storm that was gathering around them.

The men spoke in hushed tones, their voices subdued by the weight of anticipation. Edmund had spent much of the time sharpening his sword, checking the straps of his armour, and quietly praying for strength. Jamal, ever at his side, had busied himself with mundane tasks, his mind buzzing with thoughts of the coming conflict.

On the morning of the third day, as the mist began to lift from the fields, a rider appeared on the horizon. The messenger, clad in the colours of Baldwin, spurred his horse forward, his arrival breaking the monotony that had settled over the camp. Without dismounting, he delivered the long-awaited news: Baldwin's army had arrived and was setting up camp just over a league away.

Edmund wasted no time. He called for Jamal, and together they climbed a nearby hill that offered a clear view of the surrounding countryside. As they crested the top, they were greeted by a sight that took their breath away.

Stretching out across the plain was the full might of Baldwin's army, a host of soldiers and banners, as far as the eye could see. At the centre of it all, they could see men erecting the command tents, large and imposing, their brightly coloured pennants fluttering in the breeze. The largest bore Baldwin's personal banner, flanked by those of the great lords who had sworn fealty to him. The tents themselves were made of thick canvas, reinforced to withstand the elements, and decorated with the emblems of the noble houses that had come to fight under Baldwin's command.

The knights of the army, clad in chainmail hauberks, were arrayed in orderly ranks, their warhorses stamping the ground impatiently. The air was filled with the sounds of the encampment, metal striking metal, the low murmur of voices as orders were given, and the clatter of wooden poles being driven into the earth to support the walls of tents. Nearby, squires and servants scurried about, setting up campfires and preparing the noon meal, while cooks began to tend to large pots suspended over the flames, the smell of boiling meat wafting through the air.

Alongside the knights were contingents of foot soldiers, mercenaries, and crossbowmen from the various regions of the empire. These men wore simpler garb, leather and rough-spun wool, but their expressions were no less serious. They were seasoned veterans, hardened by years of fighting in the Crusades and the various conflicts that had erupted across the fractured remnants of the Byzantine Empire.

Off to one side, the siege engineers were already at work, assembling the towering trebuchets and other siege engines that would soon be brought to bear against Adrianople's walls. Massive wooden beams, iron-banded and reinforced with thick ropes, lay on the ground, waiting to be hoisted into place, and piles of stone ammunition were being stacked nearby, the rough-hewn rocks destined to batter the city's defences.

In the distance, the baggage train stretched out like a serpent across the landscape, wagons laden with supplies, weapons, and provisions for the coming siege. The oxen that pulled them moved slowly, their burdens heavy, but the men directing them were purposeful, knowing that the success of the siege depended on their efforts.

Edmund and Jamal stood in silence for a moment, taking it all in. The sheer scale of the army was overwhelming, a stark reminder of the power that Baldwin wielded and the determination with which he intended to take Adrianople.

'It's... magnificent, my lord,' said Jamal. 'I've never seen anything like it.'

'Aye,' Edmund replied, his tone a mix of pride and solemnity. 'This is the might of Christendom, assembled for one purpose. But do not let its grandeur fool you, Jamal. War is as much about endurance as it is about strength. What we see here is the beginning. The true test lies ahead, within those walls.'

As they stood watching, the sun climbed higher into the sky, casting long shadows across the plain. The banners of Baldwin's army caught the light, a sea of colours against the green and brown of the earth. It was a sight that would be etched into their memories, a moment of calm before the storm that was about to break over Adrianople.

----

On another hill, just a few leagues away, Boya Sigritsa sat astride his restless horse watching Baldwin's camp grow as if from nothing. His gaze swept across the plains, taking in the full expanse of Baldwin's army, now setting up camp with the precision and discipline that spoke of seasoned commanders and well-trained men. The sight sent a ripple of unease through him, a feeling that settled deep in his gut.

From his vantage point, Sigritsa could see the banners of the Latin Empire fluttering in the breeze, the knights moving in organized ranks, their warhorses snorting and pawing at the ground. Siege engines, monstrous in their size and power, were being assembled by crews of engineers, their towering frames casting long shadows over the encampment. Everywhere he looked, there was motion, purpose, and strength.

Sigritsa's hand tightened on the reins as he took in the scale of the army. Baldwin had come prepared, bringing with him not just a force capable of laying siege to Adrianople, but one that could potentially break the city's defences with brute force and relentless pressure. The boyar had fought in many battles and had seen armies come and go, but this, this was different. There was a determination here, a sense of purpose that went beyond mere conquest. Baldwin's men were not just here to fight; they were here destroy the city.

The boyar's horse shifted beneath him, sensing his rider's tension. Sigritsa patted the beast's neck absently, his mind racing with thoughts of what this meant for Kaloyan and the defence of Adrianople. He knew that the Tsar had expected a significant force, but the reality was more daunting than anticipated, and Sigritsa couldn't help but feel a twinge of doubt. Could they truly hold against such an onslaught?

He lingered a moment longer, committing every detail to memory: the placement of the command tents, the location of the siege engines, the disposition of the troops. He needed to report this to Kaloyan as soon as possible. The Tsar had to know what they were facing if there was to be any hope of countering the attack.

With a final, lingering glance at the camp, Sigritsa turned his horse northward. The animal responded eagerly, sensing the change in its master's intent, and soon they were galloping away from the hill, the rhythmic pounding of hooves the only sound breaking the stillness of the morning.

By the time the sun had climbed high into the sky, Sigritsa had left the sight of the Latin camp far behind. The boyar's heart was heavy with the burden of the news he carried, but his resolve was firm. He would reach Kaloyan by nightfall, and then they would decide how best to confront the threat that now loomed over them. Baldwin might have brought the strength of the west to bear, but Sigritsa knew that Kaloyan was no stranger to war, and one thing was certain, if he could not defeat them with strength, his military mind would explore every option available to succeed with cunning and bravery.

----

Two days later, Baldwin walked with purposeful strides through the heart of the camp, accompanied by Louis of Blois, their chainmail glinting faintly in the morning light. As they walked, the men took notice, many pausing in their tasks to watch their leaders pass by. The presence of Baldwin and Louis, two of the most respected figures among the crusaders, commanded respect and quiet reverence.

Long lines of tents stretched across the plain, their colours marking the origins of the various contingents that had joined the crusade. Knights and men-at-arms were busy preparing for the coming siege, some sharpening swords and lances, while others adjusted the straps of their helmets and hauberks. As always, the clamour of the blacksmith's forge rang out in the distance, mingling with the murmur of voices and the occasional neigh of a warhorse.

As they passed a group of archers, Louis noticed one young man struggling with his bow, his brow furrowed in concentration as he tried to string it correctly. Stepping forward, Louis laid a hand on the archer's shoulder, causing the young man to startle and turn, eyes wide with surprise.

'My lord,' he began, but Louis silenced him with a gentle smile.

'Easy, lad,' he said, his tone warm and encouraging. 'Here, let me show you.' He took the bow from the archer's hands and, with practiced ease, strung it in one fluid motion. 'It's all about confidence. Trust in your training, and your hands will follow.'

The young archer nodded, his face flushing with a mix of embarrassment and gratitude. He took the bow back, his fingers steady now as he tested the string.

'Thank you, my lord,' he said, his voice filled with newfound resolve.

Louis clapped the archer on the back, his smile broadening. 'You'll do well, I'm sure of it. And remember, every arrow you loose brings us one step closer to victory.'

As they continued their inspection, Baldwin and Louis moved through the ranks, offering words of encouragement and guidance to their men. Everywhere they went, they left behind a sense of purpose and unity. The soldiers, already hardened by years of campaigning, felt a renewed vigour in their hearts, the presence of their leaders a powerful reminder of the cause they served.

When they reached the siege engines, Baldwin paused again, his gaze fixed on the massive trebuchets that were being assembled at the edge of the camp. These machines, capable of hurling massive stones over great distances, were the key to breaching the walls of Adrianople, and the engineers worked tirelessly to prepare them for the assault, their hands moving with precision as they tightened ropes and secured beams.

'Are we on schedule?' Baldwin asked one of the engineers, a grizzled veteran who had seen more sieges than most men had battles.

'Aye, my lord,' the engineer replied, wiping sweat from his brow. 'The trebuchets will be ready by tomorrow's light. We'll be able to start battering the walls by midday, God willing.'

Baldwin nodded, satisfied.

'Good. Ensure everything is ready. The city must fall, and soon.'

With that, Baldwin and Louis made their way back toward the command tents, the sun now fully risen, casting a bright light over the camp. The soldiers, reinvigorated by the presence of their leaders, continued their preparations with renewed energy, knowing that the time for action was drawing near.

As they walked, Louis turned to Baldwin, his voice low.

'The preparations proceed well,' he said, 'but I want a second camp formed nearer the city, a smaller, fortified camp that will hold our vanguard.'

'Is that a good idea?' asked Louis. 'Surely there is strength in numbers?'

'There is, but this camp is too spread out to defend properly, and anyway, it is too far away for any serious threat from the city. I want our best men nearer to the walls and ready to move without the hindrance of camp followers hanging about their heels. Form a forward camp housing knights only, and make sure it is well fortified. We will join them there with the vanguard, and while our engineers destroy the city walls, our knights will patrol the roads and make sure there is no threat from Kaloyan or his allies.'

'As you wish, my lord,' said Louis, and he turned away to make the arrangements.

----

# CHAPTER THIRTY-FOUR

## Kaloyan's Camp

The torches in the Tsar's giant tent flickered, casting long shadows on the fabric walls as Tsar Kaloyan sat upon his wooden throne, draped in furs and deep in thought. The chill of the evening air seeped through the walls, but the tension that filled the space was enough to keep the cold at bay as Boyar Sigritsa approached. The boyar's face was lined with exhaustion, but his eyes were sharp with urgency.

Kaloyan straightened, his gaze fixed on his trusted commander.

'Speak, Sigritsa,' he commanded, his voice low and resonant. 'What news do you bring?'

'My Tsar,' began Sigritsa, his voice steady despite the gravity of his report. 'The Latin forces under Baldwin have arrived. They are many thousands of knights and foot soldiers, disciplined and well-armed. Their banners stretch across the plain, and their siege engines are being assembled even as we speak. They mean to take Adrianople by force, and they have the strength to do it.'

Kaloyan's eyes narrowed, his mind racing as he absorbed the boyar's words. 'How many?' he asked, his tone betraying no emotion.

'By my count, at least five thousand, perhaps more,' Sigritsa replied. 'Their knights are well drilled and mounted on powerful steeds. They are supported by infantry, archers, and siege engineers. Baldwin himself leads them, alongside Louis of Blois and other lords of the Latin Empire. They are confident, my lord, too confident, I would say.'

The Tsar was silent for a moment, his mind working through the implications of what Sigritsa had told him. The Latin army was formidable, but Kaloyan had faced difficult odds before. He knew the strength of his own forces and, more importantly, he knew the land and its people. The Latins were invaders, unfamiliar with the terrain and the tactics that had kept the Bulgarian Empire strong against all foes. He leaned forward, his eyes gleaming with a calculated resolve.

'They may be strong, but they are not invincible,' he said, his voice firm. 'The strength of their knights lies in their heavy armour and their powerful charges. But they are slow, cumbersome. We will use that against them.'

Sigritsa nodded, understanding where his Tsar's mind was leading.

'What would you have us do, my lord?'

Kaloyan stood, his presence commanding as he moved toward the map that lay spread across a table nearby. The map depicted the region around Adrianople, with the city's walls and the surrounding plains carefully marked. He placed a hand on the map, his fingers tracing the paths that led through the forests and marshes around the city.

'We will not meet them in open battle,' Kaloyan declared. 'Not yet. Instead, we will draw them into the terrain where their knights will be at a disadvantage. The marshes north of Adrianople, there, we will strike.'

He turned to Sigritsa, his eyes sharp.

'Summon the Cuman leaders. They are the key to this strategy. Their mobility and skill with the bow will turn the tide in our favour.'

Sigritsa bowed and quickly left the hall, leaving Kaloyan to contemplate his plan. The Tsar's thoughts were focused, his mind a web of strategies and contingencies. He knew that defeating the Latins would not be easy, but he also knew that their arrogance could be their undoing. They believed themselves to be invincible, but they had never faced a foe like Kaloyan.

Within the hour, the leaders of the Cuman forces were brought before him. The Cumans, with their distinctive fur-lined cloaks and long bows, were a stark contrast to the armoured Bulgarians. Their leaders, weathered, sharp-eyed men who had fought countless battles on the steppes, stood before Kaloyan with a mixture of respect and curiosity. Kaloyan wasted no time.

'You have heard of the Latin army encamped near Adrianople,' he began, his tone commanding their attention. 'They are strong, yes, but they are slow and unfamiliar with this land. I intend to use that against them. You, my Cuman allies, will play a crucial role in our victory.'

The Cuman leader, a grizzled warrior named Qutlugh, stepped forward and inclined his head.

'We are ready to fight, Tsar Kaloyan. Tell us what you would have us do.'

Kaloyan smiled, a cold, calculating expression.

'I want your riders to close in on the Latins and harass them from a distance. Use your bows, but do not engage them in direct battle. Instead, lead them into the marshes north of the city here.' He pointed at an area clearly marked on the map. 'Remember, do not allow them to pin you down. I need them to follow you all the way.'

'And once they are there?' asked Qutlugh.

'Leave that to me,' said Kaloyan. 'All you need to do is get them there.'

The Cuman leaders exchanged looks, their confidence in the plan evident. They understood the strategy well; it was a tactic they had used many times before, on the open steppes and in the forests of the Balkans. Kaloyan watched as the Cumans departed, his mind already anticipating the coming battle. As the hall emptied, he returned to his map, his gaze fixed on the terrain around Adrianople. He turned to Sigritsa.

'Mobilise our army to head south,' he said, 'but use the hidden ways, the ravines and valleys and goat paths. Take them to the forests surrounding the marshes and ensure they are not seen.' He indicated the location on the map.

'As you wish, my lord,' said Sigritsa.

'One more thing,' said Kaloyan as his boyar turned away. 'Make sure they each carry a digging tool.'

'Digging tools?' asked Sigritsa, his brow creasing with the question.

'You heard me,' said Kaloyan. 'I will explain everything when we get there.'

'Yes, my lord,' said Sigritsa and left the tent, leaving Kaloyan alone with his thoughts.

'Their strength will be their downfall,' murmured the Tsar to himself, his voice filled with the certainty of a man who had already seen the outcome. 'And when they fall, the world will remember the name Kaloyan for the rest of time.'

----

Far to the south, Cronin stood on the dock in the port of Ainos, bartering with a trader for one of the many horses tethered on the dockside. Ordinarily, the price would have been prohibitive, but with time running out, he had no other option and paid the merchant with the last of the money he had been given in the commandery.

Up above, on the ship, the rest of the knights gathered along the rail, watching the situation unfold. For the last few days, all imagined barriers between the healthy and the infected had fallen away, and they now stood alongside each other, brothers once more despite the risk of cross-infection.

'He is a very determined man,' said Sir Geoffrey, 'but I fear his is a quest doomed to fail.'

'And why is that?' asked Sir Raymond at his side.

'To find one person in the midst of war is an impossible task,' said Geoffrey, 'and even if God guides his path, he has to travel at least thirty leagues alone through enemy territory, one man against a nation.'

For a few moments, there was silence as they watched Cronin climb into the saddle. Once settled, he turned to salute the men on the ship.

'Stay strong, my brothers,' he called, 'and one day we will ride together across the fields of heaven.' Without another word, he turned his horse and rode out of the port, headed for Adrianople.

'They say he is a great knight,' said Geoffrey after Cronin was out of sight, 'and spent most of his life serving others before himself. He deserves better than this.' He looked down at the rest of the horses in the trader's paddock.

'What are you thinking?' asked Raymond.

'I am thinking that perhaps there is something we can do to help. I have a promissory note from the commandery for a great deal of money. Perhaps that trader will accept it for some horses.'

'Are you saying that you are going after him?' asked Raymond.

'Yes,' said the knight, his voice becoming more assertive. 'I think I am.' He turned to his fellow knights standing nearby.

'Fellow knights,' he called, 'I am going after Cronin and offer you the chance to join me. I have enough money to pay for horses, but you should know that if you follow, there will be a great penance to pay when we reach Acre, ' He paused for a moment as he realised what he was asking before correcting himself. '*If* we reach Acre. So, what say you, brothers? Do we stay here and watch one of our own face adversity and certain death alone, or do we stand by our vows and face it together?'

As one, every healthy knight on board took a step forward, and Geoffrey's heart raced. It was going against all his orders from those above, but sometimes the call of the brotherhood was greater than that of their political overlords.

'So be it,' he said. 'Gather your things, brothers. We are going to Adrianople.'

----

Within the hour, all twelve of the healthy knights were mounted on horses down on the dock, ready to gallop after Cronin. Geoffrey looked up at Raymond and lifted a mailed fist in salute, a mutually understood sign of respect and brotherhood. The leper knight crossed himself and returned the gesture before watching the knights ride away.

For a few moments, the ship was silent, and as Raymond turned back to join his comrades, he was surprised to see them all gathered together, waiting for his attention. One of them held a folded green blanket in his arms, topped with a heavy pair of sail shears.

'Brother Raymond,' he said, stepping forward. 'We need to talk.'

----

Down below on the dock, the horse trader counted his money and examined the promissory note from the Templar knight. Everyone knew that such notes were guaranteed and certainly a much safer way of conducting business than carrying coins. With a satisfied smile, he hid his earnings beneath his cloak. It had been a good day, but unbeknownst to him, it was about to get a whole lot better.

----

# CHAPTER THIRTY-FIVE

## The Vanguard Camp

The vanguard camp, freshly constructed nearer to the city walls, was unusually quiet, the kind of quiet that comes when men let their guard down, lulled into a false sense of security by routine and familiarity. The wooden palisades and deep trenches surrounding the camp meant they were relatively safe from any unexpected attack, especially as they were manned by plenty of guards, each keeping a sharp eye out for any potential threat.

The Easter celebrations would soon be upon them, and although the soldiers were far from their homes, many sought comfort in the familiar traditions of the holy day. The air was thick with the smell of roasting meat, and the soft murmur of conversation filled the spaces between the tents.

Around the campfires, men laughed and talked, their spirits buoyed by the thought of the coming celebration. Platters of food were passed around, bread, cheese, and whatever else they had managed to gather on the march. The tension of the past few days seemed to have lifted, replaced by a rare sense of camaraderie and peace.

Jamal sat near the edge of the camp, his back to a large oak tree, chewing thoughtfully on a piece of hard bread. Beside him, Sir Edmund was more relaxed than Jamal had ever seen him. The knight's sword lay at his feet, and he cradled a wooden cup of wine in his hands, his usually stern features softened by the flickering firelight.

'They say the city will fall within days,' Sir Edmund mused, taking a sip of his wine. 'Those trebuchets are magnificent, and we'll be inside those walls before the week is out. Before we know it, this whole campaign will be but a memory.'

Jamal nodded, though his thoughts were elsewhere. The camp's relaxed atmosphere felt out of place, as if they were forgetting that they were deep in enemy territory. He couldn't shake the feeling that something was amiss, but he didn't dare voice his concerns. Sir Edmund had already chastised him earlier for being too nervous, too cautious.

'Enjoy the quiet while it lasts,' Sir Edmund had told him, 'for when the battle comes, you'll long for a night like this.'

But Jamal couldn't relax. He glanced around the camp, noting the clusters of men, the shadows cast by the fires, and the guards standing at the perimeter, their gazes fixed on the darkened plains beyond. The guards were alert, but even they seemed more at ease than usual, their stances less rigid, their expressions less vigilant.

A sudden shout broke the stillness, and Jamal tensed, his hand instinctively reaching for the hilt of his sword. The shout was followed by another, and then the unmistakable sound of hoofbeats, fast and furious, pounding the earth in a chaotic rhythm.

Before anyone could react, the sky was filled with arrows, the first volley falling upon the camp like deadly rain, striking down men where they sat, their laughter cut short by screams of pain. Panic erupted as soldiers scrambled to their feet, knocking over plates and cups in their haste.

'Get to your horses!' roared a voice, slicing through the confusion, and Edmund was on his feet in an instant, pulling Jamal up with him.

Jamal's heart raced as he followed Sir Edmund to the picket line where the horses were tethered. The air was thick with smoke and the cries of the wounded. More arrows flew from the darkness, loosed by unseen enemies, and men fell as they ran, their bodies crumpling to the ground.

The Cumans had struck with terrifying precision, their mounted archers riding along the palisades with unsurpassed skill, firing arrows into the mass of disorganized soldiers. They appeared like phantoms out of the night, their horses barely visible in the gloom, the only sign of their presence being the deadly shafts they unleashed.

Jamal fumbled with the reins of his horse, his fingers shaking as he tried to mount. All around him, knights and squires were doing the same, their faces set with a mixture of fear and anger. Sir Edmund was already mounted, his sword drawn, and he glared into the darkness, searching for the enemy.

'Hold your ground!' Sir Edmund shouted, trying to rally the men. 'Form up, damn you!'

But the Latin soldiers were too scattered, too caught off guard to form a coherent defence. The Cumans kept up their assault, their arrows finding gaps in the chainmail, their horses weaving in and out of the darkness, always just out of reach.

'We need to stop them!' one of the knights yelled, his voice filled with desperation. 'They'll pick us off one by one!'

In the chaos, the decision was made without a word being spoken. The anger and frustration of the knights boiled over and Jamal barely had time to swing himself into the saddle before Sir Edmund gave a fierce cry and led the charge, his warhorse surging forward with terrifying speed.

Jamal's heart pounded in his chest as he followed, his horse galloping after the others. The knights, their lances lowered, and swords drawn, hurtled toward the Cumans, their rage driving them forward. They sought revenge for the men cut down by arrows, and they intended to make the enemy pay.

The Cumans, however, had anticipated this reaction, and as the Latin knights charged, their riders pulled back, retreating into the night. The knights pursued them, their war cries echoing across the plains, but the Cumans led them on, deeper and deeper into the darkness.

Jamal clung to the reins, his eyes straining to see through the night. The campfires were far behind them now, and all around was the sound of pounding hooves and the wind rushing past.

Several times, they gained ground on their attackers, but each time, the Cumans increased the distance between them before turning and again loosing their arrows into their pursuers. It was almost as if they were toying with the Latins, knowing that their lighter and more agile horses could easily outrun the heavily armoured pursuers.

The ground became softer underfoot, the horses' hooves sinking into the earth as they galloped on. The knights at the front of the charge cried out as their horses stumbled, the marshy ground sucking at their hooves, pulling them down. Jamal's horse skidded to a halt, nearly throwing him from the saddle. He gasped, pulling at the reins as his mount struggled to find footing in the treacherous terrain.

'Fall back!' Sir Edmund shouted. 'Back to the camp! It's a bog!'

Jamal turned his horse, urging it to move through the marshy ground, but it was slow going.

Sir Edmund reached Jamal, his face grim.

'Stay close to me,' he ordered, and Jamal followed, his heart pounding as he fought to stay close to his lord. They pushed through the marsh, their horses struggling with every step, until finally, they broke free from the worst of the bog and joined the others as they headed back to the relative safety of their camp.

Jamal's breath came in ragged gasps as they finally neared the campfires, the light flickering like a beacon of hope in the night. But even as they reached the camp, the damage was done. Bodies lay strewn across the marsh, knights and horses alike, cut down by the relentless Cuman archers.

As the surviving knights regrouped, panting and bloodied, Sir Edmund turned to face the dark plains, his face a mask of fury.

'Damn them,' he spat, his voice filled with anger and frustration. 'They lured us out, and we played right into their hands.'

Jamal said nothing, his body trembling from the adrenaline and fear. He glanced around at the others, seeing the same shock and exhaustion mirrored in their faces. The Cumans had shown them a different kind of warfare, one that did not rely on strength or honour, but on cunning and precision.

----

Within the hour, with the palisades reinforced and extra guards posted, Baldwin stormed through the camp and called a meeting of his senior knights and nobles. As they gathered, he paced back and forth, his rage evident.

'This was a disaster,' he said, eventually coming to a halt. 'Those men looked like steppe horsemen, and we did exactly what they wanted us to do. We played right into their hands, and there was no way we could match them out there in the dark. Who called the order to attack?'

He looked around, his face like thunder.

'Well?' he shouted. 'I'm waiting.'

'I do not believe there was such an order,' said Louis at his side. 'Everyone just assumed that would be our response, and we acted accordingly. There is no disgrace in attacking an enemy, no matter how strong the opponent.'

'There may not be any dishonour,' said Baldwin, 'but what did we gain? Nothing but dead comrades. It was a stupid response and one that we will not repeat. If they come again, we will form up in defensive lines and wait for them to commit to a frontal assault. Is that clear?'

When there was silence, Baldwin raised his voice, demanding an answer.

*'I said, is that clear?'*

'Yes, my lord,' shouted the gathered commanders.

'Make sure it is,' demanded Baldwin. 'For tonight, we lost good men for no reason except misplaced pride. Make sure it does not happen again.' With that, he stormed away, leaving the knights to ponder the disastrous response.

Edmund and Jamal returned to their fire and sat down with their backs against two trees.

'Will they come again?' asked Jamal.

'They will,' said Sir Edmund, his voice low but firm. 'But next time, we will be ready. Their mounts may be quicker, but there is no way they can beat a line of knights in open battle. Baldwin is right, we deployed the wrong tactics and didn't play to our own strengths.'

'At least we know they will not come tomorrow,' said Jamal.

'And why is that?' asked Edmund, turning his head to stare at the young man.

'Because tomorrow we celebrate Easter,' said Jamal, 'and despite his fight against Baldwin, Kaloyan is a Christian and he would never desecrate the holy day of our Lord.'

Edmund stifled a laugh.

'You have a lot to learn about war, young man,' he said eventually, 'for any combatant will see advantage wherever it is to be found, holy day or not. And besides, Kaloyan may be Christian, but I suspect those horsemen were from the steppes, and many have yet to find Christ. No, we need to stay alert, my friend, for if we do not, then this whole situation will have only one outcome, and it's not the one we seek.'

----

Back in the main camp, the news of the attack spread like wildfire. Whispers became shouts, and shouts became a cacophony of disbelief as the wounded started to trickle in from the vanguard camp and the horror of the night's events began to surface. The survivors, the wounded still able to speak, told of the relentless arrows, the treacherous terrain, and the cries of their comrades as they fell, one by one, to the arrows of the steppe horsemen.

'They caught us off guard,' one of the survivors stammered, his voice thick with shame and despair. 'The Cumans... they came out of nowhere. We couldn't see them... couldn't reach them.'

More of the wounded began to arrive, carried on makeshift stretchers or slumped over the backs of horses. Their faces were pale, bloodied, and etched with pain. The camp's healers rushed to their aid, but the sight of so many injured men, knights who had been the pride of the army, sent a chill through those who had believed in the invincibility of their forces.

Sumeira and Hunter were among the camp followers when the first whispers of the attack arrived. Sumeira was tending to a small fire, warming a pot of water, when she noticed the sudden shift in the air. The camp, usually alive with the sounds of preparation and chatter, had gone eerily quiet. She looked up, her heart skipping a beat as she saw men hurrying past, their faces grim and anxious.

'What's happening?' she asked, grabbing the arm of a passing servant. 'What's going on?'

'The vanguard,' the servant muttered, shaking his head in disbelief. 'They were attacked last night. The Cumans... they ambushed them in the marshes. Many are dead. The survivors are just now coming in.'

Sumeira's blood ran cold.

'The vanguard?' she whispered, the words barely escaping her lips. 'Jamal...'

She felt as if the ground had opened beneath her. Her son was with the vanguard. The realization hit her like a blow to the chest, and she staggered back, her breath coming in short, panicked gasps. Jamal, her only son, the boy she had risked everything to find, was out there, in the midst of the chaos and the bloodshed.

Without thinking, she began to move, pushing her way through the crowds of people who had gathered to see the wounded brought in. Her mind was a storm of fear and desperation, her only thought to find Jamal, to see him with her own eyes, to know that he was safe.

The scene before her was one of horror. The wounded were laid out on blankets or the bare ground, their groans of pain filling the air. Blood stained the earth beneath them, and the healers worked frantically to bandage wounds and set broken limbs. The smell of sweat and blood was overwhelming, and Sumeira's heart pounded in her chest as she searched each face, praying that she would not see her son among the injured.

'Please, Jamal... where are you?' she whispered to herself, her hands trembling as she continued her desperate search. Sumeira felt sick, her stomach churning with fear. But she forced herself to keep moving, to keep looking, driven by the hope that she would find Jamal alive. She approached a young man, sitting on the ground, his arm wrapped in a bloodied bandage, his face ashen. She rushed to him, her heart in her throat.

'Have you seen a boy called Jamal?' she asked, her voice shaking. 'A squire like yourself? Is he alive?'

The squire looked up at her, his eyes dull with pain. He seemed to struggle to focus, as if her question was too much for his weary mind to process. But then, understanding dawned, and he nodded weakly.

'Yes, 'he said weakly, I know him. We sailed from England on the same ship. He's... he's still out there, I think. We got separated when the Cumans attacked. I... I don't know if he made it back.'

Sumeira's heart clenched in her chest. He was still out there, somewhere in the chaos of the battlefield, or worse, trapped in the marshes with the dead and dying. She felt a wave of dizziness wash over her, and she had to steady herself against the squire's shoulder.

'Thank you,' she whispered, though her words were barely audible over the noise of the camp.

She backed away, her mind reeling. Jamal was still out there, still in danger. The camp was no longer a place of safety; it was a reminder of the peril that awaited those who dared to underestimate the enemy. The Cumans had struck fear into the heart of the Latin army, and now that fear was consuming her, choking her, making it hard to think, hard to breathe.

She turned, her eyes scanning the horizon, as if she might somehow see Jamal through the fog of war. She knew that there was no way any woman would be allowed to go to the Vanguard camp, but she had a skill that just might buy her passage. She headed back to her fire and was joined by Hunter.

'Where are you going?' he asked.

'To the vanguard camp,' said Sumeira, packing her medical supplies into a roll. 'Jamal may be there, and besides, they may just need my skills.'

'You will never get out of this camp,' said Hunter. 'The road is too dangerous.'

'When they find out I am a physician, they may let me go,' she replied. 'Besides, I have you to protect me, remember?' She flashed him a pleading smile, and he knew that he could not allow her to go alone.

'Of course,' he said. 'Let me get my things.'

Minutes later, they approached the camp perimeter and were surprised to find the gate guards were all gathered around a messenger, listening to his account of the previous night's battle.

'Come on,' said Hunter quietly. 'Now is our chance,' and as the guards' backs were turned, they slipped out of the camp and headed across the plain toward the city.

----

A few leagues away, hidden amongst the ravines and hills of the northern mountains, the campfires of Tsar Kaloyan's forces flickered like distant stars. The night was cool, the air filled with the scent of pine and the faint rustle of leaves in the breeze. Hidden away from the prying eyes of the Latin scouts, Kaloyan's army lay in wait, the dark shapes of his soldiers blending seamlessly with the landscape. The Tsar himself stood at the edge of the encampment, his sharp eyes fixed on the city in the distance, its ancient walls barely visible in the moonlight. He and his entourage had moved from their secure camp further north to be almost within touching distance of Adrianople and the battle that was destined to take place at its walls.

Kaloyan was a man who thrived on the thrill of strategy, a ruler who knew that patience and cunning were as important as strength on the battlefield. His dark, fur-lined cloak draped around him, he exuded an aura of quiet confidence, the kind that comes from years of hard-won victories. But beneath that calm exterior, there was a fire, a relentless drive to see his enemies brought low.

Footsteps approached, and Kaloyan turned to see Boyar Sigritsa emerge from the shadows. There was a glint of satisfaction in his eyes as he drew closer to his lord.

'Tsar Kaloyan,' Sigritsa said, bowing slightly. 'I bring news. The first attack by the Cumans was a success. The Latin knights were drawn into the marshes and suffered heavy losses. Many were killed or wounded, and their morale has been shaken.'

Kaloyan's lips curled into a smile, a flash of satisfaction crossing his features.

'Good,' he said, his voice low and measured. 'Perhaps they have learned, they underestimate me at their peril.'

Sigritsa nodded, his expression one of grim approval.

'The Cumans carried out their task well, my lord. They struck swiftly and retreated before the enemy could organize a defence. The knights chased them into the marshes, just as we planned, but pulled up short of the wolf pits.'

Kaloyan's gaze returned to the distant city, his mind already working on the next move in this deadly game.

'We have bloodied them, yes,' he said, 'but we must do more.' He turned to face Sigritsa fully, his eyes gleaming with fierce determination. 'The Cumans have done well, but I need them to strike again, this time in daylight to tempt the Latins further to the north. Even if it means sacrificing hundreds of their own men, it is essential they lead them past the wolf pits.'

Sigritsa listened intently, ready to carry out whatever orders the Tsar gave. He had served Kaloyan long enough to know that his mind was as sharp as any blade, his strategies often as ruthless as they were effective. He bowed again, his respect for Kaloyan deepening with every word, and as he turned to leave, Kaloyan called after him.

'And Sigritsa,' he said, his tone carrying a note of warning, 'remind the Cumans that their reward depends on their success. If they fail, there will be no gold, no plunder, only the wrath of a disappointed Tsar. It is all about the wolf pits. Get Baldwin's men amongst those, and the result is a foregone conclusion.'

Sigritsa nodded grimly, understanding the weight of the message.

'I will make sure they understand, my lord.' With that, Sigritsa departed, disappearing into the night to carry out his Tsar's orders.

----

# CHAPTER THIRTY-SIX

## The Road to Ainos

Cronin leaned forward in the saddle, urging his horse to greater speed as they thundered across the rugged countryside. The wind whipped at his face, stinging his eyes and tugging at his cloak, but he paid it no mind. The landscape was wild, dotted with forests and hills that could easily conceal bandits or worse, but Cronin had no time for caution. He had pushed his horse hard, stopping only briefly to rest and water the animal before pressing on. Every delay, every obstacle, felt like a knife twisting in his gut, a reminder that time was slipping away.

The horse beneath him was a sturdy beast, but even it was beginning to show signs of wear. Its breath came in heavy snorts and sweat darkened its coat. Cronin knew he was asking a lot from the animal, but he had no choice. He couldn't afford to lose a moment. Sumeira's life depended on it.

The landscape blurred around him as he rode, his eyes fixed on the distant horizon. He knew the Latin camp was somewhere ahead, sprawling across the plains before Adrianople's ancient walls. But he also knew that the enemy was near.

As the hours passed, the landscape began to change. The rolling hills gave way to flatter ground, and Cronin knew he was drawing closer. The thought gave him a surge of energy, and he spurred his horse on, ignoring the ache in his own muscles and the fatigue that gnawed at his mind. He had to reach her. He had to.

He was close now, so close he could almost taste the dust kicked up by the thousands of men and horses gathered for the siege. But with that nearness came a fresh wave of dread. The camp was enormous, a labyrinth of soldiers and camp followers. Finding Sumeira in the midst of it would be like finding a single leaf in a forest, especially if she had already moved to follow Jamal.

Cronin urged his horse onward, feeling the animal's exhaustion mirrored in his own bones. The camp grew larger, more defined, and soon he could make out the sounds, the clatter of armour, the murmur of voices, the distant clang of a blacksmith's hammer. But even as he drew closer, he felt the weight of uncertainty settle over him. What if he was too late? What if Sumeira had already left the camp, or worse, what if she was...

No. He couldn't allow himself to think like that. He had to believe she was still safe. He would not fail her. Not now.

As he reached the outskirts of the camp, he slowed his horse, taking a moment to catch his breath and steady his thoughts. The camp was bustling with activity, but there was an undercurrent of tension, a sense that the men here were no longer as confident as they had been when they first set out. The news of the ambush had clearly shaken them. Soldiers moved with a purpose, their faces grim, and Cronin caught snatches of conversation as he rode past, a mention of the Cumans, of knights lost in the marshes, of the uncertainty that now hung over the entire campaign.

Dismounting, he led his horse through the camp, his eyes scanning every face, every figure that passed by. He tried to remain calm, to think logically, but his heart pounded in his chest, the fear that he was too late gnawing at him with every step.

Finally, he reached a cluster of tents where the camp followers were gathered. Women and children, servants and squires, those who were not directly involved in the fighting, yet essential to the army's daily life. He slowed, his eyes searching for a familiar face, his heart aching with the hope that he might see her standing there, unharmed.

But she was not there. His stomach dropped as he realized how difficult this was going to be. The camp was enormous, and he had no idea where she might have gone. He felt the first pangs of panic rising within him, threatening to overwhelm his senses.

'Please,' he said, stopping a young woman who was passing by, her arms full of linens. 'I'm looking for a woman named Sumeira. She's with her son, Jamal, a squire in Sir Edmund of Bristol's service. Have you seen them?'

The woman looked at him with wide, fearful eyes.

'The physician? Yes, I've seen her... She was looking for her son... I think she headed toward the Vanguard camp to help with the wounded.'

Cronin's heart skipped a beat. The wounded. Of course. She would have gone to the wounded, especially if Jamal was among them. But that meant she was already in the thick of it, surrounded by the chaos and pain that followed any battle.

'Thank you,' he said, his voice tight with emotion. He turned and hurried in the direction she had indicated, his steps quickening as he moved through the camp. He reached his horse and saw a groom examining its hooves.

'Out of my way,' said Cronin, 'I need to go.'

'This horse is exhausted,' said the groom, staring at the red cross on Cronin's surcoat, 'you've ridden it half to death.'

'It can't be helped,' said Cronin, 'I need to go. Stand aside.'

'Wait,' said the groom, 'you're a Templar, are you not?'

'I am, why?'

'Because my father was in the brotherhood, and one day, I hope to follow in his footsteps.'

'An admirable ambition,' said Cronin, 'but I have no time to share a conversation. I need my horse.'

'This one has nothing left to give you, my lord, but I have a destrier you can use.'

'You have a destrier?'

'It's not mine, my lord, but its owner died in the night from an illness. Nobody has claimed it yet, so if you take it, I'm sure no one will know.'

Cronin thought furiously. He was loath to take something that was not his, but the thought of having a warhorse beneath him lifted his heart.

'I will not take it without agreement,' he said, 'but I will take it on loan and swear to return it when I'm done.'

'And if you or he is killed?'

Cronin looked down at the ring on his hand before removing it and handing it to the groom.

'This is worth a hundred such beasts,' he said, 'and if we do not return, give it to the claimant or keep it yourself, I care not.'

The groom stared at the ring in the palm of his hand. His father had worn such a ring, and he knew it was worth a fortune.

'So be it, my lord,' he said eventually, 'follow me.'

----

Within the hour, Cronin mounted the destrier they had discussed, a magnificent warhorse well-trained in the ways of war. He could feel the strength of the beast beneath his body and knew it would fly headlong into battle with the slightest encouragement. Happy with the transaction, he nodded to the groom before turning away to head towards Adrianople.

'One more thing,' he said, turning the horse back around. 'Do you know the location of the Vanguard position?'

'Aye, my lord, they say it's near the northern walls of the city. Just head north, and you'll find it.'

'You have my gratitude,' said Cronin, and he turned away again, knowing his journey was almost over. But despite his good fortune and fresh horse, he was not to know that he was already too late, for in the distance, a cloud of dust raised by five hundred galloping horses was already climbing into the afternoon sky.

----

The Vanguard camp of the Latin army had been quiet all morning, the air filled with the soft murmur of prayers and the rustle of robes as the knights and soldiers gathered to celebrate Easter. The makeshift altar stood at the center of the camp, a simple structure adorned with a white cloth and a wooden cross, a symbol of their faith amidst the chaos of war. The priests, clad in their vestments, led the devout in solemn chants, their voices rising to the heavens as the first light of dawn bathed the camp in a golden glow.

Baldwin stood among his men, his head bowed in reverence as he listened to the prayers. The past days had been difficult, but today was a holy day, a day to seek the blessings of God before the trials that lay ahead. His thoughts were heavy with the memory of the ambush in the marshes, the cries of the wounded still echoing in his mind. He had given orders to his men to be vigilant, to be ready for another attack, but on this day of all days, the camp was more relaxed. They believed they were safe for the moment, allowed a brief respite to honour their faith.

But the Cumans had no such reverence for the Latins' holy day.

The first sign of danger came not from the makeshift watchtowers around the perimeter of the camp but from the distant sound of horns, their shrill notes cutting through the peaceful morning like a blade. Baldwin's head snapped up, his eyes narrowing as he listened. The sound was unmistakable, battle horns, echoing across the plains. And then, the earth began to tremble, the faint but growing thunder of hooves pounding against the ground.

A shout went up from the perimeter, followed by the clanging of alarm bells, and the camp erupted into chaos as the realization set in. They were under attack. Again.

The priests' prayers faltered, their voices drowned out by the sudden cacophony of panic. Men scrambled to their feet, abandoning their prayers as they rushed to grab their weapons. Chainmail was hastily donned, swords drawn, and horses mounted as Baldwin barked orders, his voice cutting through the confusion.

'Form up,' he shouted, his face twisted in anger and frustration. 'As we practiced! Get into formation now!'

But the camp was still in disarray, the men disorganized and panicked by the suddenness of the attack. The memories of the previous ambush were still fresh, and the fear that had been planted in their hearts had not yet been uprooted. The Cumans had chosen their moment well, striking at the very core of the Latin army when they were most vulnerable.

And then, over the rise, they appeared. Five hundred Cuman horse archers, a dark wave of death moving as one across the plain, their mounts galloping at full speed. The Cumans rode with terrifying precision, their bows already drawn, arrows nocked and ready to unleash. The sight of them, their fur-lined cloaks billowing in the wind, their faces obscured by the shadow of their helmets, struck fear into the hearts of the Latins.

The Cumans let out a series of blood-curdling battle cries, their voices rising into the air, a sound meant to unnerve and terrify. The Latin knights, who prided themselves on their courage and strength, felt a chill run down their spines. The Cumans were like phantoms, appearing out of the mist, their horses thundering across the plain with relentless fury.

270

The first volley of arrows arced through the air, a deadly rain that fell upon the unprepared knights and soldiers. Screams of pain and terror erupted as men were struck down, the arrows piercing flesh and bone. Some fell where they stood, others crumpled to the ground as they tried to reach their weapons, their blood staining the earth beneath them.

'Shields up!' Baldwin roared, his voice hoarse with the effort to be heard above the din. 'Form a line!' But there was no time. The Cumans were too fast, too precise. Another volley of arrows followed, and then another, each one sending more men to their deaths.

The knights struggled to form up, as Baldwin had ordered the previous day, but the panic was too great. Horses reared and bolted, their riders unable to control them in the chaos. Men stumbled over the bodies of their fallen comrades, their movements frantic and uncoordinated. The discipline that had been drilled into them on the training fields seemed to evaporate in the face of the Cuman onslaught.

Sir Edmund, his sword drawn, shouted to Jamal, who was fumbling with his helmet nearby.

'Stay close to me, lad! Do not break rank!'

Jamal's heart pounded in his chest as he pulled the helmet over his head, his fingers shaking as he tried to fasten the chin strap. The terror of the previous night's ambush still haunted him, and now, with the Cumans bearing down on them once more, that fear threatened to overwhelm him. But Sir Edmund's voice brought him back to the present, grounding him in the reality of the battle.

'Yes, my lord!' Jamal shouted back, forcing himself to focus.

The Cumans continued their assault, their horses circling the camp like predators. They fired their arrows with deadly accuracy, each shot a calculated strike meant to sow confusion and panic among the Latin ranks. The knights, who had been taught to face their enemies head-on, were unprepared for this kind of warfare, one that was as much about terror as it was about killing.

Baldwin, seeing the disarray, cursed under his breath. He had to regain control, had to rally his men before the Cumans turned this into a slaughter. He spurred his horse forward, cutting through the chaos, shouting orders to the knights who could still hear him.

'Hold the line!' he bellowed, his voice raw with determination. 'Hold the line, damn you! They cannot break us if we stand together!'

But the Cumans were relentless. Their arrows continued to rain down, and with each volley, the Latin ranks thinned. The ground was littered with the bodies of the fallen, the once-proud knights now reduced to bleeding, dying men, their faith and courage shattered by the fearsome assault.

Jamal could barely keep his footing as the knights around him struggled to form a shield wall. He raised his own shield, trying to block the incoming arrows, but the force of each strike sent shudders through his arm. He could hear Sir Edmund shouting nearby, trying to rally his own command, but his voice was drowned out by the screams and the thunder of hooves.

Suddenly, the sound of horns rang out, Latin horns, blaring a countersignal to rally the scattered knights. A cheer broke out from the camp, and the lines opened to let a column of mounted knights gallop through, determined to change the nature of the fight. At their head was Louis of Blois, his face a picture of rage as he led his men into the counteroffensive, encouraged by the cheers of those who had suffered the brunt of the Cuman onslaught.

'What is he doing?' Baldwin roared, his voice filled with the authority of an emperor. 'My orders were to form a defensive line!'

Despite the disobedience, the counterattack paid dividends, and the hail of death from iron-tipped arrows fell away as the Cumans turned their horses to avoid the heavily armed knights.

Baldwin's eyes blazed with fury as he watched half of the remaining Vanguard pursue the retreating Cumans. His orders had been to stay put, but now that there had been a counterattack, he knew they would soon become isolated and would need to be supported.

'Everyone to horse!' he roared, 'Form up outside the camp!'

Moments later, the survivors of the brutal assault, a few hundred strong, mustered around their emperor.

Baldwin stood up in his stirrups to be easily seen and heard.

'You just saw what happened,' he roared, 'they attacked us on Christ's day, a time of peace and reflection. Where there should have been bread, there was torn flesh. Where there should have been wine, there was blood. Yesterday we let them enjoy their victory, but today there will be no turning back. Today there will be nothing but retribution. Take steel in hand, my fellows, and let God strengthen your sword arms.'

He raised his own sword and pointed it towards the dust cloud left by Louis of Blois and his men.

'In the name of God himself,' he roared, 'onward to glory!' And as the the remainder of the Vanguard roared their own battle cries, the last of the knights thundered after the retreating Cumans…which was exactly what Kaloyan had hoped for.

----

Half a league to the north, columns of dust billowed into the air as Louis of Blois and his heavy knights thundered across the plain, closing in on their Cuman attackers. Their horses pounded the earth, nostrils flaring and muscles straining under the weight of their armoured riders. The knights could see the Cumans just ahead, their wild, fur-lined cloaks flapping in the wind, the light of the afternoon sun catching the tips of their curved bows.

The chase had been relentless, stretching across the undulating plains near Adrianople. Each time the knights seemed to close the distance, the Cumans would spur their horses forward, just out of reach, taunting their pursuers with the promise of a fight that never quite came. Louis gritted his teeth, frustration building as the elusive enemy seemed to slip through their grasp time and again. The knights were seasoned warriors, but the tactics of the Cumans were unlike anything they had faced before.

The Cumans, masters of mounted warfare, slowed their horses just enough to keep the knights on edge, making them believe that a clash was imminent. Yet, each time, as the knights leaned forward in their saddles, eager to engage, the Cumans would quicken their pace, leaving the knights grasping at nothing but air. It was a cruel game, and the knights, driven by pride and the heat of battle, were determined not to let their quarry escape.

The landscape began to change subtly, the ground becoming more uneven. The Cumans, aware of every dip and rise in the terrain, expertly guided their horses around hidden dangers. They seemed to float over the earth, their horses barely breaking stride as they led the knights deeper into unfamiliar territory. To the knights, blinded by the dust and the thrill of the chase, it seemed as though the Cumans were faltering, their speed diminishing as they neared what appeared to be a natural bottleneck in the landscape.

Louis, at the head of the column, urged his men on, confident that they were about to catch the enemy at last. The Cumans looked over their shoulders, their expressions inscrutable, as they rode ever closer to what the knights believed would be the final engagement. The trap, however, was already in place, the Cumans steering their pursuers toward a carefully prepared killing ground, and the knights, eager for glory, followed without hesitation.

----

Moments later, as the Cumans reached a seemingly impassible cliff face, they turned their horses around and lined up as if ready to engage their pursuers in a final, full-frontal battle.

The knights surged forward, their battle cries echoing from the surrounding hills. But just as they urged their mounts into the final attack, their battle cries turned into screams of terror as the ground beneath them gave way.

In an instant, what had seemed like solid earth crumbled, revealing the carefully concealed wolf pits that yawned open like the jaws of a beast. Horses reared, their shrill cries echoing across the plain as they lost their footing, plunging into the hidden traps.

The first to fall were thrown violently from their saddles, the weight of their armour turning what should have been a stumble into a catastrophic descent. Men hit the bottom of the pits with sickening thuds, their bodies impaled on the sharpened stakes below. Horses flailed desperately, their legs shattered or caught in the splintered wood, crushing their riders beneath them. The air was filled with the sound of snapping bones, the wet crunch of flesh meeting steel, and the agonized wails of the fallen.

Louis, who had been at the forefront of the charge, felt his horse lurch beneath him. The animal screamed, its front legs giving way as they plunged into a pit. He was thrown from the saddle, the impact driving the breath from his lungs as he crashed into the earth. Pain shot through his body as he tried to move, but the weight of his armour pinned him down. Around him, the scene was one of utter chaos. Knights who had moments before been charging with confidence now lay in twisted heaps, some impaled, others trapped beneath the thrashing bodies of their own mounts. The carefully ordered ranks had dissolved into a tangle of broken limbs and shattered steel. Those who hadn't fallen into the pits found themselves surrounded by the dying and the dead, their horses panicking, eyes wide with terror as they tried to avoid the same fate.

Fear gripped the hearts of those still alive, their minds reeling as the full horror of the trap set in. The ground that had seemed so secure was now a field of death, and there was no clear path to safety. Men called out for help, their voices breaking with panic, but there was no one to answer.

Confusion reigned as the knights struggled to comprehend what had happened. In the midst of the chaos, the realization that they had been led into a trap spread like wildfire, but it was already too late. The pride and discipline that had driven them forward had been replaced by a primal instinct for survival, each man now fighting not for victory, but for his life.

Above the cacophony, the Cumans' war cries could be heard, signalling the next phase of the assault. As the Christians tried desperately to climb from the pits, Bulgarian foot soldiers poured from their hiding places amongst the rocks to cut them down with spears, pikes, and daggers. It was nothing short of slaughter, and as brave men died in their hundreds, Kaloyan looked down from one of the nearby peaks, entranced by the massacre unfolding before him.

----

Just a short ride away, Baldwin and his men galloped hard, the distant sounds of battle growing louder with each passing moment, and as he crested the final rise, the battlefield unfolded before him like a scene from a nightmare.

The sight that greeted him was one of utter carnage. The once-proud vanguard of knights lay scattered across the field, their formation broken and twisted. Men and horses alike were caught in a grotesque dance of death, many impaled on stakes or writhing in the shallow, blood-filled pits. The screams of the wounded pierced the air, a haunting symphony of agony and despair that echoed across the plain.

Baldwin's eyes widened in horror as he took in the scene. Proud men who had once ridden into battle with honour and courage beneath colourful banners now lay splattered with mud and blood, struggling to free themselves or crawling helplessly in search of escape. The bodies of those who had perished already lay strewn about, twisted in unnatural positions, their lifeless eyes staring blankly at the darkening sky.

Beyond the pits, Baldwin saw the Cumans, moving with deadly purpose. They swarmed around the trapped knights, their bows singing as they loosed arrows into the exposed ranks. Some wielded spears, plunging them into the helpless men who had avoided the pits, while others moved in with ropes and poles, dismounting any knight who still clung to their horse. The Cumans showed no mercy, their faces grim with the cold efficiency of slaughter.

A surge of rage welled up in Baldwin's chest as he heard the cries of his men, their pleas for help mingling with the guttural sounds of death. He could see them reaching out, some with broken arms, others covered in the blood of comrades or their own, their hope fading with each passing second. The realization that they were being butchered like animals drove him to the brink of madness.

Baldwin turned in his saddle, his eyes blazing as he urged his men forward.

*'For God's sake, charge!'* he roared, *'we must save them!'*

His knights spurred their horses into action, the sound of hooves pounding the earth as they raced toward the battlefield. But as they closed the distance, the true scale of the disaster became apparent. The ground ahead was treacherous, littered with the bodies of their fallen comrades and the hidden pits that had claimed so many lives.

Baldwin knew there was no time to hesitate. With fierce determination, he led the charge, his sword drawn as he shouted commands to his men. They would need to navigate the deadly traps, avoid the Cumans' relentless onslaught, and somehow pull their trapped brothers from the jaws of death.

But the battlefield was a hellscape and as they reached the front lines, Baldwin's men quickly found themselves entangled in the same chaos that had ensnared the first wave. Horses balked at the sight of the pits, and knights had to pull up sharply to avoid plunging into the same traps. The screams of the dying filled the air, and everywhere Baldwin looked, he saw the faces of men he knew, twisted in pain and fear.

The Cumans, seeing the reinforcements arrive, did not falter. They redoubled their efforts, targeting the newcomers with precision. Arrows rained down on Baldwin's men, and more knights fell, their cries of pain adding to the cacophony. The trap had been perfectly laid, and now it threatened to consume them all.

But Baldwin pressed on, his heart heavy with the knowledge that every moment they delayed meant more of his men would die.

'Fight!' he roared. 'Fight for your brothers,' urging his men to push through the chaos. Yet even as he charged forward, the grim reality set in. The battle was slipping from their grasp, and the day would end in blood and ruin.

Up above, Kaloyan gasped in relief, realising that his tactics were working. Raising an arm, he signalled to a distant commander below, and the last part of his strategy rolled into action. From the surrounding woods and ravines, hundreds of Bulgarian horses burst from their hiding places and thundered across the open fields to surround the Latin reinforcements, and within just a few moments, their fate was sealed. There was no escape; all they could do now was fight for their lives.

----

# CHAPTER THIRTY-SEVEN

## The Vanguard Camp

The scene that greeted Cronin as he approached the Vanguard camp was one of grim horror. What had once been a bustling hub of activity, full of men preparing for battle, was now a graveyard of burning tents and scattered bodies. The ground was littered with the dead, their bodies twisted and bloodied from the brutal Cuman attack that had struck less than an hour earlier. Smoke drifted lazily from the remains of fires that had long since died, and the only sound was the groaning of the wounded, who lay where they had fallen, too weak to move.

Cronin dismounted and walked through the camp, leading his horse by the reins, and as he rounded a corner, he saw a figure kneeling beside a wounded man, her hands moving swiftly as she tended to his injuries. Sumeira. His heart skipped a beat at the sight of her, alive and unharmed. Beside her, Hunter stood guard, his sword drawn, eyes sharp and wary as he watched for any sign of danger. The big man's face was grim, a testament to the horrors he had witnessed.

'Sumeira,' Cronin called out, his voice rough from the dust and exhaustion.

She turned at the sound of his voice, her eyes widening in shock. For a moment, she simply stared at him, as if unsure whether to believe what she was seeing.

'Cronin?' she whispered, her voice trembling. 'You're alive?'

He nodded, his expression softening as he approached. 'I am.'

Sumeira rose to her feet, disbelief written across her face.

'We heard… We were told you died in England. There were letters, reports… How can this be?'

Cronin paused, the memories of the treachery of the king's men flashing before him.

'It's a long story,' he said, his voice heavy with the weight of what he had endured. 'But I survived, and now I'm here.'

Before he could say more, Sumeira took a step towards him, her hands reaching out as if to confirm that he was real.

'I thought I'd lost you,' she whispered, her voice breaking. 'After everything, to hear that you were gone… it was unbearable.'

He took her hands in his, feeling the warmth of her touch, a stark contrast to the cold, death-ridden air around them.

'I'm here now,' he assured her, his voice firm. 'and I won't let anything happen to you.' He looked around, nodding to Hunter, the man who he had shared so many years fighting alongside.

'Good to see you again, Hunter,' he said, 'and thank you for looking after her.'

'Sometimes I think it was the other way around,' replied Hunter, 'but we are alive, at least for now.'

'And Jamal?' asked Cronin. 'Is he also safe?'

Sumeira shook her head, the motion small, almost imperceptible, as if she was afraid to voice her worst fears.

'I don't know,' she murmured. 'We know he rode with the Vanguard from Constantinople, but I have searched this camp for his body. He is not here, so I can only assume he rode out with Baldwin to fight. I… I don't know what to do, Cronin. I have come all this way to find him, but I am too late. He is lost to me. There is nothing more I can do.'

Cronin stepped closer, his heart heavy with the weight of her words. He could see the fear in her eyes, the dread that was slowly consuming her. He reached out, resting a comforting hand on her shoulder. 'We'll find him, Sumeira,' he said. 'Until there is a body to bury, there's still hope.' He turned to Hunter. 'Come with me.'

Both men walked a distance away, and Cronin looked earnestly at his old friend.

'Listen,' he said. 'I am going after Jamal, but there is something I need you to do for me. When I was in London, King John tricked me out of the lands given to me by King Richard. There is nothing I can do about that, and I can certainly never return to England on pain of death. However, what he did not know was there were two properties given to me, one at Fallswater and one at Cragsmere.' He reached beneath his cloak and produced a leather wallet.

'Within this package are the legal deeds to that property. They are worth a fortune, and if I fall, I want you to use the sale to set up you and Sumeira in a safe place for the rest of your days, Jamal too, if I can get to him.'

'This is a fool's errand,' said Hunter. 'There is no way you can survive out there. Jamal is dead, and the sooner you both accept that, the better.'

'I disagree,' said Cronin, 'and even if that is the case, I have to try. You are a good man, Hunter, and I know that if I die, at least Sumeira is in good hands. I have seen the way she looks at you and also know you can make her a better husband than I ever could.' He pushed the wallet into Hunter's chest. 'Promise me, my old friend, swear that you will do me this one last favour.'

'Cronin,' started Hunter, but his friend cut him short, raising his voice.

'Swear to me, Hunter!' he shouted. 'Do this for me, lest I die wondering what fate will befall her. You are the only man I can trust.'

Hunter stared at his old friend, knowing this was probably the last time they would ever speak.

'I so swear,' he said eventually. 'As God is my witness, I will do as you ask.'

Cronin grabbed Hunter's wrist and stared into his old comrade's eyes.

'Goodbye, my friend, and if we do not see each other again in this life, I will wait for you at the gates of Heaven.' Without another word, he turned away and strode back to his horse.

'Cronin!' shouted Sumeira as he passed, 'where are you going?'

He stopped and looked down at the only woman he had ever loved.

'I'm going to get Jamal,' he said eventually. 'I'm going to get our son.'

----

Deep amongst the carnage of the battlefield, Sir Edmund gritted his teeth, his sword arm heavy and aching, as he fought off yet another Cuman warrior. The clash of steel against steel echoed through the rocky outcrop where he and a handful of men had made their last stand. Blood dripped from a deep gash in his side, soaking into the mail beneath his surcoat, but he pushed the pain aside, knowing that to falter now would mean death for them all.

Around him, the few remaining knights and squires fought with grim determination, their backs against the cold, unforgiving stone. Jamal, his young face streaked with dirt and blood, stood beside Sir Edmund, his sword trembling in his hands as he parried a blow that would have taken his head. The boy was brave, but the fear in his eyes was unmistakable.

The Cumans pressed in from all sides, their numbers overwhelming, their faces twisted with the thrill of the kill. They moved with the precision of seasoned hunters, their curved swords and long spears flashing in the dim light. Sir Edmund knew that their position was untenable. The rocky outcrop had provided some cover, but it had also trapped them, leaving no room to retreat and no chance of escape.

'Hold fast!' Sir Edmund shouted, his voice hoarse from the battle. 'We make them pay for every step!' But even as he spoke, he knew the words were hollow. The Cumans were too many, their resolve too fierce. One by one, his men were being cut down, their desperate cries swallowed by the chaos of the fight. A knight to his left fell with a spear through his chest, his body crumpling to the ground. Another, a young squire who had fought valiantly, was struck down as he tried to run, his body falling limply among the rocks.

Jamal, still at Sir Edmund's side, fought with all the strength he could muster, his face a mask of concentration. But the boy was tiring, and Sir Edmund could see that it was only a matter of time before his energy gave out. As another wave of Cumans advanced, Sir Edmund made a decision, one that tore at his heart but was necessary if even one of them was to survive.

'Jamal!' he shouted, grabbing the boy by the shoulder. 'You must run!'

Jamal's eyes widened in shock. 'But, '

'Go!' Sir Edmund commanded, his voice fierce. 'There's no time! Run, and don't look back! Find a place to hide in the rocks, now!'

Jamal hesitated for only a moment, his young face torn between fear and duty. But then, with a final, desperate look at the battle raging around him, he turned and fled, his small form darting between the boulders and crags of the outcrop.

Sir Edmund turned back to the fight, raising his sword to meet the next attacker, but within moments, he too succumbed to the overwhelming enemy numbers, and he fell screaming in pain and terror, skewered by a Cuman lance.

----

Jamal ran as fast as his legs would carry him, the rocky terrain tearing at his boots and sending sharp pains shooting through his feet. The sounds of battle faded behind him, replaced by the pounding of his own heart and the ragged gasps of his breath. He didn't dare look back; he knew the Cumans would be close behind.

His lungs burned, and his legs screamed in protest, but he pushed onward, scrambling over rocks and ducking under low-hanging boughs. He could hear them now, his pursuers, their harsh voices carrying on the wind. They were close, too close, and Jamal knew he couldn't outrun them forever. Desperation drove him forward, his mind racing as he searched for a place to hide, to disappear into the landscape.

Ahead, he spotted a narrow crevice in the rock, just wide enough for him to squeeze through. Without hesitation, he dove into it, pressing himself against the cold stone, his breath coming in shallow, terrified bursts. The darkness of the crevice enveloped him, and he huddled there, trying to make himself as small as possible, willing his body to remain still and silent.

Outside, the Cumans drew nearer. Jamal could hear the crunch of their boots on the gravel, the low murmur of their voices as they searched for him. His heart pounded so loudly in his chest that he feared they would hear it, that it would give him away. He bit down on his lip, tasting blood, trying to stifle the sob that threatened to escape.

The footsteps grew louder, the voices closer. One of the Cumans, a tall man with a scar running down his cheek, passed by the crevice, his eyes scanning the rocks with deadly intent. Jamal held his breath, his entire body trembling as the man paused, just feet away from his hiding place. The Cuman tilted his head, listening, his sharp eyes narrowing as he surveyed the area.

Jamal squeezed his eyes shut, praying silently, his fingers digging into the cold stone at his back. The Cuman took a step closer, and for a heart-stopping moment, it seemed as though he would reach into the crevice, would find Jamal and drag him out into the open.

But then, another voice called out, and the Cuman turned, grunting in response before moving on. The footsteps receded, the voices growing fainter as the Cumans continued their search elsewhere. Jamal remained frozen in place, too terrified to move, even as the sounds of his pursuers faded into the distance.

He didn't know how long he stayed there, pressed against the rock, his body trembling with fear and exhaustion. Tears welled up in his eyes, and he allowed himself to cry quietly in the darkness, the weight of what he had seen, of what he had lost, crashing down on him. He was alone, hidden among the rocks, with no way of knowing if anyone else had survived or if he would ever find his way back. He was alone in a foreign land with no hope of survival and knew that only a miracle from God Himself could save him now.

----

Cronin rode hard from the Vanguard camp, his mind heavy with Sumeira's grief. The air was still, filled only with the distant echoes of battle and the cries of the wounded carried on the wind. As he pushed onward, cresting a small rise that overlooked the battlefield, the sight that met his eyes was nothing short of a nightmare.

Below him, Baldwin and his remaining men were surrounded. The knights, once proud and unstoppable, now fought desperately against the encroaching Cuman forces. The enemy moved like a swarm, their numbers seeming endless as they closed in from all sides. Baldwin's banner, still flying but tattered and bloodied, was barely visible amid the chaos. The knights were outnumbered and outmanoeuvred, fighting a losing battle as the Cumans pressed them further into the centre.

Cronin's heart pounded in his chest, a mix of horror and helplessness washing over him. He could see Baldwin at the centre of the fray, his sword flashing in the dim light as he rallied his men, trying to hold the line. But it was clear, painfully, terrifyingly clear, that they were being overwhelmed. The Cumans attacked with a ferocity and coordination that left little room for hope. Horses and men fell under the onslaught, the ground turning to mud under the relentless trampling of hooves and the spilling of blood.

Cronin's hands tightened on the reins, his knuckles white with the force of his grip. Every instinct screamed at him to charge down the slope, to join the fray, to do something, anything, to help Baldwin and the others. But he knew the truth, a bitter reality that gnawed at his resolve. Alone, he could do nothing. He was just one man, and the force before him was a tide of death that would swallow him whole in an instant.

He cursed under his breath, frustration and rage warring within him as he watched the horror unfold. The cries of the dying reached his ears, the sounds of steel on steel, the desperate shouts of men who knew their end was near. Cronin felt the weight of futility bearing down on him, the unbearable burden of knowing that he was powerless to save his comrades. He had survived so much, escaped death, endured the worst the world could throw at him, only to find himself standing on this ridge, forced to watch as his fellow Christians were slaughtered below, and amongst them, somewhere in the brutality of battle, was Jamal, out of reach and condemned to a bloody death.

Just as despair threatened to take hold, a noise behind him broke through the din, faint at first but growing louder, more defined, a rhythmic pounding, like the beat of a distant drum. Cronin turned, his heart leaping into his throat as he saw them.

Emerging from the haze of dust and smoke, a force of twelve Templar knights rode towards him, their white mantles marked with the blood-red cross. Cronin's brow furrowed in confusion. As far as he knew, there were no squadrons of Templar knights in Thrace, or anywhere near Constantinople, and even if there were, they had certainly not declared for Baldwin, preferring to concentrate their efforts in the Holy Land.

As they got closer, the man at the front lowered his hood, revealing his face to Cronin. It was Sir Geoffrey, the knight who had sailed with him from Normandy, and suddenly all became clear. These were not just any knights; these were the men he had sailed with on the plague ship. His heart missed a beat as they closed in, their faces grim, their swords at the ready as they rode in perfect formation, a disciplined and unyielding force in the face of chaos.

Sir Geoffrey raised his sword in salute as they approached.

'Cronin!' he called, his voice strong and sure above the roar of battle. 'We're with you, brother!'

Cronin's breath caught in his throat, a surge of hope and determination flooding through him as the knights drew closer. He recognised them all, men like him who had faced death and had never flinched. They had come for him, brothers in arms, a glimmer of salvation in the darkness of the battlefield.

'Geoffrey,' gasped Cronin, 'what are you doing here?'

'We could not sail away and watch you die alone,' said his fellow knight. 'We all took the same oath, and it is God's wish that we fight alongside you here and now.' He looked down at the battlefield, and the thousands of men fighting and dying in the late evening sun. 'Though what it is you expect to achieve against such numbers escapes me.'

'There is nothing we can do,' said Cronin. 'Jamal is somewhere amongst them and even if we knew where, we would never reach him. It's a slaughter down there. Baldwin and his men… they're nearly finished.'

Both men stared at the battle, knowing full well they could not change the outcome. Hope for Jamal's safety faded away, and as they watched, the last of the surrounded men lay down their arms, surrendering to Kaloyan's overwhelming numbers.

'It is done,' said Geoffrey. 'We should get out of here while we still can.'

----

Across the valley, Jamal huddled in the darkness, his heart still pounding in his chest, each beat a reminder of how close he had come to being discovered. The silence that now enveloped the rocky outcrop was almost oppressive, the absence of the Cumans' voices and footsteps allowing the fear to settle deep in his bones. He knew he couldn't stay hidden forever, but the thought of moving, of exposing himself to the dangers outside, filled him with dread.

Slowly, he inched closer to the edge of the crevice, peering out from his hiding place. The rocky landscape stretched before him, bathed in the fading light of the setting sun. The bodies of fallen knights and Cumans alike were scattered across the ground, a grim reminder of the battle that had raged only moments before. Jamal's breath hitched in his throat, and for a moment, hopelessness threatened to overwhelm him. He was alone in the midst of a war that had claimed so many lives, and the chances of survival seemed impossibly slim.

But then, as his eyes scanned the horizon, he saw them, a force of twelve Templar knights standing on a nearby rocky outcrop, their white mantles stark against the darkening sky. Jamal's heart skipped a beat, a flicker of hope igniting within him. The knights were not far, their swords drawn, their posture tense as they scanned the battlefield for any remaining threats. They hadn't seen him yet, but if he could reach them, if he could somehow make it across the open ground, they might save him.

Jamal hesitated, his mind racing with the possibilities. He knew that if he stayed where he was, hidden among the rocks, the Cumans would eventually find him. But if he made a break for it, if he ran for the Templars, he might be caught and killed before he could reach them. The thought of leaving the safety of his crevice filled him with fear, but the alternative, dying alone and unnoticed in the dark, was far worse.

Taking a deep breath, Jamal steeled himself. He had no other choice. If he stayed, he was as good as dead. But if he ran, if he could just make it to the knights, there was a chance, however slim, that he could survive.

With a sudden burst of energy, he sprang from his hiding place, his legs pumping furiously as he raced across the valley. The wind whipped at his face, and the ground seemed to blur beneath him as he ran, his eyes fixed on the distant figures of the Templars. His heart pounded in his chest, each beat echoing in his ears as he sprinted towards the only hope he had left.

Behind him, he heard the shouts of the Cumans, their voices rising in alarm as they spotted him. He dared not look back, but he could feel them closing in, the thunder of hooves growing louder with each passing second. Panic surged through him, urging him to run faster, to push his tired, trembling legs beyond their limits. As he neared the outcrop, tone of the Templars finally noticed him. They turned as one, their eyes narrowing as they spotted the lone figure racing towards them and Jamal's heart soared with relief, but it was quickly replaced by shock as he recognised one of the knights at the front of the group.

'Cronin!' he cried out, his voice hoarse with fear and desperation. 'Help me!'

----

# CHAPTER THIRTY-EIGHT

## The Battlefield

'That's him!' shouted Cronin from the top of the hill, 'glory be to God, that's Jamal!' He turned his horse back towards the battlefield and dug in his heels, sending the destrier galloping down the slopes towards the exhausted man.

Behind him, his fellow Templars paused briefly before Sir Geoffrey called out, 'Well, my brothers, what are we waiting for? This is why we came!'

Digging his heels into his own horse, he too galloped down the hill, closely followed by the rest of the knights from the ship. Within moments, they were on level ground, heading for the boy that Cronin had travelled halfway across the known world to rescue.

----

Out on the plain, Jamal's lungs burned with every desperate breath as he raced across the rocky terrain, his legs numb with exhaustion. The shouts of the Cumans grew louder behind him, but he dared not look back. His heart pounded in his chest, fear driving him forward as he darted between boulders and across uneven ground. Every muscle in his body screamed for rest, but he knew that if he stopped, if he faltered for even a second, it would be the end.

Just as his strength began to wane, Jamal's eyes caught sight of movement ahead, a blur of white and red, like a beacon of hope in the desolate landscape. The Templars were coming.

Relief flooded through him, a wave of emotion so intense that it nearly brought him to his knees. He had made it. He was going to survive.

Cronin led the charge, his face set in a determined scowl, his eyes locked on Jamal.

The sight of his friend, alive and charging towards him, brought tears to Jamal's eyes. It was as if all the terror, all the pain of the past hours, melted away in that moment. Cronin was here, and with him, hope.

Jamal stumbled, his legs barely able to keep him upright, but he forced himself to keep moving, even as his vision blurred and his strength gave out. The Cumans were closing in, their war cries filling the air, but Jamal could only focus on the Templars, on Cronin, who was coming to save him.

As Cronin drew near, he reined in the horse, the trained warhorse coming to a sudden stop. With a swift motion, he jumped down from the saddle, his boots hitting the ground hard. Without hesitation, he reached out, lifting Jamal from the ground with one powerful motion. The boy was light in his arms, trembling with exhaustion and fear, but alive.

'You're safe now,' Cronin said, his voice a gruff reassurance. He hoisted Jamal onto the horse's back, securing him in the saddle before swinging himself up behind him. 'Hold on tight!'

Jamal barely had the strength to nod, his arms wrapping around the horse's neck as Cronin turned his horse back towards the hill, the rest of the Templars charging past them to engage the Cumans.

The sounds of battle erupted behind them, the clash of steel on steel and the cries of men in combat filling the air. But Jamal could only hold on, his body pressed against the warmth of the horse, his heart thudding in his chest. The relief of being with Cronin, of being lifted from the ground and carried to safety, was overwhelming. Tears streamed down his face as the adrenaline ebbed, leaving behind only exhaustion and the lingering tremors of fear.

The battle raged on behind them as they climbed the hill, the Templars fighting valiantly against the Cumans. Cronin pushed the horse hard, his focus solely on getting Jamal to safety, and as they reached the cover of the trees, Cronin slowed, allowing the horse to catch its breath as he surveyed the battlefield below.

The Templars fought with unmatched ferocity, cutting down their enemies with skill and precision. But the Cumans were relentless, their numbers too great. One by one, the Templars fell, their white mantles stained with blood as they were overwhelmed. Jamal watched in horror as some of the knights were struck down, their bodies trampled by the Cuman horses. But six of them, six brave men who had fought through the chaos, managed to break away and join Cronin and Jamal amongst the trees, breathing heavily from the exertion of battle.

Cronin dismounted, helping Jamal to the ground. The boy's legs nearly gave way beneath him, but Cronin caught him, steadying him with a firm hand on his shoulder. Jamal could only nod, his body too exhausted to do more. He leaned against a tree, his eyes closing briefly as he fought to dismiss the horrors he had witnessed. But even in his weariness, he knew the battle wasn't over.

Cronin and the surviving Templars looked back over the ridge, their eyes widening in disbelief. From the far side of the valley, another Cuman force emerged, a sea of warriors stretching as far as the eye could see. Thousands of them, their banners fluttering ominously in the wind. They moved like an unstoppable tide, their numbers dwarfing the small band of Templars who now hid amongst the treeline.

Cronin's heart sank as the realisation hit him. There was no escape. No reinforcements would come, no miracle to save them from the fate that awaited. They were doomed.

'There's just too many,' said one of the Templars. 'If we stay here, we will be found and killed, and if we flee, they will overwhelm us before we reach safety.'

Cronin nodded grimly; his gaze fixed on the approaching enemy.

'Then we fight to the end,' he said quietly, his hand tightening on the hilt of his sword. 'We fight until the last heart stops beating, the last drop of blood stops flowing.'

The Templars murmured their agreement, their resolve unshaken even in the face of certain death. Jamal looked up at Cronin, his eyes wide with fear and exhaustion.

'What do we do?' he whispered.

Cronin looked down at him, his expression softening. 'We hold our ground, lad. We fight for every inch. And whatever happens… know that you're not alone.'

Jamal nodded, drawing strength from Cronin's calm resolve. The fear in his heart was still there, but it was tempered by the presence of the men around him, by the knowledge that they would face this together.

As the Cuman horde advanced, the Templars prepared themselves for the final stand. Swords were drawn, shields raised, and a heavy silence fell over the small group as they awaited the inevitable clash. Jamal clung to Cronin, his heart pounding in his chest, knowing that this might be the last time they stood together.

----

The air was thick with tension as the remaining Templars stood amongst the trees, their gazes fixed on the approaching Cuman horde. The sun had nearly disappeared beyond the horizon, casting long shadows over the battlefield, and the once distant roar of the enemy was now a deafening thunder in their ears. The Templars knew their time was running out.

Sir Geoffrey stepped forward, his expression resolute.

'We can't just wait here to be slaughtered,' he said, his voice low but firm. 'Let me lead what's left of us in an attack. It'll be a diversion, enough to buy you time to escape with the boy.'

Cronin turned to face him, a frown creasing his brow. 'Geoffrey, six of you against thousands will be nothing more than a momentary nuisance. The Cumans will brush you aside like leaves in the wind.'

Geoffrey met Cronin's gaze, his eyes hard with determination.

'A few moments are all you need. It will be dark soon and if we can draw their attention, even for a short while, you and the boy might make it out of here alive.'

Cronin opened his mouth to argue, the futility of the plan weighing heavily on him. He knew the courage of Geoffrey and the others was unmatched, but the odds were insurmountable. The thought of leaving them behind to face certain death gnawed at his soul. But before he could voice his doubts, another voice spoke from behind him.

'Six may not trouble them,' the voice said, calm and assured, 'but twenty would.'

Cronin spun around, his heart leaping in his chest at the unexpected sound. There, emerging from the trees, was another group of knights, their cloaks white like the Templars', but with a key difference: the red cross of their order had been crudely covered with rough green crosses, hastily sewn over the original insignia. They were the Lazarus Knights, the men who had sailed with them from England.

Cronin's eyes widened in shock as they approached, Sir Raymond riding at the front. Despite his affliction, his presence exuded strength and unwavering resolve. The other Lazarus Knights, scarred and battle-hardened, rode behind him, their expressions grim but determined.

'You followed us,' Cronin said, his voice thick with disbelief. 'Why?'

Sir Raymond dismounted, his boots crunching against the earth as he approached Cronin.

'Because, brother, your fight is our fight. We may be afflicted but we are knights still and would rather die for a good cause with a sword in hand than suffer a rotting death in the backstreets of Jerusalem. ' He grabbed Cronin's forearm, gripping it tightly. 'Our swords are your swords.'

Cronin's heart swelled with gratitude and newfound hope. Twenty knights, still a small force against the Cuman horde, but far more formidable. The Lazarus Knights had always been a group apart, men who had been exiled or sent away due to illness or injury, yet they were still fierce warriors, unyielding in their commitment to the fight.

Geoffrey's expression softened slightly, though his resolve was unchanged.

'Twenty, then,' he said, nodding to the Lazarus leader. 'It's still a slim chance but it might just be enough to gain him enough time to escape. We will ride in tight formation, deep into the heart of the Cumans, cutting through them like a knife as we did at Montgisard against the Saracens.'

'I was there,' said Raymond. 'A truly magnificent day, and while I fear the outcome may not be the same, the pride and valour will be rekindled one last time.' He turned to Cronin. 'We will buy you the time you need, Cronin. Get the boy out of here. He's too young to die in this place.'

Cronin glanced at Jamal, who stood by his side, wide-eyed and silent as he took in the scene. The boy's face was pale, but there was a flicker of courage in his eyes, the same courage that had kept him alive through the horrors of the day. Cronin knew that Jamal's survival was more important than anything else now. The boy represented the future, a future that could not be allowed to die here.

'We will do it,' he said, 'but there is one condition. Someone else will take Jamal back to his mother, perhaps the youngest amongst us, with their life still to live. I have lived mine, and I know that it is soon to come to an end, one way or another. I have no doubt that we will strike fear into the hearts of the Cumans, even for the briefest of moments, but when we do, I will be at the heart of the charge.'

'An admirable intent, Cronin,' said Geoffrey, 'but there is no need. Take the boy back to his mother.'

'No,' said Cronin, 'I have done what I came to do, and now it is time to face my own destiny. Nominate one of your men to take him, and I will join you in the charge. But hurry, time is running out.'

'So be it,' said Geoffrey and turned away to speak to his fellow Templars. As he did, Cronin walked back over to Jamal.

'My journey ends here, Jamal,' he said gently, 'but you still have your life to live. When you leave here in a few moments, ride like the devil himself is after you and head for the vanguard camp. Hunter and your mother are there and will look after you. But tell them what happened here and that they have to get back to Constantinople as soon as possible. They will not be safe if they stay here.'

'Come with me, Cronin,' pleaded Jamal. 'My mother needs you.'

'She is a strong woman, Jamal,' said Cronin, 'and with you and Hunter at her side, she will face down anything the world has to throw at her. Now get ready, you have to go.'

One of the knights walked over with two horses and Cronin lifted Jamal into the saddle.

'Tell her I loved her, Jamal,' he said as the men prepared to ride. 'I always have and always will, but it was never meant to be. Now go, and let God add wings to your steed.'

Jamal nodded, and as the young Templar knight turned his own steed away to the south, Jamal followed, knowing he would never see Cronin again.

Cronin watched them disappear into the gloom before mounting his own horse and riding across to join the rest of the assembled men now looking down on the Cuman horde.

Cronin drew his sword, its blade catching the last light of day as he looked across at the men about to sacrifice their lives for someone they had only just met.

'Brothers, he said calmly, our numbers may be few, but let our hearts be steadfast. Our brotherhood binds us, stronger than any chain, deeper than any fear. We may fall, but we will not falter. Let our loyalty to each other be our legacy, our final stand a testament to the unbreakable bond between us. Today, we fight our last battle, and let our enemies know that even in the face of certain death, there is a loyalty that will never be broken!'

Sir Geoffrey and Sir Raymond rode across to form up either side of Cronin with the rest of the knights lining up to either side.

'Let's give them something to remember,' Geoffrey said, a grim smile, and as the sun started to dip behind the western mountains, Cronin dug his heels into the flanks of his horse to lead the charge down the hill.

----

In the distance, the young Templar knight and Jamal paused on the crest of a hill. They had managed to get away unnoticed, but as they looked back, they could see hundreds of burning torches forming a circle in the darkness, no doubt shedding light on the slaughter of the last of the knights. His heart ached, and he knew he would never be the same again. Those men, Cronin and the Templar and Lazarus Knights, had given their lives for this moment, for the chance that he might survive.

'We have to go,' said the young knight at his side eventually, and as he turned away, Jamal made a silent vow, to make sure their deaths would not be in vain and to make their sacrifice worth something, even if it was the last thing he ever did.

'One last thing,' he said, still staring at the battlefield in the distance, 'what were those words they shouted as they charged the Cumans.'

The young knight followed Jamal's gaze, his heart aching with sorrow and pride.

'They were *Deus Vult*, my friend, 'he said, '*God wills it*. Now, let's get you home.

----

# EPILOGUE

## Off the Coast of Constantinople

The sea stretched out endlessly before them, a vast expanse of blue-grey that seemed to merge with the sky at the horizon. The ship cut through the water with a steady rhythm, its sails full with the wind as it made its way from Constantinople towards Acre. On the deck, the passengers stood in silence, each lost in their thoughts, the recent past weighing heavily on their hearts.

Hunter leaned against the railing in the stern, his eyes fixed on the distant shore that slowly faded from view. The journey had been brutal, and the losses at Adrianople were horrendous. News had arrived that Baldwin himself had been captured at the battle and would now rot in a Bulgarian dungeon, hoping for someone to pay a ransom for his release, a distant hope, but one infinitely better than the fate of the thousands who had died in and around the wolf pits.

His hand crept to the satchel beneath his cloak containing the deeds to the valuable farm in England. Although he knew that all he had to do was wait for King John to be replaced, he also knew that all three of them belonged in the Holy Land. It was the place where they felt comfortable, and despite the ever-present dangers, it was the place they had each called home for many, many years.

Sumeira stood beside him, her hand resting gently on the railing as she gazed out over the water. The wind tugged at her dark hair, whipping it across her face, but she paid it no mind. Her thoughts were with the men who had sacrificed everything so that she and her son could escape. Cronin's face came to her mind most vividly, the way he had always seemed so strong, so unyielding, even in the face of certain death. She had never had the chance to thank him properly, to say goodbye, and the weight of that loss sat heavy in her chest.

Jamal sat a short distance away, his small form huddled on a wooden crate, his knees drawn up to his chest. He stared out at the sea, his young face pale and drawn. The events of the past days had aged him in ways that could not be measured by years. He had seen death up close, had felt the terror of battle and the sting of loss. But he had also witnessed courage, the kind of courage that left a lasting mark on the soul. Cronin had saved him, had carried him from the jaws of death, and Jamal knew that he owed the man his life.

As the ship sailed onward, leaving the blood-soaked land behind, the three of them were united in their grief, their thoughts turning again and again to the brave men who had stayed behind. They had fought for a cause greater than themselves, and in doing so, they had given the others a chance to carry on, to live, and perhaps one day find peace.

The sun began to dip lower in the sky, casting long shadows across the deck as it sank toward the horizon. The light danced on the waves, turning the water into a shimmering tapestry of gold and orange. Hunter turned to Sumeira, his voice low and filled with quiet resolve.

'They'll never be forgotten,' he said, the words more a promise than a statement.

Sumeira nodded, her eyes shining with unshed tears.

'No, they won't,' she agreed, her voice barely above a whisper. 'Their bravery will live on in our memories, in the stories we tell. They gave us everything… we owe it to them to live well.'

Jamal looked up at his mother, his eyes searching her face for reassurance.

'Will we be safe in Acre?' he asked, his voice small, tinged with the uncertainty of a child who had seen too much.

'We will be safe,' Sumeira said, her voice stronger now as she placed a comforting hand on his shoulder 'And we will make a new life there, for all of us. But we will carry the memory of those who protected us with us always.'

The three of them fell silent again, the only sound the gentle lapping of the waves against the hull and the occasional creak of the ship's timbers. The shore of Constantinople grew more distant, a thin line on the horizon, until it finally disappeared altogether, leaving only the open sea and the promise of what lay ahead.

----

Back on the battlefield at Adrianople, the sun had nearly set, casting the land in a dim, orange glow. The once fierce and chaotic battlefield was now eerily quiet, the cries of the wounded replaced by the stillness of death. Bodies lay scattered across the plain, knights and Cumans alike, their weapons discarded where they had fallen.

A group of old women picked their way carefully through the carnage, their eyes sharp and calculating as they searched for anything of value. They moved slowly, their hunched forms and ragged clothing blending into the desolate landscape. For them, the aftermath of battle was an opportunity, a chance to find something, anything, that could be sold or traded in the markets. They had seen war before, had scavenged from the dead and dying, and they knew where to look.

One of the women, her back bent with age and her face lined with deep wrinkles, paused as she walked between the bodies. Something had caught her eye, a faint movement, so slight that she almost thought she had imagined it. She squinted down at the figure lying before her, his face pale and streaked with blood. The other women moved on, but she knelt beside the body, her gnarled hands reaching out to touch his neck.

She gasped, her heart skipping a beat as she felt a faint pulse, the weak but unmistakable thrum of life. The knight's eyelid fluttered, the faintest of movements, but it was enough to confirm her suspicion.

'Here!' she called out, her voice rough but urgent.

'This one... I think this one is still alive!'

The other women turned, their eyes widening in surprise as they hurried back to her side. Together, they carefully rolled the knight onto his back, revealing more of his bloodied face. His breaths were shallow, his chest barely rising and falling, but he was alive.

The first woman looked into his face, her breath catching in her throat as she recognised the surcoat beneath the blood.

'It's one of the Templars,' she whispered, her voice filled with a mix of awe and disbelief.

The others murmured among themselves, uncertain of what to do. But the first woman, her eyes sharp with determination, made a decision.

'We need to get him out of here,' she said firmly. 'If he survives… there may be a reward.'

Carefully, they began to strip away the knight's heavy clothing, working quickly but gently. The sun had nearly set, and they knew that they had little time before the darkness would make their task impossible. As they worked, the knight's eyelid fluttered again, his lips moving in a faint whisper, but the words were lost to the wind.

They lifted him as best they could, their frail bodies struggling under his weight, and began the slow journey back to their village, where they would nurse him back to health, or at least try.

As they moved away from the battlefield, the last light of the sun dipped below the horizon, plunging the land into shadow. The knight's fate was uncertain, but as long as there was life, there was hope, a hope that perhaps, against all odds, he might live to fight another day.

----

**THE END**

## Author's Notes

As usual, in this novel I have tried to weave an engaging tale of the characters we have all come to love, set against real events of the time. Wherever possible, the dates, times, and real characters are as accurate as they can be and have been thoroughly researched. However, on occasion, if it was needed to help the story flow, there may have been some artistic licence, and I doff my cap to all those historians out there who may feel frustrated over the detail. I hope I have struck the correct balance and believe this is a wonderful way to say goodbye to all those characters and events that have made up this series. I hope you have enjoyed them as I have loved every single minute of writing them.

### Basil the Bulgar Slayer

In AD 997, the second son of Tsar Peter I of Bulgaria, Samuel, succeeded his father and became the new Tsar. For the next seventeen years, he spent most of his reign defending the Bulgarian Empire from the ambitious Byzantine emperor, Basil II Porphyrogenitus. During that time, despite the constant military pressure from Basil, Samuel managed to inflict several major defeats on the Byzantines, launching many offensive campaigns into their territory.

But Basil was a clever ruler and had been fighting the Bulgarians for over forty years. It wasn't long before he regained the initiative and managed to lure Samuel's main army into an ambush at a place called Kleidion near the Bulgarian border. The result was an overwhelming victory for the Byzantines, which effectively ended the reign of Samuel, who died of a heart attack a few days later.

During his reign, Basil's ruthless approach earned him the name of 'Basil the Bulgar Slayer', an epithet that struck fear into the Bulgarian population for over two hundred years.

### The Battle of Kleidion

Under pressure from Basil's army, Samuel created a strong position in a ravine at a place called Kleidion. He created a huge palisade between the walls of the ravine and made his stand there with an army tens of thousands strong.

Despite their constant attrition, the Byzantine army could not break down the defences until one of their generals, Nikephoros Xiphias, found a hidden route through the rocky mountains, led an army to the rear of the defences, and fell upon them from behind. The result was a slaughter, with countless dead and over 15,000 prisoners taken. However, despite his reputation, Basil the Bulgar Slayer did not have them killed. Instead, he blinded 99 out of every 100 men, leaving one one-eyed man in each cohort to lead the rest back to their ruler, sending a devastating message to the whole of Bulgaria. It is said that upon seeing the terrible state of his returned army, Samuel collapsed and died of a heart attack.

## Baldwin of Flanders

After the sacking of Constantinople, the Crusaders had to make an important decision, as Alexios III, the true Emperor, had fled to avoid the battle. Coming to an agreement regarding the division of the city, the various factions first offered the imperial crown to Enrico Dandolo, Doge of Venice, who refused it. The choice then lay between Baldwin and the nominal leader of the crusade, Boniface of Montferrat.

While Boniface was considered the most probable choice, due to his connections with the Byzantine court, Baldwin was young, gallant, pious, and virtuous, one of the few who interpreted and observed his crusading vows strictly, and the most popular leader in the host. With Venetian support, he was elected on 9 May 1204 and crowned on 16 May in the Hagia Sophia at a ceremony that closely followed Byzantine practices at the time.

As emperor, he sought to consolidate Latin rule over Constantinople and its territories, facing immediate challenges, including resistance from the Byzantine Empire's remnants and the need to establish control over the newly conquered lands.

His efforts to subdue these challenges were cut short at the Battle of Adrianople in 1205, where his forces were defeated by Tsar Kaloyan of Bulgaria. Baldwin was captured during the battle and later died in captivity, marking a premature end to his reign.

Twenty years later, in 1225, a man appeared in Flanders claiming to be the presumed-dead Baldwin. His claim soon became entangled in a series of rebellions and revolts in Flanders against the rule of Baldwin's daughter Jeanne. A number of people who had known Baldwin before the crusade rejected his claim, but he nonetheless attracted many followers from the ranks of the peasantry. Eventually unmasked as a Burgundian serf named Bertrand of Ray, the false Baldwin was executed in 1226.

### Kaloyan the Roman Slayer

Tsar Kaloyan was the Tsar of Bulgaria from 1197 until his death in 1207. In 1201, after the successful siege of the city of Varna, he had the defenders and governors of the city tied and thrown into the moat of the fortress walls and covered with dirt. After they were buried alive in this way, Kaloyan declared himself a Bulgarian avenger, adopting the moniker 'the Roman Slayer' in retaliation for the atrocities committed against his own people by Basil II the Bulgar Slayer two hundred years earlier.

Kaloyan was keen to obtain Papal support and the recognised title of Emperor from Pope Innocent III, but when the papal envoy, Cardinal Brancaleoni, only acknowledged the Tsar as King of all Bulgars and Vlachs, Kaloyan continued his war of attrition against what was left of the Byzantine Empire. Kaloyan subsequently scored a significant victory at the Battle of Adrianople, where the Bulgarian army defeated the Latin knights and captured Emperor Baldwin I of Constantinople.

### King John

King John of England, also known as John Lackland (1166–1216), was the youngest son of King Henry II and Eleanor of Aquitaine and the brother of King Richard I (Richard the Lionheart). He ascended to the English throne in 1199 after Richard's death, despite the existence of more direct heirs, due to Richard's nomination and the political manoeuvres of his mother, Eleanor. John's reign was fraught with difficulties from the start, including the significant loss of Normandy and other lands, weakening England's position in Europe.

When his nephew, Arthur of Normandy, asserted that he had a better claim to the throne, John marched rapidly to Mirebeau to confront him and achieved a remarkable victory. The battle ended with Arthur and several of his key allies being captured and was a significant strategic win for John, as it effectively neutralised one of his most potent rivals.

### Arthur I, Duke of Brittany

Arthur was indeed the posthumous son of Geoffrey II, Duke of Brittany, and Constance, Duchess of Brittany, and was the nephew of Kings Richard I and John of England. When Richard the Lionheart died in 1199, Arthur's claim to the English throne was supported by some factions, leading to a power struggle with King John.

There are many different theories about Arthur's demise, but it is widely believed that in or around 1203, after being captured and imprisoned, he was murdered on the orders of King John to eliminate his rival claim to the throne. His disappearance and presumed death have sparked various theories, but most historians agree that he died as a result of foul play linked to the political machinations of his time. There is no evidence that he fathered any children before he died.

### The Cumans

The Cumans, also known as the Kipchaks, were a nomadic Turkic people who played a significant role in the medieval history of Eastern Europe and the Eurasian Steppe. From around the 11th century until the 13th century, they were prominent across the vast territories stretching from the northern shores of the Black Sea, across the steppe regions of what is today southern Russia, Kazakhstan, and Ukraine, and into the Balkans. They were often hired as mercenaries. In the Battle of Adrianople, they fought alongside Tsar Kaloyan of Bulgaria against the Latin Empire. Their role was crucial in the Bulgarian victory, showcasing their military skills, especially their expertise in mounted archery and hit-and-run tactics, which were highly effective against the heavily armoured but less mobile Latin knights.

## The Column of Theodosius

Often referred to as the Column of Arcadius, the column is a significant historical monument located in Istanbul, originally part of the Forum of Theodosius in ancient Constantinople. It was erected in honour of Emperor Theodosius I, who ruled the Eastern Roman Empire from 379 to 395 AD, marking his achievements and the reaffirmation of Constantinople as the capital of the Eastern Roman Empire. The monument symbolises the might and continuation of Roman authority in the East during a period marked by political division and external threats.

The column itself was majestic and crafted from porphyry, a type of igneous rock known for its purple colour, which was rare and valued highly in the ancient world. Porphyry was often reserved for imperial use in the Roman Empire, symbolising royal or divine status. The column stood approximately 40 metres high and was topped by a statue of Theodosius I, possibly depicting him in a triumphant pose or in the attire of a conqueror or deity. The base was adorned with reliefs that likely depicted scenes of Theodosius' military victories, legislative reforms, and religious endorsements, such as his support for Christianity and his role in making it the state religion of the Roman Empire.

Some historians report that after his capture, Alexios Doukas, the deposed Emperor of Constantinople, was thrown to his death from the top of the tower, while others believe he was made to stand at the top of the tower until he fell from exhaustion.

## The Knights of Lazarus

The Lazarus Knights, also known as the Knights of St. Lazarus, were a medieval military order with a unique and sombre distinction: they were primarily composed of knights who had contracted leprosy. The Order of St. Lazarus was founded in the late 11th or early 12th century, during the height of the Crusades, and it was dedicated to both the care of lepers and the defence of the Christian faith.

The origins of the Order of St. Lazarus are closely linked to a leper hospital in Jerusalem, established around 1120 near the Church of St. Lazarus. This hospital was one of several founded by Christian institutions to care for those afflicted with leprosy, a disease that was both feared and deeply stigmatised in medieval Europe. Leprosy was seen not only as a physical affliction but also as a spiritual curse, often leading to the social isolation of those who suffered from it.

The Knights of St. Lazarus emerged from this hospital, initially as an order of hospitallers dedicated to caring for lepers. However, as the Crusades intensified and the need for military defence grew, the Order took on a military role. The Lazarus Knights were unique among the military orders of the time because many of their members were themselves lepers. These knights, despite their illness, participated in battles and defended Christian territories, particularly in the Holy Land.

The Order was known for its bravery and determination, with its members often fighting with a sense of desperation, as many of them knew they had little to lose.

Leprosy did not necessarily impair a person's ability to fight, at least in the disease's early stages. Many of the Lazarus Knights were seasoned warriors who continued to serve even after contracting the illness. They were often stationed in the more perilous positions in battle, partly due to the belief that, since they were already marked by leprosy, their lives were considered less valuable. Despite this harsh reality, the Lazarus Knights earned a reputation for fearlessness.

Today, the Order of St. Lazarus survives as a charitable organisation, with various branches around the world. Its historical legacy as a military order that included lepers remains a poignant reminder of the harsh realities of medieval warfare and the extraordinary resilience of those who fought despite severe illness. The Lazarus Knights stand as a unique example of how faith and duty could transcend even the most debilitating conditions in the medieval period.

## The Battle of Adrianople

The Battle of Adrianople, fought on 14 April 1205, was a pivotal clash between the forces of the Latin Empire, led by Emperor Baldwin I, and the Bulgarian Empire, commanded by Tsar Kaloyan.

Kaloyan had also secured the support of the Cumans, a nomadic Turkic people renowned for their horse archery.

Baldwin's army was composed primarily of Western European knights, many of whom were veterans of the Fourth Crusade. The Latin knights were known for their powerful charges, which could break through enemy lines with devastating effect. However, their heavy armour made them less mobile and more vulnerable in difficult terrain.

When Adrianople declared allegiance to Kaloyan, Baldwin knew he had to take the city back due to its strategic location at the meeting of three rivers, and he mobilised his army. Once there, as his engineers started to prepare mines and assemble the siege engines, Baldwin joined his vanguard and moved closer to the city.

On 13 April, the Cumans launched a surprise attack on his camp and then pretended to flee from the knights' counterattack, engaging them from a distance with their archers, causing many casualties.

Realising their own foolishness, the knights returned to their camp to prepare for the battle they knew would surely come. That same night, Baldwin called a meeting with all of the present barons and leaders of the Fourth Crusade. They decided that, in the case of a new attack by the Cumans, the army must not follow, instead forming a battle line in front of the camp.

On Thursday, 14 April 1205, during the celebration of Catholic Easter, the Cuman light cavalry made another sweeping attack on the camp of the knights with arrows, loud yells, and the ringing of steel. Outraged by this sacrilege, the knights armed, mounted, and got into battle formation. Count Louis I of Blois disregarded the plan made the night before and led his unit after the Cumans, and the other soldiers, already blinded by anger, followed his lead. The Cuman cavalry once again fled the field, outpacing the Latins, until they reached a plain located between high ridges and forests.

On the far side of the plain, the Cumans turned around, apparently offering a serious fight. The knights charged in their characteristic formation but were checked when many horses and riders fell into hidden pits called 'Wolf Pits', prepared by Kaloyan's army over the previous few days. In the ensuing turmoil, the Bulgarian infantry emerged from the surrounding trees and rocks and fell upon the knights, using ropes and hooked polearms to unhorse the riders, before finishing them off with swords, hammers, and axes.

Despite their broken formation and inability to coordinate, the surrounded Latins put up a hard fight which lasted until late in the evening, but by its conclusion, the main part of the Latin army had been annihilated and Baldwin I captured.

----

Next Book

## DARK EAGLE

### **Rome**

One of the largest and most successful empires in history. A brutal superpower whose military machine was one of the greatest the world has ever known. For generations, her forces were second to none and millions of people across the known world trembled at the sound of the marching legions.

Their story is well-documented but what if there were others just as important. Just imagine for a moment that as well as their all-conquering legions, there were much smaller units who were just as, if not more important to the success of any mission.

What if there had been special groups of men whose contributions had huge influence on Rome's continued greatness yet left little behind in the way of records and receiving little if any recognition for their service.

Wouldn't it be fascinating if they had used special forces to achieve their outcomes, elite units that scouted the way for the main legions, often working in total secrecy behind enemy lines, thriving on subterfuge and secrecy. Wouldn't that be fantastic.

Well, guess what, they did!

*...and this is their story.*

## Description

In the grandeur of the Roman Empire, Centurion Marcus Antonius Maecilius is a man of honour and valour. Yet, fate deals him a cruel hand when he is falsely accused of cowardice and sentenced to serve as an oarsman on a bireme, a slave to the rhythm of the waves and the lash of the overseer.

Broken and embittered, he resigns himself to the monotonous toil of the galley, until the day a mysterious group of five men board his ship in Hispana with orders for the captain to take them to Belgica in the northern seas.

Unbeknownst to Marcus, these elite operatives, selected from the best of the exploratores, are on a clandestine mission deep into the heart of Germania, and when the ship is forced to engage a Gallic pirate ship, his bravery shines through, catching the eye of Seneca, the man in charge of the exploratores.

Offered a chance to join their elite ranks, Marcus must make a decision that will change his life forever. Does he stay and live out his sentence before seeking justice, or does he join these secretive men, who, by their own admission, doubt they will come back from their mission alive?

Set against the backdrop of the ancient world's most formidable empire, Dark Eagle is a dramatization of the secretive world of those who fought for Rome in the shadows. Unknown to most, their battlefields were often behind enemy lines, clandestine missions to seek information and, where necessary, dealing death without hesitation.
In today's world they would be called special forces but back then, they were known as the Exploratores.

**More books by K M Ashman**

**The Exploratores**
Dark Eagle
The Hidden

**The India Summers Mysteries**
The Vestal Conspiracy
The Treasures of Suleiman
The Mummies of the Reich
The Tomb Builders

**The Roman Chronicles**
The Fall of Britannia
The Rise of Caratacus
The Wrath of Boudicca

**The Medieval Sagas**
Blood of the Cross
In Shadows of Kings
Sword of Liberty
Ring of Steel

**The Blood of Kings**
A Land Divided
A Wounded Realm
Rebellion's Forge
Warrior Princess
The Blade Bearer

**The Road to Hastings**
The Challenges of a King
The Promises of a King
The Fate of a King

**The Brotherhood**

Templar Steel  – The Battle of Montgisard
Templar Stone  – The Siege of Jacob's Ford
Templar Blood  – The Battle of Hattin
Templar Fury  – The Siege of Acre
Templar Glory  – The Road to Jerusalem
Templar Legacy – The Search for the Shroud
Templar Loyalty – The Battle of Adrianople

**The Otherworld Series**
The Legacy Protocol
The Seventh God
The Last Citadel
Savage Eden
Vampire

Printed in Dunstable, United Kingdom

68152533R00178